# HANGING TIME

Also by the same author
from Bantam Books

*Burning Time*

# HANGING
# TIME

## LESLIE GLASS

BANTAM BOOKS
NEW YORK TORONTO LONDON SYDNEY AUCKLAND

HANGING TIME
A Bantam Book / October 1995

*Book design by Claire Naylon Vaccaro*

Library of Congress Cataloging-in-Publication Data

Glass, Leslie.
Hanging time / Leslie Glass.
p.    cm.
ISBN 0-553-09712-1
I. Title.
PS3557.L34H36      1995
813'.54—dc20      94-27275
CIP

*Published simultaneously in the United States and Canada*

Bantam Books are published by Bantam Books, a division of Bantam Doubleday Dell Publishing
Group, Inc. Its trademark, consisting of the words "Bantam Books" and the portrayal of a
rooster, is Registered in U.S. Patent and Trademark Office and in other countries. Marca
Registrada. Bantam Books, 1540 Broadway, New York, New York 10036.

*For Charlotte,*
*and in loving memory of*
*Harrison Salisbury*

*And lovelier things have mercy shown*
*To every failing but their own;*
*And every woe a tear can claim,*
*Except an erring sister's shame.*

LORD BYRON

# ACKNOWLEDGMENTS

I want to thank everyone at Bantam Books who wanted this author. Irwyn Applebaum, Nita Taublib, my editor Kate Miciak, Jamie Warren-Youll, Linda Biagi. And others in publicity and sales whose names I don't know. Years ago, when Bantam was showing the world a whole new way of packaging books, I worked there as a copywriter. It was at Bantam that I first thought I might try to write a novel. No one I knew then is there now, and publishing is no longer a small, gentlemanly, family business. But some things I experienced in the old Bantam are still there: teamwork; a fierce fighting competitive spirit that I fervently hope will never die; and the love of books as well, occasionally, as of those who write them. Thank you, Bantam, for having me back.

Even in fields such as journalism and science, where a person ought to be able to count on a few solid facts, there is very little absolute truth. With no apologies, the novelist tries for the best view of a relative truth. Those who guide her in her studies toward that end are precious and deeply appreciated. Perpetual thanks to Dr. Richard C. Friedman, my psychology professor and consultant on human behavior. Thanks to Arthur Goldman, D.D.S., odontologist and former President of the American Academy of Forensic Science. Thank you, Acting Dean Lawrence Kobilinsky, John Jay College of Criminal Justice. Thank you, Nick Petracco, dust and fiber expert, and Captain George Cockburn for details and corrections. Thanks to Thomas Lacalamita, computer expert, for his recovery skills.

And always first and last: thank you, Lindsey, for the trip, thank you, Alex, for growing up. Thank you, Sarah Jane Freyman, my agent, for waiting so long. Thank you, Edmund, for the photo ops.

# HANGING TIME

# 1

It was the dog that caught Maggie Wheeler's eye and ended her life. If it hadn't been the cutest dog she'd ever seen, she wouldn't have spoken to the woman. The very last thing she intended was to smile, pull the latch, and open the door for another customer. At six minutes past seven on a hot August Saturday night the cutesy boutique called The Last Mango was closed. Maggie was finally tidying up after a long, exhausting day that started badly at ten when Olga Yerger, the other salesgirl, didn't show up and never called to say why. Maggie figured Olga had met some guy and taken off for the weekend. It wouldn't be the first time. Olga was a blond beauty from one of the Scandinavian countries, who was in New York to find a rich guy to marry. Even when she was in the store she didn't do much work. And now Maggie couldn't find the store keys. If she left without the keys, her boss, Elsbeth Manganaro, would kill her. Maggie just couldn't imagine what she had done with them. They were always right there, either on the counter or in the drawer. Shit.

Maggie wasn't feeling good about the human race. Her legs ached from running up and down the tight circular staircase all day, attempting to please difficult customers who wanted to try on more expensive originals than could be displayed in the tiny showroom downstairs. The staircase to the loft storeroom was so narrow it caught the sides of hangers and sleeves, and Maggie's arms and elbows, too. She had a number of bruises. In addition, in the great long-ago of last winter, the owner of the store had enticed her into taking the job by promising Maggie she would never have to work on Saturdays in August.

"The Last Mango will always be closed on weekends in August," Elsbeth had said vehemently, clutching a fox coat around her shoulders even though the heat was on high in the boutique. "My customers and my girls always go away Friday nights."

Mrs. Manganaro wore many noisy accessories with her skirts and blouses, had the strangest hair color Maggie had ever seen, and made it seem as if she and the salesgirls were all so well off they didn't need to work.

"Call me Elsbeth," she had said. "I like close relationships."

Well, she lied about weekends off in summer, and a few other things, too. Maggie's mouth soured as she remembered. Nothing was going well for her just then. She wouldn't mind taking off for a weekend to think things over. She looked around to see what else needed to be done before she could get out of there.

The store was attractive in a spare, trendy kind of way. But nothing was efficient about it. The space was cramped. The display area for clothes was not nearly big enough. Maggie had to keep running up and down the circular staircase to the storeroom upstairs to show the stock, and then to put the rejects away.

The good things were the store was on Columbus Avenue near where she lived, and the owner was lazy, let her do almost everything. Maggie figured she was learning a lot. Hurriedly, she folded the last of the gauzy, wildly colored printed skirts and glittering hundred-dollar T-shirts, sequin-studded with the stars and stripes and other stirring symbols on them. All afternoon she had kept hoping Olga would find it in her hard foreign heart to turn up after all and cover for her so she could go out for something to eat. But Olga never did.

Maggie didn't dare close the boutique on her own, in case Elsbeth came by to check up on her. She was more than a little afraid of Elsbeth. Her boss was a fiftyish shrew with so much blue in her red dye job, her hair was almost purple. Elsbeth wore glasses in the shape of wings that magnified the deep wrinkles and puckers around her eyes, and she drew her lips on way over the natural line. She was the epitome of the tight-fisted, bullying employer who used the fat settlements from her various marriages and divorces to buy buildings and set herself up in small businesses.

Maggie was a birdlike person with blunt-cut short brown hair and a nose and chin too sharp for her tiny face. She was from the little town of Seekonk, Massachusetts, and frightened easily. It never occurred to her that ordering out was a legitimate way of getting food even though she saw other people doing it all the time. She was afraid of delivery boys and a lot of other things. People were always telling her to relax and smile more, but neither came naturally. Maggie was a mournful sort of person, now very hungry and anxious about losing her job when everything was such a mess in her life.

The sudden awareness of sharp tapping on glass made her look up. Peering at her through the window, a would-be customer had been knocking on the door for some minutes. There was a "closed" sign right in the middle of it that no one could miss seeing.

Maggie shook her head at how stupid people could be sometimes. Quickly folding the last of the T-shirts, she looked up and mouthed the word "closed," gesturing to the sign.

As she pointed to it, Maggie caught sight of the small poodle. The dog was in a canvas bag slung over the shoulder of the would-be buyer. All that could be seen of it was its curly head and neck. At first glance it almost looked like a baby lamb. But then Maggie saw it had soft ears and an enchanting pointed muzzle with a bit of a mustache at the end. It turned its head this way and that, trying to take in everything, eyes extraordinarily bright.

"Oh." A little gasp of delight escaped Maggie's heretofore tightly pursed lips.

Her feeling of betrayal at being left alone all day, and her disapproval at the banging on the locked door, eased instantly at the sight of the puppy. She was sure it was a puppy by the way it studied everything so intensely, its head cocked first to one side and then the other. She could see its tiny teeth. Its mouth was slightly open as if in a smile. Maggie moved over to the window to get a closer look. The poodle followed her movements, almost as if it had heard her speak. The bright black eyes winked as the knocking on the door became more insistent.

The woman at the door pointed at something in the window and then at her watch. Just a minute after closing, a tiny minute, she pantomimed.

Maggie clicked her tongue. It had been a long day. She wasn't in the mood for the kind of person who didn't care about the rules. Maggie knew she had to follow all the rules to be safe. All too painfully and well did she know what happened when she slipped and didn't follow the rules. Still, it occurred to her that if she opened the door, she could find out the vital statistics of the dog. It looked so much like a lively monkey.

One thing she had learned in her short time in New York was that dog owners were the only people who truly enjoyed being approached and talked to on the street. They loved having their babies admired. If she let the customer in, she could probably play with the puppy.

Without considering the matter any further, Maggie smiled and unlocked the door. "We're closed," she said. "What an adorable dog."

"Well, the sign's up, but you're still here. Can't you make an exception for a few seconds? I wanted to buy that shirt for a friend's birthday." The woman was tall, imperious. She pointed at an array of blouses in the display window. "I've been meaning to drop by all week, but just haven't had a minute to come in for it. I'm going away," she said peevishly, "and if I don't get it now, I won't ever be able to."

Through the half-open door, Maggie reached out to pat the dog's head.

The woman smiled and pushed in. She backed Maggie into the store, moving her shoulder at the same time so the dog in the canvas bag was out of reach. The door clicked behind her.

Maggie's attention was on the puppy. It was definitely a tiny poodle. The fur was still as fluffy as unspun silk, and she wanted to touch its baby softness. As she reached out to pet it, the puppy's velvety tongue darted out to lick her. "Oh," she cried.

"Don't touch the dog," the woman said sharply. "You going to sell me the blouse or not?"

"Which one is it?" Maggie asked, putting her mind on the sale. There were several blouses in the window. Then, unable to resist, she added, "What's its name?" about the dog. "How old is it?"

"Right there. The white one. Hurry up, I don't have all night."

"It's the cutest dog I've ever seen," Maggie cried, unable to take her eyes off it. The pale puppy fluff stood on end, as if it had just been brushed, or electrified. She reached out one finger to touch it.

"Can't you *hear*? I said don't touch the dog." The woman backed away angrily. "Are you going to get me that shirt, or am I going to have to complain to your boss?"

Maggie flinched at her tone, suddenly uneasy. The woman's face had frozen into a mask of fury. Maggie hesitated. What would Elsbeth want her to do?

"What's your problem? I asked for that shirt. Get it for me."

"The one in the window is a petite. I don't think we have any white ones in your size left," Maggie said slowly, glancing toward the back room by the dressing room, where only the blouses and cotton sweaters were stored. The door was open, but from where she stood she couldn't see the shelves stacked with colorful items in plastic bags. She couldn't remember if there was a white one left or not. In any case, she didn't want to leave the woman alone in the shop while she looked. There was something odd about her.

"Well, go and look. Hurry up, I don't have all night," she repeated.

Well, Maggie didn't have all night either. She was hungry and tired and getting anxious about the way the large, pushy woman was talking to her. A muscle jumped in her cheek and now she was looking around as if she planned to take something the minute Maggie turned her back. If the woman stole something, Maggie would have to pay for it with her salary. What did the woman want? All kinds of things happened in New York. Maybe she was a criminal. Maggie hesitated, unsure what the right thing to do was. She didn't want to make the wrong move. But what was the right move with someone like this?

The puppy winked at her, its head cocked to one side.

Angrily, the woman moved closer. "Just get me the damn shirt and I'll get out of here."

Okay. That was it. New Yorkers were something. They had to have what they wanted when they wanted it and didn't care how they got it. Maggie decided to get the damn shirt. As she turned toward the closet, her elbow accidentally brushed the canvas bag. The puppy, poised like a panther, its front paws together and head drawn back, suddenly leapt out of the bag. Maggie caught it in her arms like a short pass in the end zone.

It was unbelievably soft and sweet. Like a baby, it clung to Maggie's neck and covered her eyes, lips, and nose with warm, velvety kisses. They were the last kisses she would ever receive.

The woman grabbed the dog, wrenching Maggie's arm in a fury.

"Ow." Maggie's eyes filled with tears. "Let go."

"Damn bitch. I told you not to touch my dog."

"Hey, what're you doing? Don't. You're hurting me."

The woman seemed to have forgotten the dog. The dog was on the floor, sniffing around. "You get it for me. You hear me? You *get that shirt for me.*" Ranting, she shoved Maggie toward the storeroom.

One of Maggie's arms was twisted so badly she was sure her shoulder was dislocated. "Stop." Suddenly frantic, she tried to pull away, get to the front door, and push the alarm. The woman was much stronger than she was. She pushed Maggie the other way, toward the back room.

Maggie resisted and felt something give in her shoulder.

"Help!" she screamed, but the door to the street was closed and locked. On the other side of it, the sidewalk was empty. No one was window-shopping. There was an alarm button by the money drawer. Maggie was dragged away from that, too. She couldn't reach anything. For an instant she saw the dog sitting on the floor in the shop, watching her struggle with great interest. Then it squatted and peed. Maggie's last thought before she was shoved into the back room and the door slammed on them was that the dog was a girl.

"Bitch," the woman cried. "I'll teach you to touch other people's things."

"Ow." Maggie clawed at the door with her uninjured hand.

"Stop that." The woman started shaking her so violently that her head snapped back and forth. "Stop that! Stop taking my things. You can't have my things."

"I didn't—I don't— No!"

The woman let go of Maggie's shoulders and gripped her throat. With both hands she started shaking her by the neck.

"Always taking my things. Can't have my things. Think you can fool me. No. You can't fool me."

"Agggh." Maggie was choking. Her eyes bulged. "Agggh." She kicked out, trying to scream, to get away. She blacked out for a second, then revived when the pressure eased.

"Bitch!"

Pain exploded in her head for the last time. The woman had slipped a cord around her neck and was yanking hard.

Twenty minutes later Maggie Wheeler hung from the light fixture in the storeroom in a five-hundred-dollar size-fourteen flowered summer dress that hung way down over her shoulders and hid her feet. Purple lipstick and blue eye shadow, grotesquely applied, further disfigured her mournful little face. The air conditioner, set on high and blowing on her, ruffled her hair and skirt, and gave her the appearance of eternal living death.

## 2

What was left of the former potato field stretched over several acres at least, flat and vegetation-free. Set back a hundred or so feet from the newly created road, the house in progress soared over the emptiness, straining for even a tiny glimpse of the ocean, a quarter of a mile to the south.

Charles stopped the BMW at the construction site with a jerk and jumped out excitedly.

"What do you think?" he demanded of his oldest friend in the mental health field.

Jason Frank, author of scholarly texts, teacher, and psychoanalyst, got out of the passenger seat slowly, as if both of his long, well-muscled legs had recently been broken and were not yet fully healed. For a minute he took in the Portosan, the construction trailer, the advertising signs of the architect, builder, landscape architect, and the dozen suppliers that littered the site. Without going a step closer he could tell that the eleven-room house would be fully air-conditioned, would have a tennis court and swimming pool, and was already alarmed against vandals and thieves. This was some beach shack for a psychiatrist whose hourly fee was fixed, like Jason's, at a hundred and sixty-five dollars for those who could pay, and less for those who couldn't. There was no way he could afford such a house on his earned income.

The familiar twinge of jealousy, now almost twenty years old, threatened to seize Jason in the region of his heart, probe around for the weakest place, and strike him down with despair. Charles was independently wealthy, had all the glamour and worldly goods, and Jason was stuck with the driving ambition to do something important and leave his mark on the profession.

Charles fixed Jason with the same look of eager anticipation that had charmed him when they met and became friends at the Psychiatric Center the first day of their training. Jason had just returned to New York from medical school in Chicago and Charles was finally home from Yale. Both were eager and idealistic about psychiatry, their chosen specialty; and both were unhappily married to their high school sweethearts.

The similarities between them went a little further. They looked like they could be brothers, were six feet tall and athletic. Jason had the body of a runner, the brain of a scientist, and the all-American good looks of a Kennedy. For him it was an unlikely mix, bred from five thousand years of dark Jewish angst in northern Europe, an unhappy childhood in the Bronx, and the iron will to do better than his forebears. His parents, his grandparents, and their grandparents had all been poor, struggling peasants. Brilliant and intense, Jason was not only tall, light-brown-haired, and handsome, but the first financial success in his family.

Charles, on the other hand, was more of the Mediterranean type. He was dark-eyed, dark-haired, passionate. He was also less angular in his features than Jason, had more of a nose, more flesh in his face and body, and was a good deal more hedonistic in his approach to life. The pampered only son of a rich Westchester family, he had always been able to do exactly as he pleased, and never hesitated to do it. While Jason was still struggling to support his family and first wife, Charles already had two children, two cars, and a house in the suburbs that he wanted to be rid of. Now, nearly fifteen years later, Charles had four children, two belonging to his second wife, Brenda, three cars, three houses, and, Jason suspected, a mistress. Charles couldn't be happy with one of anything. He was also secretive. He never said a thing about this new plaything in all the months of its planning and construction.

Jason looked up at the looming structure with a sick feeling in the pit of his stomach. If he hadn't been so heavily focused on his teaching, his patients, and his writing all these years, he might have at least a few possessions, too. He was on the brink of forty, and three months ago his second wife, the actress Emma Chapman, went to California to make a movie. After the shooting stopped, she told him she wasn't coming back.

"Is this the living end, or what?" Charles demanded when no awed praise from Jason was forthcoming.

He put a protective hand on Jason's shoulder as if to say, We've been through a lot together—two divorces, two remarriages, Emma's kidnapping in the spring. Hell, we'll find a way to get through the separation, too.

Jason nodded. It was the living end all right.

He glanced over at Milicia Honiger-Stanton, who had hung back for a moment to get the fifty oversize pages of house plans out of the car. He watched her reach in, leaning all the way across the back seat, so that her short, tight skirt hiked up and displayed long, shapely legs and an extremely well-formed derriere. Charles caught the direction of Jason's gaze and raised an eyebrow in approval.

"That's it, take an interest, get the blood flowing again," he murmured.

Jason turned away, frowning. When he first got off the train that morning and saw Charles and Milicia together waiting for him at the station, Jason suspected that the tall and extraordinarily dramatic Milicia, of the wild red hair and deep green eyes, must be the mistress Charles had hidden somewhere in the woodwork of his life.

It would be just like Charles to go so far as to actually build a house to provide a project for the architect he lusted after. Jason couldn't imagine any other reason to construct a house in the Hamptons when he already had one in Bedford. Then they got to the house Charles and Brenda were renting while their new one was being built. When Brenda ran out to greet him all excited and pleased in a way he hadn't seen her in a long time, he realized the house was for her. And Milicia was a red herring. He shook his head at himself. He missed the cue. Must be losing his grip.

As Jason crunched across the pebble drive, Brenda ran out to meet him, waving enthusiastically. "I'm *so* glad you came. I've been thinking about you."

She was all in white—big white blouse, flowing white skirt. They made her dark hair and tanned skin stand at attention. She reached out her arms and engulfed him in a cloud of some floral-mix perfume that was both unidentifiable and immensely appealing. Jason had always liked her. Brenda was a small, elegant woman with a lovely shape and at least as much intelligence as her husband. Her embrace at that moment was devastating. Jason worked in a field where no one touched. He hadn't received a hug in some time. He released himself from it quickly to stop his heart from breaking.

"How are you doing? I can't not ask," she said almost apologetically.

"You can ask. I'm fine. Fine." He nodded to show how fine he was.

"I think about you and Emma all the time. What do you hear from her?" She took his arm as they walked to the house, shaking her head, as if baffled by Emma's desertion after what Jason did for her.

The situation with Emma wasn't what Brenda thought. Jason looked around, trying to hold on to his equilibrium. It was a pretty place. The rented house was surrounded by rose gardens, all in bloom. A wave of sadness swept over him as he thought how much Emma would have liked it. The smell of the roses, the smell of the sea, everything. He pulled himself together.

"She lets me call her on Fridays. We have a scheduled time. We talk. She's still—" Traumatized, of course. He shrugged and changed the subject. "What about you?"

"Well, this is me. I feel good here." Brenda laughed ruefully, letting the bruises from a difficult second marriage that she had expected to be heaven show for just a second.

"You know how I never could stand all those woods and trees. So closed in. Wait till you see *my* house. It's everything I like—decks and sun and sky everywhere. Funny-shaped rooms with light streaming in from above."

Jason smiled at her pleasure. No, he had no idea she didn't like Charles's stone house with a fireplace in every room, very little light, buried deep in a heavily wooded area. What was this, revenge? The harbinger of the end of the marriage?

He hoped for both of them that they could work it out. Brenda was perfect for Charles, wealthy herself, independent, lively, thoughtful, deeply caring of his two children, and certainly at least as clever as he. Her eyes hardened with her awareness that he was studying her.

"Sorry, I'll stop." It was an occupational hazard. He constantly evaluated everyone. Emma used to say every time he looked at her she felt as though he were taking her emotional temperature. Ever the shrink, checking for sanity.

"It's okay. I like you, too. If you ever want an ear, I'll listen."

Touched, Jason smiled. "The same to you."

"Listen," Brenda said. "I won't go with you to the house. Take a look at it on your own, and don't mind Charles's matchmaking. Milicia's an interesting person, quite talented, I think. But after Em—" She paused, confirming Jason's own personal view that his estranged wife, should she ultimately decide not to return to him, would not be easy to replace.

Brenda looked over at her husband, leaning against his car, deep in conversation with the beautiful architect, and shook her head as if she were truly puzzled.

"It always amazes me how a really good shrink like Charles could be such a jerk about women," she said.

Jason wondered if she were speaking about him as well. He had had everything he thought he wanted in a woman, and was too busy healing other people to make her happy. From three thousand miles away, Emma twisted the knife a little more and pain shot through him.

He couldn't get over the irony. How often had he heard his patients describe the black hole, the bottomless pit of agony they felt when they failed at love, were left behind in the empty apartment, with the empty bed, and the days stretching out into an eternity of aloneness. Countless times. How many times had he empathized, never for a second thinking it could happen to him.


"Here we are." Milicia bundled the plans under her arm and hurried up to them, flashing Jason a brilliant smile that, lovely as it was, failed to warm him.

Again Charles put his hand on Jason's shoulder as if to say, Come on, old man. Get back in the saddle again.

Jason shook his head. Thanks anyway, he had other fish to fry and had no interest in getting to know any new people.

Still, several hours later, after they had looked over the house three or four times, taken a walk on the beach with Brenda, and had the requisite barbecued steak ritual, Jason was feeling better in spite of himself. When Milicia offered to drive him back to the city just as dusk was falling, he nodded, grateful to accept.

## 3

*S*pan *of control, unity of command, delegation of authority, positive discipline, negative discipline, lost time management.*

Detective April Woo, Detective Squad, 20th Precinct, New York City Police Department, gathered up the pile of index cards she had made of the management aspect of being a Sergeant. She zipped them into a pocket of the looseleaf notebook she had created over the last three months as a study guide for her police Sergeant promotion test, which was coming up in less than two weeks. The notebook contained hundreds of notes on job tasks associated with being a sergeant, as well as procedures and investigation techniques, department rules and regulations. The note-book was open to the section on leadership styles. Theory X and Theory Y management behavior, autocratic leaders, free-rein leaders (*laissez faire*). April didn't know any leaders in the last category. She closed the book.

The clock beside her bed read 6:01 and already the sunlight streaked halfway across the room. She could tell summer was on the wane by the fact that only a few weeks earlier the patch of brilliance had been in the same place nearly an hour earlier. In a month or so the light wouldn't be waking her up early enough to study before work at all, but by then it wouldn't matter. She will have taken the test, and her fate would be decided. On the sergeant's score anyway.

April knew she'd have to have an overall score of 95 or 96 to get it. One of her professors at John Jay had told her she had to want it bad. She knew that already. The same professor had also quoted an old Chinese proverb. "Learning is like rowing upstream; not to advance is to drop back." She already knew that, too. Also, that she would not have another chance at promotion for five years. That was a scary thought. She was

determined to be Sergeant Woo. And maybe even Lieutenant Woo someday. She shook herself a little to get going, and didn't get anywhere.

Downstairs, April could hear her mother and father already squabbling in Chinese in their half of the two-family house they shared. They
had financed the house with their combined incomes for different reasons. Woo parents said they wanted house so they could live Chinese-
American style, together-apart in great happiness someday soon when
April came to senses, left the police, married a Chinese doctor with a good
practice, and had many babies.

April knew they said they'd be happy only if every one of their ten
thousand most-wanted blessings were granted, but in fact their most
important dreams had already been fulfilled. April had helped them buy
the house so they could live well, period. Never mind who she married.
Or even *if* she married, which most days she was pretty sure she wouldn't.

The beam of sunlight inched over, pressuring her to get moving. She
slid out of bed and padded into the bathroom. It had green ceramic tiles
and a white curtain blowing in the open window. She was glad no one
ever had to see the bathroom shelves loaded with cosmetics, moisturizers,
bath oils, and small, shiny objects of decoration.

In fact, her own home was the only place she didn't have to convince
herself she was glad to be single. She liked not having to fight over who
got the sink, or who was going to break down and wash it out afterward.
As she began her exercises, she thought it would be terrible for someone
to see her doing her hundred and fifty sit-ups, her squats and leg lifts, the
work on her upper body with the free weights, and the grip exercises she
did to keep her .38 as light as chopsticks in her hand.

She began to sweat after the thirty-fourth crunch. She was five foot
five, which was not as bad genetically as it could have been, but slender as
a reed, like her father, a cook in one of the better Chinese restaurants,
who ate all the time and never gained an ounce of flesh. She took a break
for three minutes to wash her face and assess herself critically in the
mirror. It was hard to tell an Asian's age, she knew.

At nearly thirty, April looked ten years younger. She had a perfect
oval face, and a well-defined but not too pointed chin, small mouth, long,
delicate neck, and a short layered haircut that had been singed pretty
badly in the explosion but was nearly grown out now. In the mirror her
eyes looked calm and determined, protected by their mongolian folds and

years of training. As a cop she was supposed to feel normal no matter what terrible things she saw, or happened to her. But it was no secret that the police had a very high suicide rate, a lot of alcoholics, and multiple marriages with bitter endings.

April didn't feel normal yet. She was still thinking about the case every day. She could still feel the scorching blast that knocked her and Sanchez, the Sergeant supervising her, through a door and sent them crashing down a flight of stairs into the garage below. If they'd hit the wall of the upstairs room instead, they would not have survived the fire. Sanchez lost his mustache, his eyebrows, some of his hair, and had burns on his ears, neck, and forehead. He had shoved April behind him at the last second even though she had her gun drawn and could have shot him. So there were no scars on her face, only on her hands and ankles. She owed him.

In her first days of being a detective, when April didn't have to wear the blue uniform anymore, she had tried dressing in skirts, like a woman. In the summer she wore short sleeves on the street. After a few experiences of scrambling around garbage cans, trying to catch a mugger, her legs all scratched and hanging out, and getting a favorite skirt caught in the barbed wire somebody had put on his back window in Chinatown to discourage intruders, she knew better. Now she wore long-sleeved blouses, jackets, and man-tailored trousers all year around.

Sometimes when she looked down at the scars on her hands that might never match the brown of her skin, she thought the blouse, the jacket, the pants, had spared the rest of her. But deep inside she knew it was really Sanchez's macho reflex—to protect the women at all costs—that saved her. She often wondered if he would have made the same move if she had been a male detective, or a Sergeant like himself.

Today Sanchez would be back from a week's vacation in Mexico. He'd probably be unbearably Spanish for quite a while. April swallowed some hot water with lemon in it, old Chinese remedy for she didn't even know what, and started her leg lifts. She wasn't sure exactly when flesh had gotten to be such a point of interest to her. Sometime in the year since she was transferred from the 5th Precinct in Chinatown to the Two-O on the Upper West Side she started working out more.

She still missed Chinatown. She was born there, lived there most of her life, was posted to the 5th after eighteen months on street patrol in Brooklyn. She was promoted to Detective 3rd grade after only two years

14

in Chinatown, then Detective 2nd grade, which earned her Sergeant's pay but not the supervisory rank. She had expected to remain, a social worker with a gun, in Chinatown forever. The move to the Upper West Side made no sense. In a police force of over thirty thousand, with only a few hundred of that number Asian, it seemed absurd to be assigned to a precinct that was overwhelmingly white, African American, and Hispanic. Of course, if she hadn't been transferred, she would never have met Sanchez, and who knows, might even have married Jimmy Wong and been unhappy the rest of her life, not to mention just a Detective 2nd Grade with not so many ambitions for a higher rank and a college degree.

April finished her exercises, showered, dressed quickly, and set off from Astoria, Queens, hoping to get into Manhattan before Sanchez did.

The traffic on the Fifty-ninth Street Bridge was a thick clot as usual but light on Eighty-fifth Street, crosstown through Central Park. She made it to the Two-O by 7:50 and parked her white Chrysler Le Baron in the police lot next to the precinct. Mike's red Camaro was already there.

Upstairs in the squad room, Sanchez was working the phone, feet up on an open drawer, wearing his usual combination of gray shirt and darker gray tie, light gray trousers. He liked to mix his grays. A gray linen jacket hung over the back of his chair. His black hair and bristly mustache were as lush as ever, and he was, as April had predicted, very dark from the Mexican sun.

For a week the squad room had smelled like old steel furniture. Now a familiar odor charged the air again. Sanchez was back. In the early morning his aftershave was strongest, powerful enough to sweeten a garbage dump.

"Hi." April breathed in and whistled. "Wow."

He grinned and put his hand over the receiver.

"Miss me?"

She shook her head.

"Aw, and I thought you were *mi querida.*"

"Yeah, yeah," she muttered.

"Close enough." He took his hand off the receiver. "Yeah, yeah, I'm here. What day did you say you saw Elonzo with the car in question?"

April slung her bag down on her desk and went through the motions of getting the files of her current cases together. Sure she missed Sanchez, and he knew it. But she would never say so. It would give him even more ideas than he already had. Although she'd heard there was a lot of Chi-

15

nese-Mexican mixing in California, the combination would never work for her. Not with her hopes for the future, and the kind of family she had.

Anyway, no matter what their private feelings, Sanchez was a detective-sergeant on the way up. He'd fixed it so that she worked under his "close supervision" a whole lot of the time. Nobody in the precinct had any doubts about what that meant. Sanchez had monkey business on his mind, and he was in a position to hold her back or push her ahead. She had to be careful about a lot of things, and falling in love with him was absolutely out of the question.

"Yeah, but Thursday of what month?" he asked. He made a note on the paper in front of him.

"Oh, now it's *this* month. Can you give me a date on that? A date. Like Thursday the fourth. Or Thursday the twenty-second."

At ten o'clock April Woo and Sergeant Sanchez were the first detectives to see Maggie Wheeler.

## 4

"Oh, God, she's in there!" the woman cried, pointing to a door at the back. "Oh, God, the poor kid. Who could do that? How could that happen? Oh, God."

April looked quickly around, saying some comforting words she wasn't even aware of. The store was only two blocks from the precinct and already blue uniforms were swarming around outside. It was one of the expensive boutiques that April noticed every day and never went into because she couldn't afford anything there. Right now it had some colorful shirts that probably couldn't be washed, hanging on a clothesline in the window. Below the clothesline there were some piles of sand on the floor. Like everyone was supposed to be at the beach wearing shirts like this, April supposed.

The woman started screeching at her.

"What kind of city is this that two young women can't even work in a store without getting killed?"

*A terrible city,* April didn't have time to say.

"And hundreds of cops only a block away. What the hell were you all doing when this happened?"

In a second April had taken in the soft, pouchy skin all blotched with relocated makeup, hair redder than anything nature ever intended, the funny figure with its skinny legs and thick middle, big breasts straining at a lime-green silk shirt tucked into matching shorts with a big twisted rope belt that emphasized the nonexistent waist. April estimated her age at late fifties or early sixties. Understandably hysterical. The woman said it was her store, and yes it was all right if April took a look around.

"Here, sit down," April suggested. "I'll be right back."

Crime Scene had already been called, but there was no way of knowing how many homicides the sixty-man unit was working just then. There were about six homicides a day in New York City. She and Sanchez could be body-sitting for ten minutes or three hours, depending on when a team was available. April headed where the woman said the body was. Two? Was it two bodies now?

There was only a tiny space at the back, hardly big enough to be a storeroom. The door was open. April hesitated for a second and then pushed it open as far as it would go, careful not to leave a print.

"Oh." She recoiled involuntarily at the sight of the dead girl.

The corpse's eyes and mouth were open in a mute scream, lips pulled away from the teeth as if in a huge grimace. The eyelids looked as if they had been propped open with toothpicks. Around the eyes and mouth, deep blue eye shadow and plum-colored lipstick had been crudely applied, the way makeup is on a clown. A long dress hid the girl's feet; a price tag hung from a ruffled sleeve. April could see the price, which had been written in by hand. Five hundred and twenty dollars. That was a lot of money for a dress that was made of—rayon. The price tag said that, too. Too bad it didn't say why the girl was wearing a size fourteen when she was probably only a two. This was no suicide. It was the work of a psycho.

April saw everything in an instant, and took it in the way she had been trained. She would never forget it. She would always be able to describe that scene.

The air from the air-conditioning vent blew the hair away from the dead girl's face and lifted the hem of the dress. Goose bumps covered the skin on her arms and shoulders as if the corpse could still react to cold.

April shivered, pushing away the normal person's desire to vomit. She was a cop. She wasn't supposed to be normal. To counter the urge, she reached for her notebook and oddly recorded the price of the dress first, as if that had anything to do with it. Then she crouched down and lifted the hem of the dress. The girl's feet were bare.

Mike pushed in behind her.

"Oh, shit," he muttered.

April switched her attention to the girl's little hands curled tightly into fists. Tiny red spots dotted her knuckles. Lividity. The third finger of her right hand had a small gold ring in the shape of leaves on it. One pale blue stone was set in the middle of the gold leaves. Caught on the prongs holding the stone was a tuft of some kind of peachy textile. It looked like wool.

April studied the tuft for a second and then looked quickly around for a sweater, for the girl's handbag, for the makeup that was on her face. She didn't see an orange sweater. The handbag was on a chair. It didn't appear to have been opened. April didn't see her shoes. She didn't touch anything.

"How do you think she got up there?" Mike asked, ever the prompting supervisor.

April shook her head.

The ceiling was only about seven and a half feet high. The light fixture was wrought iron, had two twisted arms decorated with a pattern of leaves on a vine. April frowned. More leaves. The girl was hung up on the chandelier by a short length of clothesline that looked like the kind in the window. Just kind of hung on it by the chin.

Her feet dangled barely a foot above the ground.

"Oh," April said again, trying to process what she saw without feeling so sick. She turned to Mike suddenly. "Where's the other one?"

"The other what?" He frowned.

"She said there were two girls here. Didn't you hear her?"

"Shit."

They left the storeroom and went back into the store. The woman was sobbing into a sodden tissue.

"No one's safe anymore. And with you just across the street. I got to get out of here. Move to Florida or someplace. I checked the register. It wasn't even money." She cried some more.

"You said something about another girl."

"I don't know where she is. Maybe she got away. Maybe they took her someplace else. I bet she's dead, too."

Mike made a face at April and went up the circular staircase. In seconds he came down again, shaking his head. No bodies upstairs.

"Was she raped?" Elsbeth Manganaro cried. "Poor thing. Was she raped?"

"We'll know that later," April said, and nodded as the crime-scene unit arrived. She looked at her watch. Twenty minutes. Must be some kind of record.

Mike went out, and April turned to the store owner.

"Mrs. Manganaro? Why don't you come across the street with me?" she suggested.

"Are you a cop?" the woman demanded, blowing her nose and finally focusing on April.

April nodded. "I'm a detective."

"You don't look like a cop." Elsbeth frowned, examining April's navy trousers and navy jacket, pale blue and white printed rayon blouse, with its soft bow at the neck.

"I'm a Chinese cop," April said. Uptown people found that surprising.

"You don't sound Chinese."

The woman wouldn't give up. Was it still so unusual for an Asian to speak English? April was an ABA—American-born Asian. In Chinatown there were clubs of them. They met and networked. Asian networking didn't work too well in NYPD. In fact, there weren't enough of them in enough high places for them to network at all.

"I was born here. I could run for president."

"Oh." The woman blew her nose again, apparently satisfied for the moment.

Mike had returned and was watching this exchange. His amused grin brought a flush to April's cheeks. With Crime Scene there, the store had crowded up.

April took the store owner's arm and helped her up. "How about a cup of coffee?"

"Are you going to question me?" Elsbeth demanded.

"I'm going to ask you some questions."

"What about my store?" the woman cried.

"Sergeant Sanchez will watch it for you."

Mike nodded gravely. April introduced them.

"You won't let them take anything." Elsbeth frowned suspiciously, now looking Sanchez over. He appeared to be Spanish and his eyebrows weren't even. The left eyebrow was only half there. There was a scar where the rest of it should be.

"No, ma'am," Sanchez assured her.

The only things that would be taken away were the corpse, the evidence, and the belongings of the victim. April turned to Mike. "I'll take her statement and meet you back here." She glanced at her watch again. "An hour at the most."

She wanted to get back before they moved the body. Sanchez nodded. "Welcome back," she murmured. It was the best she could do. She'd been taught to watch her back and save her face, hide her feelings no matter what, so persistently, over such a long period of time, she had a lot of trouble figuring out what her true feelings were.

# 5

ason watched Brian leave, pleased to note that for the third week in a row, he was taking with him all the possessions he came with. Jason gave himself five minutes between Brian, his ten o'clock patient, and Dennis, his ten-fifty patient.

He closed the door to the waiting room, returned to his desk, and carefully tucked a piece of blotter paper under one leg of his newest skeleton clock. Earlier, with some irritation, he had watched the hammered brass pendulum slow down and finally stop at the same time Brian stalled in the middle of a sentence and stared off into space. In the past, at such moments, Brian's eyelids used to droop and he actually drifted off for a few minutes. But he was slowly getting better.

Today he turned his head suddenly and said, "The clock stopped."

"It must be slightly off balance," Jason replied. "Balance is everything in these old clocks."

"Is it a new one?" Brian asked.

"Yes," Jason answered. He'd bought it about three weeks ago.

"Can you get it going again?" The pendulum had a brass sun on the end. Brian frowned at it.

"Yes," Jason said. Some of his patients knew about his passion for clocks and some didn't. Brian did because it helped him to know that Jason could make broken things work.

Jason started the pendulum swinging again. It might stop in five minutes, an hour, five hours, or not until he next left town and wasn't there to wind it. He watched it swing back and forth. Maybe the tiny adjustment would be enough.

It was Monday, a long time from Friday, when he was scheduled to speak with Emma again. Jason didn't know whether to look forward to the phone call or not. He turned to another, more reliable clock, trying to shake off the pervasive feeling that too much was wrong with his world. Now the feeling included a vague uneasiness that lingered from the previous day in Southampton.

Something about it was odd, and even way after midnight he hadn't felt comfortable letting Milicia Honiger-Stanton drive him all the way to his building. He had no reason to ask her to let him off at Columbus Avenue, several long blocks from his apartment on Riverside Drive, but he did. He figured it was some kind of symbolic thing that had to do with Emma. He lived alone now, wanted to walk home alone. Crawl home like an injured animal was more like it.

He had gotten out of the car and was surprised to hear Milicia say, "I'd like to see you again."

He didn't reply immediately, and she hesitated, as if she weren't used to having to say those words to a man herself, much less follow them up.

A faint breeze stirred the air. Somewhere a siren howled.

"Hey, man, got a quarter? I got to get me sumpin' to eat."

The plaintive voice of a large black man with long, matted hair rose to a wail as he menaced a young couple halfway down the block. Jason stiffened, ready to move in their direction. Sometimes he had Mace in his pocket, but not today. Not having the Mace didn't bother him. Even from where he stood Jason could tell the man was unsettling but not dangerous. He didn't have to rescue the couple though. On the hot summer night there were still a lot of people on the street. A cop emerged from the dark and moved the man along.

Jason returned his attention to Milicia. He was startled by how beautiful she looked in the dark. The glow from the streetlights backlit her red hair, giving it the appearance of a fiery halo. Her face was as pale as the moon, which at the moment hung low in the sky over Central Park and seemed to hover over her head, very ripe, and just a day or so short of being full.

Her wide-eyed look of sudden shyness and innocence was belied by the display of deeply tanned thighs, visible almost to the crotch, and parted with the business of dealing with a gearshift. Jason noted that her old Mercedes needed a tune-up. It idled high in neutral. The woman's whole being exuded a powerful sexuality. No thanks, he wasn't buying.

"Thanks for the ride," he said coolly.

She caught her bottom lip with her teeth and struggled a little with her breathing. "I need someone to talk to," she said faintly.

"Oh?" Jason hesitated although he was already long gone, preoccupied by a thousand important matters to avoid thinking about what weighed most heavily on his mind.

Right then he was thinking about his schedule for the next day, the precious hours he had wasted going to Southampton to see Charles and Brenda when he should have been working on the paper he had to present at a conference in Baltimore at the end of the week. He was aware that the black man was now lurching in their direction.

He smiled a bit grimly to himself at one of those gender differences between men and women that kept turning up to complicate the simplest things. Women took a lot longer to say good-bye, often had trouble letting go of the moment. Men liked to walk away without looking back. He wanted to walk away.

He and Milicia had had an uneventful drive back. They talked about the house she designed for Charles and Brenda, architecture, New York City rent-controlled apartments, the firm she worked for. It was pleasant, but by no means one of those luminous, unforgettable events like the first time he met Emma.

Jason had interviewed Emma Chapman for a paper he was writing on adults who had been moved from place to place when they were children. Emma's father had been an officer in the navy before he retired. Jason and Emma were instantly drawn together, as if some kind of bond between them had always existed.

Jason started to sweat. Jesus, how could that be over? He was distracted for a second, thinking of Emma. He had no intention of seeing this woman again. Why did she suddenly need someone to talk to after he was already out of the car? She was very beautiful. Maybe she was just used to more gratification. He couldn't tell by the way she said she wanted to see him again if she meant professionally or socially. How annoying.

"You mean you want to see someone professionally?" he asked.

He was awkward now, standing on the street. Why had she waited until he was out of the car?

"Not exactly, but I do need some advice."

"What about Charles? He's very good at advice. Have you asked him?"

Milicia hesitated some more, then shook her head.

Ah. So there was a bit of conflict there. Maybe Charles had hit on her. Jason felt a second of sympathy for her.

"You're a shrink, right?" she asked.

Jason nodded. She knew he was.

"Well, I have a very sick sister."

Oh. Jason relaxed. It was professional. He pulled a pen from his pocket and scribbled his number on a scrap of paper. "Sure I'll talk to you. Here's my number. Call if you want." He handed her the paper and headed home as if he had averted a potentially difficult situation.

The pendulum on the new clock stopped again at ten forty-eight. The phone rang. Shit.

Jason had two minutes to Dennis. He decided to answer the phone and reached for the receiver. "Dr. Frank," he said.

"Hi. It's Milicia."

"Who?"

"Milicia Honiger-Stanton. I drove you home from the Hamptons last night. Have you forgotten already?"

"No, no. Of course not."

"Remember I said I'd like to talk to you? Can I buy you lunch?"

"No, thanks. I thought you wanted a consultation."

"Can we consult over lunch?"

Jason frowned, his eyes on the motionless pendulum. "No," he replied. "Not really."

"How about dinner?"

"I don't consult over dinner either. Would you like to make an appointment?"

"Oh, all right," she said. "But you're making me think I have bad breath or something."

"If you need advice," Jason said gently, "that's a professional matter. Professional matters have to be dealt with in a professional way."

"All right," Milicia repeated. There was now a slight edge to her voice. "We'll consult. But don't think of me as a patient."

"Fine," Jason said and took out his appointment book. "When would you like to meet?"

"Today?"

He flipped the pages in his appointment book. A Monday patient was on vacation in Paris. He sighed. "Five-fifteen. Is that all right?"

"Where are you?"

He gave her the address. Then he hung up and stuck another piece of paper under the clock leg.

# 6

Igor Stanislovski of Crime Scene shook his head at April's barrage of questions that couldn't wait for the lab reports and couldn't be answered without them. What about this sand? She had asked about the sand in the window display. Would it be worthwhile to go through it grain by grain?

"Don't touch," Igor said irritably.

"I didn't touch," April said.

"Well, you're hanging around, bothering me. Don't you know you're supposed to get lost?"

"I don't get lost," April said. "Maybe you won't think of the questions I want to ask. What about the sand?"

"It's my job to think of every question. I've already thought about the sand. I'm doing it last with a different bag." Igor crawled into a corner and vacuumed the same stretch of woodwork for the second time, which meant he was desperate. It was almost unheard of to get anything of great value from vacuuming.

"Not much here," he muttered. "Not even a stray spiderweb."

"That's what's wrong with this picture. It's all too clean," April said.

No blood splattered in revealing patterns. No open window in the basement with muddy footprints leading up the stairs. No shards of glass to speak of violent confrontation. No tool marks on the door. There was probably nothing in the sand either. The sand was in the display window. Anybody going out there would be seen from the street.

Igor had bagged the contents of the wastebasket. Just bits and pieces of paper. It was odd there were no leftovers from lunch in it, nothing to indicate two girls had been working and snacking there all day on Saturday. There wasn't even an empty coffee cup anywhere. Didn't she eat anything, April wondered. Did she go out for lunch, and what about the other girl? What was the murder weapon? There were some bruises on the dead girl's arm, but April didn't see a gunshot wound on the body, a bump on the head, or anything else. Of course there could be something she didn't see under the dress. There was some bruising on her neck. It did seem fairly clear the rope that hung the girl up there was not what killed her. The noose was not in the same place as the marks on her neck.

"Stop that," Igor said crossly from across the room as April moved toward the counter.

"You did this already," she murmured, peering into the open money drawer.

There was a fair amount of money in it. Apparently robbery had not been the motive. Sometime during the day one or more customers had bought something with a hundred-dollar bill. There were several of them stacked in the drawer, along with a thin pile of tens and twenties and a number of credit card receipts. At least there were names on those. April would have to find everyone who came in throughout the day on Saturday, and for weeks before that. The receipts for items bought were dated Saturday, two days before. Mrs. Manganaro had told April the store was closed on Sunday. The girl must have died on Saturday. It looked like the time of death should be later than that. The body was in very good condition for the middle of summer. But it was very cold in the storeroom. Maybe she'd been refrigerated.

April checked the girl's handbag. Her wallet was in it, some pieces of paper, an address book, a five-dollar bill zipped into a small pocket. A pink lipstick, not the plum that was on her face, no other makeup. A medium-size Swiss Army knife. An inhaler. Ventolin—prescription medicine for asthma. Maybe Maggie died of an asthma attack. Sure.

Igor bagged the purse. He had laid out all his kits for fluid samples but hadn't had any use for them. There was no blood or other fluids to collect. The dead girl had her underwear on. It seemed unlikely that she'd been raped. Rapists didn't usually dress their victims up afterward.

"Igor, was she dressed like that before or after she was killed?" April asked.

"No spots on the floor. You tell me."

No spots on the floor under the body indicated someone had taken the time to clean up. In death, the bladder and lower bowel evacuated. There was a toilet in the storeroom. The murderer could have cleaned up with the paper towels in there, and gotten rid of them down the toilet. Murderers didn't often do that. What kind of killer was this? Cleaned the

floor, put oversize clothes on the corpse, and messed up her face. April
had the strange feeling she was trapped in the shop with a crazy person
who wouldn't speak. What had happened here? What was the message?

Until they had started going over it and dusting the place with gray
powder, the tiny boutique had looked incredibly tidy. It looked as if
someone had wiped it clean and carefully vacuumed up after the murder.
But there wasn't a vacuum cleaner in the place. April shook her head. She
had forgotten to ask the owner who cleaned, and when.

"How do you kill somebody, change their clothes, put makeup all
over the face, and get out without leaving any traces? Whose makeup and
where is it?" she muttered.

"I just collect," Igor said.

"And where are her own clothes?"

Igor didn't bother to answer. If her clothes weren't there, whoever
killed her took them away.

April crossed to the front door and looked at it again. No signs of
forced entry.

"Did you find anything here?"

Igor carefully pulled some fibers out of the rug and put them in a
plastic bag that he neatly labeled with the location the sample came from
as well as its source. He moved across the floor to do the same in front of
the door.

"Not on the outside. There's a partial on the inside, and of course a
ton of prints in here. Lot of them probably hers."

He spoke with a trace of an accent from one of the Slavic countries
that didn't exist anymore. April liked him more than the other crime-
scene people she had met uptown. Igor was a small person with a large
head covered by a rarely mowed field of wheaty hair. He had big jaw,
wide set, arresting blue eyes, and a slight list to one side from an injury he
had received several years before in the line of duty.

"Don't touch," he said again as he got to his feet. He picked up a
hemplike piece of fiber with his tweezers and studied it.

"I'm not touching," April said. He was almost finished anyway.

There was a thin film of sticky powder all over the place.

"Did you see the fluff on the ring?" she asked.

"I saw it."

"What about the fingernails?"

Igor bagged the girl's hands with brown paper bags. His partner had already photographed everything, both with and without measuring tapes to show distances and heights. They never knew what they were going to need in court when they got the guy who did it. As well as photographing, he also sketched everything, including views of the building, the sidewalk, and the trees in front.

"You know I don't touch the body," Igor told her.

"You took a look, didn't you?"

"Yeah, I *looked,* but that doesn't mean I can tell you anything. That's for the M.E., you know that."

"Can I sit here?"

She indicated the stool by the money drawer. Polished wood. It had already been dusted and still had a fine layer of gray grit on it. Lots of prints, as Igor had said.

Igor glanced up. "Yeah."

April sat on the stool. This was where the girl must have spent her free time, where she wrote up the sales slips. A stool with no back. From her first encounter with Mrs. Manganaro, April gathered Elsbeth was the kind of boss who wouldn't want her salesgirls comfortable. There was no way anyone could catnap on this stool without falling off. Nice.

Two ambulance people wheeled in the gurney. It was an awkward maneuver in the small shop. Five or six people were crowded in the back room, including someone from the M.E.'s office who had arrived to pronounce the body dead. April could hear a discussion going while the girl was finally taken down from the chandelier.

April had asked Mrs. Manganaro if the door was kept locked during the day. She told April there had been some trouble a few years before with high school kids. Now the door had an automatic latch. It appeared the girl had let in her own killer. April looked out at the street.

With the ambulance, a number of unmarked cars, and the crime-scene tapes all over the place, it was hard to imagine what it must have been like for the girl looking out from this stool on Saturday. Who had seemed safe to Maggie Wheeler? Most likely it was someone she knew.

April thought of her own Saturday. The past week had been unlucky for her. Saturday was her day off. She had wanted to study all day. But Sai Woo, her skinny dragon mother, had bullied her into attending her cousin Annie Chen's wedding. Annie Chen was five years younger than April, a bank teller, and not even her real cousin. So April hadn't exactly been dying to see her celebrated and feasted. And her mother didn't make it any easier.

"No mistake Annie's Chinese name Rucky Girr," Sai Woo had remarked. "Sometimes gods smile and sometimes don't," she added grimly.

"Very profound," April muttered. So chubby Annie, who still had a number of zits on her face, married a postal worker from Brooklyn. What was so lucky about that?

Her mother poked her in the ribs with the toothpick she was still using to clean spare-rib gristle out of her teeth.

"Nice boy, good steady job, that's what's so rucky. But not so good food." She frowned at the spare-rib gristle clinging to the toothpick before depositing it on her plate.

April agreed. All that luck, and the food still wasn't good.

Maggie Wheeler had a worse Saturday. She was murdered and hung up in the storeroom sometime on Saturday. Now it was Monday morning. April looked out at the street.

Columbus Avenue was two parking and three traffic lanes across. The shops were so far apart, you couldn't really see what was happening in them. How well did people in these shops know each other? Out in Astoria, where April lived, everyone in the neighborhood knew everyone. Same in parts of Chinatown. But it was a different story up here. Affluent. Indifferent.

Mike walked out of the back room with Sergeant Joyce, supervisor of their detective squad. April had a feeling Sergeant Joyce didn't like her and would rather not have her around. Sergeant Joyce was thirty-eight years old, the mother of two young children, and had already passed her test for lieutenant. She was waiting for a big enough group to accumulate to warrant the ceremony. She was already commander of a squad but was not yet getting commander's pay. Sergeant Joyce was frowning now, probably worrying about how not solving this case, if they didn't solve it, would affect her salary. Getting the raise was a political and production thing. And April knew Sergeant Joyce needed the money. April also knew how ambitious she was. Sergeant Joyce wanted to rise in the department, maybe to captain and command a precinct of her own.

Sergeant Joyce was a big deal now. She had been on television, taking the credit for solving April's last case while April and Sanchez were in the hospital getting their burns treated. Still, Sergeant Joyce was kind of a hero to April. Joyce had been married to an Irish cop who threatened to divorce her if she became a cop. He'd proved as good as his word. She'd been in Sex Crimes before she became a supervisor. Where she'd go next was anybody's guess. Taking credit for other people's work was sly, but good manipulation of the system. April could not fault her for it.

Sergeant Joyce was shorter and plumper than April. She had a round face, thin lips, a pug nose, blue eyes, and a special affinity for plaids with green in them. April knew men found the sergeant cute and sexy. Today she was wearing a green and pink plaid suit that was both too short and too tight around the butt. A deep frown creased her forehead and the corners of her mouth. She dragged her fingers through her badly cut, badly bleached hair and cocked her head at April.

"Ready?" she demanded.

April nodded. "You think it's some kind of sex crime?"

"How the fuck should I know? Let's get out of here."

April stole a glance at Mike, wondering if he found Sergeant Joyce cute and sexy. But he only raised an eyebrow when the three of them left the store as the body was being bagged.

## 7

At the precinct the press invasion had already begun. Cars and vans with NYPD plates and the names of news agencies painted on their sides, as well as a great deal of rubbernecking from civilian cars, had created near gridlock on a street already crammed with police vehicles. Half a dozen blue uniforms were trying to clear the street.

Swearing, Sanchez finally pulled the unmarked red Chevy Sergeant Joyce had brought to the scene back into the NYPD lot next to the precinct. Sergeant Joyce got out of the front seat. "Should have walked," she muttered.

Yes, she should have, April agreed, getting out of the back.

As they headed inside, April could see a number of reporters clamoring at the desk for information about the homicide around the corner. As if there were a whole lot to give at this point.

Across the street at The Last Mango, the video-cam crews were probably just now finishing taping removal of the corpse in its earth-colored body bag to an ambulance from Roosevelt Hospital, which would take it to the M.E. to await autopsy.

Before they reached the door, Joyce turned around abruptly. "Better go over her place. See what you can turn up, and get a name to notify." She cocked her head at the reporters, clumped around Chummley, the large and balding desk sergeant who looked a lot like a bulldog. It was clear she wanted to handle them herself.

April stared after her. It wasn't a hard one to figure. Once again she and Sanchez were being sent out of the press's way, just as they had been after they had solved their last big case. Oh, well, for five minutes Sergeant Joyce would have the scene. Then, after that, a spokesman for the case would be assigned by the department. It would be a Lieutenant from downtown. That cheered April up.

Mike looked at her and smiled. "You really care, don't you?"

April shook her head, figuring a headshake wasn't a lie. Thing was, as long as she had worked in Chinatown, she had mostly been interested in being a good cop. It was the principle of the thing. Now that she was on the Upper West Side and knew better how the system worked, she wanted to be a good cop with a high rank. Rank had something to do with being a good cop. It was still the principle of the thing, but she didn't think Mike would see it that way.

If she had been willing to talk about it, she would have said, see, up here it wasn't always so much a question of the case, but the public relations aspect of the case. How visible it was, how prominent the victim, how great the threat appeared to the public. Meaning important public, not little-people public. But she wasn't willing to talk about it, so she shook her head.

"Then let it go," Mike advised. "You'll live longer, have a better digestion."

April made one of her sounds, "hah," thinking of Sanchez and the kind of digestion he must have, considering the heavy Mexican food smothered with chilis and cheese he liked to eat. Asians didn't eat cheese. Even ABAs like herself, who could handle pizza, didn't go for melted or grated cheese all over things. She didn't say it, but she was glad Mike was back for this one.

She stood at the door, watching Sergeant Joyce talk to reporters who had their notebooks out and were hanging on her every word.

Mike touched her arm to get her attention.

Yeah, he was right. The clamor was only beginning. It would heat up all day and continue heating up, until they had some facts. Right now they couldn't even release the victim's name until her family had been notified, and they couldn't notify the family till the family could be located. First things first.

"You want to go down and get the warrant or find the landlord and say we're going in?"

April gave him a brief smile. "It's your first day. I'll give you a present. I'll go down and get the search warrant."

It was one of those unavoidable, waste-of-time things. If they didn't go to the courts downtown and get a search warrant to go into the girl's apartment and find her telephone book, a lot of really uncomfortable things could happen, including their being charged with theft if anything was missing later. They went upstairs so April could type up the warrant request.

Maggie Wheeler had lived in a brownstone, a walkup. There were six apartments in the building. An hour and a half later, April and Sanchez stood in the airless vestibule, studying the list of names on the intercom. There was only one name by 3. Wheeler.

Sanchez tried the buzzer just in case Mrs. Manganaro had been wrong about Maggie's living alone, or someone had turned up since they tried the phone number.

No response.

The place smelled of mold and wet plaster. There was a wet patch in the ceiling plaster that looked as if it was ready to come down on someone's head any second. Maggie's keys, along with the rest of her belongings, had been paper-bagged and tagged. The landlord said he couldn't get there, but if they had the warrant, it was okay with him if they just went in. They went in.

Once a really nice brownstone, the building was now all chopped up into small apartments. The doors to apartments 1 and 2 were on the first floor to the right and back of the stairs.

"Three must be on the second floor," April murmured.

They turned to the wide staircase. April ran her finger over the thick, gracious mahogany handrail that capped the sturdy banister, then started up. The tan paint on the walls was smudged, and worn carpeting covered the sagging treads of the stairs. Maggie lived on the second floor in what must have been the brownstone's former living room. Double doors flanked the entrance. The building was silent. No one was around to see the two detectives enter the apartment.

Inside, the lights were off; shades covered the bay windows that fronted on the street. April reached for the light switch, and the personality of Maggie Wheeler was revealed.

Mike whistled. "Wow."

The room was no more than sixteen feet square. It had clearly been cut in half in the middle. The back wall rose up to chop off half of an elegant decorative molding in the ceiling that must once have surrounded the centered chandelier. Now a cheap fixture hung there. Along the wall and at least a dozen years old, a tiny stove, refrigerator, and sink had been tacked on. Four small cabinets were centered above them. No dishes, dirty or otherwise, were visible.

A small, neatly made double bed covered with an old red quilt was pushed against one wall. Three matching pillows had been carefully arranged at the head. There were no clothes on the floor or the one armchair in the room and no decorations. No TV, just a clock-radio. No photographs. No art. No lists of things to do or groceries to buy. The place was empty, really empty, as if Maggie had just arrived or didn't plan to stay long.

April quickly went through the cupboards and closet. There were enough plates and cups for four people if they didn't eat much, a few pots and pans, and a toaster, all very clean. In the closet her clothes were neatly arranged. Nice clothes, colorful dresses, blouses, and skirts. Well, she worked in a clothing store. They had to be attractive. April fingered the belts. There were six of them hanging on a hanger, different styles and materials. April's clothes were very businesslike. A cop couldn't accessorize. She checked out the bathroom. Here was a surprise. Maggie used expensive soaps and bubble baths, expensive makeup in pale colors, not like the garish stuff that had been smeared on her face after she died. She'd hung up some wire shelves that were loaded down with cosmetics.

Mike was going through a letter box covered with decorative paper when April came out of the bathroom.

"It was under the bed," he said.

Her valuables consisted of a Chemical Bank checkbook, canceled checks, pay stubs, paid and unpaid bills, an address book, a calendar with an appointment book, two gold bangle bracelets, a teddy bear pin with amethyst eyes, and a few personal papers. Sanchez opened the address book and found Wheeler in Seekonk, Massachusetts, then turned to the telephone.

"Look at this," he said, pointing to the answering machine under the phone. "She didn't have a TV, but she had an answering machine."

April took the address and appointment books and put the box with the rest of the things back under the bed for the time being.

Mike pushed Play. There were five messages on the machine. Four were from her mother, first asking Maggie why she hadn't called as she promised, then demanding that she call right away. Sandwiched between her mother's calls was one from a man who didn't leave a name. April stood beside Mike as they listened.

"Hi," the male voice said. "It's me. Don't think you can get away with it. No one is on your side. And no one will ever forget." *Click.*

"What the hell is that?"

Mike pushed the rewind button and played it again, then popped the cassette out. "Let's hope his number is in her book."

Neither said much on the way back. It was too early to speculate.

# 8

Within a second of Milicia's entrance the air was charged with her perfume. Jason knew it would still be there in an hour, and his next patient would remark on it. What was it—woody, herbal, spicy? Not his favorite aroma. He made an effort not to sneeze.

Milicia slowly appraised his office, turning around, showing him her back so he could study her if he wanted to. He didn't. He had long ago learned to focus on one of the clocks or the window, even his cuticles if absolutely necessary, anything but the bodies of his female patients when they walked around his office.

Well or sick, a large number of women these days took the position that men looking at them any way whatsoever was a kind of sexual harassment. Jason never let any of them make that an issue with him.

So he focused on the pendulum of the clock on his desk. But even watching its measured process back and forth across four inches, Jason did not miss any of the many attributes of Ms. Honiger-Stanton. As indeed she did not wish him to.

In a red blouse open at the neck that in no way disguised her ample breasts, and a short red skirt, she had a statuesque presence. Everything about her signaled a difference from the ordinary, including her level of self-confidence. Her perfume was definitely spicy, not flowery or herbal, Jason decided. Maybe it was Opium. He didn't like Opium.

The perfume reminded him of the day he dared to ask his skinny, discontented father for a baseball glove. He got more than no for an answer. His father, already a bitter and defeated old man, shook several tobacco-stained fingers at him, warning if Jason got what he wanted, it wouldn't make him happy.

In ominous tones Herman Frank illustrated his point with a story about how Jason's mother, Belle, had spent a great sum of money, "more than a week's worth of food, on some gardenia perfume," Herman said, "to please me on our wedding night."

He inhaled his cigarette down to the very end, and fiercely stabbed it out, still angry over that long-ago extravagance.

"And you know what?" he demanded, blowing smoke into his son's puzzled face.

"What?" Jason remembered the smoke choking him.

"It smelled so bad I couldn't stand to be near her. Made me vomit." Herman ended the story in triumph, hacking up a lump of brown phlegm and spitting it into his grimy handkerchief.

It took Jason a long time to figure out what his father's vomiting on his wedding night had to do with Jason's being denied a baseball glove fifteen years later.

Milicia examined his environment critically, as if it were an architectural disaster in need of complete rehabilitation. Jason felt a stab of insecurity. His office was comfortable, had a bit of a view into himself in it—his clocks, gifts from his patients that included small sculptures, watercolors, needlepoint pillows, paperweights. The paint was beginning to peel in a number of places on the ceiling. It was clear to anyone with an eye for these things that the place had never seen a decorator.

Her striding into his office, posing for him, demanding attention, and smelling as if she'd doused herself on the way up in the elevator was very far from the usual nervous and highly stressed behavior of a person in need of psychological counseling. His clinician's sensitive antennae bristled.

Finally she finished her visual tour of his furniture, which was the usual collection of aged leather, semi-matched pieces, Oriental carpet on the floor, objects on his desk and windowsill. His bookcases were far from adequate for his growing collection of reference material. Books and periodicals of all kinds covered every available surface.

"I like this building," she said, finally settling into the Eames chair behind Jason's analyst's couch and crossing her legs.

Jason nodded and took his desk chair opposite her. For many years he had liked this building, too. It was a jewel, a copy of the kind of buildings in Paris and Austria that were built before the turn of the century. It had a sandstone façade in the front and a heavy wrought iron and glass front door. The centerpiece of the ornate lobby was an elaborate staircase that wound around a central space open all the way to the top floor, where there was a stained glass skylight. The elevator was a cage with a folding gate that had never been replaced with anything more modern. Now that Emma was gone, Jason was seriously considering moving, growing a beard. He stroked his chin in a rabbinical sort of way, waiting for Milicia to reveal her reason for being there.

She swiveled from side to side, showing off her long legs.

"I feel a little nervous," she murmured. "It's an odd situation, particularly since we met socially. . . . Of course, you must get this all the time."

Jason smiled neutrally. So far Milicia had revealed that she was sophisticated. She could appropriately identify the awkwardness of the situation and relate it to the present social context. Saying he got this all the time was meant to flatter him by enhancing his professional identity. His impressions of her were camera clicks.

She knocked over her handbag with her foot, leaned over to right it, showing off her cleavage and a black lace bra.

He had an uneasy feeling. Her flaunting was about on the level of a man carrying on a conversation with his hands in his pockets, rattling his change. *Guess what I've got in here.*

Milicia did a lot of rattling her change. Jason wondered why.

Her eyes slid around the room again. "Your books are reassuring. I've always loved books. If you've read them all, you must know what you're doing." She laughed briefly.

"The clutter is nice, too," she went on. "It means you're not one of those uptight people without any real feeling. You're not a plastic person." She studied him intently, a smile playing on the lower half of her face.

Jason didn't respond to this foray either. He was clicking the camera on her. And also on himself as he measured his reactions to her. It wasn't clear to him what was going on.

"So. Why don't you tell me what's happening with you, and what you think I can do to help," he said.

There was a long pause while she gazed at him some more, as if trying to decide if she could trust him.

"There's nothing wrong with me," she said finally. "I need some advice, that's all. I didn't want to talk to Charles about this. He's a client.

I'm sure you understand about that." She shrugged. "You impressed me the other day. I figured I could ask you."

Jason nodded. "Go ahead."

"I'm very worried about my sister." She crossed her legs the other way, and readjusted the handbag at her feet. Once again the blouse fell open.

Jason picked up a new black and white notebook from his desk. "What worries you?"

"Her behavior, her moods. She's very sick, and I have no one to help me manage her. I'm afraid she'll hurt herself, or someone else."

"What makes you think so?"

"Oh, God. She's out of control. She's depressed, moody, violent. She's had a problem with alcohol and drugs for years. When she drinks she's vicious, screams at people, hits them—why are you taking notes?"

Jason looked up. "Does it bother you?"

Milicia frowned. "It gets in the way."

Jason closed the notebook. "Is there a special urgency about your sister right now?"

"What do you mean?"

"I get the impression this has been going on for a long time. Why are you seeking professional help now?"

Milicia bristled. "What kind of question is that?"

"Just asking if something special has happened, a crisis?"

"What if something really awful has happened? What do I do?"

Jason glanced at his notebook but didn't open it. He didn't have to. He was trained to remember everything he saw and everything he heard. He waited for her to go on. In a second she did.

"Do you know how hard it is on a family when there are two perfect children and then one of them starts going off? It's like at the Olympics on the balance beam when the first back flip is straight on the mark and the next one a centimeter to the left. After that, a gymnast can't get it back. She keeps going crooked until she falls off."

She was silent for a second.

"And then the whole system comes crashing down, and nobody is left whole."

Jason nodded, touched by the way she said it, by the image of the child gymnast doing it right to a certain point and then faltering, failing to be "normal," thus destroying the careful façade of the family front.

41

"I know what that's like," he said gently.

He looked at her with his inner eye, searching for the real person under the cloud of flaming red hair and dusky perfume, the perfect makeup and bravado. Who was really in there and what piece of music was being played?

"Tell me," he said to Milicia, "about falling off the balance beam."

# 9

Sometimes on very sunny afternoons spikes of light forced their way through the few clean patches in the cracked basement window. Today the light looked to Camille like white grass growing up through a cracked pavement. The floor was crunchy where fallen plaster from the ceiling and walls got walked on for many months before anybody bothered to sweep up. Bare bricks showed through everywhere, discolored and chipped.

It was very damp down there, even in summer, and the smell of urine was getting worse now that the puppy was older. Bouck said she had to do something about the smell.

Camille sat on the floor with her back pressed into a corner, waiting for the bright light to fade. She could hear Jamal on the other side of the wall, polishing crystal with the sonar machine. There was kind of a whine, or a hum, that she sometimes thought was human. As long as she could hear it, she felt safe.

Jamal wasn't supposed to come on this side of the wall. The best chandeliers were in here, hanging from the low ceiling. On very bad days Camille stayed here, too, unable even to take the puppy out. The hum stopped, and she tensed.

*He wasn't supposed to come on this side of the wall.* Jamal smoked some kind of dope—hash or cocaine or something. And he touched her if he could get away with it. After he found out there were times she couldn't move, he came in and touched her hair and her breasts. Now he wasn't ever supposed to come on this side of the door.

Bouck told Jamal he would kill him. Bouck had three guns. Camille thought he would do it. He would kill for her. No doubt about it. But Jamal didn't care about the guns. He wanted to touch her fine hair, that pale, pale reddish gold that was so rare. It was a color and texture Jamal had never seen in Haiti, or Trinidad, or Jamaica, or wherever he came

43

from. Camille didn't like to talk to him. His hair was all matted and he smelled worse than the dog. Some religious thing. He listened to reggae through a Walkman that Camille knew was the devil singing in his ear.

The light moved just a little bit, and she turned her head. Upstairs in the shop she could hear the phone ring and someone answer. It wasn't Bouck. Bouck was at an auction. No, no, somebody died. Bouck was looking at a dead person's estate. Sometimes he went and took things out of dead people's apartments before the IRS could get there to tax them. Sometimes he bought the whole estate. Bouck had a lot of money. He gave her money all the time and laughed when she forgot where she put it.

"Easy come, easy go," he said.

A few weeks earlier Bouck shot somebody who was trying to get into the shop. It was Puppy that first heard the noise.

Then Camille heard it. Nights were sometimes good for her and Bouck let her move around. That night she was free.

"Bouck."

"Huh." He jerked awake as if lightning had struck him.

She stood outside his door because she didn't like to go into his room at night no matter what.

"Somebody's downstairs."

He was up before the light was on, the .38 already palmed. He was down the two flights of stairs and in the basement within a few seconds, with Camille not far behind.

It turned out to be a kid trying to jimmy the window in the basement. He didn't even get inside. Before the window was all the way open, Bouck shot him. The bullet knocked him flat even though it didn't kill him. Bouck would probably have shot him again, but the guy got up.

Together Bouck and Camille ran up the stairs and watched out the window of the shop as the thief staggered down Second Avenue, bleeding all over the place. Bouck told her later the kid must have lived. There was nothing about it in the paper. He had Jamal wash down the sidewalk the next day, but no one ever came to ask any questions. Camille thought about the way Bouck had shot the boy. Even with Jamal around, Bouck always made Camille feel safe. Bouck could make war.

She listened for him.

Today wasn't such a very bad day. The animal she called anguish was only a tightness in her chest, a weight holding her down, just above the level of hell. Today the animal was an almost manageable pain. She could think a little. By sundown the weight might lift enough to allow her to go upstairs. But then again, it might not lift for days. It all depended.

On good days it got better in the evenings. By six or seven her mind drifted back into focus and she started thinking she might be all right until the next day. Then it would start again with the dawn.

Madness seemed to come in the mornings, hitting her like a hurricane of wailing furies so loud and so ferociously violent, sometimes she shook all over. Sometimes she screamed and clawed at the wall. Bouck didn't like her to do that.

When it was very bad like that she knew she would have to die to make it stop. Dying seemed like a good idea about eighty percent of the time. But Bouck kept pushing death back for her. She thought about dying every day. More than once she tried to get there. She just couldn't find her way to the peace of death, though, where her parents were waiting to take her back. Whatever she did to end herself, Bouck kept pushing her back. Sometimes she knew death would come to her only if Bouck went first.

Camille knew where two of Bouck's guns were. One was in his belt, and one was in his boot. On good days he let her play with his guns. The third gun, the automatic with the kind of bullets that exploded inside and could blow a man's head off, was hidden somewhere else. She was pretty sure someday she'd find it.

The puppy lay across her lap, its head hanging over her knee. It could stay like that for hours, sprawled and boneless, just like Camille, almost as if the puppy, too, could die inside with the soul death of its mistress.

Then when Camille was finally able to stir herself after hours of inertia, the puppy would get up and race around. Round and round, up and down the stairs faster than any human could run. Camille knew if Puppy got away, no one could catch it. It was fast, very fast. She loved Puppy. More than Bouck. More than anything. She couldn't live without Puppy. Upstairs the shop bell tinkled. The day was taking a long time to end.

# 10

ight of them were squeezed into Sergeant Joyce's office, which was about the size of a walk-in closet. The window was on an air shaft. From time to time Sergeant Joyce tried to brighten the place up with a few pots of English ivy. There were two such plants on the windowsill now, dwarfed and brown-edged with neglect. April counted three crunched-out cigarette butts in the potted dirt and knew there were likely to be more below the surface. The tiny room with its three chairs was as close as the detective squad got to a conference room. Sometimes they sat in the locker room, where there was a refrigerator and a table. Sometimes, when it was quiet, the detectives gathered in a questioning room and questioned each other. Now, hours before the crime-scene photos were available, before the autopsy report told them exactly when and how Maggie Wheeler died, they assembled to get organized.

There were two women in the room. Only one got a chair. Sergeant Joyce sat behind her desk. April leaned against the windowsill near the dying plants. Healy and Aspirante, always the self-appointed honchos, sat in the two visitors' chairs in front of Joyce's desk. Aspirante's beady eyes and large nose were moist with ambition and a lot more heat than the room's air conditioner could handle. He was skinny, not a centimeter taller than April, and pugnacious to compensate. Now he was holding forth about psycho-killers he had known, not saying anything because he hadn't ever known one, but pushing noise out his mouth all the same.

"It's the guy on the tape," Aspirante said. "All we gotta do is find him."

Healy, at twice Aspirante's height and girth and possibly half his intelligence, nodded his agreement.

Joyce put her hand over the receiver. "Shut up," she said.

46

April glanced over at Mike. He was nonchalantly holding up the back wall as if nothing about anybody's behavior bothered him in the least. It was their case. Theirs. They were the first men in, the ones who answered the call and found the girl. And Mike had to know there wasn't a detective in the room who wouldn't do anything in his power to upstage them and complicate the process as much as possible.

Mike nodded at her, a small smile teasing the corners of his mustache. Clearly he was thinking the same thing and coming up with a different take on it. She knew how he thought. Life is short, take a chill. Hah, some philosophy.

But April felt a sudden shock at the eye contact and the way he raised his chin at her. The jolt was unfamiliar and a little unnerving. All the time Sanchez was away experiencing his roots yet again, April hadn't just missed him. She actually felt anxious, as if a part of her were missing. She didn't like the sensation a bit and was pretty sure she wouldn't feel that way if they hadn't almost gotten blown up together last May.

Now she had to worry about the effects of gratitude on this relationship that Sanchez called "close supervision." She didn't like it. She had always felt safer just a little isolated and separate from everybody. "Watch your back" was not a sufficiently cautious approach to either life or work for her.

Maybe it was the effect of all those years hearing her mother's litany of every possible danger of being alive in Queens, America, as well as constant replays of the violence and chaos, starvation, and family separations in China when she was young. In the fifties, in the Cultural Revolution, Tienanmen Square, now.

"Never forget best friends, even *Chinese* best friends, stab in front easy as back."

April went to bed with those words in her ears the way she knew American children did the prayer "Now I lay me down to sleep, I pray the Lord my soul to keep."

She and Mike hadn't talked yet. Maybe they wouldn't have a chance today. She couldn't help noticing how tan he was, must have spent his whole ten days in Mexico out in the sun with some Maria or other. Suddenly April was aware that Sergeant Joyce had hung up the phone and was frowning at her, as if already she had done something wrong. She hadn't done anything wrong. All she did was take a call, cross the street to a fancy boutique—where neither of them could even think of shopping—and find a dead salesgirl in the storeroom. April wasn't responsible for killing her, or hanging her up on the chandelier.

She clenched up inside, but refused to look down. It was a daily trial to her that Sergeant Joyce, who was so tough and so good with men, and smart enough to pass every test, didn't seem to like her. Every day April was aware Joyce could orchestrate her removal to some other precinct, and this kept the edge on April's anxiety nearly all the time. She didn't want to go back to Brooklyn or Queens or the Bronx and get lost in the backwater. She wouldn't mind being assigned to a special unit. Special Crimes, Sex Crimes. DEA. Even go home to the 5th in Chinatown. But not now, sometime in the future.

After a full year in the Two-O, April had seen a lot of things she had never expected to see, met people she never would have known. In Chinatown she spoke the language of the powerless and ignorant, the prey of every kind of predator. She knew how they thought, where to go to ask the questions. No matter what the case, she knew the path to follow, knew the secrets. And she had never known that she was one of them, as powerless as they, until she was summarily moved up to the Two-O.

Now she was in a different world, a world of random violence, where rich, educated whites tried not to rub shoulders with the disenfranchised blacks and Hispanics all around them. And the people of color refused to be ignored, pounded white heads whenever they could. But this homicide was no street crime.

April held her ground as Joyce stared at her with apparent hostility. "Have you located the other salesgirl?" she demanded. "Maybe she knows who the guy is."

When in the world would April have had time to check out the second salesgirl? It took her and Sanchez three hours to get someone from the Sheriff's office in Seekonk, Massachusetts, to locate Maggie's parents. It was the part of the job she hated most. She was glad this time she didn't have to be the one to knock on their door and tell them.

April had learned that the Wheelers had six kids, but the number of kids never made the slightest bit of difference. She once knew a Chinese couple who had five kids. Baby drowned in the Central Park reservoir, where they were picnicking in a rowboat. Afterward, the mother went crazy, sat in a chair staring at the wall. Never recovered even though she had four other children to care for.

"I've got her number and her address," April said about the missing salesgirl. "She was first on my list."

Joyce nodded. "Okay, get the hell out of here and find out what she knows."

April shoved off the windowsill with a small sigh of satisfaction. Released without bail. Wow. She pushed through the crush of detectives, who didn't exactly make way for her because Joyce gave her the show in front of everybody. It felt good. Two minutes later Mike was at his desk, and they began trying to find the other salesgirl, Olga Yerger.

It was an hour later when they finally located her. She wasn't at home and the girl she lived with didn't want to say on the phone where she was.

"Gee, I don't know a thing. Monday's Olga's day off. I have no idea where she goes," her roommate said with so many hesitations and pauses, April was pretty sure she did. "How do I know you're really from the police?"

"You can call the precinct and ask for me. You want to do that?" April asked. "Or do you want me to come over and show you my badge?"

"How do you spell your name?"

"W-o-o. How do you spell yours?"

"Ah. We just share the rent. I hardly even know her. Do you want to leave a message?"

"No. I need to talk to her now."

"Why, did she do something wrong?"

"Someone's been killed in the store where she works."

"Jesus."

There was a pause. The girl didn't ask how or when.

"Now will you tell me where she is?" April said.

"I'll call around and see if I can find her. I'll call you right back," the girl promised nervously, and hung up.

April threw her notebook in her bag and turned to Mike. "Want to take a drive?" she asked.

"That was easy." He reached for his jacket. "Where is she?"

"Doesn't want us to know. She's probably working without a green card. Let's try the roommate."

It was seven P.M. on the first day of a big case. The squad room was riotous and smelled strongly of sweat and stale coffee. Five people in the detective squad day shift were still there, the seven-man evening shift had long since arrived, and both shifts were jockeying for desk space and the phones. April and Mike's departure opened up two desks and phones. In the barred cell which was the main decoration of the room, an outraged mugger screamed obscenities.

# 11

"Well, what did you do for a whole week without me?" Mike said as soon as they were in the car. It was hot, maybe eighty-five degrees. They took the unmarked red Chevy Sergeant Joyce had used earlier even though the air conditioner was broken. They didn't like to use their own cars while they were on duty, and taking a blue-and-white was beneath Sanchez's dignity.

"Pined away," April answered lightly, busy with her seat belt.

It had taken him all day to get personal. It always happened when they were in a car together.

"No kidding." He pulled out of the police lot. "Where to?"

"Prince Street."

"Hah. Your old neighborhood."

Hah. Now he was making the same sounds she did.

"Hah, yes indeed. My old neighborhood. I'll try not to hyperventilate when we get there."

He turned at the corner and headed down Columbus. Yellow crime-scene tapes still sealed The Last Mango. April knew she and Sanchez were both having the same thought. That someone should die so young and so grotesquely not even a block from the precinct was an offense that was hard to take.

Sobbing off what was left of her mascara, Elsbeth Manganaro had said that of all her stores, she felt safest in this one. "Because of the police next door. And what good was that?" she added for the fourteenth time.

"How many stores do you have?" April had asked to make the question go away.

"Four, but two of them are on the Island."

"Long Island?"

"Where else?" Elsbeth demanded.

April lifted a shoulder. There were other islands.

Now she was silent. The beginning of each case was like walking into a fog so dense you couldn't see to the corner, couldn't even see your own feet on the ground. Everything was unknown. You didn't know what kind of awful thing you might find when you put your hand out. What piece you might miss if you didn't ask the right question. Or look in the right corner when the light was just right. Sometimes the fog didn't lift to reveal the puzzle pieces for a long time. Sometimes it never did. Anxiety about finding some pieces in the murk caused April's thoughts to jump around like a bird hopping from limb to limb.

Who would kill a girl with police cars parked all over the place just outside? Sometime on Saturday, probably just after seven when the store closed, but maybe later. The girl could have waited for someone who was picking her up. Maybe there were no police cars out there. Maybe they were all on call. What else happened on Saturday night?

"So where were you on Saturday night?" Once again Mike's thoughts echoed her own.

"Not on duty. I don't know what was going on here."

"I know. I checked."

"Checked what?"

"I checked to see if you were on duty."

It was really hot in the car, even with the windows open and the wind blowing through. It was almost theater hour. Columbus Avenue was jammed.

April bristled. "What did you do that for?"

"I don't know. Maybe you were here and saw something."

"I wasn't," she said flatly.

There was an opening in the traffic. Mike speeded up.

"So where were you?" he asked after a minute.

"I was off duty, like you." She frowned. "Why?"

"I've been away for a week. I just want to know what *mi querida's* been up to." He turned to look at her and smiled.

Very engaging. Very Spanish, just what she needed.

"I could ask you the same thing," she snapped.

"Go ahead, you want to know what I did? I'll tell you everything."

"Some other time. Right now we have a dead woman to think about."

"She's not exactly going anywhere. You could take a second to ask me if I had a good time and tell me you missed me."

April looked out the window. Lincoln Center was lit up like a Christmas tree. She had walked around it with forty other eleven-year-olds on a class trip once, but had never been inside. Mike sped past it.

"I had a wonderful time, thanks for asking," he said.

She had never been to Mexico either. There were a lot of things she didn't know. "How's Diego?" she said to prove she was up on something.

"Diego? Diego, who?"

"Diego Rivera. That painter you told me about."

"Wow. What a memory. Diego's dead, but the paintings are fine." Mike accelerated through a yellow light. Months before he had told her about the art and literature of Mexico to let her know he wasn't just some Latino from an island with a short history and not much art. His culture was as old as hers.

"Guess I should have sent you a postcard," he said.

She shrugged as their progress stalled again around Forty-second Street. He held out his hand, wiggling his fingers. Without having to ask, April knew he wanted the turret light. It was on the floor by her foot. She handed it to him. He reached out his window, stuck it on the roof, then hit the hammer halfheartedly a few times. Cars ahead of them moved over slowly at the sound of the siren.

"So?" he asked after a few minutes of silence.

"So what?"

"So, where were you on Saturday night?"

"What's the damn difference?" April fumed for a second, then relented. "Okay, I was at a wedding." She finally blurted out the hateful fact. "Not mine, are you happy now?"

A gust of hot air ruffled her hair as she turned her face back to the window.

"Oh, *querida*. I had no idea you wanted to get married." Mike was silent about his part in her breakup with Jimmy Wong.

Last spring he had checked Jimmy out, maybe found something, maybe not. Anyway, he had raised April's suspicions enough about Jimmy's activities on the night team in Brooklyn for her to end the three-year relationship.

"I don't," she said quickly. She didn't want Mike to think she was indecisive, had any regrets. She didn't have any regrets, just a lot of things to wonder about. One of them was that the person "closely supervising" her had a lot of sex appeal. She didn't know how to feel about that.

Skinny Dragon Mother said men and women shouldn't be partners. She made an explosive spitting sound when April assured her she and Sanchez *weren't* partners. "Detectives don't work as partners, Ma. You know that. He's my supervisor."

"Can't be superwhatever, can't be friends either," Sai Woo insisted. "You got big trouble."

And Skinny Dragon Mother wasn't the only one who said it. The whole thing made her uneasy.

As they neared her old neighborhood, April's stomach rumbled with the hunger of remembered childhood happiness. No, better not think that, she told herself. Just rumbled from plain hunger. With all the excitement, there hadn't been time for lunch.

"Here we are," she said suddenly.

FUCKING LESBO, SUCK MY DICK was the exhortation on the door of the formerly brown sandstone building where lucky Olga Yerger had emigrated.

Mike parked the car in front of a hydrant, and they got out. Prince Street was both run-down and fixed up in the extreme. The street was narrow, crowded, and dirty. The loft buildings all around were crumbling. Not more than three or four stories high, many of them had been old sweatshops and warehouses. Now expensive façades on restaurants, art galleries, and clothing stores winked at the shabby street. Upstairs there still could be anything.

April nodded at a gallery window featuring small wire sculptures of body parts. "This is it." The door to the building had recently been painted a color April knew as Chinese red. She opened it.

Inside, a metal cage door blocked access to the stairs. Even from the door April could see the treads dipping and sagging just the way they did in the building where she grew up. Also like home, the light was poor and the walls were coming down. Only here there wasn't the pervasive smell of cooking food, garlic and ginger and scallions frying in peanut oil, duck roasting in honey and hoisin sauce. No sounds of squabbling families.

Mike pushed the button beside the label that said Yerger. Instantly the metal door clicked open.

"Third floor." The voice on the intercom had no accent and invited them in without asking who was there.

Mike and April exchanged glances. Even when expecting company, not many people did that in New York. They passed through the metal door, letting it clang shut behind them, then trudged up the three extraordinarily narrow flights of stairs. On the third floor there was no bell for the only door. Mike knocked on it.

The dark-haired girl who opened it looked surprised to see them. She was wearing very short cut-off jeans and a halter that pushed her small breasts up. Her red lips puckered into a startled "Oh. What—?"

"Detective Woo. I called a little while ago." April showed her badge and cocked her head at Mike. "Sergeant Sanchez."

"She's not here," the girl said.

"Who?"

"You said you wanted Olga, didn't you? Well, she's not here."

"Do you mind if we come in and wait for her?" Mike smiled engagingly.

The girl looked him over. "Actually, yes. It's not a convenient time. I'm expecting company. I thought you were—"

"We need to talk to Olga."

"Why? She hasn't done anything."

"Then she won't mind talking to us, will she?" Mike crowded her a little, moving forward so that she had to retreat.

She backed into the apartment, protesting. "Hey, I said you can't come in."

They came in. So did a huge Viking of a woman. She was over six feet tall and slender, with blue eyes and a mane of fine, pale hair almost down to her waist, which was a long way. Her choreographed entrance had her clicking through a beaded curtain. The first glimpses of her through colorful plastic that tried but did not succeed in looking like glass gave the impression that she was nude. But in fact she wore a short black leather skirt and matching leather bra.

She, too, let out a surprised little "oh," at her mistake, dropped her pose, and turned anxiously to her friend for help. The friend shook her head. The blond woman was a massive Scandinavian with a very little brain.

In one take, on the girls and the place filled with soft sectional sofas and beaded curtains, April knew they were hookers. The cast-iron tub and shower was a featured item, right in the middle of the room with a standing mirror in front of it. The large TV screen and VCR were no doubt for dirty movies.

"Olga?"

The Viking nodded. *"Ja."*

"This is Sergeant Sanchez, and I'm Detective Woo of the New York Police." Once again April displayed her badge. Before she had a chance to say anything more, tears began gushing out of Olga's Delft-blue eyes.

"Please," she sobbed. "Don't turn me in. I only yust started. *Yust* started."

"Shut up," the other girl snapped. "They're not here about that."

The waterworks stopped abruptly. Olga smiled tentatively.

April glanced at Mike. He was choking on a cough.

April said, "Tell me about Saturday."

"Saturday?" Olga darted an anxious look at her mentor. "You said—"

The girl rolled her eyes.

"We want to know about the shop The Last Mango. Who came in. Who bought things. We want to know about Maggie, okay?"

Olga frowned. "Maggie?"

"Maggie Wheeler, the girl who works in The Last Mango with you."

A look of pure amazement crossed Olga's otherwise vacant face. "Is she whooking, too?"

"No, she's not whooking. She's dead. Someone killed her on Saturday evening in the store."

This was clearly news to Olga. She collapsed onto several sections of sofa. "Wow."

"So we need to know everything that happened in the store that day."

"I don't know that."

"What don't you know?"

"I don't know what happened in Lost Mango. I didn't go Saturday." Glance at mentor.

"She had a cold," mentor explained. "She stayed in bed all day."

"I'll bet," Mike said.

"*Ja, ja.* Sneeze, sneeze all day."

"Looks like you recovered enough to get back to work today." Sanchez was getting impatient.

"Don't go Moonday. Moonday day off."

"I meant your *other* work," Mike said pointedly.

"Huh?" Olga gaped at them.

April shook her head. This wasn't getting them anywhere. "Why don't you tell us everything you know about The Last Mango and Maggie Wheeler."

Olga turned to her friend for guidance one last time and nodded okay when none was forthcoming. April took out her notebook and wrote the date, the time, the place, and Olga Yerger's name. The buzzer sounded from downstairs. Ah, their customer had arrived. The mentor with the brain hurried out the door to head him off.

# 12

The outer door clicked shut as Milicia departed. Jason returned to his desk and checked the skeleton clock. It was six o'clock and still running. He had a fifteen-minute break. A patient was due at six-fifteen and another at seven. His stomach rumbled. He had eaten the last English muffin for breakfast, and as far as he knew, his kitchen had nothing else in the way of food. After his last patient, he'd have to go over to Broadway or Amsterdam to get something to eat. He dreaded the prospect of sitting in a restaurant alone.

Evenings were the worst for Jason. The worst was going out the door of his office, turning right to the door of his apartment, twisting the key in the lock, and finding the lights off, the air still. No sounds of activity reached out to him from the kitchen or bedroom. No discernible human odors hung around to comfort him. At nine-thirty, when he finally went home, his patient hours over and his many procrastinations all used up, the soothing aroma of that morning's coffee had dissipated some fourteen hours before. With the air conditioner off, the temperature rose to the eighties by noon, baking the dust and emptiness into a stuffy animal's den that his return didn't seem to diffuse.

Every day without Emma was a new shock. He had always felt a couple could negotiate for anything—lifestyle, time, attention, love. He had been wrong. There was more to a good relationship than tough bargaining for the satisfaction of needs. Some things had to be given gratis, with no expectation of return. Jason felt a little dizzy, even nauseated, as he remembered how resentful he used to feel at the banalities of domesticity. Now what he faced every night in the different rhythms of his many ticking antique clocks, and smelled in the nighttime gloom of his airless apartment, was despair.

He was comforted by the thought that he didn't have to worry about going home for several hours. His work wasn't over. He sat down at his desk and reached for the black notebook he had started for Milicia Honiger-Stanton.

There was the little look of triumph that came over her face when she asked him not to take notes and he slapped the notebook shut. Her expression did not escape him. He knew what body language and the order of words meant. He knew what to watch out for and what to ask. He did not need to take notes to remember what Milicia said, or the order in which she said it. He took information in and swallowed it whole, processing and saving it like a computer. He had fourteen minutes now to re-create what Milicia had told him about her family. He got to work, writing quickly.

Milicia and Camille Honiger-Stanton grew up in Old Greenwich, Connecticut, where, as she put it, "nobody was poor." They lived in a big house on the road to the public beach. Milicia described their mother as German in origin, slavish, and depressed. Their father was an alcoholic. The father's family was English. In Connecticut such things mattered. The Stantons were the ones with the culture and the money. Hilda Honiger, Milicia told Jason, probably started her career in America as a maid. She never conquered her accent. Milicia said she didn't know when, or why, her parents' names were joined by a hyphen. She thought it must have amused her father to annoy his family. He liked turmoil, she added.

"Did your mother or father ever get treatment for their problems?" Jason had asked.

Milicia laughed. "Are you kidding? They didn't think they had problems. Camille had problems."

"Camille is older or younger?"

"Than me? Two years younger. She's twenty-eight now."

"When did her problems start?"

"Eighth grade." Milicia said it firmly.

Well, Jason had asked himself: if Camille had problems dating back to eighth grade, why the urgency now, more than a dozen years later?

"So what were Camille's problems?" he asked.

"Oh, God. What weren't?" Milicia pursed her lips. "She had screaming tantrums. Uses foul language. She's sexually promiscuous, does kinky things with black men."

Jason mentally noted the change in tense.

"She was accident prone, always hurting herself. She's tried suicide. She drinks a lot. Takes drugs, too. What else?" Milicia shook her head. "I told you about the tantrums. Um, she screams at people and throws things, hits people. Of course, you wouldn't know it if you looked at her. She looks beautiful, vulnerable. That's her thing. But she's really vicious. She thinks she's ugly and starves herself. She's been bulimic. I don't know what else."

"Does she hear voices, see things?"

"I don't know. Uh, I don't think so."

"Does she feel anyone is out to get her? Strangers, or people she sees on the street?"

"Yes, yes. That's probably so."

"Who does she think is after her?"

Milicia thought about it. "Oh, you know, she gets really frustrated and hurt when a man dumps her. Resentful. She starts to look at men funny, really crazy. She says men are out to get her, hurt her."

That didn't sound so crazy to him. "You seem very convinced there's something terribly wrong with your sister. What exactly is your concern?"

"She can be dangerous. There's nobody to look out for her but me. What if she hurts someone? I wouldn't want to be responsible."

"What about your parents?"

"They're dead." Milicia had said it flatly, tapping her foot with impatience at him.

Why impatient, he wondered. Maybe it was her own perception that her sister was crazy. Maybe she was the one in need of help. "Both of them?"

"Yes, they died in a car accident about a year and a half ago."

"That's rough."

Milicia chewed on her lips and nodded. He felt sorry for her then. She described having to sell the house she had grown up in and most of its contents. She told him about her fury at the IRS for expecting so much money. What was left would be split between her and Camille, but that was a ways off.

"You don't get the money until the estate is audited. The IRS has three years after the death to do it. Anyway, the money is in trust. Camille can't do anything crazy with it," Milicia said.

Jason asked her if she was worried about that. Maybe her concern here was really money.

"No, no," Milicia assured him. It wasn't the money that bothered her. She was afraid of Camille herself, afraid of what she might do.

It was then that she told him how she'd seen Camille kill an animal. "We were baby-sitting together—I used to go with her sometimes. She didn't have a lot of tolerance for little kids, so I'd go to keep a lid on." She shrugged.

"This time one of them—it was a girl, about five—got to her while they were playing with a pet rabbit—Camille's anger seems to be focused on girls. Well, she grabbed the rabbit and threw it at the wall so hard, it didn't get up. Then she put it back in the cage and told the girl's parents it died in its sleep. So, you see, I'm concerned."

Jason did not have time to ask Milicia what her part was in that baby-sitting experience when her younger sister lied to the parents of her charge about the death of her pet. The forty-five minutes were over. He did try to get her to pinpoint her reason for coming to a professional, for choosing him in fact—apparently out of the blue—when their parents had died nearly two years ago, and Camille's problems, if indeed they existed, were many years old. At this point he had no reason to either believe or disbelieve what Milicia told him. He was just listening, trying to figure out what it was all about.

Milicia was impatient at him for not getting it. He asked her if she would like to come back and talk about it some more.

"Well, I have to, don't I? There's this *thing* that's happening, and you haven't told me what to do yet."

"I can give you the name of a good psychiatrist for Camille," he said.

She shook her head. "I need to talk to you. There's more to it than that."

"My fee is a hundred and seventy-five dollars an hour for consultations."

"I told you I don't care about money. I care only about my sister. She's all I have left."

Jason remembered all of this and a great deal more. What he wrote was: *Woman, middle thirties. Concerned about behavior of sister. Informant does not present herself as a patient in need of help for herself. Eloquent, expressive, sexually seductive. Too much perfume—Opium. Story about sis-*

*ter is difficult to conceptualize symptomatically. Informant says sister's paranoid, possibly dangerous. No delusions or history of assaultive behavior or OMS. Impression deferred.*

He heard the outer door close and looked at the clock. It was six-thirteen. He placed a call to Charles to ask him about Milicia. Charles's answering machine was on. Jason left a message, then checked the skeleton clock again. Six-fifteen exactly. He got up to open the door. He had two more patients and a number of phone calls to deal with before he had to face looking for food and going home. He had heard many stories like Milicia's. They were always puzzles; their true meaning came together slowly over a long period of time. Milicia could very well be a hysteric looking for attention for herself. It was way too soon to tell. He dropped Milicia's notebook in the filing cabinet under his desk and closed the drawer. By the time he opened the door for his favorite patient, Daisy—a twenty-five-year-old affective schizophrenic he'd been seeing for many years—he was no longer thinking about Milicia.

# 13

It was still light at eight o'clock. Downstairs, three reporters hung around, hoping to get more details on the case before their deadline for the morning papers. At two, the NYPD spokesman from downtown had read from a statement about what the reporters were now calling "the boutique slaying." The information had come too late for that day's papers and left a whole lot of questions unanswered, including the victim's identity. By five that information was released so Maggie Wheeler's name could appear on the six o'clock news along with the clip of her corpse bag being loaded into an ambulance.

April and Mike didn't have to see the news to know what was in it. As they came in, the desk sergeant was busy with a huge woman in a black silk dress. A thick coating of a white powder covered the woman's face like a mask. She was claiming that a calico cat in the neighborhood was Christ.

"What would you like me to do about it?" the Desk Sergeant asked politely.

They headed for the stairs, passing the reporters camped out in Reception without being stopped. That was one advantage of not being in charge.

Upstairs in the squad room, the noise level was high, and the air conditioner wasn't up to its job. The accused mugger who had been so disruptive earlier was no longer in the pen. Two other detectives, both older men with their stomachs sprung and their hair going, were sitting at the desks April and Sanchez had used on the day shift. They didn't look up from their typewriters as April and Sanchez headed straight for the squad supervisor's office without stopping first to check for messages.

Sergeant Joyce was still there, the phone receiver plugged into her ear. She looked as if she'd been in a dogfight, short hair on end, eyes bloodshot and pouchy, blouse a mess. She hadn't given up her office to the night supervisor, probably had to kill him for it, April thought.

Hah, considering her boss's concentration right then, Sergeant Joyce was probably talking to the Mayor himself. April had to revise that speculation when Joyce banged the receiver down at the sight of them. "Well?"

"Scratch Olga," Mike said, taking a chair. "She didn't go in that day and says she doesn't know a thing."

"Didn't work at all Saturday?"

"Oh, she worked, just not at the store."

April took her usual place on the windowsill so that Sergeant Joyce had to turn her head to address her.

"What the fuck does that mean, Sanchez?" Joyce didn't have a lot of patience. This was the kind of case that drove everybody nuts. Columbus Avenue, just around the corner from the precinct, was an upscale neighborhood. Lot of wealthy people lived and shopped there. Reporters in bush jackets no less were hanging around downstairs, cluttering up the place and making everyone nervous with their expectation of a break in the case at any moment. The press was like having a bunch of the other team's cheerleaders jeering "Do something, do something. When are you going to *do* something?" all day long while the detectives on the case tried to ignore them and get their work done.

Word had come down that the Captain wanted this one tied up in a day or two, like the cop found shot in the head in the marshes out by LaGuardia Airport, or the millionaire lawyer stabbed in a motel in the Bronx. Both cases were highly visible; both were nailed within forty-eight hours.

On the windowsill, April got the frigid blast from the air conditioner full force in the face. Reminded her of Maggie Wheeler's hair blowing in the cold wind and the skin on the dead girl's arms raised in goose bumps. April knew the goose bumps were a post-mortem thing, had nothing to do with the girl's being refrigerated for several days. Still, it was unnerving. The corpse seemed to be alive and suffering still. No question her spirit was still there. April shivered. If Maggie were Chinese, her family would try to coax her spirit out of the storeroom and into a joss stick so she could have a peaceful afterlife. But no one would do that for Maggie Wheeler.

April worried that she had no gut feelings about this, only a strong appeal from the girl herself to do something about it. Thing was, the older a case got, the more unlikely they'd find the killer. Ninety percent of the time, if they didn't get a break in the case fast, the perp had a good chance of getting away with murder. No one wanted to let this one get away. She could see Joyce's mind working. They didn't have anything, couldn't even do a 24-24 on the victim. Without statements from people who had been with Maggie in the twenty-four hours before her death, they couldn't put together what she had done, whom she had seen.

And forget what happened in the twenty-four-hour period after the murder. The store had been closed.

"Olga got another job," Sanchez said.

"High-class call girl." April spoke for the first time.

"Great." Joyce raked both hands through her hair like a man and turned to April, scowling. April's skin and eyes still looked fresh. Her pale blue blouse was neatly tucked into her well-tailored navy trousers after twelve hours on the job. It was clear April was a devoted cop. Her favorite color was blue.

"She give you any background on the girl?" Joyce directed the question at April.

"Olga said she was very quiet, worked hard, kept to herself."

"That all?"

April shook her head. "She said Maggie had been looking unhappy lately, like something was bugging her. What have you got?"

"Haven't come up with anybody who saw anything yet." Joyce wasn't too happy about that.

Nobody mentioned the guy on Maggie's answering machine. It occurred to April she might go back to Olga with the tape to see if she'd heard that voice before. Olga said she didn't know anything about Maggie's luff life, as she put it. Apparently Maggie didn't talk about things like that. But maybe the guy had been in the store and the sound of his voice would jog Olga's memory. It was a long shot.

She also wanted to talk to the mother. They'd been on it for twelve hours. Sergeant Joyce told them to go home.

# 14

Camille hummed a little to calm down as she tried to get dressed. Milicia had called today and said she was coming. That made Bouck mad. He was sure Camille got worse when Milicia came because Milicia kept telling Camille she was sick and needed medicine.

"Milicia should mind her own fucking business," Bouck said. Bouck wore a pistol in his boot, and another one in his shoulder holster. More than once he threatened to shoot Milicia if she ever tried to take Camille away from him. Milicia said Bouck was crazy. She didn't know enough to be afraid of him.

So far Camille had managed to get her bra and panties on. Bouck liked black, with lots of lace, so that's what they were. She pulled on one of the stockings he had bought for her and attached a garter. On her right, way in the corner, Bouck sat in the semi-darkness, watching her. His face and upper body were obscured in a deep shadow. Only his legs and the bottoms of the black boots showed clearly. She never knew which boot had the pistol.

His legs stuck out a long way because the chair was too small for him. This was the first time he tried this particular chair, and he was pretty sure it was the right one. Camille couldn't remember whether it was the fifth or sixth he had tested. The others all had something wrong with them, even though he bought them for a lot of money. Too high or low off the ground. The seat wasn't the right shape once he got it home and sat in it. The wood wasn't the right shade in the dark. Something.

The chair he wanted had to be a bergère, more than a hundred years old. The kind of upholstery didn't matter absolutely, but he felt he needed the blue medallion, preferably in the original. He wouldn't reupholster the chair. He wanted it to be worn so thin, it looked like a spiderweb in places.

The chair he was sitting in was a signed piece nearly two hundred years old, with the faded blue medallion silk so thin the pattern could barely be recognized. Camille had seen it at an antique show. The dealer was using it himself and didn't want to part with it.

Slowly she drew on the other stocking. Bouck made a sound. She tried not to listen to his sounds. She was turned to the dressing table and couldn't see him because the lights surrounding the mirror on the dressing table lit only her face and not what was around her.

He made another sound. Her heart started beating faster and she could feel the panic rise. There were different kinds of panic that made her do different kinds of things. That much she had figured out. But they all started as pressure, and she never knew, when the pressure began, where it would take her. She concentrated on the dressing table. It was from a later period than the chair. Art deco, inlaid all over with ivory and ebony. It was the best one she had ever seen. She had examined the dressing table carefully for flaws before she allowed Bouck to buy it. He had a thick wad of thousand-dollar bills and paid for it in cash.

These days he gave her only hundreds. Bigger bills were too hard to cash, and when she tried to save them, she forgot where she put them. Bouck had lots of money, but neither the money nor the guns made her feel absolutely safe all the time. The risk was always there. It was there now in Bouck's heavy breathing, there in the colored glass perfume bottles on her tray. Some were art-deco period and some new. Sometimes she broke them and tried to stab herself with the pieces. Bouck didn't like it when she did that. Bouck couldn't stand the sight of blood.

Camille cocked her head and peered at herself in the mirror. Sometimes this was all right to do, and sometimes it wasn't. She could hear Bouck making the sounds that terrified her.

They were trying it again.

Her face was white, bleached with terror, as she reached for the new comb. It was plastic with the teeth set wide apart. Her hair was getting very long now, and hard to manage. It was thick hair with enough curl in it so it didn't just hang down straight. It fanned out from her head like hair from a Botticelli. Bouck wouldn't let her cut her hair. It was red-blond, like the hair of Venus on the scallop shell. Puppy liked to jump up and play with it. Puppy was apricot. Puppy thought Camille's hair was hers to tangle. Camille raised the comb but could not pull it through her hair. She heard the zipper.

She heard Bouck breathing hard. Her stockings were white. So was her skin because she didn't like the sun to tan her face. Camille had a degree in art history and was an interior designer when she could work. Now she worked only for Bouck. She had come into his store on Lexington Avenue one day, looking for a crystal chandelier.

He was sitting behind an English desk in the back, a big man with a smooth, round, wrinkle-free baby face and benign blue eyes. His pale hair sat limp and lifeless on his head.

"I don't have a Botticelli," he said, looking up at her with surprise.

"Who does?" she replied. She was having a good day that day, was wearing a printed silk dress, teal blue with a graceful skirt, and a hat with a brim.

"You do. You're a Botticelli. I'm going to keep you."

She shook her head. Above her, sixty crystal chandeliers fragmented light into thousands of brilliant, winking pinpoints. The diamond sky blinded her. The words and the pinpoints of light stopped her cold. She went into one of her states and froze under his gaze for more than an hour, would not move or answer or blink her eyes.

Bouck wasn't upset though. He sat there behind the desk, watching her be a statue, and was enchanted. Wanted her even more. She was a work of art, a walking painting. He said he'd pay her anything to have her.

"I can't be touched," she said in her first lucid moment.

"Neither could Beatrice."

He understood. He embraced the idea of becoming Dante, making Camille his Beatrice, the adored one he would follow forever and never quite attain. He couldn't believe his luck. He wanted to guard Camille, do battle with her devils, and rescue her.

But the relationship made Milicia furious. Milicia told Camille that Bouck was about as bad for her health as anything could be. She was sure Bouck drugged Camille and did sick things to her, touched her where no one should touch her, and hurt her so bad she might never recover.

Camille thought of Milicia and tried to function. She had to comb her hair, put on her clothes because Milicia said she had to. Until Bouck, Camille always did exactly what Milicia told her. Now she was stuck in the middle. Every day she felt more stressed as Milicia tried harder to separate her from Bouck.

Camille did not want to listen to the sounds Bouck made when he watched her. Even though she couldn't see Bouck in the mirror, and he promised he wouldn't ever get up and do those things to her, Camille was terrified by the sounds he made. Sometimes she got so upset and crazed, he had to give her a pill to calm her down.

Camille never knew what happened after the pill put her to sleep. But when she woke up, sometimes more than twenty-four hours later, there were many bruises on her body. She was sore in strange places and couldn't speak for a long time. Sometimes it was a full week before she could speak again.

Her brain broke down at the thought of touch. Bouck promised he would never, never touch her. If she asked about the bruises, he always told her she'd tried to hurt herself again. She'd gotten out of control, and he had to save her. Bouck said only *he* could save her, and she wanted to believe him. He was the one who gave her money to go shopping, and he was the one with the guns.

But even with his protections and his promise not ever to let Milicia take her back, Camille was afraid nearly all the time. She felt crushed between heavy weights like the stones that killed the Salem witches. Bouck and Milicia were fighting for her. Bouck told Camille the only way she'd really be safe from Milicia would be to marry him.

And that sent Milicia up the wall. The idea of Camille married to Bouck, at his mercy, unable to stop him from doing whatever he wanted with her, was more than Milicia could take.

"Bouck is a predator, like a shark or a lion. He'll eat you alive, Cammy," Milicia told her. "Is that what you want?" Milicia got so upset, she cried real tears.

The tears made Camille feel guilty. All Camille wanted was to keep the furies back and hold on to what was left of her mind. She heard the doorbell ring. Bouck's sounds stopped. He hadn't finished. Camille's terror receded, even though she knew he'd make her do it again later. Trembling, she reached for her dress.

# 15

Camille had the dress on but couldn't manage the buttons. The front was open. Her hair was tangled and wild. The doorbell rang again. She touched the dress fabric, trying to find a name for it. It was very thin, transparent, turquoise in color, printed with a pattern. Camille felt as if she were under water, was drowning a lot of the time. She liked to cover herself with sea colors, seaweed. This dress had shells on it. She tried to button a button.

Bouck sat in the dark and wouldn't go open the door. He said Milicia was Camille's devil, the cause of all her troubles.

She heard a raspy noise. Her breath was coming too fast. The doorbell rang over and over even though she talked on the intercom, said she was coming. She couldn't make the sound stop. The sound caused the panic to rise again.

"I'm coming," she cried. She was panting heavily now as she negotiated the stairs from their bedroom. If she moved too fast, she got dizzy and fell down. Bouck told her he found her at the bottom of the stairs once. He said she'd fallen and hit her head.

Now she stepped carefully, moving one heavy foot in front of the other, stepping over the bugs she thought were in the way as she painfully choreographed her path down the stairs and finally crossed the green living room with its collection of ill-matched furniture. She headed toward the door, dodging a table and a chair.

Bouck owned the whole building. They lived on the second and third floors. The shop was on the first floor, the workshop in the basement. Camille had been buying antique furniture for Bouck. He said she knew more about antiques than anybody.

She liked to buy good pieces and then cram them in so that they formed an obstacle course, hard to get through. She liked how Bouck let her do whatever she wanted. She hadn't finished the place. It was still in the colors of green Bouck had it painted years earlier. She couldn't have the walls glazed the way she liked them because she couldn't stand men working in the apartment. The kitchen was still primitive, always would be. She never went in there.

The bell rang again. It was a harsh, grating sound, not like a bell at all. Camille didn't know why Milicia kept buzzing. All it did was make Puppy dash down the stairs and paw at the door, barking wildly.

"Shh, Puppy," Camille cajoled. She got to the door and rested her head against it, forgetting for a moment why she was there.

"Camille." Milicia's voice came at her through the door. "Open up. It's me."

Slowly Camille's breath began to even out. She opened the door. Milicia rushed in before she could close it again.

"Are you all right? What took you so long? I got scared." Milicia's red skirt and blouse clashed with her hair. Her makeup looked to Camille as if it had been spread on her face with a trowel. She reached out, but Camille backed away. The dog was at Milicia's feet, jumping all over her and nipping at her ankles.

"Hi, cutie." Milicia hunkered down to pet her.

"Don't—" Camille screamed. "Don't touch my baby."

Milicia stood up, frowning. "You kept me waiting out there for twenty minutes. You scare me to death, Camille. I almost never get to see you. I worry about you all the time, living with that"—she dropped her voice to a whisper—"madman. I call you. No one answers the phone. When he answers the phone, I know he doesn't tell you I called." She paused. "I didn't touch your damn dog."

Her face changed again when she registered what Camille was wearing. Camille's see-through dress hung open all the way down, revealing the black lace bra and panties, the black garter belt and white stockings. No shoes on her feet.

"Oh, God, Camille, what are you into now?" Milicia looked around. "Where is he?"

Camille shook her head. She was feeling tired. Milicia's voice came from a long way away.

"Where is he?"

Camille shrugged. Who was she talking about?

"Oh, baby—it's so dark in here." Milicia reached for the light. "Can I turn on the light?"

Camille shrugged again. Milicia hit the light switch with her palm. The chandelier in the center of the ceiling blazed into a fireworks of glittering light. Camille flinched.

"What's the matter?" Milicia moved toward her, making a gesture toward the dress. "Let me button you up."

Camille shook her head. "No." She and her sister were almost the same size, but Milicia still seemed huge to her. She'd start screaming if Milicia touched her.

"Camille." Milicia studied her. "What did you take?"

Camille shook her head back and forth. Forth and back.

"I want to help you."

Back and forth, forth and back.

"What's going on? Can you speak?" Milicia moved another step forward. "This is not the place for you. You're getting worse, can't you tell? Can't you feel it?"

Camille picked up her puppy and held it tight. Milicia wouldn't take this puppy from her. No way.

"Don't touch my puppy," she whispered.

"I don't want to touch your puppy. Camille, you can't go on like this. You have to get some help. Don't you want to get better?"

Camille saw the words come marching out of Milicia's mouth like little soldiers on a parade ground. Milicia was looking around nervously as she spoke. Looking for Bouck, who said he'd kill her. Camille let out a little giggle. Bouck was in the chair upstairs. He could come down if he wanted to.

They stood by the door on the edge of the living room. Camille giggled again. For the first time in her life she lived in a place where Milicia was afraid to come in.

"I met someone who can help you get better. Camille, can you hear me?"

Camille shook her head. Couldn't hear a thing. She saw Milicia's big red mouth moving, saw the words marching out, wanted to stop them once and for all.

"Will you come with me and meet this man? He knows how to help people like you. Please, Camille. I have a bad feeling. I have this really bad feeling something's going to happen that can't be fixed. You don't want anything to happen, do you?"

Camille looked at Milicia and backed away. "What?"

"What? What?"

"What?"

"You mean, what's going to happen—I don't know, Camille. Only you can know," Milicia said wildly.

Camille saw the tears in Milicia's eyes, shook her head, holding the puppy tight. Don't touch.

"*You* know. Please, I can't deal with this by myself. You have to help me."

The stairs creaked. Milicia started. "Oh, God, this place is so creepy. I don't know how you can stand it."

Camille had flinched, too.

"I know you've taken something. I can see it in your eyes. He gives it to you, doesn't he? You're scared of him, aren't you? You can't help it. I know it's not your fault, Camille. Whatever is happening with you, I know it's not your fault."

Camille stopped seeing the words come out of Milicia's big red mouth. Her eyes felt very heavy. She was holding Puppy, leaning against the back of a chair. Stiffly, she moved around to the other side of it and crumpled into the chair, closing her eyes. Puppy stretched out across Camille's lap and put her head down.

# 16

The phone rang. It was seven in the morning. A thick fog blanketed the street and Jason's head. It always took him a half hour to wake up, and he wasn't there yet. His second cup of coffee sat on the counter in front of him, black as ink. He had forgotten to buy milk for the third straight day.

He yawned and picked up on the second ring. "Dr. Frank."

"Hi, it's Charles. Sorry I didn't get back to you last night. I was out late. What's up?"

Jason snapped into focus. "Just wanted to thank you for Sunday. Great day. Congratulations on the house, it's really something."

"Glad you like it. We hope you'll come out often. You know Brenda thinks the world of you."

"I think the world of her, too. Listen, ah, about your architect, Milicia."

Charles laughed. "So that's what's up, you old rogue. I should have known."

"Just wanted to know what your take on her is," Jason said.

"Since when do you need that?"

"She's building a house for you, Charles. You've been working closely with her for some time. . . ."

"Over a year."

Could have fooled me, Jason thought. He hadn't heard a word about it until the house was half up.

"So?" Jason prompted.

"So she's a beautiful and talented girl. Go for it, you old dog."

"That's what you always say." The last thing Jason was was a dog, but he didn't want to explore the subject with Charles. "Aside from looks and talent, what do you think of her?"

"I don't really know her that well." Charles paused. "She's certainly

74

powerful. Gets what she wants . . . There is something about her that's—"

"What?"

"I don't know, a little offputting. Something that doesn't quite fit."

"Oh?" That was interesting. "Like the way she dresses, the way she acts?"

"No, not the way she dresses. She is one of those phallic women though. Go for it."

"Same old Charles. So what doesn't fit?"

"Hmmm, research, old pal? Or something bothering you about her?"

"Call it research, Charles. What about the way she thinks?"

"No, it's not her behavior, and not the way she thinks. I can't put my finger on it. It's just a feeling."

"Thanks."

"Have I helped you?" Charles sounded doubtful.

"Oh, yeah, you've helped me."

"Well, good luck, and let's get together soon." Charles rang off.

The inky coffee was cold. Jason poured it down the sink and tightened the knot on his tie. It was a nice deep blue with red French horns on it, the first tie Jason's fingers had touched when he reached in the closet for his tie rack that morning.

He rinsed out the coffee cup and left it in the sink. His stomach growled. He ignored it. He was thinking that Charles always knew what was off about somebody. His not being sure about Milicia might mean simply that Charles couldn't relate to the powerful aspect of her. But the concept of falseness might come from the woman herself. It was something to think about. The carriage clock on the hall table chimed the hour. It was fifteen minutes late. Jason sighed. He didn't have time to go out and get milk before his first patient showed up at seven-thirty.

# 17

The alarm didn't have to scream at April for her to know it was time to wake up. She always heard the click before the alarm sounded. Sometimes she was up before the click. Last night she had fallen asleep studying her notes, and now their contents were the first thing she thought of as she pulled herself out of bed.

No one was allowed to take anything home from a case. All evidence had to be carefully labeled and locked up. Only thing you could take home was your notes. April took a lot of notes. She studied them at night, working on questions, angles, speculations, hypotheses. Every case to her was like being in training for the police Olympics. Every morning she started thinking before she could see. That morning she was thinking, who killed Maggie Wheeler? Was it a random thing—some crazy off the street—or somebody involved with the girl herself?

April drank some water, pulled on her tights, and started exercising. Last night she'd had Maggie's address book copied, took the photocopy home with her, and made a few calls. She was rewarded for that bit of ingenuity by not being able to get through to anybody. She tried always to do things right. There was a rule of procedure and a reason for everything the department did. But doing everything right took a lot of extra time and wasn't always so easy to do.

Not everything happened the way it was supposed to. For one thing, no one was supposed to go into a crime scene but the cops who caught the run and the two crime-scene people. The catching cops were supposed to rope off the area and keep everyone out, but it didn't work that way. Call came in on a homicide like this, and twenty, maybe thirty people from the bureau wandered through, wanting to see the corpses and check out the murder scene. Problem was thirty cops and detectives wandering through a murder scene couldn't help but contaminate the evidence quite a bit.

No way could anyone keep the bureau out.

In the Wheeler case ten squad cars rolled up before Crime Scene got there. The new Captain of the precinct, an uptight Irishman of the old school who wore blue shirts with white collars, and half a dozen ranking officers from the Two-O were among those "having a look."

The hordes of Europe tramping around didn't make too much difference in a gore-spattered scene where the murder weapon was visible and a picture of what happened was pretty clear by the marks on the body, the way it was lying, the pooling and spatters of blood around it. But here, where there was nothing, it was a different story.

"How many?" was the first question Igor had asked when he and his partner, Mako, named for the shark, entered The Last Mango.

"Many," Mike said.

"Shit. When are you people going to learn?"

Old gripe of the science people. They said the whole story of every murder was right there on the spot, even if the dumb cops couldn't see it. It was there in traces of dust and fiber and hair and grease and stains. All they had to do was collect, identify, and match. But ninety-five percent of trace evidence was contaminated or left behind. Five percent was collected, and maybe one percent used to nail the suspect. April was taking a course on this and knew how to look at things through a microscope.

"Hey, what's that?" Skinny Dragon Mother opened the door to April's apartment with her own key, not bothering to warn her with a polite knock. Right away she started in on her in Chinese.

"What's that?" she demanded again in case April hadn't heard her the first time.

"Hi, Mom. What are you doing up so early?" April was on her hands and knees on the floor, doing leg lifts with a book open in front of her.

"Have to be early bird catch this worm," she said in Chinese.

This was the time of day that showed Sai Woo was not so new-style Chinese as she claimed. She was wearing black pants and black canvas shoes with absolutely no embroidery on them, a plain blue peasant jacket. Summer version, not padded. Very skinny woman, eyes narrowed with deep suspicion at the book on the floor. April knew her mother dressed like a peasant in her own home to fool the gods into thinking she wasn't so well off and fortunate. Clearly there was something on her mind.

"What worm is that?" April asked, lowering herself to her elbows for the next set, which was a lot harder.

"Worm daughter."

Great, she had a big new case, her Sergeant's test in less than two weeks, and exams in the summer courses she was taking at John Jay. She couldn't qualify for Sergeant without two years of college, but she already had three and a half and was hoping to graduate this year. And now her mother was calling her a worm.

"Why am I a worm, Mom?" April tried to concentrate on the leg.

"What's *that*?" Sai demanded, pointing at the book.

April sighed. So it was the Sanchez thing again. Ever since Mike had driven her home in the red Camaro that first time, her mother had been thinking the worst. "It's Spanish, Mom."

"Ayeiiii, I knew it," Sai cried, still in Chinese. "I knew it."

"You don't know it, Mom. The department wants everybody to speak Spanish. It's a new thing. You want to get ahead, want to get a degree, you have to speak another language."

Sai Woo switched suddenly to English to show she was bilingual, too. "You speak other ranguage. You speak Chinese."

"Doesn't count. Have to speak Spanish."

"This New York. Not Miami, not Rrr.A. Not so Spanish here, every kind people in New York."

"That's true," April agreed, finally rolling over and sitting up. A lot of people thought like her mother, didn't like this new Spanish thing, thought the Spanish should learn English.

"Not Spanish lestlant on every brock. *Chinese* lestlant on every brock. Chinese best food, best people." Sai pounded her tiny fists on her flat chest to indicate her pride.

April smiled. "That may be, Mom. But the department still wants everyone to speak Spanish."

"Humph." Sai turned her back and touched the little table beside the couch. It slanted a bit on the floor.

"What's bugging you, Mom?" April closed the book guiltily because her mother was right about one thing. This, of all mornings, she didn't have to be studying Spanish during her exercises. She could be doing management styles, or preparing the oral answer to such questions as:

78

*Crime analysis is an important tool for the police supervisor. Please explain to this board the purpose of crime analysis and how you would use this information as a police sergeant.*

"Taber no good. Maybe taber bad spilit in your rife."

All her hope and confidence fled in an instant. April frowned, the dread of bad luck in her exams, her life itself, descending like a pall over a wedding. "I don't have a bad spirit in my life."

"Yes. *Dr.* George Dong says he'll meet you—no promises—you no rant meet him. Must be bad spilit in this house."

"Maybe the bad spirit is downstairs. I never heard of the guy," April protested.

"He no guy. He docta."

"That's great, Mom. But I never heard of him."

"Now heard of him." Sai picked up the table and moved it to the other side of the room. "There, taber frat. Now spilit happy. You two can meet, mally, have many babies. Some boys, some girrs."

April nodded. Great, now her mother was a feminist. She must really be desperate, never used to pray for girls.

"Mom, I have a new case. Want to hear about it?"

Sai nodded, padded across the room to April's kitchen, and started rattling around. Feng Shui over, match made. Now she would make worm daughter's breakfast and solve the case. April sighed and headed for the bathroom to take her shower.


She arrived at the precinct before seven-thirty. The Desk Sergeant who'd been on night duty was still there. He nodded at her. Upstairs the squad room was empty. It still smelled of old smoke. The evening shift were all smokers. The day shift were all trying to quit. It smelled disgusting. April had never tried smoking. She dusted the piles of cigarette ash off her desk, sat down, and punched out the number of the M.E.'s office to see if the autopsy report was coming in today.

No one answered, so she took out the copy of Maggie's address book and dialed one of the numbers she'd tried the night before. The phone rang a bunch of times before a grumpy voice answered.

"Yeah."

"Is this Bill Hadgens?"

"Yeah."

"This is Detective Woo from the New York Police Department."

"Yeah, well, I didn't do it."

"Didn't do what, Mr. Hadgens?"

"I didn't kill old Maggie. That's what you're calling about, isn't it—hey, is this for real?"

"Yes, this is for real. Where are you located? I'd like to talk to you."

No reply for quite a while. "How did you get my number?"

"It was in her telephone book."

"So that doesn't mean anything. We come from the same town is all."

"I didn't say it meant anything. I'm just trying to locate people who knew Maggie. Trying to find out what happened to her."

Bill Hadgens thought it over for a while, then spoke. "I saw it on the news last night. Eleven o'clock. Really weird."

"What was weird?"

"I don't even watch the news. Last night I watch the news, and someone I know got killed. Weird."

It wouldn't be so weird to watch the news if he already knew what would be on it. She took Hadgens's address, then called the M.E.'s office again. This time someone with a friendly voice picked up the phone, listened to April's identification and questions, said, "Just a minute, please," and put her on hold for five minutes.

Then a less friendly voice came on that seemed to come from a different department. April repeated the same things about being the detective on the Maggie Wheeler case and needing the autopsy yesterday afternoon. She got put on hold again. Finally someone came on who knew something. The Wheeler autopsy was scheduled for right about now, and they should have the report by early afternoon. April offered to go over and pick it up and was told that wasn't necessary. She decided not to argue.

April looked at her watch. Eight-fifteen. The place was filling up. Sergeant Joyce, in a black skirt and apple-green blazer, her hair sticking straight up in a style that defied description, stopped by April's desk and peered at the pile of papers she had laid out.

"Early afternoon for the autopsy report," April said. She resisted the impulse to cover her notes with her hand.

"Bastards," Joyce said. "Anything else?"

Sure. "I'm checking out the boyfriends. Where's Sanchez?"

"Twentieth Street."

"What's he doing there?"

Sergeant Joyce shrugged and walked away, either didn't know or wouldn't say. Maybe Sergeant Joyce was the bad spirit in her life. Muttering under her breath, April picked up her bag and headed out to meet Bill Hadgens on Fiftieth and Second.

# 18

"I never went out with her," Bill Hadgens insisted for the third time, eyeing April uneasily. "I can't tell you anything about her."

He lived in a filthy one-room apartment overlooking Second Avenue above an old-fashioned plumbing supply store. The furnishings consisted of a nasty-looking bed and a wooden chair. Dust balls had collected around piles of dirty clothes on the bare wood floor. Four or five years of grime clung to the windows, long since replacing the need for curtains. One window boasted a rasping fan that didn't have enough power to stir the dust.

Bill Hadgens sat on the edge of his bed with his hands on his grubby bare knees. He had not bothered to pull himself together in anticipation of a visit from the police. After April's call he had clearly gone back to bed. He was wearing cut-off jeans and no shirt. The side of his long, horsey face was sheet-creased and didn't appear to have been troubled by a razor in some time. His shoulder-length brown hair was tangled and dirty. He didn't look sullen so much as completely unconcerned, as if people he knew got knocked off every day.

"Why bother with me?"

"I told you. She's a murder victim. We bother with everybody. Maggie had only a few male names in her telephone book. Yours was one." April took a look around as she spoke. Guy looked like he didn't eat much and hadn't been out of bed in days. How many days—since Maggie's death?

It had taken him a while to get to the door when she rang the bell. Then he looked surprised to see her there. He was grumpy and seemed to have forgotten she was coming. Guy was really whacked. She made a note to herself that she could always come back and take him in for possession if he didn't want to cooperate.

"Yeah, well, we went to the same school. I knew her years ago is all."

"What was she like?"

He shrugged, pursing his lips in a show of contempt. "She was kind of a dog, know what I mean?"

April shook her head. "Explain it to me."

He shrugged again. "A dog. You know what a dog is."

"If you thought she was such a dog, how come you're in her phone book?" April crossed the room to the window and looked out. Not much to see. She wondered where the stuff was. His eyes were pretty dilated. Must be around somewhere.

"Who knows."

"Then how'd she get your number?"

"Fuck if I know. Maybe somebody gave it to her."

"You have any idea who that might be?"

"No—hey, what're you doing?"

She took her hand away from the pile of clothes on the chair. "You have a problem with my sitting down?"

"Don't touch anything, okay?"

April moved away from the chair and changed tack. "What do you do for a living, Mr. Hadgens?"

"Huh?"

"I asked how you support yourself."

"I, uh, freelance—I'm a writer."

"Oh, yeah? What kind of writing do you do?"

He stared at the chair. She figured the stuff was there.

"I'm working on a novel."

"No kidding." She didn't see a typewriter. "When was the last time you saw Maggie?"

"I don't know. Long time. Months, maybe years. I lose track of time."

"I bet you do. You want to tell me about Maggie's other friends? She have a boyfriend?"

"No way. Maggie was lunchmeat."

Okay. "Mr. Hadgens, where were you last Saturday?"

"Nowhere near Maggie Wheeler. I can tell you that. I don't go to the West Side."

"Thanks." April moved toward the door. She didn't think Hadgens was telling her the whole truth, or even half the truth. Guy was a druggie and a liar. No point in pursuing the subject now. She'd try him again later.

It stuck in her mind that he had described Maggie as lunchmeat. Nice. The girl was dead. Why make such a point of her lack of attractiveness in the distant past when he claimed to have known her and they went to the same school? Was the real story the reverse—that he liked Maggie Wheeler a lot and got rejected by her? Did he go visit her in the boutique last Saturday, have a fight with her, and fix her up for all time? April tried that scenario out, played it through as she descended the grimy stairs to the street.

Nah, this guy didn't look organized enough to do all that with the dress many sizes too big and the makeup on the victim's face. That was really weird stuff. This guy looked whack, but not particularly weird. Still, he wasn't telling the truth. Maybe he didn't do it, but had some idea who did.

Out on the street the temperature was climbing steadily. It had to be close to eighty-five. April decided to go over to the police labs on Twentieth Street and find out what Sanchez was up to.

## 19

"Hey, Mike, whatcha got?" Fernando Ducci, known as Duke, finished the last of a Snickers bar and tossed the wrapper into his wastebasket. At eleven o'clock in the morning, it was his third candy bar of the day. He wore a blue shirt with a white collar of the kind Captain Higgins liked, the sleeves rolled all the way down and buttoned. His dark blue tie was Italian silk. There was no shoulder holster on his person. Duke did not like to carry. He kept his gun in his locker. With his smooth round face and thick black hair, he looked more like an aging choirboy than a cop in the hair and fiber section of the police labs.

"Stuff from the M.E.'s office." Mike Sanchez dropped the brown cardboard box on Ducci's desk.

Ducci looked past him toward the door. "Hey, where's the pretty one? She avoiding me, or what?"

"She's out."

"I'm hurt. I want the stuff from her. We like continuity around here."

"Yeah, well, I'm continuity. I could have just let them put this shit on the shelf and forgotten it like everybody else. You're always saying you want everything in the beginning. Well, here's everything."

"Ah, well." Ducci tapped on the box. "Hey, go ahead, keep me guessing. What case are we talking about?"

"Same as yesterday. Boutique thing."

"Oh, and here I thought something else came up. Shit, why can't you guys get your act together and give it all to me at once?" He knew damn well why they couldn't, but liked to annoy.

Ducci was a man who hadn't gone outside for the last twenty years. He had a slide collection of every kind of dirt, asphalt, stone, fiber, head hair, pubic hair, leaf, pine cone, bird feather, tree bark, grass he'd ever come across. He'd analyzed so many things from so many cases, working over the years in so many departments in the labs, he now believed he could tell what park a grass stain on a pair of pants came from, and what activity the wearer was engaged in when he got it. Some people said he had a bit of an ego problem.

Before Mike tossed the box on it, Ducci's desk had already been piled high with folders, odds and ends, boxes of slides, relics of various sorts. Now it was definitely overburdened. Ducci looked around for another place to dump the box, debated putting it on Bryan's desk for a little while just to piss him off when he came in. Right next to his in the long, narrow room with windows across the other side, Bryan's desk was clear.

Ducci thought Bryan was a real asshole, kept everything so god-damned neat, no one could ever find anything he worked on. Ducci was the brilliant one, and Bryan was always complaining, saying he couldn't work in the same room with such a pig. Judy, who was a scientist and not a cop, was the mediating agent on the hair and fiber team. But she wasn't there. She was on vacation in a canoe somewhere in Wisconsin.

Mike pointed at Ducci's other chair. It had a pile of papers with a skull on top of it. Some of the teeth in the skull were missing. The ones remaining indicated quite a lot of tooth decay and no visits to an ortho-dontist.

"Mind if I sit down?" he asked.

"Hey, no problem."

Ducci stepped around some debris from another case he was working and removed the pile of stuff from the chair. He placed it on the empty chair in front of Bryan's desk. Bryan used the phone in there, but most of the time he worked in another lab. Hair and Fiber had three desks and three sets of shelves in it, all facing the wall opposite the windows. The tile walls and floor were sea green.

In the old days, when there were fewer people in the police labs, there had been just one desk to an office. Now with three, it was hard to get around, hard to make calls, hard to think. And even with three, they didn't have anywhere near enough people for the workload.

Ducci had a whole lot of complaints about the system. Every case in the city that had hair and fiber evidence came through this lab. Coordina-tion between detectives and the scientists was not so great. A lot of things got messed up. Ducci had fantasies of a different setup, police labs with only scientists and absolutely no police at all.

He himself was a cop who had found his calling by accident in college. After six years of writing parking tickets and getting two degrees at night, he discovered he liked science. When he was asked if he wanted to go into the labs, he jumped at the chance. Though of exactly the same mold, his office mate, Francis X. Bryan, was not, Ducci believed, cut of the same high-quality cloth as himself. Bryan wore his gun all the time and was still more cop than scientist. Ducci had fantasies of forcing him back to the streets, where he had started as a foot patrolman. Now he scowled at Sanchez, thinking of Francis.

"Want some coffee? Tastes like shit, but it's better than nothing."

"No thanks, I've tasted it." Sanchez sank into the cleared chair.

"So?" Ducci rubbed his stomach as if he were some kind of Buddha, or had acid indigestion. "So tell me about this little present. What is it?"

"Take a guess. You got everything from the scene yesterday. This is the stuff from the body. You should thank me. Not everybody would go over there first thing in the morning and bring it to you."

"True." Many detectives didn't have the time or temperament to collect evidence and take it through the obstacle course correctly so that when the time came to go to court the case would hold. Sanchez did. So did his girlfriend, April Woo. "Stick around."

Ducci opened the flaps on the box. A printed dress with wild purple and red flowers all over it, not even bagged, spilled out.

"Shit, what'd they do, toss it around the table, guessin' what mighta happened?" He noted the label, size fourteen, and shook his head. "How many people touch this?"

Mike shrugged. "Can't tell you that. Four, maybe five."

Ducci sifted through the rest of the stuff, all paper bags meticulously labeled. He looked at some of the labels—*Long red hair found on skirt of dress. Makeup from victim's face. Fiber taken from bruise marks on victim's neck. Victim's ring, with fibers caught on prongs.*

Very, very occasionally Ducci personally went to a crime scene if it was really important, or the morgue, to check out the marks and bruises on a body for himself. But he never dealt with the wet stuff. That was for the serology people.

"You got a cause of death yet?"

"The report's coming later today."

"Okay, so what've we got here?"

Sanchez filled him in on what they had on the case so far. Not much. "I'd like to see the autopsy report and the crime-scene sketches and photos," Ducci said, happy to be in on the ground floor for once. Most detectives didn't even tell him what the case involved or what he was looking for. "Don't keep me in the dark."

"Fine."

Ducci sat back, satisfied, and patted his stomach some more. Pleased as he was, this was about as far as he wanted to go with the case at this point. He examined Sanchez and frowned. "Where you been anyway? You look fried."

"Mexico. Went for a week."

"No kidding."

"Yeah, lots of sun. What about you? You look like you haven't seen the light of day all summer."

In the last weeks of August, Ducci's unlined face was still winter pale. His shiny black hair, untainted with gray, sat like a burnished crown on his head. He shrugged. He didn't like more of the light of day than came through the window. "You go with your girlfriend?"

"Who might that be?" Sanchez's frown appeared crooked because not all of his right eyebrow had grown back where the scar was. It made him look more quizzical than he had before. Ducci knew the plastic doctor had told Sanchez he could fix it, but Sanchez didn't seem eager to buy.

"Hey, I thought you and pretty one were a known quantity," Ducci said.

"No way, man. You know the Chinese."

Ducci shook his head. There were lots of Asians of all kinds as well as Indians in the labs. But no, he really didn't know the Chinese.

"Inscrutable," Mike said.

"What's that, some kinda disease?" He laughed, holding his stomach.

"Yeah, maybe."

"So, what did you go for?" Ducci changed the subject. He had a minute before getting back to the microscope. He was working on twelve pubic hairs from twelve different people found on the bedspread of a well-known hotel where a guest had raped a maid. Serology said they had identified almost as many different semen stains. Seemed like a lot of people were in too much of a hurry to turn back the covers.

"Hey, why all the questions?" Mike demanded.

"Just being friendly. You're pretty inscrutable yourself." Ducci was sure Mike and April had something going. So what was the big deal? "You don't want to tell me about Mexico, that's fine."

"I went to see my ex-wife, happy now?"

Mike looked so unhappy about that, Ducci didn't think he should let it go. "Want to tell me about it?"

"No," Mike burst out angrily. He glanced at the skull on the chair, shaking his head. "She wanted to say good-bye, okay? She's dying. Cancer. You happy now?"

"Oh." Ducci's face softened. Lot of times he went too far and felt like a real jerk. "Sorry," he murmured. "I always ask people a lot of questions, guess it goes with the territory."

He pulled a Snickers bar out of the center drawer of his desk, held it out to Mike as a peace offering.

Mike looked at it as if it were a dead animal he wouldn't touch under any circumstances. "No thanks. Can't afford the calories."

"So? Neither can I. Never stopped me, never will."

"Yeah, well, sign for this, will you, and I'll get that other stuff to you as soon as I can." Mike shifted the papers with the skull on top back to Ducci's chair while Ducci signed for the box and its contents.

As Mike went out the door, Duke shrugged and opened the candy wrapper.

# 20

Sergeant Joyce had made the day's assignments first thing after roll call. Five of the eight detectives on the day shift were working the Maggie Wheeler homicide. Healy and Aspirante were out in the field looking for witnesses in the neighboring shops on Columbus Avenue who might have seen something Saturday night they didn't at the time know they were seeing. Detective Stevens, a tough young black man pretty new to the squad, was working the phone, checking the boutique's Saturday receipts. With the help of MasterCard and Visa, he was putting together a list of the names and addresses of the seven people who had made charges that day. The store didn't take American Express, so that narrowed it down. They were out of luck with the people who had paid cash, but you never knew who might turn up with information later. Mike had gone to the police lab.

April got back from questioning Hadgens just around noon. Downstairs, three scraggly members of the press loitered on the metal chairs, their knapsacks and coffee cups on the floor around them, looking like homeless waiting for a meal. If there wasn't a break in the case by that night or the next morning, they'd give up on the meal there and move on to something hotter. As she passed the two eager-looking young men and hawk-faced woman on her way to the stairs, April ignored them, and they ignored her.

In the squad room Mike was on the phone. He raised his hand in a small wave. "Yeah, I want a printout of all the calls coming in and out of that number. Yeah. Thanks." He hung up. "Maggie Wheeler's home number," he said.

April dropped her bag in the bottom desk drawer. "What's new?"

He looked her over. "Not a whole lot. What about you?"

His way of examining her as if she were a storm front on a weather map made her nervous. Today his gaze was so intense, she could feel herself beginning to sweat, suddenly anxious that she had done something terribly wrong, or something was inappropriate about her makeup or outfit. That day she was wearing hardly any makeup, a pale blue cotton jacket over a white blouse and khaki slacks. Her outfit was very conservative. Not even the top button of the blouse was ever open. She didn't want anyone looking at her with monkey business in mind.

Mike knew everything. He was studying her so intently, she thought maybe he'd already heard about Dr. George Dong. It occurred to April that she'd forgotten to ask what kind of doctor Dong was. She frowned, thinking about Skinny Dragon Mother's treachery, then hauled herself back to the moment. This case was a whole lot of blanks.

"I talked to one guy in Maggie's phone book. Possible abuser of some kind. He knew what I was calling about, but said he didn't know anything more about it than what he saw on the news." She brushed at some stray ashes on the seat of her chair before sitting down. "He says he didn't call her this weekend and hasn't spoken to her in years."

Mike picked up on her doubt right away. "But you think it's possible he knows more than he's saying."

"Yeah. Maggie's boss said she's been here for only six months. How come she had his number if he hasn't spoken to her in years? Doesn't add up. What have you been up to?" She narrowed her eyes at him, preparing for a lie.

"I went down to the M.E.'s office to pick up the crime-scene stuff and took it over to Duke. Now he's got everything."

"Did you look in on the autopsy?"

"Sure. And stayed for breakfast."

"It was scheduled for this morning." Was that a lie? She looked at her watch.

"I know."

"You seem to know everything," April muttered. "Duke say anything?" Her desk was behind Mike's. He had to swivel around to face her. Now his feet were up on an open drawer and he was facing out at the pen, the holding cell in the middle of the squad room. It was empty at the moment.

Except for Maggie, it was a pretty quiet day.

"Yeah, he misses you. Wondered why you weren't the one to come and see him. It's not my job to carry evidence around."

"I didn't know the stuff was ready."

"You sore?"

April swiveled around the other way so she was looking toward Sergeant Joyce's office. The doorway was just outside the squad room, down the hall so no one could see in. No way to know what Joyce was up to. Yeah, she was sore. Second day back on the job and already Mike and Sergeant Joyce were being secretive. What did Mike know that she didn't? Hey, if she was investigating and he was supervising her investigation, he had to share whatever information he had.

"Well, it should be done by now," April said. "I'll give them an hour or so and go down and pick it up."

"What's the matter?"

April swiveled back. "I asked you if Duke had come up with anything and your response was he missed me. You holding out on me, Sanchez?"

Mike spread his hands. "What's the matter with you? I think you got a lot of potential. Why would I hold out on you?"

April chewed on her lip. There were a lot of reasons. He was a man. He had monkey business on the brain all the time. He was her superior and maybe wanted to keep it that way. And maybe he just had some reasons of his own she didn't know about.

"Lighten up," he said.

"I will not lighten up until I have some answers."

"Well, there aren't any answers. Duke hadn't even looked at what I gave him yesterday. He hasn't had time."

Still didn't have an answer. Why did Mike go to the M.E.'s office first thing this morning? It was on Thirtieth Street and First Avenue, sort of an adjunct to Bellevue. Thirty-fourth to Twentieth, then up here to Eighty-second and Columbus. Back and forth. She shrugged. Maybe there was nothing in it. Most police work was just running from one place to another—getting warrants, moving evidence from one place to another, trying to reach people who weren't home. Mike's phone rang. He swung his feet down and picked up.

April looked at her watch, then punched out the number of one of the other male names in Maggie's book. Still no answer there. She tried Maggie's mother. Yesterday Mrs. Wheeler had told the sheriff who came to her house that she'd do anything she could to help the detectives in New York. Maybe the mother was ready to answer a few questions.

# 21

The rusting yellow taxi came to a screeching halt sideways in the middle of Second Avenue, barely avoiding a nasty collision with the bicycle messenger who had cut it off without warning. Skidding into a pothole, the bike tipped over and the skinny, kinky-haired messenger with a number of gold earrings in both ears fell off it. Cars squealed to a stop around him as he got up, shaking his fist.

Out of the battered taxi lunged an Indian of some sort. He was wearing a turban on his head and making angry noises in a language that in no way approximated English. Frustrated drivers in blocked cars started honking their horns.

Milicia leaned forward across the table. "Camille, can you hear me? I can't take this."

Camille stared out of the coffee shop window at the two men arguing on the street. It reminded her of Bouck and the gun. One day Bouck was out with Puppy at night, just around here, on Fifty-fifth Street. A guy in a car cut another guy off. The guy cut off was so mad, he jumped out of his car, pulled a gun, and blew the other man away before either of them had a chance to exchange a word. Bouck said there was blood all over the street. Camille smiled, thinking about it, trying to get away from Milicia's big mouth.

*Finally, she was having a good day and Milicia had to turn up again, find her out on the street, and capture her.*

Milicia was spying on her, watching everything she did, just like she used to. Camille stared out the window. When did Milicia have time to build those buildings of hers? There was a new one on Third Avenue, with colored panels on the outside. Milicia took her to see it last spring and told her it was hers.

Camille thought it was ugly. Bouck had offered to get the light fixtures for the whole building, but Milicia said someone had already gotten the bid for that. The bag moved. Camille put her hand on it.

Puppy was in the bag. Bouck had bought her a fancy carrier from Louis Vuitton that looked like a shoulder bag so Camille could take Puppy with her everywhere. Nobody in the coffee shop knew there was a dog on the seat beside her. Her mind shifted to that but her face didn't smile. She could feel her face freezing as she tried to ignore her sister opposite her in the booth.

"What were you doing in that boutique?" For the last ten minutes Milicia kept asking her the same thing. The tuna salad Milicia had ordered didn't meet her specifications, too much mayonnaise. Two scoops of it sat untouched on a sheaf of pale green iceberg lettuce.

Camille's hands twitched in her lap. She didn't answer. She wanted to eat the toasted cheese sandwich on her plate but couldn't reach for it with Milicia there. She was thinking that Milicia probably poisoned it. Even if Milicia left, she couldn't eat it now.

"I saw you, Camille. I saw you in the window. Camille, I know you're crazy. I know you think this boutique thing is a way to get back at me, but you'll be punished. Do you understand? Look at me." Milicia's voice dropped to a furious whisper. "You'll be punished worse than ever before."

Camille turned her head. Now she could see Milicia's red mouth moving again. She wanted to put a stop to it.

"Why don't you leave me alone?" Camille finally formed the words. She found the words and her lips moved.

"You know why."

Camille shook her head. She didn't know why. She was trying on a dress. Just trying on a dress. She liked to go shopping when she could. Today she could. The sun was burning a hole in the deep blue sky. There was not a single cloud anywhere. No possibility of rain. Camille didn't like to sit in the sun or let it touch her too deeply, but she could walk in it. She had been having a good day. She'd moved from Bouck's building out into the sun. A hat with a big brim hid her face from the dangerous rays. It was the hat Bouck liked best, straw with a lavender ribbon around the brim.

She remembered working on getting outside, sneaking away before Bouck could talk to her. Sometimes Bouck talked to her, bothered her, wanted her to do something. She couldn't ever tell Bouck that she didn't like that. He got mad at the tiniest things. She pressed her lips together to remind herself what would happen if too many words came out. Sometimes she sat in the basement, hiding all day, listening to the noises in the shop above, afraid to move. Sometimes she got in trouble with herself and didn't know what she was doing. But today her head felt okay, clear enough to get out.

She had turned left on the street and headed north toward Bloomingdale's. She passed Bloomingdale's, though, couldn't go in. It was too dangerous in there. She even turned her head away as she went by it. All that stuff and the black walls did bad things to her. In Bloomingdale's sometimes she remembered her mother, stroking her head when she was little after something happened, and promising her everything would be all right. The memory gave her a headache. Other memories, too.

On Third Avenue and Sixty-first Street there was a shoe store. The boutique next to it had a dress in the window that attracted Camille. She wanted to try it on. Camille liked going into stores and trying things on. Bouck always gave her lots of money in hundred-dollar bills. She could have anything she wanted. She liked to think about the cash in her pocket. Sometimes she put her hand in her pocket, or the bag Puppy was in, to feel the money. The money, rolls of it, hidden in the house, shocked Milicia.

Milicia's mouth was moving again. "Don't you understand I'm trying to save you? Camille, you're in terrible trouble. Do you understand that? I'm trying to figure out what to do."

"Leave me alone." Camille traced the words on the paper table mat: *leave me alone.*

"I want to help you."

Camille shook her head. Milicia wanted to hurt her, had always wanted to hurt her. Milicia was there waiting to get her. Like today, when she was feeling better. Milicia came out of her office like a spider, looking for her, spying on her. Camille stared down at her knife on the table, imagined picking it up and driving it through Milicia's hand.

Milicia followed her gaze. "Don't even think about it," she said.

Camille didn't pick up the knife. It wasn't the right kind of knife.

"You need help, Camille. Bouck can't give you the kind of help you need. Only I can give you the help you need. I'm your sister. I'm the one in charge of your health." Milicia's eyes were slits.

"You don't know what I can do," Camille murmured.

"Yes, Camille. I know. I know very well what you're capable of doing, and believe me, I won't let this go on."

Milicia's voice was a razor, cutting deep with every word. Camille saw the razor at her throat.

"I know how you feel," Milicia continued. "I know what you're thinking. I know why you like Bouck, but he can't protect you from punishment this time."

"You're afraid of him." Camille found some more words, picked them out of the air, where they drifted around her mouth like the smoke from the cigarettes at the next table. Clouds of it hovered for a few seconds and then rose, dissipating in the air.

"I'm not afraid of him. He can't hurt me."

Milicia said it with her big red mouth, but Camille knew Milicia came to the house only when she thought Bouck was out of town. Last time she left as soon as she found out he wasn't in Westchester after all. He was upstairs all the time. So Milicia couldn't look for the money.

"I have to get back to work," Milicia said, checking her watch.

Camille recognized the watch even though she hadn't seen it in years. It had been their mother's. Small rubies and diamonds surrounded the pretty face, and the band was a gold bracelet. Milicia told her it had been destroyed. She said their mother had been wearing it the day their father drove the car off the road. Milicia told her the car flipped over and crashed in a deep, deep ravine. Their bodies were burned in the fire and there was nothing left of them. Camille's eyes hardened. Milicia took whatever she could get, no matter whose it was.

"Are you all right?" Milicia asked suddenly.

Camille's expression changed. She could see Milicia was afraid to walk back with her. Milicia was afraid of Bouck. Camille said nothing.

Milicia paid the bill, shaking her head. "I hate this. You're all I have, and I don't know how to reach you. What am I supposed to do? I don't want you to be punished, Cammy. I really don't."

Camille could see there were tears in Milicia's eyes, but they were fake tears. The bag moved by her side, almost tipping over. It was time to take Puppy outside.

# 22

Jason had an hour and fifteen minutes until his appointment with Daisy. He hesitated for a second just inside the door of his waiting room, then went out into the hall, turned left, and returned home.

The little entry hall, with the polished wood floor and the table where Emma always put the mail, was empty. The doors to the living room were open, revealing a generous space lit by two windows that overlooked the tree-lined street. The room was painted a pale lemon yellow and decorated with comfortable tweedy sofas. Built-in shelves on two of the walls were filled with books, souvenirs, and five of Jason's antique clocks. There were nine clocks altogether in the room. All were over a hundred years old and all were in working order. Jason never bought a clock that couldn't be made to work. Unlike human hearts, they were mechanical and could be fixed when they broke down.

It was painful for Jason to come home. Every time he heard those clocks and looked around, his heart started to race with the memories of Emma's kidnapping and his part in her ordeal. He didn't want to brood endlessly about everything. But he did. He went over and over his failure to read her, his failure to acknowledge how hurt and neglected she felt. His failure to read the script of her first film, the little thing that came along and destroyed their life.

He brooded that his insensitivity to Emma's unhappiness might have made the difference. If he'd been thinking of her needs instead of his own, they could have had a baby by now. They'd be living in the suburbs. Forty had always meant the crossover to old on his life timeline. He'd be thirty-nine in a few days, and had no family except a set of parents he saw only a few times a year. Work was always the driving force in his life, but he loved Emma. Never wanted to hurt her. Never expected to be so desperately lonely. On the other hand, he knew that even if she had been happy, she might have made the film with the same tragic results anyway.

Jason brooded. He came from a long line, maybe five thousand years old, of serious brooders. There was a reason he was an analyst. He took in and processed information in big chunks, but it took him a long time to come around to action. He hung around the hall table, shattered by the emptiness of his home and the heat of the New York summer. The apartment was hot and musty. He turned to the kitchen, beginning to sweat. The inch of aged coffee in the coffeepot on the counter by the sink seemed a testament to his domestic misery. All around was the sound of clocks.

Living in this apartment in this building had always seemed to him like living in Europe in another century, when there were no telephones or faxes, no computers or copy machines. People communicated by mail which came twice a day, morning and afternoon. Men like Freud went home for lunch, and their wives tolerated them no matter what they did. In those days no one who ran away lived happily ever after.

Ask anybody, Jason thought bitterly, and they'd say that times were better now. He stood in the hall outside the kitchen, paralyzed with grief, wondering if his wife was finding happiness in L.A. after what happened to her. He didn't think she could recover without his help.

The hall carriage clock chimed the hour. Emma used to say he spent more time with his clocks than he did with her. And it was true he had thought of them as his friends, his link with the past and the future, his grasp on time. Now he knew they had been his little hedge against mortality, substitute for a lot of things.

Shaking his head, he shuffled down the hall to the bedroom. Emma had left most of her possessions and all of her souvenirs around the house, indicating a certain ambivalence about clearing out for good. Jason didn't know whether to hope for an eventual return or not.

Depression was a dangerous state for a psychiatrist. A dozen years of training had taught Jason all about the management of troubled people. The main thing was that every second of every session counted. There were no time-outs, no moments for the doctor to escape into his own dreams, his own thoughts, his own agenda. There could be only the patient and his needs, for even the silences spoke loudly and with meaning. An empathic lapse of even a few tiny moments could bring about a cataclysm in a patient's life. Jason's primary responsibility was to his patients. He knew he was depressed, and there was no one he could trust with it.

Never mind his years of training, his expertise at listening to the other voice in sick people. A lapse on his part could be fatal. He worried about the safety of his patients. Jason brooded about the past. He had left his first wife, his high school sweetheart, after five years of utter misery. Emma, his second wife, had left him even though it could be argued he had saved her life. There were no blessings to count when he tried to get to sleep at night. He didn't have children to prove his ability to love and nurture. He couldn't know for a fact that he was truly competent.

No matter how many patients he had had over the years, or the fact that those who had the potential to get better under his care always did, he was still afraid that the failures in his personal life made him unfit to advise others.

And yet he knew he was better than most. His patient Daisy was the daughter of a colleague he didn't know, who had resisted and resented her getting help. Daisy's father was one of those psychiatrists who practiced with deep cynicism, not believing in what he did and deeply suspicious of everyone in the field. He had done everything he could to prevent Daisy's getting help even though she had been a very sick girl and might even have died of anorexia and depression years earlier if she hadn't found someone to intervene.

At twenty-five, after five years of therapy, Daisy was finally in her first precarious year of college. But she was still so sick, she was unlikely ever to function on her own. She was the only long-term patient Jason had who would never really get well. He would never take on another.

He put on a white Nike T-shirt and white shorts. His running shoes were two years old and needed to be replaced. He left the apartment and ran down the open staircase that spiraled down from the twelfth floor to the lobby. Jason lived on the fifth floor. Sometimes at the end of his run in Riverside Park, he staggered up the stairs. Sometimes he didn't.

Downstairs he nodded at Pete, the tiny, balding ex-marine who manned the door.

"Hot out there, Doctor," Pete said, opening the door.

Hot air hit Jason in the face. "Yes, it is," he murmured, heading west toward the river.

He went out for the click, the moment after twenty minutes of loping along at four miles an hour when the endorphins kicked in and the black hole of despair lifted briefly. When he got back to his office forty-five minutes later, there was a message from Emma on his answering machine. She wasn't in when he returned the call.

# 23

At nine o'clock in the morning on the third day of the Maggie Wheeler investigation, Sanchez followed Sergeant Joyce out of the Captain's office. His expression was grim. Captain Higgins was new to the precinct, and it was common knowledge that Higgins had been recently promoted from Organized Crime Control in order to open up his former post for someone else. The Captain had almost no experience in administration and knew next to nothing about running a precinct. His arrival in June had been heralded with little enthusiasm. Since taking over the command, he had done nothing to raise anybody's hopes about strong leadership in the future.

A taut, wiry man of middling height with gray skin, graying hair, and a nervous twitch in both brown eyes, Higgins looked like a hyperactive mole in expensive shirts. He was used to being on the move without a thousand eyes evaluating his every gesture. Commanding his own precinct seemed to have stamped him very quickly with the bewildered, unresigned expression of an innocent man sentenced unfairly to life inside The Big House.

Higgins's response to his own confusion was to dress better and call unit heads frequently into his office, question them closely about their jobs, and then tell them some other method of doing them. In this way he gave the appearance of being on top of everything while keeping everyone else off balance.

Ethnic diversity had kicked Higgins upstairs. After the election of the first African American mayor of New York, racial diversity became an imperative. Everybody had to speak Spanish, and suddenly there were lots of black and Hispanic Commissioners everywhere, in health, education, the school system. In the Police Department there were new black

Deputy Commissioners of the Transit Police, Housing Security, and other special commissions.

Higgins's old job, in which he had been happy and for which he was well suited, had gone to a black Lieutenant who knew next to nothing about organized crime. That was how the system worked. When a person moved up, he usually moved away from what he had been trained for and knew best.

Sergeant Joyce stumped down the hall, muttering. Captain Higgins was of the old school and reminded her of her former husband, a cop who believed there were certain places women didn't belong, and the NYPD was one of them. Joyce liked to say that her former husband's attitude was one of the reasons her ex was still *Police Officer* Joyce, a foot patrolman in the Bronx. But Higgins's rise to the top clearly disproved this theory.

Captain Higgins had called Joyce into his office and told her with no preliminaries that he was getting pressure from downtown. The Deputy Commissioner had even hinted to him a few minutes before on the phone that if they didn't get a break in the boutique killing soon, he was going to put a Lieutenant from the Bureau on over Sergeant Joyce to supervise the case, and add some new blood from outside. "I don't want that to happen, do you?" the Captain asked.

"No, sir," Sergeant Joyce replied. "We can handle it."

"Sure you can handle it. You're the hotshot who solved the tattooer case." Higgins ignored Sergeant Joyce and jabbed a well-chewed pencil at Sanchez.

Joyce scowled at the slight.

"I had some help," Sanchez said modestly.

"Well, I'm counting on you to come up with something on this one. You caught it. You solve it." That would look good. Sanchez was Hispanic, on the way up.

Though asked to sit down, Joyce had remained standing, gritting her teeth as if she had stomach cramps. It was clear as they flanked the Captain's heavy old desk that had probably been in use since the turn of the century that Higgins had called Sanchez into his office not because he had solved the tattooer case, which he hadn't exactly. No, Higgins had Sanchez in there with his Detective Squad Supervisor because the squad supervisor was a woman, and Higgins preferred talking to a man.

And this was no isolated occasion. Every time Higgins called her in—

and he called her in a lot because he had never once set foot in the squad room—he had Sanchez come with her. Joyce fumed.

"We're a good squad, sir," she said now. "We have an excellent clearance rate."

"I'm sure you do, Sergeant." Higgins's eyelids twitched as he kept his focus on Sergeant Sanchez, not Sergeant Joyce. "And I expect quick results on this one, because if I don't get them, you know what will happen. You'll have detectives from downtown swarming all over the place, doing everything all over again and making you look like assholes, especially if they come up with something you missed, like the perp."

"I have every hope we'll find him, sir," Joyce said quickly, then added, "But we don't have a hell of a lot to go on. He didn't exactly leave his calling card." A touch of sarcasm crept into her voice.

"How do you know, Sergeant Joyce? You don't even have the autopsy report." Higgins finally turned his twitching eyes on her.

She blinked helplessly back. Did he think the calling card was in the body? It was a strangling case. Some psycho thing. They were checking out the crazy angle, looking for psycho cases like it, recently released mental patients, paroled nutcases put away for the short term. Hell, they'd even called Interpol and the FBI to see if there was anything else out there like it. They weren't exactly letting the thing slide.

"We're working every angle, sir."

And then his phone rang and he asked them to report back later.

"Yes, sir," Joyce said politely, then cursed softly as soon as the door was closed. "Report what? He doesn't know a damn thing about investigations."

Sanchez kept his mouth shut.

They turned left and headed for the stairs.

"Shit, we don't need any new blood. We got perfectly good blood already."

At least she and the Captain agreed on one thing. They were both trying to hang on to the case. This was the Captain's first big case since taking command. He needed his people to solve it not to seem a helpless fool himself. Joyce needed it for the grade pay. She muttered some more. And Higgins couldn't even command the attention of the M.E.'s office.

"What's your take on why the autopsy report didn't come in yesterday as promised?" She plunged down the middle of the staircase, ignoring the traffic around them. "What's the hang-up here?"

She stopped suddenly as if challenging Sanchez to bump into her. "You think it's gone somewhere else?"

Sanchez gripped the handrail to stop himself from charging into his boss. He shook his head. "Nah. If it had, they'd have asked for the file. May just be bureaucratic shit. Why don't I go down there and goose them on it?"

"I get the feeling the Captain doesn't have a fix on what's going on," Joyce muttered. "They could still ask for the file."

They turned into the squad room. With all the phones in use, the noise level was very high. Still frowning, Sergeant Joyce stopped at April's desk. "What's new?" she shot out.

April looked up from her notes. It was the first time she had seen Sergeant Joyce that day. The Sergeant was all dressed up in a lime-green shirtwaist dress and black linen blazer with gold buttons. Apparently for good luck she had put on her gold four-leaf-clover earrings, which were thin discs the size of small pancakes. Her thin, pink-frosted lips were pinched together as she glowered at April, passing along the distrust of women, from boss to underling.

April glanced at Sanchez as if he had betrayed her for the thirty-fourth time, then turned to Sergeant Joyce. "We have a confession," she said.

"No shit. Who is it?"

April referred to her notes. "A bookkeeper, and get this. It's the guy who does the accounts for the store across the street."

"Where is he?"

"I've got him downstairs in a questioning room. I thought you'd like to hear what he has to say."

Joyce nodded. She motioned at Sanchez. "Let's go."

April raised an eyebrow at the guy who kept saying he wanted to be her best friend and kept edging her out every time he got the chance.

Sanchez shook his head. She just never got it. Women.

"So what happened up there?" April asked, her voice neutral as they trooped to the stairs. It was hot out in the hall. The heady smell of precinct sweat filled the corridor.

"Asses on the line." Sergeant Joyce gave her a hard look. "It would be nice if this were the guy."

. . .

104

In the questioning room, Albert Block sat in a metal chair, chewing on his nails. A chubby blue uniform the size of a fullback guarded the door.

"Howya doin', Herne?" Sanchez said.

Hernando Silvera nodded. "He's a live one all right."

Sanchez looked in through the wired window at eye level and snorted, then opened the door for Sergeant Joyce.

"That was my initial reaction," April said softly.

They filed into the green room, with its ancient peeling paint, one lone table, four chairs, and smudge marks on the wall. Albert Block jumped to his feet. He was all of five five and weighed in at no more than a hundred twenty-five. His scraggly brown hair was gathered into a short ponytail that just brushed the collar of his bright red-and-blue checkered shirt, which was tightly buttoned at the wrists and open at the neck. Black jeans, black motorcycle belt with silver studs. On his feet were a pair of expensive green lizard cowboy boots. In contradiction to the boots, the ponytail, the motorcycle belt, and the strongly colored shirt, his face was shuttered down and timorous in the extreme. Block had watery blue eyes, thin chapped lips, and a receding chin. He was small and pale. His hands were tiny and freckled, the size of a child's. He looked a lot like Woody Allen after the fall.

April put the tape recorder she had brought down on the table. "Mr. Block," she said politely, "this is Sergeant Joyce and Sergeant Sanchez. You can sit down."

He nodded and plunked himself back in the chair, eagerly regarding the tape recorder. "Thank you," he said.

Sanchez and Joyce looked at each other. What the hell was this? This guy couldn't lift a five-pound sack of flour, much less press a hundred-and-five-pound corpse a foot and a half over his head and hang it up on a chandelier. What'd he do it with, a winch? Sanchez coughed into his hand.

April ignored him.

"Mr. Block, why don't you tell the sergeants here what you told me about Saturday night."

Albert Block nodded again, stuck his thumb in his mouth, and looked from one cop to the other, checking out their faces, three, four times, as if testing their patience. No one moved. He had them in thrall.

Finally he removed the thumb from his mouth and started to talk.

## 24

"What's that for?" Albert pointed at the tape recorder.

"So we can remember what you said."

"I'm confessing." Albert frowned at the tape recorder. "Where's the D.A.? If I confess, I know the D.A. is supposed to be here. I don't want to talk to that. I want to talk to him."

"We have to do everything properly, Mr. Block," April said pleasantly. "Right now we're talking. We're establishing what, if anything, you know."

"I told you I did it." He became belligerent. "What else do you want?"

Sanchez and Joyce glanced at each other.

"Why don't you just tell the two sergeants here what you told me about Maggie," April prompted, "and we'll worry about the D.A. later."

"Who are they?" Block crossed one black-jeaned knee over the other and jiggled a green lizard cowboy boot nervously.

"I told you. This is Sergeant Joyce, Supervisor of the Detective Squad in this—"

"Did you read him his rights, Detective?" Sergeant Joyce interrupted.

"Yes," April said, "I did. Twice."

"Do it again, Detective. For the record."

Albert kneaded his freckled hands.

April read his Mirandas for the tape. "You have the right to remain silent, you have the right to be represented by a lawyer. If you cannot afford one, one will be provided for you. Anything you say can and will be used against you. Do you have any questions, Mr. Block?"

"No," he said faintly.

"Would you like a lawyer?" Sergeant Joyce asked gently.

"Who's doing this, you or her?" Block flared up, his moment of weakness gone in a flash.

"Who would you like to do it?" Sergeant Joyce asked.

Sanchez coughed.

"Shut up!" Albert slammed his hand on the table.

Okay. The guy was a nut with a temper.

April took a deep breath. "Why don't you just tell us about Maggie, Mr. Block. You knew Maggie."

"Maggie?"

"Yes, tell us how you met Maggie."

Block sniffed. "Will you get the D.A. in?"

"No promises. Just tell us the story." April kept her eyes on him. He was weird. Earlier the words had just come tumbling out. Now he was acting like a hardcase. She should have taped him then.

"Okay." He lapsed into silence, staring off into the far distance, where the green wall had a long crack down the side that resembled the California coastline. "Fuck you" was scrawled over Mexico. There was no window in the room except the wired window at eye level in the door. It was getting stuffy and tense.

"I met Maggie last winter."

Silence.

April licked her lips. They waited.

"Uh-huh. Could you give us the time frame on that?"

"Huh?" Block shifted his gaze.

"When you met Maggie."

"Oh, in February. Right after she moved here. I decided to go out on my own."

Silence.

"What do you mean, Mr. Block? Did Maggie convince you to go out on your own?"

"I was working for a firm. You know the kind of tight-assed kind of place." He looked at them expectantly. They didn't.

"I'm an accountant. Harry encouraged me to go out on my own. Harry's the owner of All Dressed Up. That's the store on Columbus next to the bookstore." He waved a tiny hand in the direction he thought it was.

Sergeant Joyce nodded. They knew where it was.

"I had his account. He told me to go up and down to all the stores and restaurants on Columbus and ask if they were happy with their accounting. Nobody's ever happy with their accountant, you know." He challenged them to disparage accountants.

Sanchez and Joyce kept their faces neutral. It was the last thing they would do. They didn't know a lot about accountants. Their taxes were easy. One source of income, no bookkeeper necessary. Joyce glanced at April. April had the feeling she'd be toast if this guy kept Sergeant Joyce there for hours and gave them nothing. She shifted uncomfortably in her chair. Don't rabbit on me now, Block, she prayed silently.

"Harry said to tell everybody I could do it faster and cheaper and he'd back me up. Then I should go to Amsterdam and Broadway, you know."

"So you went to The Last Mango, looking for work," April said softly, "and there you met Maggie."

He shook his head. "No, first I quit my job. Got some new clothes. You know, for my confidence."

"Then you went to The Last Mango, looking for work."

"Yeah."

He relapsed into silence.

"Jesus," Sanchez muttered.

"Hey, you want me to tell the story or not?" Albert turned on him furiously. "I don't like this guy. I want the D.A."

April took a deep breath. "The D.A.'s office is very busy. We can't just get somebody to come over every time someone comes in to talk to us. Please, Mr. Block, just tell the sergeants here what you told me about Maggie."

"And then you'll get the D.A.?"

What was his thing about the D.A.?

"Look, I watch TV. I know you don't indict without the D.A."

He wanted an indictment. The guy had no priors, no sheet of any kind. He hadn't ever caught so much as a speeding or a parking ticket in his whole life, and he wanted to be indicted for the murder of Maggie Wheeler.

Sergeant Joyce checked her watch and made a move to get up. "Why don't you give me a call later," she said.

Block twitched. "Okay, okay. You don't give a guy a break, do you?"

"Yeah, you have our full attention," Sergeant Joyce told him, leaning back in her chair. "I'm here if you want to talk. I'm gone if you don't."

He looked at the wall again, rubbing his palms together. Now April could see he was sweating into his plaid shirt.

"Like I said, I went into The Last Mango, looking for the owner. Maggie had just come to work there, maybe a week before. She wasn't the manager yet."

"Did she become the manager?" Elsbeth Manganaro never said she was the manager.

"Oh, yeah, Maggie did almost everything in the store. Except she couldn't fire that stupid bitch."

Sanchez raised an eyebrow at April. Well, that part was true. Olga Yerger was no rocket scientist.

"Who would that be?" April asked for the tape.

"Olga, the helper. It's her fault Maggie's dead."

"How is that?"

"I don't know." He looked down at his hands. "We used to have lunch together—oh, every couple of weeks. It was kind of a regular thing. I stopped in on Saturday. Last Saturday, the day she—uh, died."

April nodded.

"See, she liked to eat late—but Saturday she wouldn't go out. That bitch hadn't turned up again." He shook his head as if he still couldn't believe it. The ponytail bobbed from side to side, and his face flushed with rage at Olga. "I told Maggie to just close the store for an hour, what's the big deal? But she wouldn't do it. She was scared Elsbeth might come by, see the store closed in the middle of the afternoon, and fire her. I don't know. Elsbeth would do anything for Olga, but Maggie—I don't know, she took advantage of Maggie. It happens to short people. It made me—" His little hand curled into a fist.

"So why didn't you order in?" April had noticed there were no food containers in the wastebasket in the store.

"She was working. She didn't want me around," he said bitterly.

"So you left."

"Yeah, I left."

"When was that?"

"Around one-thirty."

Again Sergeant Joyce shifted in her seat. Her stomach growled.

"But I came back," Block added quickly.

April nodded. Okay, now they were getting to it.

"I was really upset. I, you know. I liked her. She was—different." He wiped his nose with the back of his hand. "She was from Massachusetts. Anybody in the world ever heard of Seekonk, Massachusetts?" He shrugged. Nobody.

"We had a fight, kind of. We'd go out to lunch like I said. We'd talk. We had to talk. I was going to do the accounting, at least I think I was. Maggie introduced me to Elsbeth, and you know. Elsbeth was going to try me out."

"So what happened?"

"So I felt bad. I kind of ripped into Maggie about Olga. I told her if she wasn't going to tell Elsbeth about Olga, I was. And then we got into this fight. So I came back later to make up."

Nobody moved. The room had become hot and still. He liked the girl. There was the ring of absolute truth about that.

"I, uh, wanted to take her out to dinner. I knew she was hungry, she didn't have lunch. So I—asked her." He flushed, trying to swallow down the humiliation. "She said she already told me she wasn't going out with me. I guess I lost it. I went crazy . . . I killed her."

He was flushed all over, face purple, nose running unchecked. Hands shaking. He had confessed, and he was finished.

"Now can I see the D.A.?"

"How did you kill her?" April asked.

"What do you mean?"

"How did you kill Maggie?"

He looked at her as though she were stupid, pulled a red handkerchief out of his pocket, and blew his nose twice. "I, uh, strangled her."

He could have read that in the newspapers. It was not good enough. April shook her head.

"How did it happen? When you got mad. What exactly did you do? What did Maggie do?"

"I told you—she didn't want to be with me—you know, that way. So I lost it. I strangled her. What else do you want?"

Information that did more than put him on the scene. Something more than a slender motive. Something that connected him physically, directly with the crime. Something he could tell them that no one but the killer could know.

"Details," April said quietly. "We want details."

"You mean about the dress?"

"What dress?" Sanchez blurted out.

"The printed dress, size fourteen, she was wearing when I hung her on the chandelier." A look of pure triumph galloped across Block's homely, pinched little face at their electrified reaction. Got 'em. "Can I have a sandwich? I'm starved."

Again he looked from one to the other.

April jumped up and went to the door with the window in it so she could place a lunch order with Officer Silvera. "Of course. What would you like?"

Neither Sergeant Joyce nor Sergeant Sanchez moved. Suddenly they had all day.

## 25

"But I did it," Block protested, his whole body twitching with anguish and outrage when April finally said he could go, three hours and forty minutes later.

"Life's tough, but stick around. We'll get back to you," she said as if he were applying for a job. Which in a sense he was.

"Stick around here?" he asked hopefully, lagging behind at the door of the stale questioning room guarded by a uniformed cop big enough to break his neck with one hand if he got out of line.

April shook her head. Why anybody would want to be indicted for murder, stand trial, and go to prison was beyond her. "Unh-unh, just don't leave town."

"But what else do you want?" he whined. "You know I did her." Tears flooded the corners of his eyes and threatened to fall down his pale cheeks. He wiped them with the now-damp red handkerchief.

"Unh-unh," April said again. "We just know you were there. You didn't tell us how you killed her, Albert. Or what you used, or where her clothes are. Lot of things we still don't know. You tell us everything, and you're our man."

"You're letting me walk right out the door. I don't believe it."

Well, it wouldn't be the first time the police questioned a killer and let him go. It wouldn't be the last. April stood on the sidewalk outside the precinct with some blue uniforms, watching Albert trudge dejectedly to the corner, just to make sure he really left. She was pretty sure he didn't do it, even if he knew something no one else knew.

April saw him reach Columbus and turn the corner, then she went back inside. Three detectives would now start checking the background and activities of Albert Block. He'd eagerly agreed to a search of the rental apartment where he lived. Maybe something would turn up.

She wearily climbed up the stairs to the squad room, thinking it over. Block had the motive and the opportunity. He had the temper, and he felt guilty. But she didn't figure him for a killer. She just didn't. And she knew Sanchez didn't either. She headed down the hall to the ladies' room.

It smelled like a war zone. There was some kind of pink face powder peppering the bottom of the sink. It reminded her of the makeup smeared on Maggie Wheeler's face. Not exactly done by an expert. Could that be Albert's work? April wiped out the basin with some toilet paper, then splashed cold water on her face.

Since there didn't appear to have been a robbery at the boutique, she figured it had to be someone who knew Maggie. Either Albert Block, or Bill Hadgens or some other guy they hadn't a line on yet. April made a mental note to ask Elsbeth if anything—anything at all—was missing from the store.

She dried her face with more toilet paper. It was the cheapest city issue and felt like sandpaper. Still, they were lucky to have it. In the ladies' rooms in the criminal courts downtown, there often wasn't any paper at all.

On the other hand, maybe this was something else altogether. The murder had the composed look of a ritual, something a crazy would do for reasons of his own that weren't rational, or easily explainable like Albert's reasons. Most people who committed murder didn't do weird, sadistic things to their victims afterward.

Well, Block was nuttier than Hadgens. She'd gone back to see Bill Hadgens a second time with a tape recorder an hour after her first visit to ask if he had any further recollections about Maggie. He hadn't changed his clothes or gotten up since she first spoke to him, and didn't seem to have many thoughts about anything. She taped his surly answers. She'd compared his voice with the one on Maggie's answering machine. It was negative for a match. She had the suspicion Albert Block's would be, too.

So far they had *nada* that even connected Block and Maggie as lunch pals. The whole thing could be a figment of Block's imagination. April had heard of cases where a psychic revealed one thing, one tiny detail, about a case that gave everything else he said a weird kind of credibility. She'd heard stories of hopeful detectives feeding a psychic (like they'd fed Albert Block), talking for days, trailing off on a bunch of wild goose chases, only to find out in the end that the one tiny thing the psychic "saw" was just a fluke. Could be that way with Albert. She had to check him out with the owner of All Dressed Up. Maybe he knew about Block's relationship with Maggie.

April applied fresh lipstick and tossed it back in her black leather shoulder bag with the two interlocking C's that she got in Chinatown and looked like a Chanel. It contained her off-duty gun, her Mace, a couple of notebooks, some pens, her telephone book—most precious possession—that had all the numbers of every source she'd ever used, a couple of packages of tissues for when she had to go to court and use the un-equipped ladies' room, her badge and wallet.

Her stomach churned with hunger. During his long questioning, Albert had eaten a triple-decker turkey, salami, Swiss, and chopped chicken liver sandwich with Russian dressing and then a huge slab of cheesecake. Neither she nor Sanchez nor Joyce had eaten anything themselves. As she headed back to the squad room, she hoped Mike might want to grab a bite and talk things over.

He got to her before she hit the door. He looked as if he'd been hanging around in the hall, waiting for her. "Where you been?" he de-manded.

"Seeing Block out the door. *Qué pasa?*"

"*Magnífico. Hablas español.*" Sanchez grinned and told her *qué pasa en Español.*

"*La cosa está que arde. La autopsia de Maggie Wheeler está lista. Vamos a buscarla.*"

Something, something Maggie Wheeler. Shit. That was the problem with this Spanish thing. You said something simple and got back something totally incomprehensible. April frowned. "Huh?"

"Never mind, you just started a few months ago." Sanchez touched her arm and nodded toward the stairs.

"*Vamos?*" To lunch, she hoped.

"M.E.'s office. The Wheeler autopsy report is in."

Oh. April shook her head. She should have gotten *la autopsia está lista. Lista* meant ready. They headed out into the heat, her stomach still protesting. Lunch was clearly not on the menu.

# 26

The black lacquered mantel clock was just chiming ten P.M. when Emma returned Jason's call. He sat in the living room, still in his suit trousers and dress shirt, working on half a glass of straight gin. At eight forty-five, after his last patient had left, he wandered out onto the street and turned left toward Broadway. He was hungry to the depths of his soul, hungry in a way he had never been before.

Ironically, Teddy, his last patient on Wednesdays, had talked for forty-five minutes about a dinner he'd had last night. Teddy was a food critic for a major magazine. Jason had to endure hearing a bite-by-bite account of a four-course meal so sublime and tempting he would have given a lot to share it. Jason didn't usually let Teddy talk too much about food. It was bad for him, distracted him from his real problems and gave him a false sense of feeling better. Teddy always went to some fabulous restaurant either before or after his sessions with Jason, which Jason could never reveal drove him crazy.

Jason sipped his gin and felt the pressure ease. He had lived through therapy with surgeons who had described in excruciating detail every surgical procedure they did, with businessmen who talked about balance sheets and taxes who expected Jason to be up on *The Wall Street Journal,* with a chess player so intense and obsessed Jason had to learn the game to understand what he was talking about. There was more to his job than people thought.

Every kind of pathology was in the books on his shelves. The theory was, all manner of sickness could be described and categorized. But a whole lot of cases weren't just one thing, not just a character disorder, a personality problem, a garden-variety neurosis. Each human being was different, sang his own unique song. No matter what the books said about technique, the good doctor—the *really* good doctor—had to learn a new language and reinvent himself for each patient.

The myopic and chubby food critic's highly erotic description of last night's dinner was all the more poignant since his problem was impotence. Teddy's conflicts about food and love were right in step with Jason's own hunger for nourishment, for human warmth, and love. He certainly got no love from Teddy, who called Jason a food-and-wine know-nothing.

The remark stung all the more for being right on the mark. Jason decided to prove Teddy wrong. He headed for Zabar's for something interesting and upscale to eat. Healthy gourmet salads like tabouleh, jambalaya, rice and beans, crawfish and wild rice. The sort of thing Emma liked. He walked slowly, legs aching a little from his run earlier in the day, dying inside because his wife had called and hadn't called back. He meant to stay at home until they talked, but in the end he was starving and couldn't wait.

He turned east. His thoughts shifted to pickled herring, cajun shrimp, smoked salmon, bagels in exotic flavors. Barbecued chicken—all the things he could have carried home wrapped in white paper and eaten in the kitchen, over the sink. But he didn't go to Zabar's and buy gourmet bits and pieces, carry them home to molder in the fridge. He got to Broadway and was stopped cold.

"Jason. Hi." The voice was warm and confident.

Jason, deep in his own thoughts, swung around in surprise at the sound of his name. Then frowned reflexively as Milicia Honiger-Stanton stepped into his space, her slim hand with its blood red nails held out to him.

"How *are* you?" she said brightly, as if he and Milicia were the oldest of friends meeting unexpectedly after a long separation.

He nodded, disgruntled. He didn't like it when patients called him by his first name. Familiarity was inappropriate. Especially if the patient was a woman, lovely to look at, and definitely coming on to him.

She didn't appear to be put off. Her warm, smooth hand was in his before he could ward off the intimacy. She maintained the contact several seconds longer than necessary, gazing deeply into his eyes as if she could read his desperation there.

Jason looked away, uncomfortable with the powerful sexuality she projected. He hadn't slept with Emma since before her abduction in May;

he hadn't slept with anyone else since. A normal healthy male starts going bonkers after three or four days of physical deprivation. Couldn't help it. It was a biological thing.

From habit, before going out he'd put on the khaki jacket that went with his trousers, as if a camouflage of formality could hide the desperation he couldn't help feeling was exuding from every pore in his body, like the kind of smelly sweat that couldn't be masked by any cosmetic known to man.

"What are you up to?" Milicia's voice was throaty and low.

He smiled vaguely. "Just out."

"I saw you from the corner, and you looked very alone. Have you had dinner?"

She was wearing a purple suit, the jacket open to its one button at the waist, the skirt short and tight. Jason tried not to look at the white silk blouse she had on underneath. Cut low enough to reveal stunning breasts that were bigger than Emma's, it was embroidered with gold stars and crescent moons.

Jason's whole body stiffened defensively. He didn't like her intimate tone, her body language, her insinuations. The assault of sexuality was like Teddy's aromas from the kitchen, irresistibly tantalizing. Like a computer, he scanned his database for his true feelings. Was he attracted to Milicia, Charles's architect, who had come to his office looking for—what?

"How's your sister?" he asked stiffly.

"Horrible." The eagerness faded from her eyes. "Really horrible. I have the feeling—" She stopped.

"What?"

Suddenly tense, apprehensive, Milicia shook her head. "I—can't talk about it here."

They had stopped in front of a restaurant, an Italian restaurant, not very fancy. Milicia gazed through the window wistfully, as if she were as hungry as Jason was.

"Have you eaten? I could tell you in there."

Jason glanced at the busy restaurant with its red and green flag-of-Italy façade. The pungent fragrance of garlic and tomato sauce blew out of the air-conditioner exhaust above his head. He was tempted to go for it. Charles had suggested he go for it. He had already eaten a meal with Milicia. Hey, what did it matter? Emma had left him; he was free to go for anything. He was tempted and didn't dare look at her, didn't want her to know. She had come to him professionally. He could not do it. Probably couldn't have done it anyway.

"I'm looking forward to talking to you," he said, trying to keep the ice from forming on his words. "On Friday."

He didn't give a reason, and didn't allow himself to worry at the way her face collapsed at the rebuff. He'd already told her social and professional couldn't mix. He stood there, inhaling the garlic until she was out of sight, then he grabbed a hamburger and french fries in the Greek coffee shop. His encounter with Milicia brought him way down.

He had been on his way to eat fancy food, but guilt made him instantly slide back to the old habits of before Emma—fast food gulped on the run, pizza, hamburgers, steak. French fries with everything. He ate the takeout hamburger and fries in his kitchen, dripping over the sink. Well, Teddy was right, but he didn't exactly have a gourmet background. Jewish boy from the Bronx, not so far from the peasant past. What did anyone expect? His parents favored heavy Jewish food, the heaviest. Boiled beef, knockwurst and sauerkraut. Potato pancakes with apple sauce, and gobs of sour cream piled on top. Pastrami and chopped chicken liver sandwiches four inches thick. Matzo-ball soup and chicken in the pot, thick with noodles and chicken fat. Everything made with chicken fat. The men in his family often dropped dead before they reached sixty.

Jason finished up the fries and threw the wrappings in the garbage. Fuck his arteries. He got the bottle of Tanqueray and poured himself a healthy drink, then sat in the large pale green armchair that Emma had chosen, shuddering at the gin's fiery path down his throat. Gin had always been his drink, bitter and medicinal. It went straight to the heart of the trouble, kicking in with a jolt like nothing else.

Ebony branches stood out against a sky of midnight blue, slowly fading to gray, then black. He felt like shit, then began to feel a little better. He thought about the twilight sky. The first time he'd seen a Magritte painting of this kind of sky he'd thought the image came from the imagination of the painter. All his life he'd been too busy studying books and the insides of people to see the way light changed colors as time passed and the earth moved around the sun. Now light and colors were preoccupations of his, along with his passion for time. In a few days, he thought, he'd be thirty-nine.

The sound of the mantel clock striking nine was as deep and resonant as Big Ben. The clock kept perfect time exactly seven and a half minutes late. Every forty-eight hours Jason wound the clock and set it to the correct time. Three or four hours later it would be seven and a half minutes late again. There was no explanation for it. Clocks were not alive. They were just mechanical things that measured precise units through a series of spur gears.

Some considerable part of every day, Jason studied the way time was measured. He couldn't help being awed by what a breakthrough the clock was, the brilliance that conceived the whole idea. The falling weight, or an unwinding spring, that powered the driving wheel through a pinion geared to rotate once an hour. The driving wheel turned the two hands around the face of the clock, ensuring that the minute hand moved exactly twelve times around the dial for every revolution of the hour hand. The pinion drives the minute hand directly. The hour hand is driven through two sets of spur gears that together reduce its speed to one-twelfth that of the minute hand. Another set of gears sets the speed at which the driving wheel rotates by connecting it to the escapement, the heart of the timekeeping mechanism. The escapement was the thing that went back and forth. The tick-tock.

On the eighth strike of the tenth hour, Emma called.

## 27

"If he didn't do it, how did he know she was hanging from the chandelier? Huh, tell me that?" That was the question Captain Higgins had shouted at Sergeant Joyce when she suggested they let Block go.

" 'Let him go. Are you fucking crazy? He had to be at the scene. If he didn't do her, who did?' You should have seen her face," Mike told April. "She was fucking furious. I've never seen her so mad, and she couldn't show a thing. I thought she was going to explode. What kind of food do you want?"

April checked her watch. It was after eight and she hadn't had anything to eat since breakfast. There wasn't any time after the autopsy report came in and everybody went kind of crazy because the report said Maggie Wheeler just happened to be pregnant. That kind of changed things. And they had let their prime suspect go.

Block was being watched around the clock though. He wouldn't get very far if he changed his mind and tried to run. April and Sanchez stood on Columbus, getting a breather from the noise and chaos in the squad room. A lot of people hung out on New York's streets in summer. Already there had been two muggings and a rape reported that evening, and it wasn't even eight-thirty.

April couldn't help noticing that suddenly Mike was talking to her as though she were one of the guys. A few months earlier he held his tongue on the four-letter words like motherfucker and asshole. She ignored his question about food. She was still mad about being excluded from the meetings in the Captain's office. She was clearly not one of the guys in the ways that mattered.

"Yes," she said sharply. "I should have seen her face. We caught the case together. I should have been there."

"So we caught it together. A technicality." Mike stopped on the curb for a red light, forcing her to stop with him.

"A technicality? Is that what you call it?"

"Look, the Captain's not crazy about women. That's not my fault. So he calls me in with Joyce. I know one precinct chief that likes the whole bureau in every meeting. I know another likes to work with only one, two guys—" He looked at her quickly. "Women. You know what I mean."

"I know exactly what you mean."

"Don't get political on me, April. Each commander does it a different way. They call the shots. So this is how Higgins does it. It's not a political thing."

April shook her head. But it was a political thing. Everything was a political thing, and Mike knew it.

"Hah. Easy for you to say," she muttered, then checked his face quickly to make sure he wasn't getting too mad at her. She didn't want to cross the line with him.

Lots of lines she didn't want to cross. Didn't want to get too close, didn't want to be too far away. It was so complicated, the whole thing was dizzy-making. Or maybe she was dizzy from lack of food. Anyway, Sanchez was watching the traffic light, waiting for it to turn green, and wasn't looking at her.

She took the opportunity to examine him. She did this from time to time when he wasn't watching. He wasn't so sensitive. He stared at her quite openly whenever he felt like it. Now she looked at him like a cop, sizing him at five nine or ten, pretty tall for a Mexican. Medium to stocky build. She got the impression he worked out, had some discipline about what he ate and drank. His stomach hadn't fallen out yet. Lot of detectives in the bureau got soft and let themselves go. Didn't have the time or opportunity to eat right or exercise. Too much tension on the job, too much rushing around. Had to keep irregular hours. Mike liked gray and black, but today his jacket had a kind of greenish cast. Gray tie, drab green shirt.

Black hair cut pretty short. Distinguishing marks: angry red patches on one ear, hands, arms, neck. Eyebrows scarred and uneven. Maybe the burns had killed the hair follicles or something. She thought of them as just distinguishing marks though. Not really disfiguring. He was still good-looking to her, with his intense dark eyes and nice mouth that was always smiling. He wouldn't talk about the burns, still smiled a lot.

Sometimes she thought about his mouth, with his bushy mustache hiding the top of it, and wondered what kissing him would feel like. He was different from the Chinese she was used to. Chinese didn't smile so much. In China a smiling person probably just ate your dog. Or had a devious plan to separate you from your money. Mike looked like a bandido and smelled like a perfume counter. April's mother and aunts thought people like that—so big and smiling, with lots of hair on their bodies and smelling like women—were barbarians.

The light changed. Mike turned to her, noted her scrutiny, and smiled. She shook her head, couldn't believe she had been talking to him like that. What had happened to her? Only a few months before, a quiet little Asian from Manhattan South—way south, all the way in Chinatown—too nervous to say boo. And now she was furious because the new Captain of the Precinct was overlooking her in her own case. And thinking about kissing a superior in her squad, who happened to be Mexican. Was she crazy?

Without exactly planning to, they had crossed the street and wandered down the block to The Last Mango. They stopped in front of the window. The crime-scene tapes were gone, but the brightly colored shirts were still on the clothesline in the display window. The track lights in the ceiling were on.

Around the time Maggie died, it would still have been light outside. But not much of the inside of the store could be seen anyway. A backdrop behind the display in the window hid most of the store's interior.

"So what did she tell him?" April asked.

"Who?" He was gazing into the store, speculating.

"Sergeant Joyce. What did she tell Higgins?"

"She told him we questioned the guy for almost four hours and he couldn't come up with a single piece of solid evidence that would hold up in court.

" 'But he knew about the chandelier. He knew about the dress. He knew about the fucking *size* of the dress. Explain that for me,' Higgins screamed at her."

"That's what I say," April agreed. "So what did she say to that?"

"She said, 'Maybe Block came in after she was dead, sir.' So Higgins goes, 'And maybe he came in *before* she was dead and did her just like he said.' "

"Anyway, if it was after, how did he get in? You think the killer left the door wide open?" April asked. Elsbeth Manganaro had given April a set of keys to the shop, but they already knew it had the kind of door that locked automatically when it closed.

"Maybe he had a key."

"Where would he get one?"

They looked at each other. Maggie might have given him one.

"Maybe we better get him back and ask a few more questions. The time frames don't work for me. When he came back after she didn't go to lunch with him. When he had this so-called fight with her. How he killed her, and the time he left. If she was alive when he came in, then she might have let him in as he said. But if she was already dead, then how did he get in?" Mike asked.

"Maybe he was there with someone else, and someone else did it. None of it plays except the jealousy, does it?"

"Well, if he went in and out several times that day, somebody must have seen him. He's known in the neighborhood. Got to start all over again, talk to the other store owners, look for a witness who saw *him*."

"It sure puts a different cast on the thing."

"You mean the little fact that Maggie was seven weeks pregnant? Yeah. It does. Either everything Block told us was a crock, or else he didn't know. Maybe she wouldn't date him because she was involved with someone else."

"Yeah," April agreed. "If he was just someone she knew, why would she tell him she was pregnant?"

"Maybe she finally told him about the other guy and he had a fucking fit."

"Yeah, but maybe he's the father, but someone else still did her. At least that's a piece of physical evidence we can check. If he doesn't want a blood test, we can get a court order."

"Did the mother know who the boyfriend was?" Mike changed the subject.

"She said Maggie was kind of backward that way, wasn't really interested in boyfriends yet. I gather she didn't know her daughter that well."

"Right."

"You still think Block didn't do it?" April wasn't sure about anything anymore.

Finally Mike turned away from the store window. "We'll nail him if he did."

"I just don't want to nail him if he didn't," April murmured. That happened too. "Are you up for Chinese?"

Mike smiled. "Always."

The nearest takeout place was uptown. They walked north slowly. April knew "always" didn't have anything to do with Mike's taste in food. In the food department the only way to get along with Sanchez was to make her choice Mexican.

The streets smelled fresher now. The air was finally cooling off after the long, hot day. April stretched her cramped muscles as she strolled along. Just being outside for a few minutes helped ease the tension. The M.E.'s report said Maggie had been strangled. It was up to the science people to tell them by what. A few fibers had been taken from the wounds in her neck. Maybe the fibers would tell them something. The report also said Maggie's arms and hands were bruised and scratched. She probably tried to fight off her attacker. Her fingernails were very short though, and there were no scrapings under them. Oh, and that little thing about Maggie's having been about six or seven weeks pregnant at time of death.

April forgot about food again. She was back to business, worrying about who killed Maggie, and if it was someone they didn't even know about, like the person behind the voice on her answering machine. Poor Maggie didn't have much luck. Olga said something was bugging her before she died. It must have been the pregnancy. April wondered how the pregnancy fit into their case.

# 28

Milicia immediately picked up Jason's altered mood when she arrived five minutes early for her three-fifteen Friday appointment. Unlike the last time she had been there, the two doors separating his waiting room from his office were open. She could see him sitting in his desk chair, writing in a black and white speckled notebook. He was so engrossed in his work, he didn't look up at the sound of the door.

"Hi, is that me you're writing about?" she asked coyly, sweeping into his office without waiting for an invitation. She was eager to try again with him, had dressed specially for the occasion, and didn't want to sit in his waiting room like a patient. She was more than a patient, much more.

"Hello, Milicia." He looked up. And, wonder of wonders, he smiled, put aside the notebook, and rose to greet her.

He hadn't smiled at her before. Milicia beamed at her moment of triumph. See, he really did like her, after all. She raised an eyebrow, pleased at her success.

She had been desperately trying to figure him out, had decided to change her style of dress and see what happened. This time she was wearing a well-tailored red, white, and blue print silk jacket with gold braid, gold twisted rope, anchors, lifesavers, and other nautical symbols on it. She thought it signaled *Doctor, save my life.* Classy. The little blouse underneath was white, and her navy skirt was softly pleated.

After several unsuccessful shopping expeditions both on the East and West sides, she had finally found the suit on sale in a boutique on Lexington Avenue. She thought it might appeal to Jason, and she was right. It seemed that Jason liked the classy look.

"How are you?" she asked as he stood, waiting for her to sit down.

"I'm fine." He smiled again. It made him altogether a different person. Nicer, more attractive. Finally, accessible.

She was encouraged. She'd been afraid she was losing her touch. Until this minute Jason seriously irritated her. She was beginning to think he was a waste of time. She'd met him three times now, and throughout their encounters his face had been as closed and guarded as any she'd ever seen. He was like a poker player, cards always close to his vest. Or one of those mass murderers you read about in the newspapers—real flat, an ocean so dense, not even the shallows close to the shore could be penetrated by the naked eye. What was it with him?

Milicia didn't like getting things wrong. She needed to be liked, approved of, desired. So far her failure rate with men had been very low. What was it with Jason? She'd wondered, as she shopped for the perfect suit to wear on her second office visit, if his opacity was a side effect of his profession. She had no way of knowing. Charles was the only other psychiatrist she knew. Charles was an open book. She knew by the way Charles's eyes traveled over her body exactly what he was thinking. For Charles, as with other men, beauty and sex were the way in. She was pretty sure she could get him with the crook of a finger.

With Jason, though, something was wrong. His eyes never flickered with the lustful interest that always put her in control. She couldn't figure it out. It wasn't exactly that he wasn't engaged by what she had to say. She could see that he was listening, asking questions, thinking. But he was impersonal about it. He seemed to be looking, not at her, but *beyond* her all the time. It made her uneasy. She had the uncomfortable feeling that he might be gay. If he was gay, he'd be useless. He might not care, wouldn't do what was required.

And what was required now was to get the situation with Camille under control. This horrible boutique thing put the Camille problem in a different league. A crime had been committed. A person was dead. It had been in the paper and on the TV news. For the first time Milicia was scared, really scared. The police were involved. Even if the police didn't figure what happened, it wouldn't be all right. Camille was a time bomb that was going to go off in a bunch of different ways over and over. And with Bouck to cover for her, there was no telling how far she could go.

Milicia needed a person with authority to take over and do what had to be done. She'd been confident when she met Jason that he was that person. He was smart. He'd put the pieces she gave him together, because that was the only way. She couldn't just come out and tell him her sister had crossed the line and murdered somebody just to hurt her. She *couldn't* say that. She didn't know him well enough, couldn't be sure he was trustworthy. It all sounded too sick and crazy, even to her, who knew the truth about what happened long ago. Jason had to come to the right conclusions himself. And if he couldn't do it, she'd just have to find someone else. On the way to his office she'd decided this was his very last chance to drop his reserve and help her.

Now she felt vindicated. She stood there for a moment, basking in the feeling of happiness that he projected at seeing her. Then she sat in the chair and adjusted her skirt primly to cover her knees.

His expression changed slightly. He liked prim, reserved. She got it now, had his number.

"I was so happy to see you on the street the other day," she said softly, thinking that next time she would wear paler lipstick and tie her hair back. She looked down, suddenly shy. "Some people have that effect. They just make other people feel good."

Jason returned to his chair, the smile fading just a little as if the shift in her manner set him thinking.

Quickly she adjusted. "You seemed very busy, but just seeing you for a minute eased my distress. . . ."

"Oh?"

"Yes, I really have the feeling that you're very strong. You understand the system. You can help me."

Now his smile was gone and the penetrating examination was back. Milicia looked away from the gaze that had made her uncomfortable before. She needed help. Why was he holding out?

A tear gathered in the corner of her eye. She had thought so much about this in the two miserable years since her father did the ultimate irresponsible thing—crashed the car, killed both himself and his wife in a fiery wreck—left her with a maniac she couldn't control who was determined to ruin her life. Now there was someone who could help her, and he seemed to be holding out on her. Why? She shook her head.

Jason saw the tear. "So what's going on?" he asked gently.

She waited for a minute, still filled with the hot rage she had felt each time her parents rushed to Camille's aid at every breakdown. Camille crashed herself over and over, with all engines burning. And each time her parents had dealt with it through a boozy haze, pretending each incident was only a phase Camille had to pass through on the way to settling down and finally being good.

*But she isn't good. She's a bad seed, like a mean dog that couldn't be tamed no matter what.* Still, all Camille's life they had patted her on the back and hid her away at home in Connecticut for months at a time until she calmed down. While she, Milicia, was ignored.

Oh, yes, the pretense that Camille was not crazy had always maddened Milicia. Just as it hurt and enraged her when they pushed her, the good daughter, away just because she was strong. Milicia was the one who had to go out and conquer the world on her own. Milicia was the one they kept at bay, fading out like used up light bulbs whenever she craved love and tenderness.

Milicia's tears brimmed over, and she caught them in a tissue, gathering them tightly in her fist. It still burned her up that they never cared about the things Camille did. How Camille took over the dog given to *both* the girls for Christmas and made such a fuss about not sharing it that her parents took the puppy back to the store and punished them both. How Camille stepped on a baby bird that had fallen out of its nest, and threw the rabbit against the wall. Camille was insane, and they hadn't *cared.* They just *hadn't cared.*

And then lawyers told Milicia it was her responsibility to protect Camille and defend her, to manage the money so Camille would be secure in a dangerous world. That was how her parents had set it up. Even from the grave they were against her. Milicia had to bear the humiliation of Camille's eccentricities, her promiscuity with off-the-wall lunatics like Nathan Bouck, men who had enough money to dazzle her and to prevent Camille from getting the help she needed in a therapeutic hospital environment. Now maybe even get away with murder. It wasn't fair.

And Jason Frank didn't care either. How could so many people not care about dealing with the insane? Milicia turned her head, would not look at him again.


Jason knew all about clothes, the things they projected and said about a person. He noted the jaunty pleated skirt, less aggressively sexual, demurely covering Milicia's knees. He could see that she was correcting all the time. Now she was correcting her mistake in asking him to have dinner with her two days before. She wanted him to feel special even though he had rejected her. Underneath her supreme confidence he felt her urgency and desperation. With Milicia, Jason always had the feeling they were on a boat ride and she was at the helm. But where was she leading? And now the tears. He waited for her to speak.

Before she had come into his office, Jason had been euphoric, jotting down the flight times of his trip to California, making notes of the things he had to do. He had lost his feeling of exhaustion even though he had been in Baltimore for a morning seminar the day before, and had three patients late into the evening. His talk had gone very well in spite of the fact that his preparation had not been quite as thorough as usual. His mind was on Emma. Emma needed him. He couldn't stop hope from lifting the corners of his mouth. Emma needed him.

On Wednesday she had called for his advice about the laser treatment she was thinking about trying to get rid of the tattoo on her stomach. She said it was his thoughts as a doctor she wanted, but he sensed a lot more in the call. He offered to check it out, then after a pause offered to come out to be with her. For the first time since she had left him in May, she said she wanted to see him.

Jason watched Milicia squeeze in her fist the tissue containing her tears. "I feel so confused about all this. You give me the feeling that there's nothing we can do if a person is crazy, self-destructive, dangerous." She sniffed. "Is it true family members can't do anything about it, can't intervene and put them away where they can't hurt anybody. Is that why this society is such a mess?"

She didn't wait for an answer. "I thought you were a doctor. You could help in situations like this. I'm all alone. I have no one to help me."

Jason shook his head. "You're not alone. I'm here with you. Tell me more about Camille."

"I want to know about the laws. Aren't there laws to protect people from the insane?"

"Let's just go back. Tell me what's happening with her."

"Well, I saw her. Her dress was unbuttoned. She was wearing stockings and garters—" Milicia's face twisted with disgust. "That man was lurking around upstairs. I knew they were into something. She'd taken some kind of pill, or maybe she was drunk. I told you she'll do anything. And the furniture in the room was all jumbled together. You couldn't even get in. I knocked on the door for twenty minutes before she let me in. I think she was standing there right at the door." She paused, her face contorted, then continued.

"I told her about you. I said there was someone who could help her, and she got furious, told me to get lost. Started throwing things. I had to leave. And then the next day I saw her in a boutique. I saw her in the window. She was being abusive to the salesgirl. She does that all the time. Waiters, salesgirls. I saw her in the window." Now Milicia's face was white, as if bleached by distress because he wasn't getting it. He wasn't understanding the story.

"Isn't that terrible? She just has this uncontrollable temper. She's done other things, too. I'm telling you, she's crazy." She gave him a hard look. "I'm telling you she can kill. Maybe she already has killed somebody."

Jason's face didn't change. He understood that Milicia felt her sister was killing *her*. He kept waiting for a description of seriously crazy and dangerous, and Milicia simply wasn't giving him one. He tried again, asking one way and then another. How was Camille crazy? Did she see things that weren't there, hear things? How about her speech patterns? Could she organize her thoughts? No matter what he asked, Milicia stayed on her own track, painting an abstract picture with no shape or form that made psychiatric sense.

"Should we call the police? What do you think?" she said finally, her urgency cracking her voice.

The corners of Jason's mouth twitched into a smile at this suggestion. He thought of April Woo, his friend in the police, and what April would do with a case like this. He shook his head. April was a professional, like him. He would never get her involved in a psychiatric case unless there was a very, very good reason.

"Your sister sounds like she has a short fuse, and she may well have a lot of other problems. But I haven't heard anything about her behavior that would justify—"

"But she's already out of control," Milicia interrupted, almost out of control herself, "and then she takes drugs. And then, then she's capable of doing anything. Why won't you believe me? You don't know her as well as I do."

"Well, of course you know her better, and I can see how upsetting it is for you, but if she doesn't want to see anyone, there's nothing more I can do at this point."

Milicia took a deep breath, her eyes darting around the room, looking for help. Searching for the way in. "There's more," she said.

Jason nodded. Of course there was more. There was Milicia. "Why don't you tell me a little more about the underlying issues?"

Milicia opened her eyes wide, truly surprised. "What issues?"

"That's what I was wondering about." He glanced at the clock. "We have only a few minutes."

"Oh, God." Another tear formed in Milicia's eye. "I don't know if I can tell this kind of thing in a few minutes. . . ."

"This is the problem with my profession," Jason said gently. "I have to go by clock time. People don't live by clock time."

"I need to see you again. Can I come on Monday?" Milicia leaned forward for a tiny instant, as if to show her cleavage, then sat back.

Jason shook his head. Monday was Labor Day. He'd still be in California. "Next week is bad for me. How about the week after?"

"What? You don't have an hour in the whole week for me?" She looked appalled at the insult, crushed. How could this be?

"I'll be out of town." He opened his book. "I can see you Tuesday of the following week. Three o'clock."

Her face crumpled, then reddened with fury. "I hope for your sake it won't be too late."

She rose in a single motion and strode out of the office, her new skirt swinging back and forth across the tops of her knees. Jason didn't want the session to end this way, but she gave him no other option. He had been trained not to apologize or explain, especially with manipulative and controlling people who had problems accepting limits. He knew Milicia was deeply angry at him, but there was nothing appropriate he could do about it. His patients were either in love with him or in hate with him all the time. It was an occupational hazard. Their love and their fury had mostly to do with them. He was never the principal actor, only the stand-in for others who weren't there.

He heard the door slam, and took a moment to write up his notes on the session. His diagnosis of the situation and the subject was still deferred.

## 29

After weeks of relentless summer heat, the rains finally came on the worst possible day of the year, Saturday of Labor Day weekend. Rachel Stark thought everyone who had fled the city the day before had to be miserable now. Rachel could picture the couple who'd invited her for the weekend: sitting in their cramped, moldy house, drinking too much, playing board games, and quarreling ever more bitterly as the hours went by. She was glad she hadn't asked Ari for Saturday off, after all. Sitting inside at the beach would not have been as much fun as watching rain batter Second Avenue from the cozy safety of European Imports, where she had been working for more than three years and was very happy. Everything about the tiny store suited her. It was a relaxed place just this side of shabby, neither trendy nor uptight. Second Avenue in the Fifties was like that. Restaurants that tried to be Irish or English pubs lined the street, dishing out middling to awful food in underlit, dreary settings. The occasional little store was nestled between them in unrenovated buildings. The new office towers all had Gaps and Strawberrys and Benettons and Banana Republics in their huge downstairs spaces.

Rachel much preferred her funky environment, where there wasn't so much customer traffic and glass, and she didn't have to live in a fishbowl. At European Imports the clothes were well constructed and stylish, and she enjoyed being the only salesperson. Sometimes business was slow. She didn't mind that either. She had a favorite place behind the curtain that separated the display window from the selling space. Back in the corner there was a carpeted step where she sat when things were quiet. From there she could see the street through a gap in the fabric without being seen from outside.

Today she had spent many hours watching the water sheet down at impossible angles, driven, so the radio said, by forty- and fifty-mile-an-hour winds. At times during the day the storm had been so ferocious that people were dragged along by their umbrellas, shoved right out into the traffic or slammed into the sides of buildings. By late afternoon the tempest had worked itself up to such a wild frenzy, it almost looked like the second flood that would end the world.

At every corner the gutters had overflowed into an impassable lake. The awning of the chandelier shop across the street had ripped open and begun flapping in the wind. Three broken and twisted umbrellas, as well as a lot of other loose garbage, had caught in the drain in front of the Korean market. The workers were very conscientious there. Rachel waited for someone to venture out to clear it, but the weather was so bad, no one did.

Since early morning the plastic sides of the Korean market had been rolled down to protect the flowers and produce. Eventually the unpainted wood stands were cleared of their decorative displays of fruits and vegetables. Now the stands were all barricaded up in front of the window.

At European Imports, only one customer had been in the store since noon, and Rachel suspected the tall, red-haired woman in the silver raincoat had come in only to get out of the rain. She hadn't said a single thing, not hello or good-bye, or thank you, hadn't acknowledged Rachel at all. Rachel was a small, unassuming person whose most fervent wish as a child had been to grow to a normal size. It hadn't happened. At four foot ten and a half inches, she couldn't reach the overhead bars on the bus. Her feet didn't touch the floor when she sat down in most chairs. Worst of all, at thirty-two she still looked like a child, and even in the store where she worked she was often ignored.

Today, after fifteen minutes of desultory pretense at working the racks, the woman in the silver raincoat left without buying a thing. All afternoon Rachel considered closing up and going home. For some reason she didn't. She sat listening to the radio, happy to be surrounded by racks of lovely colorful clothes, even the smallest of which were too big for her. After five, only the deluge kept her there. She hated getting wet.

At two minutes to seven the rain was beginning to lessen, and Rachel had just started her routine of closing up. The front door was locked. She went into the tiny, crummy bathroom to pee, was just flushing the toilet when she heard the front doorbell ring. She took a second to wash her hands. Now the person outside was banging on the door as well as ringing the bell.

Rachel came out of the bathroom. It was the woman in the silver raincoat. The hood was up as before, but now the woman had a bag over her shoulder. Rachel did a double take as she realized there was something alive in it. A curly apricot head popped out and then two tiny paws. It was a poodle with winking black eyes and a pink tongue. In spite of the awning over the doorway, it was clear to Rachel that the dog was getting wet. She hurried to open the door.

"You're lucky," she said, letting the woman in. "I was just closing for the weekend."

Instantly the woman filled the space. She swirled around to survey the scene, her voluminous raincoat spraying droplets of warm summer rain in all directions. She was taller than Rachel remembered, but to Rachel everyone was tall. Certain kinds of men picked her up without warning, treating her like a toy, a doll, and she felt so humiliated with her feet dangling off the floor, there was nothing she could do to recover her dignity. Height was never off her mind. Unconsciously, she stepped back from the tall stranger.

"Was there something special you wanted to see?" Rachel stared at the dog. It was the friendliest thing she'd ever seen, seemed to be struggling to get out of the bag and leap at her. The dog was tiny, just like her. She reached out to touch it.

"Don't touch the dog," the woman said angrily.

Rachel stepped back even farther, shocked by the first words her customer uttered. The woman's voice had an edge, its tone jagged and harsh, as if she weren't used to speaking. An inexplicable undertone of uncontained fury in the voice caused Rachel's hair to rise on the back of her neck. She shivered. Prickles of fear shot down her arms and spine.

Something about the woman wasn't right. Rachel couldn't have described exactly what it was. She was dressed appropriately, didn't look crazy the way the street people did, with their several layers of clothes on the hottest days, filthy hair and faces, odd gestures and gaits. Rachel didn't open the door for people like that.

The front door had shut with a click. The woman towered over her. Now Rachel could see that there was something funny about her eyes. They were green eyes—cat's eyes, cold, furious. The woman was enraged, and Rachel hadn't done anything, didn't understand what was wrong.

"We're closed," she said timorously, regretting her impulse to spare the dog.

"You opened the door. You're open. I want to try something on. Where's the dressing room?"

Rachel's eyes shifted quickly to the room opposite the toilet, then back to the woman.

"I'm, uh, late," Rachel said. "We open at nine on Tuesday." She had a bad feeling, really bad. The woman towering over her with the poodle in a bag didn't look like a thief, couldn't be a rapist. Yet, Rachel was suddenly afraid. She wanted her out.

"No. Tuesday's too late. I'm getting on a plane. I need it now."

The dog started to bark, little sharp cries, almost like a baby. The announcer on the radio said it was nine minutes past seven.

"It's too late. I'm sorry, you'll have to come back."

"Shh, baby." The woman put the bag down and let the dog out.

Immediately it began to run around, sniffing at everything. It ran over to Rachel and jumped up on her. Rachel crouched down to pat it.

"Don't touch my dog." The woman was shouting at her. "I told you, don't touch my dog. Are you crazy? Are you deaf?"

As Rachel backed away in horror, the woman grabbed her shoulders and started to shake her. Rachel screamed as the storm outside picked up and a bolt of lightning flashed. Screamed again.

"Don't—oh, God, don't hurt me . . . don't!" Rachel's terror pierced the air of the tiny shop. Anguished, panicked, humiliated once again by her small size, she screamed, but in the storm no one could hear her.

The woman pushed her in the back, into the tiny dressing room hardly big enough for one. There was no space to move. Rachel kicked out shrieking as the woman hit her head against the mirror once, twice, three times. The little dog ran around, circling their feet in a frenzy. Rachel kicked again as the hands closed around her neck. She felt a sharp pain on her ankle before she blacked out. Her last conscious thought was that the dog had bitten her.

# 30

There was surveillance on Albert Block when April called him on Thursday with the PD's request for a blood test. Word was he hadn't left his apartment since his questioning at the precinct. He picked up the phone on the first ring. April told him who she was and what she wanted. His amazement at the request further convinced her that he had not done Maggie Wheeler.

"Blood? Was there blood?" he asked on the phone, clearly astounded. "Did I draw blood?"

Like they'd been in a duel or something. April didn't reply for a second and let his panic come pouring out of the receiver. Albert Block was in way over his head.

"What do you need my blood for?" He couldn't figure it out. "Where was blood? I didn't see any blood."

And then. "Yeah, maybe I hit her. Oh, I couldn't have hit her. Did I hit her? But—why do you want *my* blood? I didn't bleed. Jesus, what is this—a setup?" he demanded accusingly as if he hadn't come in himself and confessed.

"No, it's no setup, Mr. Block," April told him. "We just need your blood type."

"What for?" he wanted to know.

There was a long silence. April let him think it over to see if he could come up with any ideas. Why else would they need a blood type? Finally he got an idea.

"Oh, God," he cried. "Was she raped?"


"He didn't know," April told Sanchez when she hung up. "He didn't know anything."

She gathered up her stuff, then wasted several hours escorting Block to his blood test. She took a female officer assigned to the case, a woman more muscular than the suspect, name of Goldie, with her to drive. April sat in the back seat with Block, hoping he might tell her something she didn't already know. But he sat there in his jeans and green lizard boots and didn't have a thing to say. He had shut down at the prospect of the needle.

It was still August hot. It hadn't cooled down at all. The windows were rolled down, but the air that blew in gave no relief. Block was trembling all over.

"You all right?" she asked.

"I don't like needles," he muttered.

"No one does."

"Yeah, but I really don't. I don't get this at all."

Goldie stopped the car with a jerk that April wouldn't forget. This wasn't the time to tell him Maggie had been pregnant.

"We get out here."

"I don't get it," Block muttered again. "Why the blood test? You can look at me. No cuts or bruises."

Oh, so now he didn't want to be the suspect. April shook her head. They already knew he didn't have any cuts or bruises. Maggie had plenty of bruises, but her nails had been short. She either didn't have an opportunity to use them, or they were too short to do any good. Still, Block was the wrong size to overpower her. Unless she had been totally out of it, Maggie could have done him some damage.

"You're not going to tell me, are you?" It was a fact he accepted.

Block didn't know why the police were doing what they were doing, but even though he was really scared, it didn't seem to occur to him that he could object. April concluded from his passivity that he must have some sort of problem with authority. Lot of suspects objected to everything, their jailhouse lawyers forcing a new court order at every step of the way to an indictment. Block complied with everything, but he was so nervous, April thought he might wet his pants when the needle hit his vein. Some killer.

In the waiting room of the lab he wrinkled his nose at the smell of the place, the bite of ammonia cleaner with the undercurrent of iron from the metal chairs scattered around and, he insisted, from the faint smell of blood. He was afraid of getting AIDS.

His eyes darted around. "Are we in the morgue?" He was obviously under a lot of stress.

"Nowhere near."

During his long questioning he had hinted darkly that he had other information about the case. He said it again now.

"I've got the stuff."

"What stuff?" Maggie's missing clothes? The keys to the store? They were waiting on a worn plastic-covered sofa in the reception area of the lab, surrounded by a lot of people who apparently didn't believe in soap and water. Block had said he had the stuff before and had come up with nothing. He turned toward the wall, did his usual, and clammed up.

Forty-five minutes went by before he was taken into a treatment room. At one point April saw that tears had formed big puddles in his eyes and threatened to spill out down his cheeks. The man was actually crying. He turned away and dabbed at his cheeks with a checkered handkerchief he dragged out of a pocket.

Later she took him back to his apartment, then returned to the precinct. She was certain little would come of the exercise.

# 31

It was Friday, the end of a frustrating week. Other than Block, they had no leads on Maggie Wheeler's killer. April spent the morning dialing numbers in Maggie's phone book of people who hadn't answered before. Sanchez and Joyce had disappeared soon after roll call. A tall, thin-lipped, gum-chewing detective in a powder-blue jacket with a department tag proclaiming him Lieutenant Braun, Homicide, was using the phone at Sanchez's desk. As the hours passed, the surface of Mike's desk became ever more littered with green gum wrappers.

In between calls the Lieutenant sat there, staring at the ceiling, cracking his gum and ignoring everyone around him. April wondered where the hell Sanchez and Joyce were. She smoldered quietly. She could see where this was leading, and hated feeling left out.

Around midday she could smell Sanchez enter the squad room. His aftershave, or whatever it was, reached out and proclaimed his entrance.

"Ah, lover boy is here," Aspirante said, loud enough for six detectives and Gina the secretary to hear over four phone conversations and the protests of an extremely well-dressed suspect in the pen who had tried to walk out of Charivari with a lot of stock he hadn't paid for.

"This is *so* embarrassing. I didn't do a thing," he kept saying. "I don't know why I'm here. Hey, let me out of here."

"What's with him?" Sanchez tossed a file on April's desk, cocking his head at Aspirante.

"I think the suspect came on to Sol in the car on the way over. Thing with this guy is he keeps ripping off the expensive stores, and then he tells his friends. And *they* rip the stores off." She shrugged. "Sol caught the run."

The waste of time had pissed Aspirante off. The suspect would be out in a few hours. April didn't add that Aspirante, like herself, was maybe concerned that Sanchez might be moving up the department ladder on Captain Higgins's discomfort with Sergeant Joyce.

"Who's this?" Mike raised a crooked eyebrow at the man addicted to Wrigley's spearmint who sat at his place.

"Papa bear?" April shrugged. "I thought you knew."

"Not me. I've been in the field all morning. Look at this."

April picked up the file he'd put on her desk without looking at him. She didn't want him to read in her face the fact that Dr. George Dong had called her the night before. Now she had a date with a guy who wasn't in the department and just happened to be Chinese. She wasn't exactly sure how she felt about it, but she was certain she didn't want Sanchez interfering.

After she'd gotten home, she had put aside her anxiety about Maggie Wheeler and started preparing her notes to study for her Sergeant's exam. Tonight she was working on prioritized items, phone calls, and model responses.

*Crime Pattern Bulletin must be read at roll call. Information is crime- and location-specific. Put special detail in area to work problem. Depending on procedures in your department, either implement special detail or recommend it to your Lieutenant or patrol officer. Prepare routing slips.*

She was about to write up a few in-basket exercises, when the phone rang.

"*Wei,*" she said, thinking the caller was Lonely Skinny Dragon Mother on the first floor, too lazy to walk up the stairs.

"April Woo?" A male voice.

"Yes, this is Detective Woo."

Silence.

"Hello?"

"Uh, this is George Dong."

She almost said, "What's your problem, Mr. Dong," as if she were at her desk in the squad room, where no one called her who didn't have a problem. Then she realized she was the problem. Her mother had done the *feng sui,* had fixed the tilting table and exorcised the bad spirit from her apartment. And still, no good daughter resisted the chance at happiness offered by smiling God.

Even though Sai Woo expressly warned her that George Dong "may be last chance," April had forgotten to anticipate her shining future. She had completely forgotten about him.

"Yes," she said, chastened. "Hello."

Turned out George Dong had his practice in Chinatown. He was an eye doctor. Thirty-five years old. Always the suspicious detective, April asked herself what was wrong with him. Why not married? Then realized he could say the same about her.

"I'm a cop," she told Dong right away as if it were a communicable disease that must be disclosed immediately.

"I know. Dangerous, long hours, uncertain schedule, uncertain future. I've seen it on TV. You wear a uniform?"

"No. Do you?"

"I wear a white coat."

"So," April murmured. Where did that get them?

"It reassures my patients," Dong added.

"Uh-huh." She had to hang up and study for her exam, reminded herself that she wanted to make sergeant. "So," she said again.

"You have to eat sometime."

"Yes." She couldn't argue with that. They made a date for lunch in Chinatown on Sunday.

The file Sanchez had brought her was the report on Block's blood. April had the thickening Wheeler file on her desk. She pulled the autopsy report and checked the blood type of the fetus in Maggie's womb. Maggie's blood type was A. The baby's was O. She pulled Block's lab file. Block's blood type was B.

Sanchez leaned over April's shoulder to get a look. The sudden closeness and aroma of heated cinnamon, citrus, and cinnabar made her dizzy. She could feel his breath on her neck. Shit, the man was hot. She rolled her chair back and looked up at him fiercely. "Don't do that."

"What?" He straightened up, looking like the surprised innocent. "What?" He turned around and asked the room. "What?"

Nobody answered.

Why was he breathing on her damn neck? April wondered if he knew about Dr. George. How could Mike know about George? She hadn't even met him yet. But Sanchez was very smart, had some Indian blood—Mayan or Aztec or Native American. He claimed it accounted for his sixth sense.

April frowned, remembering Mike's shoving her behind him while her gun was raised, risking getting shot in the back. She couldn't get it out of her mind. He'd fallen right on top of her, a dead weight on her ankle so she couldn't walk right for weeks. The doctor who treated it said she was lucky the bones hadn't been reduced to mush. And now he was the hotshot of the squad. Cool and hot at the same time. He was smiling at her now, the old, old soul who knew everything except what Lieutenant Braun was doing at his desk.

"So, Block couldn't have been the father of Maggie's baby. Where does that get us?" She added the lab report to the file, telling herself to get a grip.

He shook his head, already knew it.

"Doesn't help us one way or the other. Anything from Ducci?" she asked.

"Yesterday he said he was working on it. Any luck with her address book?"

"Lot of surprised people. The last guy I called turned out to be a piano tuner she went to kindergarten with, hadn't seen her since, and didn't have a clue why he was in her book. Lives in New Jersey. On the night in question he was with his wife and two children on Long Beach Island. . . . Couple of numbers no one answers any time of day. The boyfriend must be one of them."

Mike shifted from one foot to the other, his back to his desk, ignoring what was going on behind him. He just wasn't about to confront the guy at his desk. "Anything new with Manganaro?"

"She was going to go over the store inventory, see if anything is missing."

"She said that two days ago."

"Well, Maggie did all that for her. Mrs. Manganaro says she doesn't know the stock all that well. She'll have to match orders and sales. It's going to take her some time."

Earlier, Elsbeth Manganaro told them Maggie had had a lot of ideas. She didn't tell them about the guest book that Maggie had bought for the store last spring. She was surprised when it turned up in a routine search of garbage cans shared by a number of stores behind the building. She had forgotten about it. That meant she might have forgotten about a lot of other things, too. It was possible Mrs. Manganaro wouldn't even know if anything else was missing from the store.

The book was covered in green and black marbleized paper. After being asked about it, the boutique owner recalled it had been one of Maggie's ideas. She always asked customers to sign it. The book had been dusted for prints. Whoever threw it in the garbage must have wiped it first. There was only one partial on it, down at the very bottom of the second page. A thumb, not Maggie's and not Mrs. Manganaro's. But Mrs. Manganaro swore she never touched it.

There were only thirty-eight names in the book, all dated since June seventh, when Maggie put the book out. Sergeant Joyce had a detective checking each one out.

"Look at this. Wilma Masters. John Dodge Road, Jackson, Wyoming. August twentieth."

"Yeah, she was here visiting her sister. Bought a belt."

"Linda Green, 860 Fifth Avenue. August twenty-first."

"She's in Maine, bought a sweater."

"Margret Smart, Sarasota, Florida. August eighteenth."

"She's in Europe."

"Camille Honiger-Stanton, 1055 Second Avenue. August fifth."

"Second Ave? That's right across the street from Bill Hadgens, the addict she knew from high school."

Sanchez shifted feet again. "Any connection?"

"I don't know. No one's spoken to her yet. The number for that address is some kind of antiques shop. The person who answered the phone said he'd have the owner give us a call."

Sanchez tossed the book back into the file. "This isn't going to get us anywhere. They're all women. A woman didn't do her. Let's go see what the Duke has for us."

April picked up her bag, nodding. Good idea.

## 32

"Come."

Ducci was sitting at his desk, sorting a box of slides, when April obeyed his command to enter. He looked up suspiciously and frowned as the door cracked open, then grinned when he saw who it was.

"Hey, pretty one, come on in. What's happening?"

April shook her head. "Nothing good. What about you?"

Mike followed her into the lab and closed the door after them. "You locking yourself in now?"

"And Mike," Ducci added less genially.

"Not 'and Mike,' Duke. Just Mike. Mike stands alone." Sanchez slouched over to the bookcase and leaned against it to demonstrate standing alone. He was in a bad mood about the unknown Lieutenant and Sergeant Joyce, who was too busy with her own sulks to tell him what was going on.

"Oh, God, man, I'm sorry." Ducci crossed himself. "May she rest in peace. When did it happen?"

April turned to Mike. "What's he talking about?"

Mike scowled. "Damned if I know."

"Huh? She don't know?" Ducci wagged a finger at Mike. "You didn't tell her?"

"What's going on?" April looked from one to the other. She thought the problem was Lieutenant Braun sitting at his desk. That's what Mike had been grumbling about in the car on the way over.

Mike shook his head at Ducci, his eyes closed in disgust.

Ducci cocked his bushy eyebrows at April. "If he doesn't want to tell you, it's not my place to."

"Damn right."

April leaned against the corner of the desk because Ducci's other chair was occupied by a lot of files, books, and a skull with crooked teeth and a hole in its cranium. She chewed her lip. What was this all about?

Ducci shrugged apologetically. "Hey, sorry. I thought you two talked."

Mike's face faded to gray under his tan. "We talk. We talk plenty. We came here to talk about the Maggie Wheeler case, okay?"

April had never seen him angry like this. She turned to him questioningly. "Uh, Mike. You want me to leave?"

He shook his head, scowling. "Stay where you are."

"Yeah, stay. Here, have a candy bar." Ducci dipped into his stash in the middle drawer, came out with a Mars bar, and offered it to her, stretching his trademark, the impeccable blue-shirted arm with its starched white cuff, across his desk.

"No thanks, not for me," April murmured.

"What about you?" He turned to Mike.

"In yours."

"Hey, man, you should tell her. Women are good at this kind of thing." Ducci gave up on the candy bar, dropped it back in the drawer. "What can I do for you?"

"Other than throwing yourself off a bridge—?"

"We came about the Maggie Wheeler case," April interrupted. "You want to tell us about that?"

"Yeah, yeah. I know what you came for. I put a lot of work into it. Overtime."

"Good. What've you got?"

Ducci pulled his case file. Across his desk he laid out two series of glossy color photos on Maggie Wheeler: the first from the crime scene, of her hanging from the chandelier in the storeroom, with and without the tape measure showing the distances from the ceiling to the floor. The second were twelve angles of Maggie naked on the metal autopsy table— with and without the ruler placed beside the ugly marks on her shoulders, on her neck, on her arms. Glossies of her hands showed short fingernails and no signs of a fight. One of her feet showed the ID tag attached to a big toe. In the photos with the makeup cleaned off, she looked pretty bad. He put the autopsy report to one side.

"Okay, this is what I can tell you. See these bruises?" He pointed with the tip of a pencil to the marks on the arms.

Mike pushed off the wall for a closer look. "Yeah?"

"Old."

"Old?" Mike repeated.

"Yeah, like antique. See, they're already healing. They don't mean nothing."

He moved his pencil to the smudges on the victim's neck. "See these bruises?"

"Yeah?" Mike leaned closer.

"New."

"Shit." Mike slammed the desk with the palm of his hand.

April pressed her lips together in annoyance. Duke was playing with them, and Sanchez was seething. What was it with these two? She thought they were friends.

"Come on, Duke. Don't jerk us around. We haven't got all year," Mike shot out.

"All right, all right. Just trying to cheer you guys up. You look worse than she does."

"If you tell us something we don't know, we'll cheer up, okay?" April said.

"Okay, okay. Here, take that stuff off the chair. Just put it on the floor. Sit. Go on, sit down so I can look at you. I don't like to talk up, know what I mean? You"—Ducci lifted his chin at Mike—"pull up Bryan's chair. He won't mind. He's on vacation."

April moved the books, the files, and the skull with the hole in the cranium to the floor. She shifted the chair over so Mike had room to sit beside her. There was so much tension in his body, she could feel him vibrating. She shot him a questioning look. *What's going on with you?* He shook his head.

"All right, so the straight line across the neck indicates the victim was murdered. The bruising would curve up under her ears if she had hung herself. And the rope she was hanging from was not the one that killed her. Too thick to match the bruises. Look how the bruises are below the rope. Also, we can see from the pictures that there was nothing for her to jump off. No ladder, no chair. There's a stepladder in the corner, but she sure wasn't the one to put it back.

"Now, these marks on the shoulders indicate the guy took hold of her like this, face-to-face, and maybe shook her." Duke put his hands out and mimed the shaking. "Maybe the person was real mad and kinda lost it. I'm just speculating here." He looked like he didn't think he was speculating. He lifted his shoulders modestly as if waiting for applause, then let them drop. Nothing he told them so far was within his area of expertise. It didn't seem to bother him a bit.

"Perp was someone quite a bit taller than her. Stand up, April. I'll show you." Ducci shoved back his chair noisily and made his way through the clutter to the other side of his desk. "What are you—five four, five five?"

"Five five." April faced him in the crowded space. Ducci's paunch stood between them like a ship's prow.

"I'm five eight." He grinned. "You smell good. What're you wearing?"

"Hell you are," Mike protested. "I'm five nine and you're at least three inches shorter than me. And I thought you were a hair and fiber man."

"Shut up." Ducci raised his hands to April's shoulders. "I'm working."

"Yeah, well, don't work too close."

"Pay attention. Here's five five and five eight. The guy held her like this, the thumbs in front, the rest of the fingers over the top. Got it?"

"So?"

"So, I'm off balance like this, not tall enough. If I want to shake April, I'm going to grab her *here,* with my hands on her arms, or the sides of her shoulders. I'm not going to reach over the *top* of her shoulders."

"You can take your hands off her now and tell us something we don't know."

"Yeah." Ducci dropped his arms and headed back to his chair.

"Maggie was barely five feet," April muttered, thinking of Block.

"Yeah, you're looking for a guy between five nine and six foot with hands—glove size about eight and a half, maybe nine."

"But what about the damn fibers?"

"Well, these neck ligatures were made by a thin braided cord with a fiber fill of some sort. What kind I don't know. We don't have any references to match, but half a dozen fibers from the fill were embedded in the neck wound. Could be the kind of cord that's in the hood of a windbreaker. Anything like that in the store?"

"We'll check it out."

"What it looks like is he shook her up and then grabbed her from behind."

"Why behind?" April asked.

"See how the marks are thicker here. The cord was crossed over double here and pulled the other way back around her neck. Looks like the guy had some trouble. There's bruising from the hand at the back of the neck, and the victim's hyoid bone was fractured and so was the thyroid cartilage. That suggests the victim struggled, the perp couldn't hold on that way, and had to resort to manual strangulation."

"Hmm."

"Now, the fibers taken from her ring look like a tuft of wool, but it's not wool. And, A—There's no clothing in the store that matches it. B—We found some fibers that match it from the taping of the storeroom and just the other side of the archway into the showroom. No similar fibers were found out by the front door. C—The M.E. found some in her nose. What does all that suggest to you?"

"Hah." April had seen the tuft in the ring. "What?"

"Take a guess."

"We're not guessing. Don't play with us, Duke."

"You guys are no fun."

"We're not paid to be fun." Mike smiled at April. She smiled back, relieved that his mood had lifted.

"So, do you want to know?"

"Yeah, and you're paid to tell us."

"Dog," Duke said proudly.

"No shit. A dog killed her." Still smiling, Mike glanced at April. "A dog between five nine and six feet."

"Remember the Tawana Brawley case?" Ducci asked.

April nodded. "Dog hairs in the feces." The police had analyzed the feces that Tawana claimed her kidnappers had used to defile her. The feces contained dog hairs, not surprisingly, since dogs lick themselves. A check of the dogs in the building where Tawana had hidden for several days showed that the hairs in the feces came from dogs in her own backyard. The dog hairs helped disprove her story.

"Now you're talking," Mike said. Then, more seriously, "What does this do for us?"

"It tells us a dog was present at the scene either at the time of Wheeler's death or very shortly before. You may well be looking for a murderer with a dog."

"What makes you think the dog wasn't in the store hours before?" April asked.

"Because the dog hairs in the victim's nose would have been blown out after a minute or two. They wouldn't have stayed in there very long if she had remained alive."

"Dog," April murmured. "Block doesn't have a dog."

"Forget Block. He didn't do it," Sanchez said.

"He was at the scene though. That bothers me. How did he get there if she was already dead?" April muttered.

"Hey, he *appeared* to have been at the scene. There's no *evidence* he was at the scene. He described the dress she was wearing but didn't say anything about the makeup. Maybe he wasn't ever there," Mike said.

"It doesn't play. Maybe the killer left the door open and Block goes in, sees his beloved hanging there, gets scared, and splits." April turned back to Ducci. "We've been over this a dozen times. The guy comes in four days after she dies and confesses. But he has no idea what happened. Face it—Block doesn't make sense. We could get a shrink evaluation of him to prove he's a nut. But we already know he's a nut."

Ducci coughed delicately, slicking back his already carefully combed black hair. He glanced down at the dots on his tie, looking offended.

"What's the matter now?" Mike shook his head at April. What a piece of work.

"Don't you want to know what kind?" Ducci demanded.

"Okay. What kind of what?"

"Dog. You want me to locate the dog for you?"

"Okay, what kind of dog, Duke?"

"Like I said, it wasn't so easy to identify. We have no known references here." He patted a stack of slide boxes. "I've got over a thousand slides of different animal hairs. Know how long it takes to go through them all, looking for a possible match?"

"Well, you knew it wasn't an elephant."

"Very funny. See, the morphology of long-haired and short-haired dogs is different. Add to that wild dogs and mixed breeds." He rolled his eyes. "Hey, and the morphology of underhair is different from the hairs on top. Not only that, underhair has no root ends."

"That's very interesting," April said politely. "What kind of dog is it?"

"The hairs found on Wheeler's ring and in her nose have a natural twist and no root ends, like underhair, or sheep hair. What does that suggest to you?"

April shrugged. "I don't know a lot about dogs. My mother wouldn't let me have one when I was little. She thought the neighbors might eat it. What kind?"

Ducci pretended to consult his notes. "From the color, I'd say a poodle. And I'd say a puppy. The twist isn't pronounced yet. This is still fluff, probably from a dog that hadn't been clipped yet."

"Size?" Mike asked.

"Small." He smiled at them. "I don't think it walked in. No traces of it by the door, see."

"Gee. That's pretty good, Duke. The dog was carried in."

Ducci nodded. "And the killer let Maggie play with it. There was dog hair in her ring and in her nose."

"What about the makeup? And those long hairs on the dress?"

He shook his head. "The hairs are human. Two of them. They don't come from a wig or anything. I can't tell you anything about them or the makeup without some references. Go get me something more to work with. Get me the dog."

"Thanks, Duke, you're brilliant." April pushed out of her chair.

Ducci nodded and stroked his tie again. "Yeah, yeah. I know."

"Everything clear now?" April asked as she and Sanchez piled back in the car a few minutes later.

"Oh, sure—we're looking for a tall guy with a small poodle. Perhaps with long red hair. What kind of a guy carries a little poodle around?" Mike slammed the car door.

Who indeed. April remembered the shoplifter from Charivari who'd been in the pen when they left. "It would complicate things quite a bit if the perp's a transvestite."

"Sure would." Mike had a new thought. "What do you say the odds are Braun is still there?"

"Probably ten thousand to one. Who's the one who said only days ago, 'Life is short, take a chill'?"

Mike pulled out into the traffic. "No one I know."

# 33

Between Twentieth Street and Eighty-second Street the traffic was pretty badly jammed up. Labor Day weekend traffic was already assembling for its mass exodus out of the city. Mike turned onto Sixth Avenue in spite of the complication of construction there and got stuck around Twenty-eighth Street.

"So, what was that all about with Ducci?" April asked.

Mike negotiated the car around a bulldozer. "Jesus, last year Central Park West, this year this. What a mess."

"Umm. So what was the 'rest in peace' all about?" she persisted.

"Ah—nothing. Let it go, April." Mike stopped at the next red light, scowling. The intersection had a big hole in the middle of it, and the green Pontiac Grand Am ahead of them had pulled into the space beside it, blocking all cars trying to cross the other way.

"Will you look at this asshole." Mike didn't bother to ask for a turret light to slap on the roof of the unmarked gray car they'd taken. He just hit the hammer. His siren screamed its little "hello-out-there" warning, and miraculously the traffic slowly opened up.

"So, what was Duke doing, huh? Putting down women?" She didn't let it go.

"No, he was putting up women. So let it go."

"He sure got to you."

"Yeah."

Mike lapsed into silence. She let it be for a whole block.

At the next light she asked, "What woman?"

Mike heaved a great sigh, punctuated by an irritated "humph" at the end. "Jesus, April, not you. My ex-wife. Okay?"

"Oh." April looked straight ahead, her cheeks flushed. What a jerk.

She just forced her way into Sanchez's private space. She shook her head at herself, wishing she were in China.

Why was it that the cause of death in a badly decomposed, mutilated corpse was the kind of thing that kept her up at night, but she didn't want to know about the frailties of the still-beating, physically healthy heart of her partner? Yeah, in a funny kind of way Mike was her partner. She looked out the window, hot all over. What was it about this love thing? She could see it, feel it in the air around her. Books and TV were filled with it. Movies showed how it was supposed to happen. But with her the phenomenon was just a ghost that passed her by.

Skinny Dragon Mother said how it happened was you meet someone with a good character and you get married. It was as simple as that. Everything else so what.

Every time April told her it didn't work that way in America, you had to fall in love first, Sai Woo would produce the shell of a melon seed she'd been harboring somewhere deep in her mouth. Who knew for how long. Maybe for an hour or so, or ever since she left China. She'd spit it out with the word "love" to demonstrate her disgust for it. "Pah. Rove. What's that? Just riry brooms one day."

Sai Woo couldn't even get the words right. She meant love was a lily that blooms only for one day. A day lily, in fact. Years ago she had planted day lilies in her garden to prove the point. April didn't get it. All her life she worried that the lost l's in her mother's English meant she, as Sai's daughter, could never find the right emotions she needed to be a true American. Couldn't fall in love and get married because Chinese didn't believe in it, and couldn't even say the word.

One thing April had noted about the lilies in her mother's garden though. It was true each one did bloom only a day so you couldn't pick them and bring them in the house. But as each flower died, another grew in its place. The lilies proliferated. The roots spread under the ground, and the clumps of lilies had multiplied until they were all over the back-yard.

So Mike had some trouble with love and marriage, too, and the last thing she could ever do was ask him about it.

"Well," he said somewhere in the fifties. "I guess you want to know why I went to Mexico."

"Uh, no. That's okay—I mean you can tell me if you want to. I—"

"You know I'm married, right?"

"Ah."

"You didn't know?"

"Yeah, I knew that." So what? What did that have to do with her? Except the shit had been coming onto her for months. So much for the heavy breathing. She blinked, her face impassive.

"Yeah, well, she was young, came to New York from Matamoros. Beautiful. Sweet, you know, not like the girls from here. I, uh, really liked her."

There it was—Sanchez in love. April bit her lip, blushing again.

"So, we got married. And you can guess what happened, right?" He turned to look at her.

April shook her head. She had no idea what happened.

"Well, she couldn't stand any of it. The noise, the weather, the rough city life. She missed growing things, the sweet perfumed air of Mexico. Couldn't really speak English and didn't want to go to school. She was scared all the time, scared of me—you know, my being a cop. . . . Everything.

"Maybe I wasn't much of a husband." He shrugged. "Anyway, after a while she went back to Mexico. And then my father died." He shrugged again, staring out at the traffic.

"I'm sorry." She couldn't think of anything else to say. "So what about her—"

"Maria? She's dying of leukemia." He shook his head. "You know, all these years she refused to get a divorce. I thought it meant she planned to come back someday. But the truth was her priest told her if we were divorced she wouldn't get to heaven. Isn't that something?"

"Yeah. It's something." Absolutely unbelievable. What kind of woman would leave a man like Sanchez for any reason whatsoever? Without thinking, April put her hand on his arm. Neither said anything the rest of the way back to the precinct.


Thirty minutes later, Gina at the desk in the squad room waved them over.

"Sergeant Joyce wants to see you right away."

"Thanks." Mike pointed at his desk. Still littered with the Wrigleys wrappers, it was uninhabited now. "Gone," he said, grinning at April. "Who said the odds were ten thousand to one? I think you owe me."

"Not so fast," she murmured, pointing to her desk that no longer had the thick Wheeler case file on it.

They headed across the squad room. Aspirante and Healy were out. The flamboyant shoplifter was no longer in the pen. In his place was one of the panhandlers on Broadway who usually launched verbal assaults on passersby, but occasionally chased one with an empty wine cooler bottle. Right now he was singing "Happy Birthday" to himself.

Sergeant Joyce's door was open. "Yeah, come in," she said when she saw them. She was sitting at her desk, her blond-streaked hair sticking straight out at the sides as if someone had been pulling at it. Her eyes were pouchy, and her skin was the color of unbaked cookie dough. Her blouse that might have been white when she put it on now looked like coffee had been coughed all over it. Both sleeves were unevenly rolled. Her lips were two thin lines of unhappiness.

April felt sorry for her. Sergeant Joyce was the kind of woman to whom stress was no friend. Everything showed on her: ambition, anger, jealousy, loss of face.

"Where've you two been?" Joyce demanded. "I wanted to talk to you." She looked April up and down, scowling some more.

"At the lab, talking with Duke," Mike replied. "What's up?"

"We've had a Lieutenant from downtown assigned to the Wheeler case."

"The guy who was sitting at my desk this morning? Lieutenant Braun?"

"Yeah, that's the one."

Mike took a seat. "Nice guy. Neat. Friendly."

April took her usual seat on the windowsill and stuck her finger in the dirt of one of the ivy plants. The leaves were drooping and the dirt was bone dry.

"How did the Captain take it?"

"Gee, I don't know, Mike. You weren't here when it happened and he doesn't exactly communicate directly with me." Sergeant Joyce glanced at April. "What's with you?"

April shook her head. "Nothing. Just thinking about what Duke said, that's all."

Sergeant Joyce turned back to Mike. "Captain Higgins called me up and told me."

"Uh-huh. Did the good Lieutenant bring his own people?" Mike asked with no trace of the resentment Sergeant Joyce was using to electrify the room.

"Unh-unh. Apparently they couldn't spare anybody else. So you're going to be working for Braun. He's got the file. I want you to cooperate with him fully." Her eyes were doing something funny. April couldn't tell if their supervisor was having convulsions or giving them a different message.

"Yessir," Mike said. "Where is he?"

"The Captain put him upstairs, three-o-four." She smiled grimly. The empty office next to the men's room had a heady odor no amount of disinfectants seemed to help. It was full of filing cabinets, and used mostly as a storeroom.

"I want you to go up there and introduce yourselves, brief him on what you've got so far." Sergeant Joyce gave Mike a hard look.

This prompted Mike to ask, "Has he done anything yet?"

"Yeah, he pulled surveillance on Block."

"Well," Mike assured her, "that was probably all right." Then he filled her in on the kind of suspect Ducci had told them they were looking for.

"You got to be kidding. He-shes don't kill. They *get* killed."

"So what about the long hairs on her dress?" April asked.

"You know how hairs stick. Shit, they could have been on the dress already." Sergeant Joyce's skimpy lips turned up at the corners for the first time since they arrived. She threw her head back and honked out a hearty laugh. "A transvestite boutique killer. With a poodle as the only witness. Ducci is really something. If you've got spatters, he's a spatter man. If you've got glass breaks, he's your glass-break man. Now two red hairs and he tells us to look for a he-she. And I thought I'd heard everything."

"What if it was a woman with a poodle?" April murmured.

Sergeant Joyce laughed again. "You find that, and I'll buy you both the best dinner you ever had."

"Deal," Mike said. He got up to leave.

April stopped him in the hall. "If that's what we find, do we have to eat the dinner with her?"

"Cute, real cute."

They trudged back through the squad room and climbed the stairs to locate the exiled Lieutenant Braun.

"This is some shithole" were the Lieutenant's first words when they appeared at the door of his assigned "office." Looking around, they couldn't disagree.

# 34

After the storm passed, the air was clear and fresh. Just before they left for Fairfield, Bouck and Camille surveyed the damage to the canopy over the store. The canvas was torn, and the exposed metal frame was pretty badly bent on one side, but it didn't look as if it would come down on somebody's head anytime soon.

Camille breathed deeply, hugging the puppy in her arms. Her own storm was over, too, and for the first time in weeks, her head was clear. The red cloud was gone. She could see, talk, eat.

"Why don't I design a new one," she suggested. "Something classy. What do you say?"

"Hey, this isn't classy?" Bouck demanded, pointing to what could be seen of the gray canvas hanging off the frame. It was years old, cracked, and dirty. The "T" and "Q" from the word "Antiques" were almost completely worn away by the constant drip of the air conditioner above.

Camille was wearing the new straw picture hat she had bought after her lunch with Milicia. It was hand-painted with lavender flowers and had a huge bow at the back. The salesgirl had admired her in it. "Not everyone has the height to carry a hat like that," she said. Camille had been so angry at Milicia, she had no idea what she looked like. The hat soothed her because it was a cover, big enough to hide her face. She could run away inside of it and not come out until she wanted to.

Now she tipped the hat down low over her face as she whispered to the puppy. After a brief consultation, she spoke from under the straw. "Puppy says the sign was never classy."

Bouck threw his head back and laughed like a pirate. He was wearing jeans and Gucci loafers, a lightweight navy Ferragamo blazer over a black T-shirt. Camille thought of him as a pirate. A big man with a round cherub's face, small pink lips, pale blue eyes, and soft hair that hung down his neck and caught on his jacket collar. She didn't know how he captured the money. But she knew he was powerful, made things happen. Kept her safe from her sister, who would kill her if she got the chance. She pushed away Milicia's evil force by hugging Puppy tightly.

At a few minutes after ten on Sunday morning Second Avenue was deserted. Only a few cars and dog walkers cruised the streets. Saturday's storm had left three feet of water in the subway and a water-main break on Broadway and Ninety-second Street. There were parts of the city where thousands of rats, forced out of the ground by high water, scurried among black plastic garbage bags, foraging for food. Puppy saw one and struggled to get out of Camille's arms.

Smiling, she murmured, "Oh, all right," and put the dog down. Puppy took off after the rat, only to be stopped short after a few feet by its retractable leash. The rat disappeared into the wet garbage that clogged the drain over the sewer on the corner.

Once the water had abated on Second Avenue, the devastation seemed to be limited to an assault of sodden newspapers and cardboard boxes that had been left out for a recycling pickup on Saturday that never occurred. Wet paper and loose garbage had blown all over the street.

"Let's get out of here." Bouck led the way across the street and halfway up the block to Third Avenue, where the garage was. He had called for the car, and it was waiting for them—a dark green Mercedes large enough to carry home most of the things they liked to buy.

Many antiques dealers were compulsive buyers, collecting at a much faster rate than they sold, and Bouck was no exception. He went to shows and auctions up and down the East Coast, with Camille beside him in the Mercedes. When she was really bad, he let her hide in the basement and didn't stay away longer than twelve hours. Today they had a handle on things, were celebrating a new phase.

Camille settled herself into the caramel-colored leather and watched Bouck burn up the Merritt Parkway all the way to Connecticut. Two or three times she felt a tremor of panic, but when she retreated into the hat, she could see Puppy curled up on her lap. As long as Puppy was there, its tiny teeth showing in a smile, the red cloud wouldn't close in over her. She knew from past experience if nothing bad happened, she would have a few good days.

Today was dazzling. The sky was deep blue, the trees and foliage that lined the highway after Greenwich thick and green. They were headed for the Fairfield Antiques Fair, which was held at a farm that was now a flea market and auction site. The traffic was light and by noon they had already parked and were beginning their meticulous study of the thousands of items offered in seventy-five small booths under three large tents in an open field.

They made a striking couple as they strolled casually from booth to booth—Camille in her straw hat and printed dress, a long and slender beauty stroking the tiny poodle in her arms, and Bouck, large and affluent with his diamond-studded gold Rolex, Gucci loafers, and benign baby face. Not visible was the small automatic tucked in his waistband, or the fairly crude Saturday night special in the small handbag that he never put down.

They appeared casual, but their search for treasure was an intense and careful process. They knew exactly what they were looking for, knew which dealers they would approach and which they would not. Bouck specialized in chandeliers, but he occasionally bought candlesticks, art glass, porcelain, unusual objets d'art, small chairs and tables, mirrors, sconces.

Camille shuddered. "Not there." She turned away from the next booth. "That woman's a witch. She wants to steal Puppy. Get away." She made a brushing gesture.

"Sure thing." Bouck steered Camille toward the barn, careful not to touch her as he moved her toward the indoor booths, where chandeliers hung from rafters.

The barn had been converted years before. Now its roof was studded with skylights. Today, the sun piercing through the grime on the windows and clouded crystals of the chandeliers gave everything a radiant, almost magical cast. Light, in tiny, dancing pinpoints, reflected everywhere.

Bouck and Camille continued their easy pace, pausing here and there to admire a piece and to chat with dealers they knew. The business had its own special language and its own insider information.

"You see the Empire piece in that corner?" Bouck nodded toward the back of one of the booths as they strolled past.

"Yes, very good," Camille confirmed. "He also has the best pier mirror I've ever seen. Look at the size of it."

Bouck glanced at the booth again quickly and then away so the owner wouldn't think they were interested. He shook his head. "I thought we agreed. Nothing too big for the Mercedes."

"Perfect for the living room. Perfect for our chandelier. Perfect for me," she said in a little-girl voice. "I bet you can get them both for seven."

"Oh, do you think so. We'll see about that."

They continued to walk, occasionally murmuring a kind word about a piece they admired but would never buy, and passing without comment the horrors and junk that comprised most of the show. This was no place for amateurs.

Fifteen minutes later, they circled back to the booth with the pier mirror in the center and the Empire chandelier in the corner. The pier mirror was nearly seven feet high. Its age could be set at over two hundred years by the way it was made. Heavy wooden panels, crudely put together, supported the huge slab of mirror on the front, the carved and gilded frame, and complicated side panels set at an angle with many mirrored insets. Like most old pieces, the visible parts were finely detailed while the undersides and back were rough and unfinished. Camille was enchanted by the piece. She paraded back and forth in front of it, swinging her skirt and preening.

Bouck smiled indulgently and examined the Empire chandelier. Its clean lines were broken with exquisitely detailed heads of horned and bearded faces and had the classic ram finials. The dealer was a short, heavyset man in his mid-fifties, wearing an orange silk shirt over his tailored khaki trousers. He was drenched in a perfume so strong that Puppy sneezed when they entered his space.

The man looked anxiously around for the source of the sound and didn't see it. He wore very thick lenses encased in the kind of owl-eye black plastic frames favored by architects. Milicia's boss wore glasses just like it. Camille hiked up Puppy in her arms. Puppy sneezed again.

The owner saw it now, squeaked, "A dog," jumping out of his chair, away from Puppy, as if it were necessary to defend himself.

Good. Camille wandered off, leaving Bouck to do business. She checked out some rococo sconces hanging on the rough wooden beams that supported the roof, took another look at the small French bergère the dealer had been sitting in when they approached. Now she could see the full shape of the chair and the delicate carving on the exposed ends of the arms.

Checking behind him nervously, the dealer was trying to concentrate on showing Bouck some small art-glass pieces in a vitrine in the middle of the booth. Camille could see Bouck wanted the vitrine and not what was in it. Good, old display cases were very hard to find. Apparently the vitrine was not for sale.

"Gallé is so difficult these days. I sell only authentic, but some dealers—" The dealer shrugged. "And it's hard to tell if you don't know what you're doing. The Koreans are flooding the market with copies, you know. Here, let me show you."

He picked up a magazine and passed it to Bouck. "Look at this, faked art glass. Daum Nancy, Gallé, Steuben, Tiffany, complete with signatures."

"We don't have a problem with that," Bouck said airily, fingering the zipper on his handbag.

"I guarantee everything I sell," the myopic dealer said quickly.

"Hmm." Bouck pointed at the yellow bud vase with the blue-green ivy pattern, clearly signed Gallé. "That's nice."

"Let me take it out for you."

The vitrine door swung open. Camille could see Bouck nodding at the way the key had turned easily in the lock and how the door swung evenly on its hinges. "Bouck?" she said.

"Yes, my angel."

"What do you think of the chandelier?" Camille turned toward it.

"I'll look at it in a second." Bouck held up the small yellow vase, turning it in the light. She could see from his expression it wasn't bad, was probably authentic. The weight was right and the edges of the pattern were not too neat, as they were likely to be in fakes.

"What are you asking for the vase?"

"Well, prices have come way down on these pieces since eighty-seven and eighty-eight. The Japanese drove the market way out of proportion and then, all of a sudden, they stopped buying. Back then this would have sold for thirty-five hundred to five thousand. Today it's probably worth half that. For a dealer, I'd say fifteen hundred." He hesitated as if he'd already said too much, then added, "I can do that because I bought it with a lot of other, larger pieces, from an estate about ten years ago, so I don't have that big an investment in it."

Bouck put down the bud vase and smiled at the dealer. "What chandelier, Cammy?"

"Oh, the Empire. That is a beauty." The dealer trotted along behind Bouck toward the corner were Camille was standing, stroking the puppy's head. He regarded the dog with distaste.

"You, of course, have excellent taste. That's one of the best Empire chandeliers I've ever had. Unfortunately, I've had it only about three months, so I can't do much on the price. But it is exquisite. Did you see the detail on the ram's heads and Pan, of course. Ah—" he squeaked. "Don't do that."

Camille had reached up to take the chandelier off its hook.

"Oh, no, no, no," he cried. "Let me do that."

Camille didn't wait. She lifted the chain, easing the chandelier gently off its hook. The profusion of heavy, dangling crystals swung into one another, clinking wildly.

The dealer rushed toward her, almost tripping over Bouck. "Oh, my God. That's heavier than it looks."

He grabbed it from her, staggering a little under the weight until Bouck steadied him. Together the two men rehung it on a lower hook, slightly below eye level. For the second time the horrified dealer backed away from Camille. Bouck smiled at his colleague's discomfiture.


Twenty minutes later Bouck pulled the Mercedes into the parking lot of a small French restaurant Camille remembered from before. The Mercedes was old enough to have the generosity and elegance new sedans lacked, the trunk ample space for the chandelier. The pier mirror was being delivered on Tuesday. The chair in which the dealer had been sitting was comfortably nestled in the back seat. Bouck had taken it for his ritual. The display case and the bud vase remained where they were. Bouck had handed over nine thousand dollars in cash.

"I'm taking Puppy in," Camille insisted.

"No, Camille," Bouck said sharply. "You can see her from here."

"I want to," she said.

"No. You'll have to leave her in the car." Bouck opened the windows and poured some water from an Evian bottle into a bowl with black paws painted on it. "She'll be fine. I promise." When she didn't move, he added, "Get out, Camille. Or I'll show Puppy my gun."

Meekly, she got out of the car and moved toward the restaurant door that suddenly opened for her as if by magic.

"Do you have a reservation?" the obsequious maître d' asked, leading them to the half-empty dining room, where he pointedly consulted his book.

Bouck's round, angelic face was serene except for a small sign of strain in one cheek, where a muscle jumped. "We'll sit there, by the window," he said.

"Um, that's reserved."

"That's where we're sitting. Go on, Cammy, that's your table."

"Oh. Well . . . all right." The maître d' followed Camille anxiously with the menus.

Bouck pushed the menus away. "I'll have a double Glenlivet. A glass of Beaujolais for the lady." He frowned, tapping the table with his fingertips as the maître d' flushed and murmured, "Right away, sir."

Bouck glanced at Camille, directing his scowl at her. She could feel the life draining out of her and clenched her fists to hold her life in.

"Don't start, Camille," Bouck said, hissing through his teeth like a snake. He smiled. "We're having lunch, remember. You've conquered the witch Milicia, don't let her back. She can't hurt you now. Don't let her creep up on you from behind.

"Come on, Cammy. I'll let you have a nice piece of salmon, not cooked too much. Whatever sauce you want. Ah, here's your Beaujolais." He waved his hand at her, commanding, "Sip, sip."

Camille reached for the wineglass as he directed, put it to her lips, did not drink. Her face was white.

"We've had a good day, hmmm?" Bouck drained his tumbler of single malt without flinching, then raised his hand for another.

# 35

Jason didn't expect Emma to pick him up at the L.A. airport, but she was standing in the crowd of welcomers at the gate when he arrived. He was caught behind a couple with two babies who had screamed all the way across the country. Now mother and father were determinedly trying to wheel the exhausted infants, in two heavy-duty strollers, through solid matter. Their maneuvering gave him a minute to realize the beauty waving at him, dressed in the buff-colored linen trousers and mint-green blouse, with the arms of a tan nubbly sweater tied around her neck like a fashion model, was his wife.

Emma looked different. Her hair was shorter than he'd ever seen it, cut bluntly around her jawline to make her look jaunty and young. It was lighter, too. She was wearing a heavy gold necklace that was clearly expensive and a large braided leather handbag over her shoulder. The way she was put together complimented her perfect figure and fine complexion without making a big deal of either. She had a fresh healthy appearance, like the classy cover girl of *Town & Country*. She did not look like a woman who'd been abducted and tattooed by a madman only three months before.

A space opened up in the crowd. Jason walked toward her, stunned. He thought he was prepared for anything. Emma hadn't been in good shape when she left New York right after an ordeal that would have turned most people into vegetable soup for quite some time. There were still bruises and burn marks on her body. Also on her feet. She had been naked and barefoot, and had to walk out of a house on fire. Weeks afterward, she was still finding it painful to cross the room.

And of course there was the unfinished tattoo. A couple of serpents curling up from her groin, stopping short just below the navel because they had been lucky and stopped the guy before he had time to finish the scenario he had planned. Emma shot him with his own gun. April Woo, the police detective on the case, shot him with hers. The bullets from both guns were found in his charred remains. But it was the fire that finally killed him.

Jason still woke up in a cold sweat, reliving the scene of Emma's rescue. Half a block of Queens on fire, the shrieking of horrified home-owners and fire equipment. The pungent odor of two barbecuing bodies. And Emma being hustled into an ambulance, covered with soot, colored all over like an Easter egg ready for dipping, protesting all the while, calling for her own doctor. For him.

And despite it all, she grabbed her big break and headed for Holly-wood anyway. Jason was still staggered when he thought about it. The man who abducted Emma had been triggered by a tattooing scene in her first film. And that didn't put her off getting up there on the screen again as soon as possible. Not at all. Quite the contrary, Emma had been afraid the producer and director would fire her when they saw her packaging was no longer flawless.

Even though they hadn't fired her, and she appeared to have made it through six grueling weeks of filming, Jason would not have been sur-prised to see any kind of deterioration in her now. What he wasn't pre-pared for was the transformation three months away from him had made. The intelligent, attractive daughter of a navy meteorologist, raised on navy bases around the world, had brought herself through her own wars, just as she said she would.

As a person who prided himself on curing the sick and wounded, Jason felt the shock of having been short-circuited.

"Hi, pal." Just barely brushing against him, Emma smiled. She lifted her lips to his cheek.

He restrained the impulse to grab her, hold her tight. Instead, he raised a finger to touch the place where she had kissed him.

"Wow, you look great. Thanks for coming."

Now she looked surprised. "Did you think I wouldn't?"

He shrugged. "I could have taken a cab." He hoisted his carry-on with one hand and his overstuffed briefcase with the other.

She stared at him. "I guess you don't think much of me. . . . Can-yon Beach is an hour and a half away."

"I think the world of you. But thanks anyway."

She flushed, her eyes flashing anger for a second.

Jason didn't know L.A., had no idea where she lived. He bit his lip, worried that he had blown it in the first five minutes. "Was that manipulative?"

"A little." She nodded, frowning, then brightened up. "Oh, well, let's go." She turned toward the exit.

He followed her, relieved. Emma had never been a person to hold grudges. He didn't know what she was like now, except that she was in a hurry. She covered what felt like several miles across the airport to the short-term parking lot at a race walk, finally stopping beside a red Mustang convertible.

"Nice." He wasn't looking at the car. He was watching Emma fumble in her huge new braided handbag for her car keys. He realized he missed her even more than he thought.

He shook his head at her hair. Emma always said she'd never color it. Once a rich honey-wheat color, her hair was now unashamedly movie-star blond. Her perfume was different, too. Spicy.

More winded than he liked to admit, Jason dropped his gear. He didn't know what to make of her. It was like meeting a stranger with a familiar smile.

"Tired?" she asked.

"No," he said quickly.

She found the keys and unlocked the trunk, looking up at him almost shyly. Showing off her car. "Like it?"

He held back a choke, managed a moderately convincing "Uh-huh."

As he had once told his friend Charles, there wasn't a thing not to like about Emma. Except now he no longer knew who she was.

She inclined her head modestly. "It's leased." She jumped in and put the top down, then turned to him questioningly, as if she suddenly remembered something.

"Any objections to my driving?"

He shook his head. How could he object?

"Good." She pulled out, had no trouble finding her way out of the airport, and was soon speeding south on the 405.

This, also, was an adjustment. Jason had been married to Emma for five years, but even on long trips he'd never thought of asking her if she wanted to drive. Now it occurred to him that she might have minded.

He looked out at the scenery, which wasn't impressive. He didn't know where they were headed, and didn't ask. They drove for almost an hour before Emma turned off onto a road leading through a small canyon that dead-ended at the Pacific Ocean. Suddenly the red Mustang was stopped at a traffic light facing a beach crowded with volleyball players. Emma turned to him with another of her smiles.

"Canyon Beach. Like it?"

"It's great, really terrific." He nodded. Yep, really terrific. A million light-years away from New York and definitely too far from the L.A. airport to take a taxi. This was more than the fragile male ego could take. Emma drove back up another hill and pulled to a stop on a steep incline that made him slightly dizzy.

A few minutes later she was unlocking the door to her rented house. "Come on in."

The way her eyes were glowing with pride made Jason suddenly realize why she had wanted him out there. It wasn't to explore new laser treatment to get rid of the tattoo on her stomach. Unh-unh. It was to show him this.

He could see the ocean from the front steps. It was just at the bottom of the steep hill. Up there, they were perched high enough for a New Yorker to get a nosebleed. Jason looked around.

It didn't take a genius to see that the house was hanging by a few sticks from the side of the cliff. He couldn't get the images of mudslides, fires raging down from the canyon above, huge earthquakes dumping the entire Tinker-Toy town into the Pacific, out of his mind.

To make matters worse, the house was not without charm. The living room melted into the dining-kitchen area. The bedroom was up several steps to one side in a clever way that allowed both living room and bedroom to have views of the sea. Another sleeping loft was carved out of the cathedral ceiling along the back of the living room. Below it was a glass wall that looked out on a rock garden planted with blooming rose-bushes.

The furnishings were simple, in earth colors that suited Emma's complexion. Throughout the place a southwestern feeling pervaded.

"Like it?" she asked when he had seen it all. It was the fourth or fifth time she'd made the query since he arrived.

Jason arranged his mouth for another, "What's not to like?" kind of answer. So, she had to get him out there to show him how gorgeous it was.

How the sun shone down on her and her red convertible, bathing her in golden serenity and the well-being of the truly self-sufficient, while he rotted unhappily by himself, locked in with the crazies of New York.

Her eyes were almost pleading. What did she want from him? Forgiveness? His blessing? He looked away, already worrying about having to sleep up there in the loft.

"It's great. Really terrific. I'm just—flabbergasted at how great it all is." Seeing how great it all was had given him a headache. He needed a drink, too.

She nodded, picking it all up right away. "Must be strange, huh? Want to go out for a drink?"

"Yeah." The frown behind his smile eased just a little for the first time. He wouldn't turn down something to eat either.

She was looking him over. His blazer and khaki pants were wrinkled. He hadn't changed his style, probably never would. "You look very thin," she concluded. "Better eat something, too."

"Yes." Everything about their relationship was different, yet the feeling of togetherness was still there. He didn't know what to think. To take his mind off the subject, he glanced over at the telephone. Emma followed his gaze, a little frown beginning to organize itself between her eyes.

He turned away from the phone. "Let's go, sweetheart."

For once in his life he decided not to call in for his messages.

# 36

At five past twelve on the Sunday afternoon before Labor Day, April slid into a seat at a tiny back table at the Dim Sum Tea House. Next to her a chubby young woman with badly permed hair cooled a spoonful of noodles in her mouth, then fed the half-chewed mess to her baby. April looked away as the baby spit it out.

George Dong shook his head and resolutely studied his menu. "Delightful. What do you feel like?"

April smiled politely. Like going right home. Right away she didn't like him. She didn't care if he was a doctor. He had to be a fool, taking her to the kind of place where mothers make baby food in their mouth, then expecting her to choose something from the menu when it was a dim sum place. It was a no-win situation, like a trick question she couldn't possibly get right. She glanced at the menu. It was a long one.

"I don't know yet." She decided the polite thing was to consider the menu. She'd been a cop long enough to know Dr. Dong was solemnly studying her as if she, too, were an item on the list.

She was wearing blue trousers, as usual, with a white blouse and red jacket. She had wanted to wear her white vest and jacket, very chic; but Skinny Dragon Mother, who came upstairs uninvited to give her advice before she left, said white was bad luck, the color of death.

"Led good ruck cuwa, wedding cuwa for blides." Sai Woo absolutely insisted on red.

There was no point in telling her blides wore white in America. It was a good ruck color here. Sai would only have argued that bad Chinese spirits can go anywhere, don't respect borders.

A surly waitress with a protruding gold tooth unceremoniously dumped a pot of tea on the table. April poured some in the two tiny cups.

In her cup one lone tealeaf drifted gently to the bottom. She hadn't waited long enough for it to steep. Probably meant she'd blown her whole life.

A few seconds later the same surly waitress stopped beside their table with a rolling metal thing that looked like a hospital supply cart. The top-shelf offering was bamboo steamers filled with some unidentifiable gelatinous mass.

George waved her away. He turned out to be the second kind of Chinese body type—five seven, maybe five eight, his physique undefined and on the pudgy side. His lightweight navy warm-up suit with red stripes down the arms and legs didn't help. April guessed he wanted to look sporty and athletic, not overdressed for the occasion. His round face was studded with wholly unremarkable features, small mouth, small nose, deeply set serious eyes that didn't want to make contact with hers. April was unimpressed and couldn't get her mother out of her mind.

"Be nice," Sai Woo had warned. "Tomolla, I don't wanna hear you stick up."

"I'm not stuck up."

"Everybody say you stick up."

Yeah, well. Chinese didn't trust the police. Even one of their own. April spotted another cart heading toward them through the crush. She watched the steamed buns filled with barbecued pork that were her favorite disappear along the way. Suddenly she felt old and remembered her mother's other warning: *Smart girl loses innocence but not hope. Stupid girl loses everything.*

Nowadays when April went to Chinatown, she saw it with a more critical eye. When she had lived and worked there, she never thought about the garbage that shopowners threw on the street. It was nothing to see fish guts floating in fetid puddles in the gutters along with crumpled newspapers, rotten fruit and vegetables, rags. Roaches and rats ran around like honored guests. Now the place looked like a slum to her. Why couldn't they clean it up? What was it with Chinese and garbage?

The cart got to them. No roasted pork buns were left.

April shook her head at the ancient fried wontons that remained. This was some place for a first date. The noise level was deafening. There were too many people in a very small space, and dozens more blocking the sidewalk outside. Along with frying smells, the air was charged with the powerful odor of old garlic from what felt like ten thousand eager Chinese mouths, all shouting and eating a mile a minute. This dim sum parlor on Doyers Street, a tiny cul-de-sac off Mott, was packed all day every Sunday. Chinese from all over the tri-state area came into town for their weekly food pilgrimage, brought the family, and ate all day long, pausing only long enough to buy more food to take home in their overburdened American station wagons.

"You wanted that?" George asked, looking her in the eye for the first time.

April shrugged. "When she comes back."

George stopped the waitress and spoke rapidly in Chinese, telling her to bring a cart of the best dim sum, not the stuff that had been sitting there in the kitchen, waiting all morning for the noon rush. "Hurry up, and don't stop on the way—" He turned to April. "How about a beer?"

At her nod he added, "And bring us two Tsing Tao."

That done, he picked up his chopsticks and fiddled with them. "So, your mother knew my mother in China. Know anything about that?"

"Might have known each other, but they didn't come from the same place," April replied. "We never met."

"They call each other sister-cousins," he pointed out.

"Yeah, well, if they're sister-cousins, how come they live in the same city and were out of touch for twenty-two years?"

His smile lit up his face. "You're the detective."

He had a nice, cultured voice. Without intending to, April smiled back. "Maybe some kind of feud. Maybe they're not such good friends."

"Then why introduce us?"

"Could be spite," April speculated. She was known to be stuck up, hard to please. Her rejecting the doctor son of an old enemy would make the enemy lose face. On the other hand, if the doctor rejected her, Sai Woo would lose face. All around it was risky. Pretty much a no-win situation.

"Could be desperation." George laughed, opening his mouth wide enough to reveal white, even teeth. "Anything for a grandson to carry on the name."

"My mother would settle for a granddaughter. Where did you go to school?"

"Queens. Then Columbia all the way."

April guessed he meant college, medical school, and all that other training. She frowned. And then he came down to Chinatown to practice when he had never been stuck here in the first place? That didn't make sense. Why would he return to a place he'd never been? Most ABAs who got to college and learned to blend married Caucasians if they possibly could. They didn't exactly come stampeding back to live with the immigrants just off the plane.

"You live down here?" she asked.

He shook his head.

The steamed buns came. April bit into one. "Ummm. Food's good."

He drank down some of his beer, nodding. "You have to be in the right mood though."

Ah, so that was it. He hadn't known what kind of girl she was, and didn't want to be seen with her if she wasn't up to a better place. She flushed, feeling put down by the Ivy League graduate. Last spring she'd laid eyes on Columbia University for the first time. She had a missing person from there. Seventeen-year-old girl. The girl was killed in California, and April Woo was the one who located her.

All right, so maybe she was a cop, a street person, not a doctor, not exactly a first-class medical school graduate. Okay. Maybe she *was* just a cop. But in a month she'd be a cop with a college degree herself. And if she had anything to do with it, she'd be a sergeant in the department, too.

"Is that a tennis bag?" She jerked her chin at the bag at his feet.

"Yes. You ask a lot of questions."

"I'm a cop. It comes with the territory. How did you get to be a doctor?"

He smiled again, sipped more beer. "I studied for a lot of years. And my parents wanted a docta." He twisted his face into old style. "You know how that is. Ten thousand pounds of steaming guilt a day. 'Have dumpring. Study book. Be docta. Take care palents.' I really didn't have much choice."

Another cart came by. This one was filled with pearl balls and shui mai. April took the shui mai. She'd heard that in old China dim sum was served in tea houses for breakfast. The words dim sum meant "touch the heart lightly." She tried to concentrate on the meaning of the words and the delicate taste of shrimp and dried mushroom. Yes, she knew exactly how much ten thousand pounds of steaming guilt a day weighed on a child's shoulders. She liked the image and his joking about the accent, liked the gold signet ring on his finger.

He drank down half the beer and looked at her appraisingly. "What made you become a cop?"

She tasted hers, considering an answer. She didn't want him to think badly of her parents for not insisting she go to Columbia. Didn't want to insult her parents by implying poverty. She put her glass down. The beer was warm. "There seemed to be a need."

In response to that, her beeper sounded from inside her lucky red blazer.

George looked surprised. "What's that?"

"My beeper. Something must have come up. I'm sorry. I have to call in."

She pushed her chair back and made her way through the crush to the front of the restaurant, where a pay phone hung prominently behind the cash register. She dialed the squad number.

"What's going on?" she asked when Sanchez came on the line.

"Where are you?"

"Doyers Street."

"Chinatown. What're you doing down there?"

"It's lunchtime, my day off. I'm having lunch." April tried not to sound impatient. "What's coming down?"

"Braun wants you in here now. Third floor, examination room."

"Yeah, what for?" Adrenaline and alarm shot through her in equal measures.

"He's got Maggie's boyfriend."

"No kidding." April's heart thudded. How did he do that, when she and Sanchez had missed him? Son of a bitch. This wasn't going to go down well with Sergeant Joyce or Captain Higgins.

"No kidding. And get this. Braun wants his team there with him."

Oh, now they were a team, great. April looked at her watch. She'd been with George Dong all of twenty-three minutes. So much for dating. "Twenty minutes max," she promised.

Sanchez hung up without comment.

April pushed her way back to the table through an even larger crowd than had been there earlier. George Dong, the doctor, was smiling at her. She noticed he was not so very ordinary-looking when his mouth turned up at the edges. As she approached the table, she had a minute to wonder if he really played tennis or if he just carried the racquet around for show. Lot of people were sneaky like that.

"You have to go, right." It wasn't even a question. He knew.

"Sometimes it happens. I'm really sorry. The case I'm working—something's come up."

"It's okay. I know how it is," he said magnanimously.

But she knew it wasn't okay. All the way uptown, she had a really sick feeling about the whole thing. She didn't know if there was any way to make it all right with him. She figured the worst case was he'd bad-mouth her to his mother. His mother would bad-mouth her to her mother and her mother would kill her. Best case he wouldn't say anything.

# 37

ieutenant Braun was still wearing his powder-blue jacket. April spotted it across the squad room when she arrived. Braun was crowding Mike's desk, talking fast, and poking a finger at the air. He turned around at Mike's welcoming smile.

"Ah. Detective Woo," Braun said. A hint of sarcasm edged into his voice.

"Lieutenant Braun."

April's desk appeared to be unoccupied by anyone on the Sunday shift. She put her bag down on it. "What's happening?"

Mike raised a crooked eyebrow, jerking his head at the farthest desk down the line. A preppy-looking young man in a seersucker sport jacket seemed to have tied his body in a knot around a telephone, and was relating to it intimately.

April took him in. Light brown hair, blue eyes, a spattering of freckles across the nose. Medium build. Looked not unlike Dan Quayle, the former vice president. Five eleven to six foot. Where did Braun dig him up?

Braun nodded. "I'm pretty hot shit" was written all over him. He smirked and folded a fresh stick of gum into his mouth. "Name's Roger McLellan. Says he left town a week ago Friday. That's the day *before* Maggie got hit. Easy enough to check out. Claims he has no idea what this is all about, none at all. He consented to come down here to help us out with whatever our problem is. But lo and behold, the second he gets here he changes his mind and decides he better not say anything without his lawyer present. Hey, does that look like a guy who doesn't know what this is all about?"

"What kind of guy that young knows a lawyer? He knew the number by heart, didn't even have to look it up. I'm running a sheet on him," Mike added.

"Maybe they're friends," April murmured.

McLellan's body was still wrapped around the telephone receiver as he whispered into it heatedly.

"Who?" Braun looked at her.

"Him and the lawyer."

"Yeah, sure. Who's friends with a lawyer?"

They watched McLellan reluctantly put the receiver back on the phone and straighten up, visibly pulling himself together. When he approached the three detectives, it was with an air of nervous belligerence.

"My attorney is on his way. He told me to tell you I have nothing to say until he gets here. Where would you like me to wait?" McLellan glanced at the barred enclosure opposite the line of desks.

Braun shook his head at the holding cell. Not so fast. "We'll go downstairs. You want something? Cup of coffee?" he asked. Real friendly.

McLellan said no. They all trudged downstairs to the same questioning room April and Mike had used to interrogate Albert Block five days earlier. April guessed Braun still wasn't thrilled with his accommodations next to the men's room.

Peter Langworth, a near-twin of Roger McLellan's right down to the seersucker jacket, appeared forty-five minutes later.

"Okay, what's this all about?" the attorney demanded.

What a pair of tough guys. April glanced at Mike, who had one of his sudden coughs.

Braun introduced himself, then nodded at the chairs. "Why don't you gentlemen take a seat. Mike, go check on the sheet you were talking about." Braun turned his back on Sanchez.

Stunned, April caught Mike's eye. What was that little power-play all about? First he gets Sanchez down there on his day off and then he sends him out of the room. She watched Sanchez's retreating back. Not one to show his frustration, Mike closed the door quietly as he left.

"Sit down, Detective." Braun pointed to a chair, then waited for the sitting and scraping to stop. Finally he addressed Roger McLellan. "You know Maggie Wheeler?"

"She's not in the movement," McLellan said. "It's my thing. She has nothing to do with it."

Braun furrowed his brow at April. What movement?

"Why don't you tell us about it," he suggested.

"Maggie has nothing to do with it. She doesn't want to be involved—"

His lawyer leaned forward. "You don't have to say anything else, Roger. Lieutenant—"

"Braun."

"Lieutenant Braun. Why don't *you* tell *us* what this is about."

"Fine. Maggie Wheeler was murdered last Saturday night—"

The gasp was audible. "What?" McLellan croaked.

April's heart plunged. Shit. The guy didn't know.

Braun went on, unperturbed. "So we're looking into who killed her."

"Maggie's dead?" The lawyer paled. So he knew Maggie Wheeler, too.

"Yes, she's been dead for a week." Braun shot them a get-real look. "If you didn't know that, how come the lawyer?"

"I've been out of town. I didn't know," McLellan protested. He suddenly got interested in his bitten cuticles, examined one finger after another. "Jesus, all I wanted was to save it," he muttered. ". . . So that's why she never called me back."

"What?"

"You want to establish Mr. McLellan's whereabouts on the Saturday Maggie died, is that correct?" Langworth demanded.

"We want to know Mr. McLellan's relationship to the deceased as well as his whereabouts." Braun had not spit his gum out. April could see it wadded in his cheek.

"I was in Albany. We had an agreement. She promised me she would wait."

"Wait for what?" Braun's face did a little dance. It was clear neither patience nor tact was one of the Lieutenant's virtues.

"Just wait a second, Roger. You were in Albany. You don't have to say anything. Lieutenant—uh—"

"Braun. Like the coffeemaker."

"Maggie had a botched abortion, right?" McLellan looked angry.

"Unh-unh. Someone strung her up on the chandelier in the boutique where she worked."

"Oh, God. My baby," Roger McLellan cried. "She killed my baby." He shook his head back and forth, horrified. "How could she do it?"

"Who's she?"

"Maggie. You said she hung herself. Oh, God, that stupid bitch—"

"No, Mr. McLellan. She didn't kill herself. Somebody killed her."

McLellan slammed his hand on the table. "That's not possible."

"Okay, Roger." Braun dropped the "mister." "Why don't you tell us about your relationship with Maggie and why she might want to kill herself?"

The young man shook his head, as if he didn't want to, then started hesitantly. "We were friends. I don't know why she'd want to kill herself. . . . Well, she got pregnant. I don't know how it happened."

"You don't know how it happened." Braun jerked his head at April to underline that particular remark in her notebook. The man had the mental and emotional awareness of a tree. He didn't know how it happened. "Got that?"

April, the secretary, nodded, repeating, "He doesn't know how it happened."

The door opened. Sanchez handed a folder to Braun. Braun opened it, looked inside briefly, then passed it to April. Sanchez took a chair and made a silent drumbeat on the edge of it with his fingers while April looked over Roger McLellan's priors. Guy had over two dozen arrests for obstructing entrances to abortion clinics, harassing clients of abortion clinics, various types of vandalism to abortion clinics, demonstrations. One B and E.

"She wanted to kill my baby, and it looks like she did."

April finished reading and looked up. McLellan had hidden his face in his hands. His shoulders were shaking with some emotion or other. It wasn't clear exactly what his regrets were. He seemed more upset about the baby than Maggie. Langworth put his hand on Roger's arm to comfort —or restrain—him. It struck April that neither of them cared what had happened to Maggie Wheeler.

"Come on, Roger, I'll take you home."

"Not so fast. We're not finished here," Braun broke in.

"Look at him. He's in no shape to answer any more questions. In any case, he was out of town when Maggie, uh, died. You can see he doesn't know anything about it. *When* he feels better—*if* he feels better—you may come interview him in my office, but only subject to a specific written request."

"You want a subpoena, fine. We'll get a subpoena."

"Do that, but don't forget: If you try to harass a prominent leader of the right-to-life movement, we'll have the press all over you." Langworth stood up. So did his client.

The demure Asian lowered her eyes to hide her reaction of total disgust. Way to go, Braun. Well handled. Tactful. Now the possible suspect will walk out of the precinct, get his lawyer pal to rip his shirt and mess his hair, then call the press and scream police brutality. She shook her head, not daring to look at Mike. The two of them would have done a lot better.

# 38

ason stood on the patio, watching the fog dissipate from the trees below, listening to the nine new messages on his machine since the previous day. He checked his watch. Eight Sunday morning made it eleven on the East Coast. Odd. Three calls from Milicia.

"What is it?" Emma came out of the glass doors holding a glass of orange juice.

He frowned, shaking his head. "Nothing."

"That's what you always say." She turned around and headed back into the house. "It's always something, and you always say it's nothing."

"Hey, don't go away mad."

"I know. Just go away."

"I didn't mean that." He followed her through the doors, still holding the phone. A Dr. Wilbur Munchin from Austria was speaking to him on tape, asking about having some meaningful correspondence about his latest paper on listening. Herr Docktor Munchin was in New York and wanted to meet. Then Charles was telling him he was in Manhattan on his own for the weekend and wondered if Jason was free for dinner. Then the fourth call from Milicia, breathless, saying she was desperately worried about her sister. It seemed that she was always desperately worried about her sister. Maybe worrying about her sister was her thing. Milicia rang off, and his patient Douglas started telling him he was having a panic attack over flying to Chicago to his father's funeral. "Do I really have to go?" came the plaintive cry. Jason pushed the button to save the calls.

"Was that for me?" he asked, watching Emma drink the orange juice he'd watched her squeeze only moments before.

"No."

"You know I have to call in."

"You have only two speeds, Jason. On and on."

"I'm off now. Look." He put the phone back in its cradle. But he felt bad about Douglas, torn between the funeral and his terror of the skies. *Go,* he said silently. *Go for it, Douglas.*

"I guess I'd feel better if I knew who they were," Emma murmured. "All these unseen rivals for your love and attention."

"The whole point is that no one knows who they are," he replied mildly. It was better not to get defensive with Emma over old grievances. He refrained from adding no one was supposed to know who she was either. And her film career had changed all that.

Emma swallowed the last of the orange juice without offering him a single sip. She would never have done that in the past. He sighed. "I miss you," he said.

She went back into the kitchen without answering. After a minute or two he looked up Milicia's number in his telephone book and dialed it. In spite of Milicia's desperate eagerness to talk to him, she wasn't waiting for his call. He got her answering machine and spoke to her on tape. Same with Douglas.

He heard the sound of the juicer and perked up. He and Emma still had a whole day and night.


Sometime between five and five-thirty on Monday morning, Jason watched the dawn slowly suffuse Emma's room with a soft gray light from the skylight over the bed. A thick blanket of fog did not descend low enough to hide the branches of the eucalyptus tree that towered over the house on the side of the back patio.

In the Bronx, where he came from, very few trees dotted the sidewalks; every building was the same squat configuration of brick and concrete. Even in comparison to Riverside Drive, with its attractive park along the Hudson River, the town of Canyon Beach was beautiful. Still it seemed a pretty fragile setup.

The first night he slept there he could see the shape of the tree, far blacker than the sky, framed in the skylight, and had to resist thoughts of it crashing through the roof of the house in a light wind. He was afraid of an earthquake, a natural disaster that would end in total destruction of the entire West Coast and most particularly this tiny portion of it. The foundation of Emma's charming house seemed unbearably flimsy, the angle of the street going down to the beach way too steep.

And he knew his anxiety about the durability of the setting was a mask to cover his grief about the fragility of his marriage, indeed the whole structure of his life. Emma told him she hated his lifestyle, his philosophy of work and being, his rigid personality. And then she let him hold her, make love to her. Indeed, kept him up half the night with the other half of her ambivalence.

Jason lay still, listening to the quiet. He was used to sirens screaming all night long, used to hostile encounters on the street. Used to the pace and the dirt and the difficulty of getting around in New York. He lived in the psyches of people who couldn't fall in love, couldn't work, couldn't face their death or their life. He worked all the time without thinking much about where he lived or what he ate, how much his back hurt from sitting so still all day. His physical comfort was not a high priority to him.

He figured that was what Emma meant about his rigidity. Even in his sleep he did not escape the tortured world of his patients. He worried about them all the time. After a peaceful dinner three thousand miles away from her he felt compelled to call Milicia again. Just in case.

"Where are you?" she had demanded angrily.

His patients were often angry when he went away. They seemed to expect him to have no life but theirs to think about. Some of them punished him by hurting themselves. Women got pregnant. Men had accidents. Emma didn't bother to ask him what made him call, or what made him shake his head when he hung up.

The next morning, watching the sun rise, he wondered if the calls from Milicia were just another attempt to get his attention and control him. He wasn't particularly worried about it. He returned to his anxiety about an earthquake and all the things Emma had said in the past three days.

"It isn't worth the effort" was the last thing she said before falling asleep. "We're too different."

He knew it was stupid to tell Emma he would change. Nobody could really change very much. The best they could do was feel better about who they were.

"Nothing worthwhile comes without effort" was his wimpy reply.

"That's just shrink talk," she grumbled.

She didn't want to admit there was anything worthwhile about him. Still, he got the picture it was no picnic being a single woman in California.

"It's no different from high school," she had remarked the first day.

"Are you surprised?" he asked. They were walking on the beach, waiting for the sun to set. Emma glanced around at the crowd gathering at the water's edge.

"I was surprised none of these pretty people has anything to say. There's no one to talk to."

So. He was still good for something. It was his first soaring indication that he would not have to sleep in the loft.

Now, as the sun rose higher on the last day, he had to prepare himself for the separation. Emma was still asleep, her body pressing his. Once again they had been up much of the night. She'd fallen asleep with her head on his chest and her shoulder somewhat painfully crushing his arm.

He hadn't wanted to disturb her by moving. Now his arm and shoulder were numb, and he still didn't want to disturb her.

"I could go for this," he murmured.

He liked walking on the beach, liked the feeling of the place, the perfume of the sea and the foliage. The brilliance of the sun. He looked up at the eucalyptus tree, wondering how long it had been there.

"What?" she said sleepily.

"The whole thing. I like the whole thing, Emma. It's all great. I love you. If this is what you want, you should have it."

He was surprised when she answered. "So?"

Now he could see that she was awake, had been feigning sleep all along.

"So we could try to work it out. I could visit. You could visit. We don't have to make any decisions now."

She sat up suddenly, brushing her hair away from her face, fully awake, totally feminine and confusing, with a logic all her own.

"I don't know what to do. You've ruined me, Jason," she wailed. "I can't trust anybody but you anymore."

He was silent for a long time. It wasn't the most romantic thing he had ever heard. In fact, she made him feel like an old shoe. Still, he wouldn't forget the way she had loved him in the dark. And trust was more than just a place to start. It was central to everything.

"Yeah," he told her finally. "Me, too."

# 39

The owner of European Imports, an Israeli who owned a number of small boutiques around Manhattan, discovered the body of Rachel Stark at nine o'clock on Tuesday morning. Ari Vittleman made the rounds of his stores every weekday, never varying his routine. He always started at European Imports and worked his way downtown to the garment district, then to the Lower East Side in the shabby yellow van with the slogan ARI ENTERPRISES on the side. His travels took him back and forth across town in a zigzag pattern that always led to a hole-in-the-wall deli on Hester Street that had been in the same family and in the same location for over seventy-five years.

Though none of it was relevant to the case, Ari explained all this to the two officers from the 17th Precinct who responded to the call at nine-seventeen. Bald as an egg, with nearly forty extra pounds on his five-foot-seven-inch frame, Ari wore a shiny silver-gray suit, a heavy gold watch, and a large diamond ring on his right pinky finger. Right from the start he wanted it known that he was a conscientious, hardworking person whose appetite and ability to sleep would be affected for some time to come and whose confidence in New York and all things American was badly shaken.

He told the officers he had served in the Israeli Army during the Yom Kippur War and had seen a few things in his time. But nothing he had ever seen shocked him as much as the sight of his former employee hanging from an exposed pipe in his bathroom.

Over the weekend Rachel's head and neck had turned a greenish red under the makeup. After twelve hours, maggots had already emerged from the fly larvae laid in her eyes and nose within ten minutes of her death. By Monday afternoon beetles could be seen working at the dry skin of her arms and shoulders not hidden by the expensive size-fourteen evening gown she was wearing.

The smell of rotting meat had drawn Ari to the bathroom. Her body, blocking access to the toilet, forced him outside to the street, where he vomited loudly in the gutter next to his van before pulling himself together enough to call the police.

It took only twenty minutes for the commanding officer at the 17th Precinct to connect this homicide with the boutique murder at the Two-O. There are twenty-two thousand law enforcement agencies and no centralized homicide reporting in the United States. If the second case had been in Staten Island or New Jersey, or Long Island, or indeed nearly anyplace else, the authorities might not have put them together. Since the first was just across town, Lieutenant Braun, the officer in charge, was located within minutes and called in his troops.

April worked the eight-to-four shift on Monday. She had spent most of those hours interviewing a dozen reasonable-sounding, wholesome-looking right-to-lifers who claimed Roger McLellan was in Albany the weekend Maggie died. Several of them had sheets a mile long for cutting phone and power lines, spray-painting and stink-bombing abortion clinics, threatening doctors and clients. Even though no demonstration had occurred at the State House, or anywhere else in Albany, during the crucial time in question, April had not been able to shake their story that McLellan had been there.

On Tuesday her hours were four in the afternoon to twelve at night. She'd started studying for her Sergeant's exam at five A.M., her hundreds of pages of notes and exercises laid out all over the bed and floor. The phone rang at two minutes to ten.

"April?"

"Yeah?" she confirmed without enthusiasm.

"Mike. There's been another one."

The adrenaline kicked in like a shot, instantly filling her with energy. With just those words she knew what he meant. "Where?"

"Little boutique on Second Avenue. Fifty-fifth Street."

"I'm on my way." The location rang a bell. It was where the other friend of Maggie's lived, the one who didn't get out of bed.

# 40

By the time April got there, over fifteen vehicles and thirty cops jammed the area that was already roped off with sticky crime-scene tape. The two beat officers from the 17th Precinct who got there first and were responsible for securing the scene were still fighting a losing battle trying to keep interested colleagues out of European Imports. At least a dozen people had marched into the store to have a look. All had come out in a hurry, green as the corpse.

The ABC news van that April had seen the week before outside the bagel store on Fifty-sixth Street must have picked up the police call while they were getting breakfast. They were already setting up for a special broadcast.

"Get them out of here!" Lieutenant Braun barked at the beat officers, pointing to the news team.

Two other officers from the 17th were trying to direct the traffic. The street was a mess. Vehicles, including half a dozen blue-and-whites from each precinct, the news van, an EMS ambulance, and a crime-scene station wagon were all triple-parked on Second Avenue, slowing the traffic to a frustrated trickle.

April had double-parked her white Le Baron a block down and walked back. She heard Braun barking orders before she could see him. The first person she saw was Igor unloading his equipment—the cameras, evidence boxes, kits, and the vacuum. Good, they called for the same team that worked the other case. She waved.

Lieutenant Braun and Sergeant Sanchez were deep in conversation on the sidewalk in front of the store.

"Ah so, Detective Woo, thanks for joining us," Braun said without turning his head in her direction.

April nodded at him, brushing off the sarcasm with a smile. She

186

figured him for a heart attack in the not too distant future and comforted herself with the thought that someday she'd be the Lieutenant and he'd be dead.

"Morning, sir," she murmured. From downcast eyes she noted that Braun's stringy hair was thinning fast. He was wearing the same powder-blue jacket he'd worn the week before. It still looked clean. Maybe he had more than one.

"How ya doing, Mike?"

He looked at his watch, then at her. "You made good time."

"Yeah, I took the tunnel."

She didn't have to ask why they were hanging around on the street. The air conditioner was on, and the unmistakable odor of a not-so-recent death pumped out to the sidewalk like the frying garlic from Chinese restaurants.

"Nobody reported this all weekend?" she asked, wrinkling her nose.

"Nope. Apparently the owner turned on the air conditioner when he got here. He said he wanted to air out the store, didn't want to lose his merchandise," Mike told her.

"Oh." They'd all been contaminated often enough to know how persistently this odor lingered in the nostrils, on the skin, in whatever clothes they were wearing. It would cling to the walls and carpets of the store itself, like smoke after a fire.

"Did he touch anything else?" Igor, loaded down with cardboard evidence boxes, stopped beside them for a second.

"Igor, do you know Lieutenant Braun?" April asked.

"We're old friends," Braun said. "Keep-your-fucking-hands-behind-your-back Stan, we call him."

Igor looked offended. "It's the rules," he muttered. "Some of you people can't keep your hands to yourself. Mess up the whole thing. It's not a hard one to keep your hands in your pockets."

He jerked his head at Ari Vittleman, standing at a safe distance down the block, surrounded by officers physically preventing ABC from attempting to get their story.

"Did he touch anything else? I got to know."

"He says no." Braun turned to April. "He says they close at seven on Saturdays. He figures it happened about then."

"Why? That was the storm day, wasn't it? She could have closed earlier." April looked around at the proximity of other stores. Who could have seen what in that rain? She saw the boutique had the kind of metal barricade that pulled down. Had it been down when the owner came? Would the neighbors have noticed anyone going in, coming out at closing time? From here she could see the plumbing supply store and the apartment above, where Maggie's friend lived. The guy who claimed he hadn't seen her in years but whose name and number were in her phone book. Her mind whirled with questions.

"That's what your pal here said. What are you, hotshots or something?" Braun demanded.

"Yeah. Or something." Sanchez smiled at April.

Braun shot her an appraising look. "Ready to go in?"

"Any time." April took out her notebook and shifted her bag from one shoulder to another.

"Clasp your hands behind your back," Igor called over his shoulder.

"What a piece of work. How am I supposed to take notes with my hands behind my back?" she muttered.

"It's the rules." Braun laughed at his joke.

April moved inside the store. She would take notes of everything—the weather, the time, the placement of each article in the small store, the whole setup. She'd never forgotten the example given in a John Jay class of a cut-and-dried homicide that was lost in court because the two detectives on the case couldn't agree whether an article of clothing, totally irrelevant to the case, had been on the bed or the floor of the room next to where the crime had been committed. The defense attorney convinced the jury if the police couldn't be trusted to agree on what was at the scene of a crime, none of the rest of their "evidence" could be trusted either. The guy got off.

April moved toward the smell.

"You going to be okay, Detective?" Braun asked.

"Yessir," April replied. Lot of them didn't know it, but after about three minutes in a very bad smell the olfactory nerves went numb. All those people who kept running in and out of horrendous crime-scene stenches for fresh air got hit with the same blast of nausea each time they returned. Anybody who lived with the pungent pickling and drying rotting smells of the Orient knew that.

But when she looked through the open door, she could not control a spasm of revulsion. This was worse than Maggie Wheeler. Clearly, it had been hot in there. The girl's body was not in good condition. It had already begun to swell from the gases forming inside. Decomposition works from the inside out.

Aware of Braun behind her, gauging her reaction, April pinched her nose and breathed through her mouth, her internal camera continuing to click. What was she seeing here? What was the story? On the grimy bathroom floor under the hanging body there appeared to be some congealed blood along with the other fluids that had leaked out of her orifices after death. April looked for an open wound that would have bled. She didn't see one. Several two-to-three-inch patches of blistered skin were visible on the dead girl's neck and shoulders, but April had seen that before and knew they were post-mortem artifacts. Bacteria was eating away the tissues under the skin.

April noted that the rope the girl was hanging by appeared to be the same kind used in the Wheeler murder. Obviously the huge black evening gown on the small body, and the tinges of blue and red makeup, partially dissolved and further distorted by feeding beetles, told the same twisted tale that was understood only by the teller. Little girl dressed up as a big girl. Strangled. But what if it were a little boy dressed up as a big girl?

She remembered Ducci's suggestion that they were looking for a transvestite. But transvestites didn't kill. So, who was it? Where did this put them with McLellan now? As April wondered if anyone had bothered to call Ducci, the cop pushed into the space, stomach first.

"Hello, pretty one. How's it going?"

She shook her head, backing out so he could take her place.

"Clasp your hands behind your back," Igor admonished from the front of the store, where he'd begun dusting for fingerprints.

"Oh, fuck off," the Duke told him.

"Nice talk." Braun turned to Sanchez, who was busy taking notes. "Well?"

"Looks similar. No marks on the door. No signs of struggle in the store. Similar rope, not tied correctly for a suicide. Although, if the other hadn't come first, this might have the appearance of a suicide."

"Yeah?" Braun moved toward the door, hot-footed it outside. Sanchez followed him.

"She could have jumped off the toilet," Sanchez said.

"Sure, and dressed herself up like that first."

"I wonder where McLellan was Saturday night."

April watched Ducci take in the scene. They were honored. His workload was too heavy for him to get out much anymore. For a half hour . he worked with Igor and Mako, collecting and labeling, putting items in paper bags and then cardboard boxes. Like April, Ducci seemed puzzled about the blood on the floor. But, not to worry, blood wasn't his business.

After the body had been sketched and photographed, Ducci lifted the black silk skirt, looking for a wound. All he could see was an irregular semicircle of small marks on the corpse's right ankle.

"Looks like a bite," he remarked loud enough to be heard in Jersey.

April looked where he pointed. From the showroom she could hear the sound of Sanchez's derisive laugh at this outrageous speculation. "Oh, sure, oh, sure. Four days later on a decomposed body he can identify a bite mark."

"Looks like the work of insects," April said.

Ducci straightened and pointed to the mottled hands. "That's insects. Just a mess with no particular pattern wounds. Here, there's a distinct pattern."

April nodded, though she had her doubts. Ducci was a trace man. It was up to the M.E. to tell them what happened to the body. Where the blood on the floor came from and what made the marks on the hands, the shoulders, and the ankle.

Sanchez called her from the street. "The Lieutenant wants us to go home now."

April took one last look around and closed her notebook.

# 41

Jason sat in his swivel desk chair. Milicia was opposite him in the chair he used with patients who liked to lie on his leather sofa. Her face was very pale. He could see a muscle twitch in her cheek. She was wearing a conservative suit and very little makeup. The sensitive skin under her eyes was dark and bruised-looking. She'd lost a few pounds. The stress in her face, and what appeared to be sleep deprivation, made her look vulnerable and seriously frightened. Jason could feel his body stiffen in defense against any sympathy that would work against his being able to help her.

"What is your real concern, Milicia?" he asked, getting to the core of the matter right at the start.

"I told you I was afraid Camille would hurt somebody, and now I know she has." Her words were angry. She spat them out at him, showing him how furious she still was at his being out of town when she needed him. She regarded him accusingly, as if it were his fault that it had taken twenty-four hours to make contact. He knew it was the time lapse she would count, not the attempts he made to reach her when she was out.

Milicia had insisted that she needed to see him Tuesday, his first day back in the office. There was no putting her off. In order to work it out, he'd had to reschedule his appointment with Jenny, the woman who did his secretarial work and bookkeeping.

He was used to hearing his patients accuse him of everything under the sun. He was concerned by the way Milicia looked, but unmoved by her rage.

"You think . . . Camille . . . has hurt someone?" he said flatly, careful to keep the disbelief out of his voice.

"*Killed* someone, Jason. Don't you listen to the news?"

He nodded. Of course he did. "So?"

She stared at him as if he were retarded, or worse. "There's been another boutique murder."

"Oh?" Her face was flushed. He could see she had begun to sweat.

"Just like the one last week," she prompted. "Right here on Columbus. Don't you remember?"

He nodded. "Salesgirl in a boutique, wasn't it?" He'd read about it.

"I had a feeling then. I had this really creepy feeling." Milicia covered her face with her fingers so he couldn't see her. "I just had a feeling Camille had something to do with it. And now there's been another one. The truth is, I'm terrified, and I feel responsible."

She dropped her hands and confronted him, green eyes flashing. "I came to you for help. I told you all about Camille, and you let this happen."

Jason didn't realize he'd been holding his breath until he let it out. He glanced at the clock on the table. He didn't have much time to calm her down.

"Milicia, let's go back a little. You didn't tell me when we met the first two times that you thought your sister was a murderer."

"How could I? You didn't even believe that she was sick."

Had he missed something here? Jason thought back to his notes, quickly reviewed them in his mind, shook his head. Milicia had been vague. She said she came to him because she wanted her sister to get treatment, wanted her removed from her boyfriend's influence and taken care of in a safe environment. But she had not been able to give any convincing reasons for intervention. And certainly no legal ones. It was very hard to put people away. You couldn't do it just because they were inconvenient.

At the time of Milicia's visits, Jason had a feeling her assessment of her sister's violent tendencies was an afterthought. Milicia hadn't known what constituted symptoms of potential violence. Certainly, she didn't mention the homicide in the neighborhood as part of her concern. If she was really worried about the boutique murder, why didn't she tell him about that right away?

"Milicia, I must confess. I was away this weekend, and I read the papers only briefly this morning. I didn't see any article about another—"

"It was on the news a little while ago. I heard it in the office," Milicia said. Defiantly, she crossed her legs the other way, showing a lot of thigh in the process.

"It happened today?" Jason frowned. But Milicia had called him on Sunday, starting very early in the morning. How could she have known if it happened today? "But you called me on Sunday."

"I called you on Sunday because she disappeared on Sunday. I told you she's been acting very strange lately. So when I couldn't reach her, I was concerned. In fact, I was frantic. Camille is autistic, catatonic—I don't know what you call it. Sometimes she can't move at all. She just sits like a stone with no reflexes. . . . She calls it soul death. And then she goes kind of wild afterward."

What was going on here? Jason's face was perfectly still, like Camille's in soul death. He was trying to figure it out. The scene wasn't playing for him. He didn't know where it was wrong.

"Have you located her since?" he asked.

"Yes. She's come back. She won't tell me where she was. I'm so scared." She looked scared.

Jason drew a breath. "What makes you think Camille is responsible for these—murders?"

"I just do, just the whole picture, the sort of killings they are. She liked to hang our dolls. In a row. Sometimes she put my clothes on the dolls and then hung them. I told you that, didn't I? Dressed them up and hung them by their necks."

Jason's head had begun to throb, but he didn't move.

"She's obsessed with death, and with hanging. She says she feels like she's choking. Often she can't eat anything because she thinks she'll choke on the food. Sometimes she chews one bite for an hour. It's disgusting to watch." Milicia's agitation became extreme as she described it.

"Look, Milicia," Jason said gently. "I can understand that all of this is disturbing. But murder is going a very long way. The two, uh, murders you've told me about happen to coincide with your own anxiety about your sister. It's an unfortunate coincidence. In any case, all the studies have shown that most murders are committed by men. Only a tiny percentage of murders are committed by women, and they're almost never stranger murders. Look, I'm not a detective, but I haven't heard any compelling evidence—"

"But I *know*—"

"What do you know?"

"I know Camille. You don't. Sometimes you just *know* things." Milicia thrust out her chin. The twitch had moved up to her temple.

He watched it jump. It was true that he didn't know Camille, and his not knowing Camille made it even more important that he be extremely careful with this. Milicia had her own agenda. He decided to try something else. He'd float an interpretation. If he was right, she'd calm down. If he was wrong, she'd dismiss it out of hand. Then he'd know what to do.

"You've told me Camille is angry," he said gently. "What she does is experience her emotions as murderous and dangerous. But that is very far from acting on those impulses. You've also told me that Camille's angry feelings incapacitate her. She's overwhelmed and becomes immobile. People like that are not capable of any action at all, much less very complicated and stressful acts of violence. Having murderous feelings is kind of like having fantasies—watching movies of oneself killing someone, smashing a car, setting a building on fire. They're wishes about committing violent acts. Wishes are not reality."

Yet as he spoke, Milicia shook her head. "You're wrong about this. You're talking theory. You're telling me what you've read in studies. I've seen you do this before. You push yourself away from what you don't want to hear. The bottom line, *Doctor* Frank, is if my sister is killing people, and if you don't do something about it, you're responsible for murder."

The woman was very smart. A door in Jason's mind closed, and another one opened. He'd made his judgment. He would no longer try to manage the patient. He'd manage the situation. Abruptly his manner altered. His warmth was gone.

"I think we can change the subject just a bit, Milicia. You've been trying to persuade me that your sister has actually committed murder. Let's presume that what you say is true. In that case, I must notify the police immediately."

"If I wanted to go to the police, I would have gone to the police in the first place," Milicia retorted, but the tension in her face began to ease. Her color slowly returned.

"I didn't want this to happen," she murmured. "Is there no other way?"

"In a matter like this it's not a judgment call," Jason said firmly. He wasn't going to negotiate. "I'm not questioning whether we should go to the police. You want me to accept your suspicions. All right, I do. Where life is at stake, I have absolutely no choice but to go to the authorities."

"You mean it, don't you?" Milicia's cheeks were red now.

"Yes, I do."

"Well then, it's out of my hands." She sat back, soothed in an instant.

Jason could feel something like a sigh of relief escape her, and suddenly her abstract design came into crisp focus for him.

"I don't want Camille to suffer," Milicia was saying, completely in control again. "I had hoped we could just take care of her quietly. But now . . ." She made a gesture of helplessness. "You say we have no choice. Calling the police is the only thing to do."

Jason thought of April Woo and said nothing. He had every confidence the police would get to the bottom of this, and a whole lot faster than he could. He couldn't talk to Milicia's sister unless she came in to see him. The police had instant access to anyone. He watched Milicia's face. Now he got it. This was what Milicia had wanted all along.

Milicia had wanted police involvement, but she couldn't get it on her own. She felt she needed an authority figure behind her. But what was the pathology? Was Milicia a variation on the kind of people who confess to crimes they didn't commit out of guilt for unrelated acts of their own? And because they crave attention. Did she crave attention? Was the twist here that she wanted to turn her sister in to the police for something the sister most likely did not do in order to punish the sister? Or did Milicia figure this kind of stunt was the route she needed to take to draw attention to the illness of a sibling she couldn't control?

Jason's brow furrowed deeply. He was well aware that he had been manipulated by Milicia in a very big way. But there was always the possibility, remote as it seemed to him at the moment, that the sister had committed the crimes.

As Jason's eyes bored into Milicia, her blush deepened.

"When do you want to do it?" she said, her voice throaty.

He continued to study her, looking for an answer. "Right now," he said coldly. "Immediately. I know a detective. Do you want to call her, or do you want me to call her?"

"A woman?" Milicia laughed.

"Yes, and very good at her job."

Jason hadn't spoken to April Woo since May, in the debriefing after Emma's rescue. But he thought about her often. He felt no hesitation about calling her now, in a situation like this.

"You do it." Milicia's voice sank to a whisper. Once again she covered her face with her fingers. "I couldn't. I'd be incoherent. I'd break down. Poor Camille. I hate to think what will happen to her."

"Fine." Jason reached for his address book and looked up the number. Even months later he realized he still knew it by heart. He glanced at the skeleton clock. It was five-thirty. Sometimes Detective Woo was there after four o'clock, and sometimes she wasn't.

# 42

It took four hours to process the Rachel Stark crime scene and get the body removed by the Medical Examiner. By the time April and Sanchez had finished their own notes and interviewed Ari Vittleman, the stench of death hung over them both, eclipsing even Mike's powerful aftershave. If they didn't do something about it, the reek would sit there in the sinuses and in the hollows of the hair shafts for a long, long time. Braun wanted to leave an hour before, but Mike and April weren't finished then. Braun wouldn't go if they didn't. Now they were ready.

"Let's go," April said, turning toward her car.

"Salsa?" Mike suggested, falling into step beside her.

She shook her head, frowning. "No way. Szechuan is much better."

"Nah, you have to eat too much of it," Mike argued. "Salsa's better. One shot goes right in there and blows the shit away. Chase that with a few peppermints—you know, the red and white striped kind—hey, and everything's cool."

They came to where Mike had parked the gray unmarked car. Braun was leaning against it, waiting for them.

"What?" The Lieutenant was staring at them suspiciously, his beaky face all pinched in annoyance at how long they had taken.

"Just a small debate over the best method for clearing the sinuses," Mike said, rattling his car keys.

"Horseradish, no question. You folks got a change of clothes at the shop?"

"Yessir."

"Then clean up. We got some people to talk to." Braun didn't get in the gray car with Mike. An unmarked black car, like the kind the FBI favored, was waiting for him. At the crook of his finger it pulled up to within an inch of where he was standing. "Say an hour," Braun said, getting in and slamming the door.

"So what did he hang around for if it wasn't the ride?" April asked.

"Nice guy," Mike remarked. "Doesn't look like he trusts us."

"Does he return in another blue jacket?" April muttered.

Mike shrugged, then cocked his head down the block, where an unsuspecting female beat officer was getting ready to tag April's Le Baron.

"Oh, no." April sprinted down Second, reaching her car with her badge out just as the officer raised pen to pad.

The officer, young, bulging out of her department-issue trousers, glanced at the badge. "Sorry, Detective. Nice car." She moved on.

Twenty minutes later April was showering at the precinct, her hair lathered for the second time with lemon shampoo. Mike might be right about peppermint after chilis, but she would swear by lemon soap for the hair. She let the water scald her skin, then got out. She didn't like lingering in the moldy shower. No telling how many kinds of fungus and rot a person could catch there. She changed into the white shirt, slightly wrinkled black pants, and black silklike jacket she stowed in her locker for emergencies. She'd been working off the chart since she caught the homicide that morning. Her desk in the squad room was now hers, and she was officially on duty.

The call from Jason Frank came in at five thirty-five, just after she had returned from a testy meeting with two warring factions that pretended to be on excellent terms. Sergeant Joyce with eight of her detectives faced off against Lieutenant Braun, who had returned in an unflattering brown jacket missing its middle button, bringing with him three new homicide detectives from downtown.

Sergeant Joyce and her people thought they were at square one on this thing. Braun and his people were pulling in Roger McLellan and Albert Block again, looking for a connection there. Nobody was in a good mood. April had begun to type up her notes, when her phone rang.

"Detective Woo," she said, picking it up on the first ring.

"Detective Woo, this is Jason Frank."

"Well, how are you, Doctor?"

"I'm just fine. I'm with someone, though, so I'm going to get right to the point."

"Fine. What's up?" She reached for a pen.

"I have someone in my office who's talking about the murder that was all over the papers last week and the one that's, uh—apparently on the news today. I haven't heard it myself." The words came out matter-of-fact. The doctor was as coldly professional as April remembered.

"I don't want to speak too quickly. I know how many calls you get. But this is a little different." He paused.

April realized she was holding her breath. "No problem, go ahead. Take all the time you need."

"The person with me is a young woman, articulate and well-groomed, no psychiatric history. She came to see me with a concern about her sister, who does have a history. I have never seen or examined her sister. You with me?"

"All the way."

"So I don't know the validity of the concern. I'm passing this along for what it's worth. The woman with me believes her sister may actually have committed these murders. I've discussed it with her at some length. The major basis for this belief has to do with the sister's motivational state and past psychiatric history. There are no other relevant positives."

"I see," April said. Instantly she understood what he was getting at. Dr. Frank was telling her that in his professional assessment of the situation, there was no evidence to suggest the sister was involved. But he was worried all the same.

Anybody else would have stayed on the phone asking dozens of questions. In this case April didn't have to. She had absolute confidence in the caller.

"I think the next step is for me to speak with this person, Doctor. Can I set up an appointment?" April asked.

"Yes," Jason said. "Hold on, please."

A few seconds later a hesitant female voice came on the line.

"Hello?" The voice was quavery and a little hoarse.

"This is Detective Woo. Dr. Frank has told me you have some information about the boutique slayings." With no reluctance she used the press's name for them.

"Well, I don't know. I'm not sure . . ."

"That's all right," April interjected quickly. "When are you available? Let's just meet and you could fill me in on what you know about the situation."

More hesitation. Then, "I guess I could do that."

"How about now?" April suggested.

This time there was a long wait. April could hear muffled sounds on the other end. She guessed Jason was talking his patient into it.

"All right," the woman said reluctantly.

"Twentieth Precinct. Eighty-second, between Columbus and Amsterdam. It's not far from where you are. What's your name?"

"Milicia Honiger-Stanton."

It sounded familiar. April's heart, which had picked up its pace with Jason's first words, started racing now. "What's your sister's name?"

"Camille—Honiger-Stanton."

April didn't dare ask what Camille looked like, how tall she was. And by the way, did she have red hair and a dog? All April said was "How soon can you be here?"

As soon as she hung up, she gestured at Mike, who was plugged into the phone himself, his hair slicked back, his Mexican tan tinged faintly pink from his own hot shower, and his whole self reeking once again of every fruit and spice known to the Caribbean.

He raised his eyebrow, but didn't hang up.

*We've got a connection to the L. Mango guest book.* She wrote it on a pad and shoved it across the desk.

"No shit." He banged the receiver down without saying good-bye.

# 43

April's mouth fell open in surprise when the tall redhead entered the squad room with a beat officer behind her. The redhead stopped short by the scarred wooden bench just inside the door. A fat woman in a purple dress took up most of the bench with several shopping bags and a battered suitcase. When she saw the newcomer, the fat woman moved over, filling the rest of the space. April glanced over at Sanchez. He was staring, too.

Even if April hadn't been called by the Desk Sergeant downstairs, she would have known instantly this was the woman Dr. Frank had in his office. She saw the woman hesitate and Officer Linda Gargiola's mouth move. The uniform was about half the redhead's size. She was heavily weighed down with all the equipment hung around her waist.

April got to her feet. On the first day of the second major homicide, the room was chaotic. All nine desks by the window were occupied. The holding cell harbored a huge white male with a number of lurid tattoos on his arms, a beer belly, and a greasy ponytail that trailed halfway down his back. At the newcomer's entrance, the clamor stopped as everyone turned to look at her.

Then, in an apparent change of heart, the woman turned and pushed past a surprised Linda Gargiola, retreating to the hall. April followed at a run. In the hall she found Linda trying to restrain Milicia Honiger-Stanton without actually touching her.

"Wait a minute. Is something the matter? Can I help you?" Officer Gargiola tried to prevent her charge from leaving.

April stepped into the scene.

"Miss Honiger-Stanton, there's nothing to worry about. I'm Detective Woo. I've spoken to Dr. Frank about the situation, and I've been expecting you," April said firmly.

At the reference to her doctor Milicia stopped. "How'd you know—?" She didn't finish the sentence. *Who I am.*

Sergeants Joyce and Sanchez, Aspirante and Healy crowded out into the hall, jostling each other as they pushed through the door. The sudden quiet in the squad room acted like a drop in barometric pressure sucking Sergeant Joyce out of her office. The Sergeant's color was high. April imagined this was the way she looked after a few beers.

April glared at them. "Give us a little air, will you?"

"Ah." Milicia looked at the cluster of detectives. "I think I made a mistake. . . ."

"No, you're in the right place. I'm Sergeant Joyce." Sergeant Joyce moved forward in a nice, friendly manner. "Thanks, fellas, you can go now," to Healy and Aspirante. They backed off, scowling.

Milicia shook her head. "I don't know what I was thinking. I feel dizzy. . . ."

"It's all right. I know this place looks a little alarming if you're not used to it." Sergeant Joyce smiled a nice, friendly smile, turning to April with a "where did this come from" look.

Mike came out and joined the little group in the hall.

"This is Sergeant Sanchez," April said, frowning at Sergeant Joyce to make her go away. The squad supervisor wasn't going anywhere. They stood there, a tight little knot, with all sorts of people wandering back and forth around them. Everyone was staring at the striking redhead.

"Why don't we go downstairs, where we can talk?" April suggested.

"All of you?" Milicia said faintly.

"Yeah, we like to keep an eye on each other," Joyce said amiably. "Would you like some coffee?"

Milicia shook her head. "I have to be somewhere. I don't have much time."

"Fine, let's get to it, then." Sergeant Joyce led the parade downstairs. April and Mike followed them.

"Where's Braun?" April asked softly.

"Upstairs."

"Think we should get him?"

Mike shook his head.

Sergeant Joyce opened the door to an empty questioning room. "Here we are. Have a seat."

Milicia's green eyes raked the room. It was even hotter than upstairs.

The paint was peeling off the walls. Plastic chairs were placed around the kind of rectangular table they have in school lunchrooms. Under the table was an overflowing wastebasket that smelled of ancient coffee. Sergeant Sanchez placed a tape recorder on the table. Milicia turned and faced them, her face white, as if she'd gotten a whole lot more than she bargained for.

"Get her some water, will you, Detective?"

April went out to the water cooler in the hall. Only one paper cup was left. The water was tepid. She filled the cup and came back. Milicia sat on one side of the table. Opposite were Mike and Sergeant Joyce. The tape recorder didn't have its wheels turning yet.

Milicia took the paper cup but didn't sample the water in it. Her face took on a remote expression.

"Thank you for coming. I have the greatest respect for Dr. Frank," April said with a quick look at Sergeant Joyce, who had no idea who this person was. "Start with your name and your address, then tell the story any way you want."

Milicia shook her head. "This wasn't ever what I had in mind," she said softly, staring at the tape machine.

Mike was closest to it. He pushed the button, told the machine their location, the date, the time of day, the names of the people in the room— except Milicia's.

"Would you tell us your name and the date?" Sergeant Joyce prompted.

"Milicia Honiger-Stanton," Milicia said. "You already said the date." Her green eyes filled with tears.

"Never mind the date." April wished Sergeant Joyce would self-destruct. Why couldn't she just let the woman tell her story? "It's okay. Go ahead."

Milicia took a ragged breath. "I went to see Dr. Frank because I have a troubled sister. I thought she needed some—supervision."

She stared down at her hands. April noticed she wore no jewelry. "She's more than troubled. She's . . . well, sick. I don't know the word for whatever it is. I thought she needed to be in a hospital, where she couldn't hurt herself or anybody else. It's a long story. My parents always used to take care of her when she had a—crisis." An expression of anger crossed her face.

"But they died a year—no, two years ago. Since then she's—deteriorated. Drugs, alcohol, fits of rage. She lives with a real—" Milicia couldn't find a word of dislike strong enough for the person her sister lived with.

"See, I went to Dr. Frank because I thought you could, you know, put people like that away. Someplace safe. Camille cut someone's face once. She's come to my office and made scenes, oh, a hundred times. I'm an architect. It's disruptive. She threatens me. I'm afraid. See, when we were little, she used to play these games. Dress up and hang the dolls, break their necks and say they were me. Know what I mean?"

Mike looked at April, but no one said anything. Sergeant Joyce had deep horizontal furrows between her eyes that made her look like a mole blinded in the daylight.

Sure, they knew what she meant.

"So when the first girl got killed—that poor girl." Milicia sniffed. "I knew it was a warning for me. It was me she wanted to kill. So I had to tell somebody. I had to do something about Camille . . . I didn't want this." She looked at them, one at a time, tears welling in her eyes.

"I didn't want this. I thought it could be taken care of quietly. But he wouldn't listen to me." She shook her head. "He just wouldn't listen."

Milicia's composure finally cracked. Her tears fell unchecked. April got up to find some tissues. When she returned, Milicia was still crying.

On the other side of the table Sergeants Joyce and Sanchez sat as still as they could, bursting with unasked questions. They waited while Milicia dabbed at her eyes.

"What are you going to do?" she asked finally.

"Check it out," April said softly. "We're going to ask you a few more questions, and then we're going to check it out."

"Would you like a sandwich? Some coffee, tea?" Sanchez asked, looking like he could use some himself.

"What?" Milicia blew her nose delicately, pulling herself together.

"Something to eat or drink?" Sergeant Joyce said.

Milicia slung her bag over her shoulder, taking a deep breath as if she'd gotten a tough job over with. "Oh, no. I've got to go. I have to be someplace."

Sergeant Joyce shook her bulldog head. *Not a chance, baby. In a homicide investigation, you don't have to be anywhere else until we say so.* She turned to April, cocking her head. *You tell her.*

April nodded at her supervisor, getting the message. "Well, just one or two more things," she murmured. "We're not quite through yet."

Mike checked the reel. Nearly finished. He switched off the recorder and turned the cassette over, then punched the play button and told the machine who was in the room, the day, date, and time. The way they played it, it was his turn to ask the questions.

# 44

Braun's face was pinched with anger. The Lieutenant took an aggressive stance in front of Captain Higgins's desk, even though the Captain had offered him a seat when he'd slammed in moments earlier. "They were going out on a new lead without me." His voice had the whiny quality of a kid who hadn't been picked for the team.

Higgins checked his watch. He grimaced. "You've got two minutes to tell me what you've got, and then I have to meet the press. It better be something."

"Well, I don't know if it's something or not." Braun glanced over at Mike, who never appeared fazed by much of anything. "Your people hold out on me. We don't like that."

"Is that the royal we, or do you have some special meaning?" Higgins carefully smoothed his tie. "Look, as far as *we're* concerned, our people are your people. We're all the same people." He inclined his head to Sanchez. "Are you holding out on Lieutenant Braun, Sergeant?"

"No, sir." Mike's mustache closed over his lips.

"I don't ever want to hear that you're holding out on the Lieutenant. We're all the same team."

"Sergeant Joyce?" Captain Higgins tilted his head the other way.

"Yes, sir." Sergeant Joyce stood one step behind Sanchez and Braun. It was clear she had combed her hair and tried to repair her face for this meeting. Apparently she knew that without a little makeup, she tended to resemble a codfish fillet.

April watched her supervisor struggle to maintain a strict air of neutrality, her hope for support from her C.O. revealed only in the shiny pink lip gloss on her mouth. The rest of her fire-hydrant-shaped body, packed into a forest-green jacket and skirt, was rigid with hate.

"Are you holding out on Lieutenant Braun in any way?"

Sergeant Joyce took a step forward. She was the supervisor of the squad. April could read her thought that she should have been standing ahead of Sanchez, not behind him.

"No, sir."

Higgins glanced quickly at April. Her lips twitched in a small smile at the triumph of her being in this exalted place for the very first time. The Captain nodded, but didn't say anything. Apparently he didn't consider her high enough in the hierarchy to hold out on Braun. She lowered her eyes in the classic gesture of submission, unable to resist the reflex action. Ten thousand thoughts juggled for position in her brain.

April couldn't help thinking that ambition, like the sucker-covered tentacles of an octopus, encircled them all, clouding every issue. And she wasn't immune in the least. Her own ambition had her slated to spend the first ten hours of the day studying for her Sergeant's exam. And the next eight hours on the job. The discovery of Rachel Stark's decomposing body had cost her precious study time. Unless somebody else was found dead at the exact moment her exam was scheduled, she'd have to take it anyway, prepared or not. And if she failed, she wouldn't get another chance at it for a long, long time.

The other four had their own careers to worry about. And there they were, jockeying for position. Three of them had spent the day very close to a former human being, someone who had a mother and a father, two brothers—way out on Long Island. Somebody who had had a life and hadn't wanted to lose it. The stench of the former Rachel Stark would stay with them for quite a while no matter how hard they tried to wash it off and ignore it. And yet they were not exactly willing to unite to find her killer.

"Okay, so what have you got?" Higgins asked.

Braun scowled at Sergeant Joyce because he couldn't attack Captain Higgins. "You tell me."

"So far we have found no connection between the suspects in the Wheeler case and Rachel Stark—"

"And this new lead?"

Sergeant Joyce hesitated. "Some kind of mental case. Female, lives across the street from European Imports; name's in the guest book of The Last Mango. It's just a lead."

"And the informant's the sister. A redhead, I heard," Braun said angrily. "I didn't get a chance to question her."

"Uh-huh," Higgins said. "Where does that get us?"

He directed his question at April. After a moment she realized the Captain expected her to answer. She wasn't sure exactly what he meant.

"Two long red hairs were found on the body of Maggie Wheeler, sir." She articulated carefully, didn't want him to think she had an accent or anything.

"Yes, yes," he said, impatient now. "I know that. So work it out. You got twenty-four hours to put it together. Two is too many."

"I can't work under these conditions," Braun protested. "I don't want my people undercut like this. We get a lead, *I* follow it up. *I* ask the questions."

"I don't have a problem with that. Do you have a problem? Sergeants?" Higgins searched the faces of Joyce and Sanchez.

Yeah, they had a big problem. They thought Braun was an asshole. He had handled that preppy McLellan with all the skill of a pile driver, had the analytical skills of an unprogrammed computer. It was their case. They didn't want any assistance from Homicide to solve it.

Mike's mustache twitched. "No, sir," he said.

Sergeant Joyce chewed off her lip gloss. It was clear to April that Joyce couldn't tell whether her team had won the skirmish or not.

# 45

The folding metal gate across the front of the chandelier shop was locked with a heavy padlock, but somewhere deep inside the store a light was on. Lieutenant Braun reached his hand through a diamond formed by the steel grate and pressed the doorbell. Sergeant Roberts, one of Braun's people, waited beside him. Like Braun, Roberts was wiry, with gray skin and lackluster, thinning brown hair. His beaky, humorless features suggested a poor digestion.

After a short wait they tried again, then walked the few steps to the entrance of the residence located above the shop. Braun rang the bell there. Then he leaned backward and looked up. The lights were off on the second and third floors of the building. Roberts stepped back and copied Braun's action. Now they both knew the lights were off. But that didn't necessarily mean no one was home. Twilight was only just beginning. The two men took a step closer to each other, put their heads together, and conferred.

In the maroon unmarked car on the corner, Mike's stomach gurgled. He coughed to cover the sound. "This really sucks."

April hadn't heard him use the term before. She couldn't stop the confirming laugh from jumping out of her mouth. "Yeah."

In fact, the situation with Braun and his people sucked so much that in the last few days Captain Higgins and Sergeant Joyce had started looking pretty good to her. Not until that afternoon had it occurred to her to think well of Sergeant Joyce. Then Dr. Frank called. It wasn't often that a civilian from an old case came back with a lead on an unrelated new case. But then, a lot of things happened out there on the streets all the time that weren't supposed to happen. Having to sit in a car and watch two homicide people from downtown follow a lead in their case was just one.

April didn't like to remember that Sergeant Joyce had not opposed her investigating her first big case. And there was one other little thing April didn't like thinking about. After Sergeant Joyce had her picture in the paper and took all the credit for the Chapman case that April had solved with Dr. Frank's help, she had suggested April start thinking about taking the Sergeant's test.

Sergeant Joyce had stood over April's desk, scowling, and spat out, "You're ready," as if all along April had been nothing more than some turkey roasting in the oven.

At the time April didn't know what to think of it. Was the Sergeant pulling rank, mocking her? Was she hoping April would take the test and fail? Failing would cause April to lose face. Succeeding would get her reassigned.

But now April considered another alternative. What if her superior acted like a shit all the time just to challenge the people around her to do things they didn't think they could do?

Braun and Roberts were taking a long time deciding no one was home.

April sighed. She didn't want to reassess her opinion of Sergeant Joyce. It put a new spin on the Sergeant's exam. What if Sergeant Joyce actually wanted April to succeed and April let her down?

Braun and Roberts hit the bell for about the tenth time. By now they were developing the defeated look that forecast some ominous new action.

"What will they think of now?" April muttered. It was after seven-thirty. Both she and Sanchez were on duty until midnight. Both of them had better things to do than follow Lieutenant Braun on their lead, not to be of help in any way, but so they couldn't come up with anything else in his absence.

Mike shook his head. "What a day." He paused for a beat, then asked, "He ever call you back?"

"Who?"

"Your lunch date." Sanchez kept his eyes on the homicide detectives.

"What?"

"Sunday," he prompted. "You had a date on Sunday. Braun called us in on the McLellan thing. Remember?"

"You know, I hate to get in the car with you. What is it with you? Get

210

in a car, and you get personal." April's face flushed with fury. "What is it with you and cars?"

"It's the only time we're alone," Mike murmured.

"So?"

"So, I know guys who get turned on in elevators. Can't control themselves."

"So?"

"So, with me it's cars. We may have to sit here for hours. Might as well, you know, communicate. Talk. You've heard of that, haven't you?"

"No," she said flatly.

"No what? You haven't heard of it, or you don't want to?"

"I don't want to talk about my personal life. It's not a good idea. You want to talk about the case, we'll talk about the case."

"So it was a date," Mike said triumphantly. "I knew it was a date."

"What it was is none of your business." April groaned. Braun and Roberts were still ringing the damn doorbell.

"I can be interested, can't I? It's not so easy to have a relationship in this business." Mike checked his watch. "Take it from me."

"I don't want to talk about it."

"So, you agree."

"It wasn't a damn date."

April glanced at him quickly to see if he bought it. He nodded.

"Yeah? He was a cousin?"

"No, he wasn't a cousin. He's the son of a sister-cousin."

"What's a sister-cousin?"

"Guess you don't know as much as you think you know."

"Never heard of it. You're either a sister or a cousin. Can't be both," Mike insisted.

"Oh, yes. In Chinese you can be both."

"How? You got some family lines nobody else in the world has?" Mike drummed his fingers on the wheel. *Hah, got her.*

"Yes. In old China the families were really big. I mean really."

"Yeah, so families are big in Mexico, too. Lots of children. Same kind of culture."

The sky turned midnight blue as the light slowly faded. The two dicks still stood ringing the doorbell. The smell of fall was in the air.

"Unh-unh. In China lots of wives for *one* husband. We're talking dozens of children, with complicated combinations of relatives you can't even imagine. Uncles and part uncles one-tenth the age of their part nieces and nephews. All living in huge compounds. Unbelievable."

"Let me figure this out. Your mother is a multiple wife and this guy Dong is your brother."

April gasped. "How'd you know his name?"

"You told me his name."

"I never told you his name," April fumed. "I never mentioned him at all. I can't stand this. You're spying on me again. I thought we talked about this. I don't ask about your life. I don't care what you do. I don't care," she insisted.

Mike regarded her with delight. "You know, we should do this more often. I love it when you get excited."

"You can't spy on me like this." April was almost choking on her fury. "And my mother wasn't—*isn't*—a multiple wife. There's no such thing as a multiple wife."

"I thought you said—"

"Forget it. Sister-cousin used to mean part of the family even if there was no real blood tie. But now it means closer than a friend. A relationship that's like a friend but has some tie that makes it more than a friend. Okay? Got it?"

Mike nodded again. "So, how did it go?"

Braun and Roberts gave up on the doorbell and approached the unmarked car with identical determined strides.

"Uh-oh. Here they come."

All the windows were rolled down. The car was facing downtown. Mike was driving. Lieutenant Braun approached April's side.

"Look, she must be out for dinner or something." He made a quick check of his watch. "We're going to go out for a bite. You stay here."

"Yessir," April said.

"If she comes back, don't approach her," Braun ordered. "I want to do this."

Neither one in the car said anything.

"Got it?" Braun demanded.

"Don't approach her," April repeated.

"Right." Braun turned away, headed downtown toward the Irish bars.

After a minute Mike said, "You know, none of this plays."

"I know."

"I mean none of it, from the beginning."

"Maybe we've just been going at it from the wrong direction."

"How about now?"

"What do you mean?"

"I don't see a woman strangling women, do you?"

April shook her head. "Not in general, but there's the makeup and dressing the body up. And did you see the size of the sister?"

Mike shrugged. "Big."

"Big and redheaded." April was silent for a minute. "I've seen women who could kill."

Mike laughed. "Their husbands, maybe."

"Other women, too. Ever see a fight in a women's prison?"

"I saw a skinny girl try to give her rival an unscheduled mastectomy with a carving knife once."

They sat watching the building as the sky darkened. After a few minutes a light went on in an upstairs window.

"Well, look at that." April opened the car door and got out.

"Where do you think you're going?" Mike demanded.

"He only said not to approach her if she came outside. He didn't say we couldn't go *in* if she opened the door."

"Right." Mike closed the windows, then got out and locked the car.

# 46

An intercom was set into the plaster next to the doorbell on the short piece of putty-colored wall that turned the corner into the doorway. The whole building was dilapidated and sad-looking, the black paint on the doorframe cracked and gray with city grit. A faint odor of urine rose from the corners of the worn stone threshold. The door looked as if the top half had once sported a glass insert of some kind. Now it was crudely paneled and painted over and had a peephole in the middle. The light bulb over the door was blackened with age.

No nameplate indicated who lived there.

April pushed the bell, then stepped back to look up at the windows, as Lieutenant Braun had half an hour before. A few feet away, Mike leaned against a streetlamp, peering up. He shook his head. Nothing.

April rang the bell again. Then a third time, and a fourth. After the second ring she thought she heard a yelp way in the back of the house.

"Come here. I think there's a dog in there."

"No kidding." Mike let go of the lamppost and approached the door.

April hit the button again. They listened and were rewarded by more excited barking.

After a short pause the intercom crackled.

"Bouck?"

April glanced at Mike.

"Bouck?"

Mike raised his chin at her, indicating that she should be the one to answer.

"Ah, no." April put her mouth close to the speaker-phone holes. "It's Detective April Woo, New York Police. I'd like to talk to you. Would you let me in?"

In the lengthy silence that followed, April thought the woman had gone away.

There was some more crackling and a faint whisper, like the sound of leaves blowing in the wind. "What did he do?"

"I can't hear you. Would you open the door?"

The voice rose to a wail. "What did he do?"

"Miss Stanton, could you open the door so we can talk to you?"

No answer, only the sound of a dog's crazed yapping.

"Jesus," Mike muttered.

"Miss Stanton, we just want to talk to you. Please open the door."

". . . I can't."

"Why not?"

There was another long pause before she answered. "He'll hurt me."

"No one will hurt you. I promise. We just want to talk to you for a few minutes. Please open the door."

"Yes, he'll hurt me."

The whisper was hoarse and intense. April had to strain to make out the words.

"Who'll hurt you?"

"I can't tell you."

"Who's Bouck?" April tried.

"He owns the house. I'm not supposed to let anyone in." The voice was timorous, more like that of a frightened little girl than a grown woman.

"Tell her to come outside," Mike suggested.

"Huh?"

"Tell her to walk the dog."

April nodded. Good idea.

"Miss Stanton. Can you come outside?"

"No, no. I have to stay until he comes back."

"When is he coming back?"

Silence.

"Did he say when he was coming back?"

"He said four o'clock."

"It's way past that now." April spoke carefully into the intercom. "What happens when he's late?"

"Uhh."

215

"Ask her to walk the dog." Mike nudged her arm.

"Miss Stanton, doesn't the dog have to go out?"

Silence.

"Are you allowed to take the dog out, Miss Stanton?"

The intercom crackled. "Of course I can take Puppy out."

"Miss Stanton, why don't you do it now?"

"Why?"

"It sounds like Puppy wants to go out."

"Puppy *always* wants to go out."

No more sounds from the intercom.

"Miss Stanton, Miss Stanton—damn." April turned to Mike. "What do you say?"

"At least we know she's in there. This guy—Bouck. Maybe we should run a check on him."

"She seems scared to death of him."

"Confirms what the sister said."

"Uh-huh." They headed back to the car to put in a call to Sergeant Joyce. "Yeah, but she also said the woman was out of it."

"She sounded scared, not exactly out of it. Give me the keys." Mike held out his hand.

"You were driving. You have the keys."

"Unh-unh. You put them in your bag."

April rolled her eyes. "That was yesterday."

Mike patted himself down, found the keys in his jacket pocket. "Oh, yeah, I knew that. Just testing your memory."

"Sure."

Mike unlocked the passenger door and opened it, then walked around to his side of the car. He got in and called Sergeant Joyce. While he was still speaking, April punched him in the arm.

The black paneled door of the building opened a crack. The woman they thought was Camille Honiger-Stanton stuck her head out and looked around.

After a second or two, when the woman didn't see anybody lying in wait for her, she came out with a tiny poodle on a retractable leash. A current of electricity, kind of like lightning, jolted through the car. April felt the familiar rush of adrenaline. She looked at Mike. It had hit him, too. His body was still, but she could feel his heart racing, his blood pressure rise at the sight of the red-haired woman walking a dog that was a hairball with a muzzle. "Holy shit," Mike murmured.

It was kind of an orange color, a bit lighter than the hair of the woman, who was even taller than her sister. April estimated her height at five eleven. She wore a long, flowered skirt with a white blouse hanging out over it. The blouse had big sleeves and reminded April of another one she had seen somewhere like it. Her shoes were black flats, like ballet slippers. Her hair was long and wild around her head. In the darkening light, with her tall, slight frame covered in billowy clothes, she looked almost ghostly.

Mike made a move to get out of the car, then stopped. "She's not going anywhere," he said softly.

"No. Look at that dog, will you?" April shook her head. Unbelievable. Ducci was going to be impossible after this call.

The poodle had fluff all over it, was clearly a puppy that hadn't been clipped into poodle shape yet. The little dog looked to April like a lamb. Immediately the puppy squatted in the doorway, then took off, leaving a little puddle behind. It raced down the sidewalk as far as the leash would go. At about twelve feet, the cord ran out, pulling the dog up short.

It stopped and turned around to look at Camille questioningly. Its mouth was open in what appeared to be a smile.

"Oh, my God, it's smiling," April muttered. "Have you ever busted a dog?"

"No, have you?"

"Not exactly an everyday thing."

They were silent, watching the woman. She did not move from the front of the building. The dog raced back to her, then ran down the sidewalk the other way, until the leash ran out just before the corner where April and Mike were parked.

"Cute," Mike muttered.

"Yeah, but what is it? Accessory to murder? Witness to murder?"

"All of the above. But it doesn't look like it's going to tell us about it."

"We don't know what Ducci will turn up from this one." April jerked her head toward the crime scene where they'd spent the better part of the day.

The store where Rachel Stark died was almost directly across the street. Some of the yellow tapes that had sealed off the sidewalk in front of

European Imports earlier were still stuck on a tree. They were still in place all over the front of the shop.

Camille Honiger-Stanton didn't seem to be aware of them. Her attention was focused on the dog, now racing for the street.

"We'll have to pick it up. It appears to be evidence."

They were both silent again, thinking their own thoughts about how Lieutenant Braun would handle this suspect and her canine accomplice. April could see how the dog could work to win over a victim, make a murderer welcome anywhere. She remembered that the Boston Strangler had gotten into his victims' apartments by mewing like a cat.

"Ohhh shit." Mike stiffened in his seat.

Finally the woman felt it was safe to move. She strolled toward the opposite corner, where Lieutenant Braun and Sergeant Roberts were returning from their dinner.

# 47

Jason checked the clock as Milicia gathered up her things. His face was rigid. She was taking a lot of time to get organized. He willed himself to appear relaxed and neutral at her resistance to leaving. Daisy was Jason's next patient. He hoped she and Milicia wouldn't meet in the waiting room. Daisy would be disturbed by Milicia.

Finally Milicia was on her feet, but she wasn't happy. Only seconds before she had been calm, as if a great pressure inside her had finally eased. Now she was hurt and angry again because Jason wouldn't drop everything and take care of her now that he understood the true nature of her crisis. She felt he had tricked her into going to the police alone. She was furious, but there was absolutely nothing he could do about it. Daisy was probably sitting in his waiting room already, and she was by no means his last patient.

He glanced down at his appointment book. Tuesdays he had patients until eight-thirty at night. The only thing that would stop him from seeing them was an actual medical emergency. One of them getting shot or hit by a bus. A suicide crisis. An accident where blood was flowing all over the ground. Nothing else.

Once a very sick patient he was visiting in the hospital became suicidal during the visit. Jason had stayed at the hospital until the patient was stabilized. He got back to his office an hour and a half later. While he was gone, the patient whose session he missed had become hysterical waiting outside his locked office door, knocking and getting no answer.

He had planned to come right back, had left the lights and the radio on in the office. The patient, a woman, saw the crack of light under the door and heard the radio. She fantasized that Jason was in there, had had a heart attack, and would die if the doorman didn't break down the door to save him. The doorman wouldn't do it. A male patient confronted by a locked door would probably have shrugged and left. But his woman patient never really felt safe with him after that.

Jason watched Milicia turning things over in her mind. How she would handle this apparent betrayal on his part, how she would manage the police. Jason was intensely aware in those moments that he didn't fully understand this situation, had no idea what was really going on.

There are so many levels to the relationship between psychiatrist and patient, so many secret recesses of the mind where events and feelings were processed but never fully explored no matter how many hours are scheduled.

Jason knew most people couldn't make connections between things, and even when they could, human communication was an iffy undertaking at best. From the first moment he saw her, Jason knew Milicia was not like anyone else. It was more than her extraordinary presence. He couldn't place her, couldn't define her, wasn't sure of her purpose, her character. His method was always to let the patient inform him of these things. But every time he saw or spoke to Milicia, something totally unexpected came out of left field. This was an uncommon thing. Very rarely did he remain perplexed for very long. With Milicia he had been perplexed ten whole days. That was as long as he had known her.

In psychiatric time ten days was nothing. Jason kept wondering if there was something he should have picked up right away from the very incomplete picture Milicia gave him when they met the first and second times.

He had a feeling of helplessness as she left the office. It was another one of those occupational hazards that went with being a shrink. He couldn't be with his patients when they made their actions. He couldn't stop them or help them, or rewrite the story as it was happening. He could only discuss it with them afterward.

Milicia walked out of his office to talk to the police about murder. Jason knew the procedure because he had been there, knew the precinct, knew how the detectives, particularly April Woo, would deal with her. He was deeply involved and yet he had to miss it.

Daisy came into the waiting room. Jason had heard the door open and close. Daisy was always difficult, a challenge.

He nodded at Milicia as she went out the door. She didn't look back.

If she didn't call him to tell him what happened, he wouldn't call her. April would no doubt fill him in.

The brass bull clock on his bookshelf hit the quarter hour with a tiny click. He waited until he was certain Milicia was gone, then came out of his office, prepared for Daisy, smiling slightly and looking as if nothing important had happened to him in a long time.

# 48

Braun sauntered up Second Avenue, in no hurry now, though he had grabbed only twenty minutes for his hamburger. April watched him unwrap a stick of gum and fold it into his mouth as he stepped up on the curb at the corner. The suspect's tiny dog ran over to greet him, sniffing at his cuff. Camille quickly jerked the dog away. Braun shook out the crease in his pants, chewing, while his mouth tried for a smile.

He passed Camille. Slowly it occurred to him. His head turned. On his second take he sought guidance from Sanchez and Woo, sitting in the unmarked car as they had been ordered to. Braun looked at them and cocked his head behind him at the tall redhead now crossing the street with the little dog.

*Is that the suspect?*

Mike and April kept their faces neutral, unwilling to commit on yea or nay to such a jerk.

Lieutenant Braun decided it without their prompting, spun around, and ran back to her. Roberts followed.

"Shit," Mike muttered.

Braun and Roberts approached the suspect like a freight train racing at full throttle. They blocked her front and back. Braun shoved his badge in her face. She cried out, reeling back.

"No! Don't touch me." She reached down to pick up the dog, then tried to get back to her front door. She didn't get there.

Sergeant Roberts's arm snaked out to stop her from resisting an officer. The suspect panicked and started screaming. April shook her head as the two men subdued her and put her in their car. Before they pulled away, Braun made a sign for Sanchez and Woo to remain where they were until further notice.

# 49

Camille's eyes darted wildly around the room. She could hear them, and she could speak if she wanted to. She wouldn't speak though. No matter what. She wouldn't ever tell them the secret, even if they sent her to prison for the rest of her life. She didn't want to think about prison. Milicia said in prison they'd do bad things to her. Really bad.

The beating of Camille's heart sounded like thunder. It was hot. She worried that the place they put Puppy was even hotter. The big one said they had a special place for Puppy, would give her back when they were finished. She didn't believe him. She stared at him, willing a knife to enter his throat. He was fiddling with something on the table. The other one was staring at her as if she were a witch. Beads of perspiration dotted her forehead.

*Yes, I am a witch. A very bad witch.*

She gnawed at her bottom lip. They told her to cooperate. She shivered.

"Okay, got it." The one who had taken Puppy away nodded at the one who grabbed her off the street.

"All right, let's begin. Would you state your name."

Camille unclenched her jaw, releasing her lip. She licked it carefully, sticking her tongue way out. He said some things into the microphone. She didn't listen to what they were.

"Uh, your name."

She didn't answer.

"Would you like something to drink?"

"Camille," she said suddenly.

"Ah. Camille what?"

"Camille Honiger-Stanton."

Camille sat back, gathered her bottom lip back into her mouth, gnawed on it while her eyes blinked open and closed. *There,* she told them.

"Where do you live, Camille?"

"Hmmm."

"Can you tell us where you live?"

Camille watched the tape recorder. She counted softly to thirty.

The taller man looked at the smaller one. Camille noticed that he had a big mole on his face. Black.

"Ten fifty-five Second Avenue."

"Okay, good. Are you married or single?"

Camille giggled. He was going to die soon. She could see it happening. The mole on his face was cancer. She didn't like being so close to it, having to look at it. Quickly she combed her hair over her face with her fingers until it was a dense curtain she couldn't see through. That was better. She sat back in the chair.

"Uh, Camille?"

"Who's calling?"

"Um, it's Lieutenant Braun."

"Did you know you have a mole on your face?" Her voice came from behind the curtain.

There was a brief pause before he answered. What the hell was this? He decided to humor her.

"I didn't know. Where is it?"

"Underneath your eye."

Camille moved her hair enough to see the man with the mole lift his hand to his cheek. She tossed her hair back, leaning forward suddenly to look closer.

"There." She stuck her finger at his face.

The man recoiled. The word "Christ" jumped out of his mouth.

"Did you know those kind of things cause cancer?"

He looked wildly at the other guy. "Roberts, do you see a mole?"

"No, sir." The other man didn't look, but he was smiling a little.

"I don't have a mole on my face." But he was a little uncertain now.

"Oh, yes, you do," Camille said angrily. She reached into a pocket in her dress and pulled out a small artist's notebook with a pen stuck in the spiral binder. She took out the pen and flipped the pages until she came to a clean one.

"What're you doing?"

Braun was alarmed. Every movement the woman made was jerky, ungainly, weird. He was afraid she might stab him with the pen. He reached over to take it away.

She moved it out of his reach. "I'm drawing your face is what I'm doing. Don't disturb me, I'm concentrating."

She stuck her tongue deep in the side of her cheek. It bulged out, distorting her face.

"Camille, we have to concentrate on these questions," Braun said. His eyes were nervous now, flitting back and forth from Camille to the guy sitting next to her, guarding the tape machine.

Camille didn't look up. She pounded her left hand on the table irritably. The recorder jumped.

"Don't interrupt. I want to preserve this moment."

"Jesus," Braun muttered under his breath.

Then he was silent for a while, watching her pen move in swift strokes across the paper. It didn't take a genius to see that she wasn't drawing anything.

He looked at his watch. "It's getting late. You must respond to these questions."

Camille laughed. His eyes were rolling all over the place, looked about to jump out of his head.

"What are you laughing at?"

He looked upset.

"What's so funny?"

Camille directed her pen at his eyes and poked across the table in their direction not far enough to touch him but far enough to make him nervous.

"It's all in the eyes. You can see it all in the eyes." She stared at him, her eyes blinking quickly open and shut. Then she dropped her gaze to her drawing, became absorbed by it. She nodded and fell silent.

Horrified, Braun looked at the woman with her head bobbing up and down.

"Okay, that's it." He gestured to Roberts to turn off the tape. He got up, his hands rubbing the skin around his eyes and above his cheekbones, turned his back on the table where Camille sat like an insect, a big insect, with hair sticking out from her head like crimped red filament wire. Cold. Weird.

"Get Woo in here."

"Yes, sir." Instinctively Roberts reached for the tape recorder and took it with him.

Braun followed him quickly to the door. "Stay here," he told Camille. "We'll be right back."

But she wasn't listening to him. She was thinking about Puppy and how frightened Puppy must be.

Camille didn't know how long she was there before a different person, a woman, came in. The woman took a look at her and said, "Stop that" very sharply.

Camille growled and continued biting at her arm.

"You can't do that." April approached her matter-of-factly and pried the arm out of Camille's mouth. A little blood oozed out of the places where she had chewed some holes in it. The bitten arm looked raw, as if it should be hurting quite a bit.

"There's no need for that," April said.

Camille gnashed her teeth, snapping at the air now.

"I guess you're having some trouble, huh?"

*"Rrrrrr."*

"I'm April Woo. You're acting like a dog. I'd guess you're worried about your dog." April stood there with one hand on her hip. She was used to crazy. It happened all the time. The police department could do it to anybody.

"Would you feel better with your dog in here?"

Camille stopped growling and fell silent.

"Will you talk to me if I bring you the dog? What do you say?"

"Yes," Camille whispered. "I'm better with Puppy."

What was so hard about that? April leaned out the door and talked to the officer who was standing outside. He hadn't been doing his job. The woman should not have been allowed to mutilate herself while in police custody.

# 50

"I want to talk to you." Sergeant Joyce crooked her finger at April and made some wiggling motions with it. "In here."

It was after nine that evening. April followed her into her office.

"Close the door."

April closed the door.

Sergeant Joyce returned to her desk. When she was settled in the same kind of old-fashioned wooden, rolling, tilting chair April had in the squad room, she turned to April. April could see that the order to stay behind in the precinct had not exactly been easy for her supervisor to take. April felt a little sorry for her.

Out in the squad room someone began screaming obscenities. "Fucking pig hit me. Asshole fucking cop. I'm gonna file a complaint. I'm gonna have your fucking ass."

The screaming stopped as suddenly as it started.

A breeze drifted in through the open window. It was cooling off and beginning to smell like fall. In the second of silence April noticed there was water in the saucers under the two plants on the windowsill. Sergeant Joyce must have been really desperate for something to do. The plants looked happier now. Sergeant Joyce didn't.

Only two hours before, Sergeant Joyce had had the pleasure of being chewed out with her two best detectives in front of the captain of the precinct by a lieutenant from downtown. For once April knew more about what was going on than she did. Sergeant Joyce didn't like not knowing what was going on. Her desk was a mess. It looked to April as if she'd spent the time since the skirmish messing up the number-coded forms and eating her fingernails.

Right now her face was screwed up into a big question mark.

"Where's Mike?" she demanded.

"Down at the district attorney's office, trying to get a search warrant."

Joyce frowned. "Any particular reason?"

"Whole thing looks suspicious."

"What about the boyfriend, wouldn't he let you in?"

"He wasn't home."

Sergeant Joyce raised an eyebrow. "So what's going on here?"

April told her how Braun and Roberts had pulled Camille off the street while she was walking her dog, brought her in for questioning and gotten nowhere, then called April in from the stakeout to see if she could do any better.

"Nice of them to inform me. Jesus, what fuck-ups. Where are they now?"

"Braun and Roberts went back to the building in question to wait for the boyfriend. They seem to think the boyfriend might be involved."

"Oh, yeah. What makes them think so?"

"The woman is—wacko. When I went in there she was chewing on her arm. And I'm not kidding. Bite wounds all over."

April stood in front of the desk, her face impassive, reporting like a soldier.

Sergeant Joyce cocked her head, nodding for her to take a seat. Reluctantly, April sat down. She could see Joyce, thinking through her nerve endings, trying to figure this one out.

Ducci had said the fibers in Maggie Wheeler's ring were dog hairs. Camille Honiger-Stanton was found walking her dog.

"Where's the dog?"

"Braun took the dog away from her. When she got the dog back, she responded better. It's still with her."

"What kind of dog?" Sergeant Joyce jumped on the question.

"Poodle. Apricot-colored. They're downstairs."

"She fit Ducci's description?"

"Kind of." April fell silent, uneasy.

"Well, what did she tell you?" Joyce demanded impatiently.

"Uh." April pulled out her notebook. It had been necessary to take some notes. What Camille had said was all on tape. But what she had done during the interview had to be written down on paper. The woman was really weird.

"She said her sister was a witch," April began.

"Millie?"

"Milicia. Said she made her—Camille—sick. She rolled her eyes back in her head. Then she told me I was going to die of cancer." April looked up.

"Oh, why is that?"

"She said there was a big cancer-growing agent in the precinct. Anyone who's in here could catch it."

Sergeant Joyce frowned. "That's not so crazy. I'd agree with her on that. What else?"

"Eyes roll back in head. Growling noise. That meant she was thinking about the dog. She said she was worried about the dog catching it, then said the dog couldn't get precinct cancer as long as she was holding it."

"Great." Sergeant Joyce impatiently tapped the desk with a pencil.

"She said the sister had been projecting radiation rays at her. She wanted to report it, but didn't think the police would do anything about it. She said the sister tried to kill her in other ways, too. I asked her what ways. She said poison, through radio waves. She has a whole list."

"Uh-huh, so why does the sister want to kill her?"

April continued reading from her notes. "She said Milicia was always trying to kill her. Said she'd be dead now if she didn't have Bouck to protect her."

"So what is this? Some kind of sibling-rivalry thing?"

"Yeah, Camille said Milicia was jealous because their parents loved Camille more. She said Milicia killed her parents and she—Camille—was the only one who knew. So now Milicia has to kill her, too."

"Okaaaay." Sergeant Joyce tapped the desk with the pencil. Two sisters and two boutique salesgirls in a dance of death with a poodle.

"Anything in that?" she asked about the murder of the parents.

April shook her head. "Milicia told me their parents died in some kind of car accident about two years ago. Greenwich, Connecticut. I have someone checking it out."

Sergeant Joyce sighed. "What about the boyfriend?"

"Name's Nathan Bouck. I'm going to run a check on him. Camille says he owns the whole building and the chandelier shop downstairs. She says he's God. He can do anything he wants."

"Must be nice," Joyce murmured.

"Yeah, even Milicia the witch is scared of him."

"So, ah, what do you think?"

April closed her notebook. Her neighbors next door in Chinatown when she was growing up had a cousin. Name of Lee Hao Chung. Fat boy, stupid-looking. His movements were jerky just like Camille's. Lee Hao did a lot of naughty things, stole the best food, tortured the other kids. Got away with everything because he was kind of crazy upstairs. April remembered Skinny Dragon Mother telling her again and again, "Lee Hao not crazy, smart. Do anything he want, never have to work in life. Family always make excuse. Pah."

Could be like that with Camille. Maybe crazy, maybe not. Maybe parents made excuses. Maybe sister not so tolerant. April could see how Milicia would not like being troubled with a sibling who covered her face with her hair whenever she got upset and talked about cancer traveling in radio waves—not that such a thing was completely impossible. April had read somewhere that power lines near farms out west had killed whole herds of cattle. And lots of people in New Jersey were getting leukemia. Could be radio waves. Why not?

"So, is she a murderer?"

April shook her head. "I have no idea. The crime scenes were very—organized. Crazy, but organized, know what I mean?"

"Yeaaah," Joyce said doubtfully.

"So the homicides look like the work of a crazy person, doesn't mean they are." April leaned forward, trying to gather her thoughts into a coherent whole. "Camille acts crazy. Lieutenant Braun was completely freaked. Maybe she's too crazy to do anything. Braun thinks so."

"What do you think?" Joyce pressed some more.

"I don't know, Sergeant. I wish I did."

"Let's go have a look at her."

"Sure." April stood. Last she saw Camille, the curtain of red hair was covering her face. Sergeant Joyce was going to love this.

# 51

Jason picked up the phone on the first ring. "Dr. Frank."

"It's Milicia."

Jason waited.

"Am I calling at a bad time?" she asked after a beat.

"No, I'm between patients. I have a few minutes."

"Jason, I'm so worried."

Jason cringed just a little. The situation slipped into the background as he worried about a patient calling him by his first name. No matter what Milicia thought, they were in a clinical setting and had a clinical relationship. He didn't allow anybody to use his first name in a clinical setting. His first name was reserved for colleagues and family members.

For a second he considered changing the footing by insisting they use last names. Then he elected to let it pass.

"Jason, what's wrong?"

What was wrong was he let the temperature drop when she put him off. Now he let it drop some more.

"What's going on?" he said finally.

"I've been so nervous since you opened this whole thing with the police. I can't contain myself."

Her voice took on a baby-talk quality. Childish was not a style that appealed to him. Jason had to remind himself that this was how Milicia acted with all men. It had nothing to do with him. She had learned to appear vulnerable because most men could be relied on to respond well to cute and cuddly. But Jason knew this girl had a steel blade for a heart.

"But you've been to the police."

"I know, but it really weirded me out."

Jason didn't say anything. He could see how it would.

"I need to see you. I need to compare notes with you. We need to be together on this."

"Why?" Jason looked at the bull clock on the shelf. He had thirty seconds before he saw his last patient. Then he was going to go out into the evening and get something to eat.

She'd already seen him that day. Why did Milicia need to see him again? He told himself that this was how she was with men. But at the same time, in the sleeping part of his mind, he thought maybe this wasn't the way Milicia acted with all men. Maybe this was how she chose to be with him.

"Remember when you were a kid, and sometimes you had to go to a scary place that seemed to have monsters in the shadows? Well, I want you to tell me there are no monsters in the shadows. I want you to tell me my fears are silly. Jason, I need to feel protected, and you're not protecting me."

Jason shifted in his chair, genuinely irritated now. He was really put off when grown women talked baby talk to him. He struggled to shake off his annoyance. This was an open clinical situation. The idea of murder—homicide—was disconcerting. It was a horrible thing. He didn't have patients who came to him worried their siblings were killers.

Milicia had held that piece of information back until the second murder. Horrible.

He felt manipulated.

"When I was there," he said suddenly, "they gave me a tuna fish sandwich. I was surprised how homey it was."

"You were at the precinct today?" Milicia jumped on the revelation. "What did you say?"

"Not today," Jason told her. "I was there for something else."

"Well, what did you tell them today? Tell me exactly what you said."

"You were here. You heard what I said."

There was a brief pause. "Are you sure?"

What did she mean? Jason couldn't let it go by. What was she really asking?

"Do you think there's something wrong with my memory?" he persisted.

"No, no."

"Do you think I'm not telling the truth?"

"No, silly. Sometimes little things slip away, that's all."

The door closed in the waiting room. His next patient was there. It was time to go. Jason did not reassure Milicia there were no monsters in the shadows.

# 52

By nine-thirty Jason was exhausted and overstimulated. He had returned from California only the night before, had seen ten patients that day, one of whom ended up at the police station accusing her sister of murder. All through his session with his last patient, the conversation with Milicia played over and over in Jason's mind. He didn't want to think about it. He had other things to think about.

When he returned home, he lingered in the kitchen debating whether to ratchet down with a beer or a martini with three olives. He'd have a drink, think about Emma and California. Later, he'd read a book.

He decided on the martini, built it, threw a frozen pizza in the toaster oven, and took his first burning swallow. Yes. Alcohol helped. He grabbed three more olives from the jar and savored the salty taste. Glass in hand, he wandered into the living room, thinking about making love to his wife. He concentrated on that, didn't want to crash with the weight of being alone again.

Sipping the martini slowly, he told himself this was okay. He didn't have to have a wife with him every second. They could live together sometimes. He tried to walk around a little with that conviction.

But underneath it all the Milicia tape played on and on. Her voice calling him silly, talking baby talk about monsters in the shadows, clicked on without his bidding.

*What did you tell them? Tell me exactly what you said.*

He turned on the television and listened to the weather report, couldn't pay attention, and turned it off. He was trained to look at time sequences for branch points without making judgments or conclusions.

At every fork in the tree he asked himself what was going on. Why did she say "We have to be together on this"?

Why was she worried about what he told the police? Why did she pretend not to know what he'd said?

He wandered around the living room, picking up one book after another, trying to unwind. He wanted to stay with Emma, think about her. Read a book. But the more he tried to escape, the harder it was to get away from Milicia and Camille.

Against his will Jason had been drawn deep into their story. That bothered him. He was a quick study. He could put together any number of disparate elements of personality and character almost from the very start. It wasn't like him not to be able to come to a conclusion right away.

It occurred to him that maybe the reason he couldn't get it this time was that Milicia was lying about something. He reviewed how she had started with him. Bits and pieces about the day in the Hamptons, the ride home in her car. How she had asked to see him. Her calls when he was in California. It was all unusual, ambiguous. Nothing in this life was truly random.

He turned away from the books, looking for another diversionary tactic. He had to calm down or he wouldn't get to sleep that night. He didn't want murder hanging over his dreams.

The martini was almost gone. He decided to have another. The phone on the table rang. He picked up on the first ring, hoping it was Emma.

"Hello, Jason?"

He sighed. It was April the detective. Now she was calling him Jason. Earlier that day she'd called him Dr. Frank. He couldn't help smiling. He knew if she was calling him by his first name, she wanted something.

"Hello, April."

"It's nine-thirty. Am I getting you in the middle of dinner?"

Jason jerked his head toward the kitchen, suddenly remembering the pizza in the toaster oven. Shit. "No, I haven't had it yet."

"Ah. Then you're probably sitting there with a gin martini. May or may not have olives in it."

"Yes, gin martini, and yes, it has olives." He looked down at the glass. Had olives. It was empty now.

"You're unwinding after a long day of patients. Am I right?"

"Yes, again." He wouldn't mind a few more martinis so he could unwind further. He had a strong suspicion by the way she was talking to him that he wasn't going to get them.

"It's really nice to chat with you, April. But I have this really uneasy feeling you're not calling to chat. And I don't really feel like chatting right now anyway. Am I right?"

"You're right. Something's come up that's a quasi-emergency—well, it's not the Twin Towers blowing up, or anything like that. But I need some input about a medical problem I have here at the precinct this minute. . . ." Her voice trailed off.

Jason heard some noise in the background. He knew this call was about the Honiger-Stanton sisters. April wouldn't bother him about anything else. The karma must be bad for his getting away from those women tonight.

He had been committed to clearing his mind and getting into a quiet place where he could refresh himself. Now a wave of nausea swept over him at the thought of having to gear up again so late in the day. The smell of burning pizza drifted out of the kitchen. Shit.

"Hold on for a second, will you." Jason put down the phone and charged across the hall.

In the kitchen, black smoke spewed out of the toaster oven. Shit. Inadvertently he thought of the burning house where Emma had been held in Queens. Thick clouds of reeking smoke jetting up into the sky. Rubble everywhere. Talking to April Woo must have triggered the association. Shit.

He burned himself yanking the small metal tray out of the oven. Tonight wasn't turning out to be so great. He raced back into the living room.

"You still there?" he said breathlessly.

"You okay?"

"Sure." Just depressed and anxious and starving. It was clear he was going to lose sleep over this and feel rotten through all ten patients scheduled for the next day. He studied the burn on his left index finger.

"You were telling me the Twin Towers are not the reason for this call."

"Yeah. This is the thing. I have your patient's sister here as kind of a suspect in a homicide investigation. You with me?"

"Of course."

"And this woman does fit the description we have of the murderer."

"Really?" Jason was appalled.

"Yeah, well, but there's something odd. . . . She's—ah, bizarre, to put it mildly. We need a psychiatric evaluation of her to determine what to do with her. At the moment we're getting a warrant to search the house where she lives and there's a BOLO out on her boyfriend."

"You lost me." Jason shifted the phone to his other ear. "What's the connection between this woman and the murder—murders—and what's a BOLO?"

"She has a dog. Similar-colored dog hairs were found on the first murder victim. She has red hair. Several red human hairs were found on the dress the victim was wearing. Bruises on the neck and shoulders of the first victim show the woman we have here is the right height to have caused them. She lives across the street from where the second victim died. We don't have anything yet on the second homicide. You still with me?"

"Sort of. What's a BOLO?" he repeated.

"Be on the lookout. Guy drives a Mercedes. We're trying to locate him."

Jason swallowed, frowning. He tried to remember what was in the paper about the murders. Not a lot. "They were hung?"

"Strangled, garotted, then hung."

"Not exactly a woman's crime," Jason murmured.

"Look, I have this feeling—"

"What's your feeling?"

"It's like this woman makes me feel weird when I talk to her, but I don't feel frightened. Does that make sense?"

"What does weird mean?"

"Ah, like stepping off the curb and there's no street there. I don't feel any human connection with her. She, like, bites herself, growls."

"What about her eyes? Does she stare? Are her eyes very wide open? Does she seem super vigilant, afraid of having anything behind her?"

"I don't think so—she's creepy."

"Do you get the feeling she's a cat, that she could strike like a panther?"

"No. I'm not an expert, Jason. It's only my intuition. But I get the feeling she's a very disturbed, brittle person. She's frightening, but only because of the way she acts. It's kind of like you're trying to soothe somebody and they vomit on you. You're horrified, but not frightened for your safety. You see what I mean?"

"Yes, I know what you mean. She's creepy, but you don't think she's dangerous. What do you need?"

"Well, this is the thing. We not getting very far in our questioning of her. We brought this woman in. Now we're liable for her, responsible for her safety. We can't let her loose and we can't hold her. We need a psychiatric interview, and it would be great if we could also get some further information about the murder."

"What's your normal procedure in a case like this?"

"That's the thing. Usually I'd take her to the emergency room at Bellevue and they'd bring in a psych team. At this hour they'd be residents. It's a very inhuman thing. I don't like to say this, 'cause they mean well. But it's very unlikely such an interview would lead to any important information for our investigation. And I hate to go there."

Jason could understand that. He was quiet, trying to control his nausea at the prospect of doing such an interview at this hour. He asked himself if there was anything illegal or unethical about it. He was being called in as a consultant. He decided there was not. Milicia was his patient, and she had already asked him to see her sister. And now it was a murder investigation. That changed things.

"How do you like Chinese food?"

"I love it." He also liked her. "You want me to come down to the precinct now, is that it? And talk to her there?"

"I'll, uh, cook you a Chinese dinner, buy you a bottle of gin, a book on Freud. Or all three if you do this huge favor for me."

April Woo didn't say that he owed her for saving Emma's life. Or that he was responsible for the woman's being there in the first place. She was a clever girl. She didn't have to say anything like that. He sighed softly.

"I'm on my way," he told her.

# 53

April met Jason at the downstairs desk. The psychiatrist looked tired but in better spirits than she had seen him last. She felt a little guilty dragging him in so late, but Sergeant Joyce remembered him from his work on the Chapman case and had liked the idea. Especially since he knew the sister. After she suggested it, April could see Joyce giving her points for it. Getting Jason to do the evaluation meant her supervisor didn't have to lose April to the bowels of Bellevue, where April would have to escort Camille and wait with her half the night until a bunch of residents saw her and made a recommendation about what should be done with her. And what they recommended might not be the right thing. This way April could return to the building on the East Side with Sanchez and participate in the search of the place where Camille lived.

"Hi." She noticed right away that Jason had lost some weight and his hair was a little longer. She had forgotten that he was a handsome man, was surprised to find she was glad to see him.

"Thanks for coming."

He smiled. "You'd do the same for me."

"Of course." It was her job though. She shrugged and turned away to hide the flush that crept up her neck. Suddenly she felt awkward in the change of clothes from her locker.

It had been a long day since Rachel Stark was found hanging in the bathroom at European Imports that morning. And even though she had showered and washed her hair twice, April couldn't help wondering if she still smelled of death.

"She's in here." April led the way to the questioning room where she had left Camille with several guards, a cup of tea, and some of the devil's food cookies Sergeant Joyce hid in her locker for special occasions when she was absolutely desperate.

After finding her gnawing on her arm, April knew better than to leave Camille alone. April had left her with Goldie. The female uniform was big and experienced enough to handle anything. April thought Camille would feel better with a woman. A male uniform stood outside the door just in case. As she made the introduction, April was keenly aware of Sanchez in Sergeant Joyce's office. The door was closed. Didn't want to leave the two of them together too long.

April nodded at the uniform, then opened the door. Camille was sitting in the same position April had left her. The dog was laid out, boneless across her lap, its head hanging over her knee. A thick curtain of long red hair covered Camille's face.

The mug of tea on the table was half empty; the cookies didn't appear to have been touched. In the corner, Goldie shook her head. Nothing had happened since April and Sergeant Joyce left.

Puppy heard the door open and sat up, barking excitedly. Camille whispered to it. "Shhh."

April approached the table with Jason beside her. "Miss Stanton, I've asked Dr. Frank to come and speak with you."

"Who's speaking?"

"It's Detective Woo," April said, feeling weird.

Camille moved her hair to one side. "Woo, I've been waiting for you. Where've you been?"

"I went to get Dr. Frank. He's a psychiatrist. It would be very helpful if you'd talk to him, you know, openly. Tell him whatever you want. He's a good listener."

Camille let her hair fall back over her face.

"Miss Stanton, is it okay if I leave Dr. Frank with you?"

"Fine." The response came through the curtain of hair.

April looked at Jason uncertainly.

"Would you prefer if Detective Woo stays?" Jason spoke for the first time. "She's very busy and has a lot of things to take care of."

Camille turned her head away and didn't respond.

"I think it would be better if I leave," April said finally.

Camille didn't object.

April turned to Jason, indicating the uniform in the corner with a jerk of her head. He nodded. Yes, she could go and yes he would deal with the uniform.

Relieved, she ran upstairs to the squad room. Maybe Mike hadn't left without her.

# 54

ike waved a piece of paper at her. "Got it. Did she say anything?" He picked up a paper bag from the desk that was his because they were now on duty until midnight.

"Who?" The suspect or Sergeant Joyce?

"The suspect."

"Oh, not a lot. She was too busy eating her arm."

"Whaa?"

"The woman is an alien. I'm not certain she can add two and two. Dr. Frank is in with her now." April eyed the bag, hoping it contained food.

"I heard. How did you manage that?" They headed downstairs.

"I asked him. Didn't want to spend the night at Bellevue and miss the fun. What's in the bag?"

"What do you want it to be?"

April waved at the Desk Sergeant, and they stepped out into the night. It was about sixty degrees, bright and clear.

"I want it to be something really spicy and hard to eat, with lots of sauce. But I'd settle for a tuna sandwich."

"Done." He handed her the bag. "Tuna salad with lettuce on white toast."

"Thanks. What did you get for yourself?"

"Something really spicy and hard to eat, with lots of sauce."

She laughed, punched his arm as he headed for the driver's side of the car. "That's twice in one day. It's my turn to drive."

"Yeah, maybe. But wouldn't you rather eat? I had mine after I met with the ADA."

"Who'd you get?"

"Penelope Dunham, no problem at all. Know her?"

April shook her head. She'd never met this assistant district attorney.

"Why are you such a nice guy?" she asked, settling in the passenger seat. Then she opened the bag. Shit. It was two chicken enchiladas with mole sauce.

Mike grinned. "Don't ever say I don't take care of you. And there's no cheese on it anywhere. I know you don't like cheese."

"Thanks," she said. "Really thanks. It's great."

She wrinkled her nose and dug into the enchiladas with the plastic fork thoughtfully provided, knowing the food would be all over her and the car by the time they got across town. Mike was trying to get her used to Mexican cooking. She had to admit she liked the green sauce made of tomatillos, but the mixture of chocolate and chilis in the mole tasted to her kind of like dirt.

"How is it?" Mike jerked to a stop at the red light on Central Park West.

A blob of mole splattered off her fork and hit the front of her white shirt.

"Great. Just great. How much do I owe you?"

"More than you'll ever know."

Yeah yeah. He accelerated through the park while she worked on the enchiladas.

Six minutes later, as Mike pulled into an empty spot on Second Avenue near Fifty-fifth Street, she crumpled everything back into the bag. The black sedan with Lieutenant Braun and Sergeant Roberts in it was parked in front of 1055 Second.

Mike killed the motor and the lights, tossed the keys to April. "You can drive home."

Her attention had been on the brown spot on her blouse. She caught the keys, but only just. Nice.

Braun and Roberts were out of the car heading toward them before they could move. "Got it?" Braun demanded.

Mike handed the search warrant over. "Any sign of him?"

"Man at the garage says the car's in there and he hasn't taken it out since Sunday."

Braun stuffed the warrant in his pocket without looking at it. "Okay, let's go in."

All four headed toward the door with the crudely paneled top half. April prayed Braun wouldn't make them stay outside as backup. Before the thought was complete, she saw he'd already thought of that. She saw him nod at his two other people, one at each corner, by the litter baskets. Oh, and there was somebody across the street leaning against the skinny tree in front of European Imports. The Lieutenant wasn't taking any chances.

Roberts opened the downstairs door with no trouble. They trooped up the stairs with Braun in the lead. He had to move aside on the tiny landing at the top so Roberts could get at the door. There were four locks on it. Roberts worked on them for about thirty seconds. He got all four unlocked, and went inside.

For a second Mike and April stood outside on the landing while Braun and Roberts, stuck in the doorway, fumbled around for a light. A single pale bulb shone over their heads.

"Weird," April murmured softly.

"Yeah what?"

"The whole setup. Guy owns a chandelier shop and look at what he's got hanging here." She pointed at the bare bulb. It flickered, as if in response.

"That's not the only weird thing. Maggie Wheeler was hung on a chandelier," Mike reminded her.

From inside the apartment came the sound of a crash as something was knocked over.

"Shit." Braun's voice sounded pained.

A light came on, the logjam was broken, and April quickly followed Mike through the door.

"Wow." Mike whistled.

The four detectives huddled together for a confused instant, frozen with surprise. The place was not exactly what they had expected. It looked like some kind of warehouse. All kinds of furniture, a huge mirror, lamps, tables, settees, chairs, and sideboards were jumbled together, apparently at random, in the room fronting Second Avenue. There was so much of it, they could hardly get through it to the kitchen and the stairs. It almost seemed as if the furniture had been assembled that way to form a barricade to block entry to the living quarters.

The place smelled dusty and stale. Braun and Roberts began picking their way through it, turning on more lights as they went.

"This is going to take a while," Braun muttered. "You could hide anything in here."

April took another route, behind a sideboard, a desk, the mirror, and three chairs to the kitchen. Positioned behind the stairs between the front room and back rooms, it was a pretty sad affair. The walls hadn't been painted in decades. The plaster of the ceiling was crumbling to a fine powder in several places. The refrigerator, sink, and stove were from another era. Dirty dishes filled the sink and covered every counter surface. April studied the dishes with interest. All fine china, several patterns. The glasses looked like crystal.

She pulled on a pair of gloves and opened the refrigerator. Inside was a loaf of moldy bread, a pizza box, two six-packs of Amstel light beer, five packages of film, and a little girl's jewelry box of pale blue leather with faded gold tooling around the top. Carefully, she removed the jewelry box from the second shelf of the fridge, reminding herself where to return it later.

"What's that?" Mike was peering over her shoulder.

She could feel him breathing on her neck again. She shivered.

The little box wasn't locked. It swung open.

"What is it?"

There were only a few things inside. A broken necklace of American Indian beading, some crudely made enamel earrings with screwbacks. A cheap gold filigree bracelet with a cameo in the middle, and a gold pin of some sort with Greek letters on it. She picked up the gold pin and held it to the light.

"What is it?"

Mike shook his head.

"It's a sorority pin," Roberts said scornfully. He had pushed in behind Mike. "You two know what a sorority is?"

"Sure," Mike said pleasantly. April could see the word *Dickhead* hanging there behind his smile. Sanchez moved out of the kitchen.

April put the jewelry box back in the fridge, then joined him in the back room. It was empty, looked as if it had been cleared for a renovation that never happened.

Braun looked around and had nothing to say. He cocked his head toward the stairs. Once again the four of them trooped up a flight of stairs in a line.

This time Braun had something to say. "Jesus H. Christ. Get a load of this."

"Isn't this fun." Mike let April go in first.

She stopped suddenly, stunned. Nothing downstairs prepared them

for what was up there. Unlike the mess on the floor below, this level had
been very carefully decorated. The floor in the bedroom was pickled
white, stenciled in a colorful pattern around the edges. An Oriental rug
filled in the center. The walls were covered with fabric. April could tell it
was high-quality silk, had a pattern of stripes and tiny flowers in pink and
gold and green. The fabric was gathered at the ceiling and pulled up to a
point at the top to look like a tent. From the center point hung an ornate
chandelier with cherubs of painted porcelain.

A king-size four-poster against one wall was made up with a rich red
brocade bedspread and topped with dozens of tapestry pillows, tassled
and velvet-trimmed. The head- and baseboards were ornately carved,
gilded wood.

There were only two other pieces of furniture in the room. A dressing
table with a mirror attached, completely inlaid with ebony and mother-of-
pearl, and a chair in the corner with faded and threadbare upholstery the
same color as the jewelry box in the refrigerator.

Speechless, the four detectives studied the room. Then they moved to
the bathroom, which had a Jacuzzi bathtub and black walls. In the closet
they found only men's clothes, and several shoe racks filled with cowboy
boots of different colored leather—ostrich, alligator, snakeskin.

Up on the third floor they found a stark white room which held an
old-fashioned cot and a painted chest of drawers. There were some rum-
pled sheets, an old quilt and one pillow on the bed, bars on the windows.
The floor was bare except for a bowl of water with a dead cockroach
floating in it, and a small white bathroom rug that was badly stained with
a lot of little yellow circles of what April guessed was puppy urine.

"What's that?"

Braun pointed to some soiled laundry in the corner. Roberts leaned
over and picked it up. His forehead furrowed with alarm as he displayed
the straitjacket, the straps showing quite a bit of wear.

April glanced at Mike. What did this picture tell?

Braun shook his head as if one ear were filled with water.

"Looks like he kept her up here in more ways than one."

April took out her notebook and made a quick note. She wondered
how Jason Frank was doing with the suspect.

## 55

After they saw the restraint on the third floor, Braun called in one of his detectives from the street to help search the house. A few minutes later he found April in the other bedroom on the third floor. She was leaning over a table, studying Camille's hairbrush and the tangle of long reddish-gold hair in its bristles. Arrayed around her were a number of rolling racks hung with women's clothes. All kind of clothes. Up there, there seemed to be a warehouse of blouses and dresses and jackets and skirts the way the downstairs was a warehouse of furniture. Some items still had price tags on them. It looked like Camille did a lot of shopping.

Braun gestured at April. "Go check out the basement. See what you can come up with."

Basement! Immediately her heart began to pound. Why the basement, when there was a treasure trove right here? She struggled to swallow the protest that jumped onto her tongue. What was wrong with this guy? Didn't he know she was the first one in on this case and knew what she was looking for?

"You got a problem?" Braun said nastily.

She turned away for a second, lowering her eyes so the hot rage didn't spill out there either. She didn't have a problem. She didn't love dark places like basements, but cops weren't supposed to admit to little weaknesses like terror, repulsion, nausea, or rage at incompetent supervisors.

"No, sir, no problem."

She had wanted to see if the missing items from Mrs. Manganaro's store inventory were in this room. And he was a jerk.

"Then what are you waiting for?"

"I'm gone." She headed for the door, leaving the gold mine of information in all those clothes. Braun didn't know about the missing white blouse from The Last Mango. Elsbeth Manganaro had just told her.

Braun would pass it by if it was there. She'd have to come back and look for it later.

Downstairs, she turned the thumb latch on the basement door and stood outside it, cursing herself in Chinese for being afraid of opening a door and entering a cave that might have ghosts in it. Only people like Skinny Dragon Mother, born in China, believed in ghosts. American-born Asians like herself knew better. Ghosts didn't cross the oceans. They stayed on the other side. She switched on the light.

After she had the light on and the door at the top of the stairs open, it wasn't so bad going down there. She could tell there wasn't anything either alive or dead in the basement. It felt damp and cold, and the smell of ammonia made her eyes tear, but it wasn't frightening. It felt the way she had described Camille to Jason—weird and upsetting, off-kilter in every way, but not frightening. Creepy.

April had a powerful sense of Camille's presence in there. Wherever Camille spent time with her dog, there was the smell of urine. Either the dog was not trained to go outside, or Camille neglected to take it out as often as it needed to go.

She tried to visualize the dog and Camille in this place. What did they do in there? The room was nearly empty. There were three smallish cardboard boxes half filled with junk that April recognized as chandelier parts, ceiling caps, chains of various thicknesses and lengths, pieces of crystal with wires through them, brass arms. April spent several fruitless minutes raking through them.

An oil-burning furnace and a rusting water heater sat off to one side. There was no furniture. No tables or chairs. As in the front entry, the ceiling light was just a weak bulb, this one set in among the maze of exposed plumbing pipes. An odd-looking bundle sat in the corner behind the furnace. April had to circle the furnace to see it. Immediately she knew this was Camille's corner. There was a piece of fraying blue carpet under the bundle. April shivered when she saw the way the carpet was positioned. From here Camille would be partially hidden behind the furnace, but able to see the barred window above. April had no idea why she could see Camille sitting there.

April studied the bundle. It was tied up by the arms of a shirt like a hobo's sack in an old movie. She didn't want to touch it. She had a feeling that everything about this place told a story just as the crime scenes in the two boutiques where the girls had died told a story. As she contemplated the bundle, she worried about what the team was doing upstairs. What if they needed another kind of expert? What if Braun was moving things around and missing their significance? She tried to put the politics of the case out of her mind, to let the little pieces of information patter down on her like rain, while she kept her own counsel and her own focus.

She'd never seen a restraint like the straitjacket on the third floor in somebody's home; she didn't have a good feeling about the bundle in the basement.

She heard the sound of voices overhead. They must be going through the kitchen. Reluctantly, she reached down to pick up the bundle. As she touched the fabric, she had the kind of bad feeling that conjured up her discovery of Lily.

It seemed like a hundred years ago that April found the sleeping bag in a Chinatown backyard that held the body of the missing child called Lily. Dozens of people on the case and April had to be the one to spot the bag. The moment she unzipped it, she recognized the white and purple sneakers ten-year-old Lily had been wearing when she disappeared. She was still wearing them when April found her.

It was the shoes this time, too. April had a description of Maggie's favorite shoes from Olga Yerger, the salesgirl turned hooker. Olga said the shoes were brown suede flats with fake alligator insets across the top and fat gold chains over the inset. Copies of Gucci, Olga added. She thought they came from a shoe store called Maraolo, and was positive Maggie wore them nearly every day because they were comfortable and went with everything she had.

The shoes had been pressed together inside the sack and fell out first when April opened the bag. They were size five and a half. In the toe of one shoe was the dark blue eye shadow. In the toe of the other was the plum lipstick. April's heart beat double-time. She shook her head, perplexed.

The voices above were loud and angry now. April retied the bundle the way it had been and headed for the stairs. It sounded as if the two factions of the department had gotten into a serious dispute over something. What a mess.

Halfway up the stairs she began to make out the words and realized it was not Sanchez fighting with Braun or Roberts.

"What the fuck do you think you're doing in here?" The outrage in the newcomer's voice had reached the cracking point. The guy was furious, almost crazed. He was in the hall, must have just come in. "You can't just break into someone's house like this!"

"Sir, if you'll just calm down, we'll work this out." It was Lieutenant Braun. He was not speaking in a calming tone, and did not get the hoped-for results.

"Are you crazy? I'm not calming down. You broke into my house. You asshole. I'm going to have your head on a platter."

"No one broke into your house. Are you the owner, sir?"

"The fuck you didn't!"

"Are you the owner, sir?"

"Yes, I am the owner."

"Is this yours, sir?"

"What the—?"

"I'd advise you to calm down."

"And I'd advise you to get the fuck out of here."

April couldn't see what was going on. At the top of the stairs, before she came into view, she put the bundle down. Then she pushed open the basement door.

# 56

Jason pulled over a chair and sat down next to Camille. The dog struggled to get away from her. Before Camille realized what he was up to, Jason reached over and took the puppy onto his lap. She stiffened, but didn't object.

"Hi there, fella." Jason scratched the dog's ears. Puppy climbed up and licked his face. Out of the corner of his eye Jason watched Camille. She had been rendered immobile by this new threat.

He reached into his pocket and pulled out his key ring. It was red and had a small knife-and-scissor set attached. He held out the keys to the dog and shook them like a rattle, ignoring the patient. The puppy hesitated for a second, its small body and front feet pulled back into a crouch. Suddenly it pounced on the key ring like a mountain lion. Funny dog. Jason laughed.

"Do you mind if he plays with this?" He finally acknowledged Camille.

"It's okay." Camille didn't look as if it was okay at all. Behind the curtain of hair, she looked rigid with disapproval.

"This is a pretty friendly puppy. What's its name?"

"Puppy."

"Hunh?" Interesting choice of names.

"I had a dog a long time ago," Jason murmured. "I had forgotten how much I miss her. What's Puppy's sex?"

"She's a girl."

Jason put the key ring on the table close to Camille. Puppy jumped at it. Jason watched Camille. She had no reaction to the knife, clearly wanted her baby back.

"Well, maybe I'll put my keys away. It looks like she wants to come back to you again."

Camille took the dog from Jason, then relaxed. "She's a good dog."

"Yes, she is. Where did you get her?"

Camille hugged her baby, regarded her fondly. "We got her from a breeder," she said in a baby voice.

"So you knew you wanted a poodle?" Jason crossed his legs the other way. This was going to take a while.

"Oh, absolutely." Camille kissed the dog again and again. Puppy licked her face.

"All I know about poodles is they're very smart; they're high-strung; and they don't cause allergies."

Camille laughed and freed her hands so that she could clap them. "Right on all counts. My sister had allergies when she was a child. I have them now. We figured a poodle was especially safe. So we both got one."

Jason leaned over. "You mean you have a poodle and your sister has a poodle?" This was news to him.

Camille laughed again. "Yes, it's the same dog, except my sister's dog lives with her and my dog lives with me. They're carbon copies, just like us."

"I see," Jason said gently. He certainly didn't see the sisters as carbon copies, and Milicia had never mentioned having a dog. "What made you get them?"

"Oh, I was lonely," Camille said vaguely. And Milicia thought being nice could get her back. It didn't work. Camille shivered and pulled a strand of hair over her face.

"Was it your sister's idea to get the dogs?"

"No, no," Camille said fiercely. "I wanted it first. She had to come with me to get it for me."

Jason nodded. He could see that Camille didn't have the presence to buy a dog. "Did you both plan to get one?"

"No." Fierce again. "I wanted the dog. Bouck didn't want a dog. He wouldn't get it for me. We had a big fight. My sister hates Bouck, so she got me the dog." She paused. "She said she'd take it if Bouck wouldn't keep it. Then I could visit it at her house."

Jason nodded again. "So you went to the breeder," he prompted.

Camille made her shrill, high-pitched sound that tried to be a laugh. "Yes, and my sister changed her mind. She had to have the same dog. Same color, same sex. Everything."

"So she has a dog?" Jason asked again, just to be sure she meant Milicia had a dog.

"Oh, yes. Same dog."

Interesting. Now he knew something about Milicia he hadn't known before. He had another piece of the sisters' puzzle.

"Dogs make great companions. Have you always had one?"

Camille responded to this by covering her whole face with her thick mane of tangled hair. She didn't answer.

He tried a different tack. "What about Bouck? I guess he didn't mind about Puppy after all."

Behind her hair, Camille giggled. "Not after the break-in."

What break-in? Jason made a mental note to come back to the break-in. "How does Puppy feel about being here?"

"She's okay as long as I'm here."

"Oh, that's good, because if she has to stay around here too long, she may get bored." He paused, waiting for Camille to relax again. "How do you feel about being here?"

Camille started swaying from side to side, so the curtain of hair in front of her face swung back and forth. "It's a horrible place. I hate it. I want to go home."

"I can understand that. How do you feel about talking to me? Would you rather the officer stays, or waits outside?"

Abruptly Camille pushed her hair back and sat up, looking around as if she were upset about forgetting the officer in the corner.

"She can leave."

Jason nodded at Goldie. "It's okay if you wait outside."

The officer hesitated, then got up and left.

Jason processed Camille's response. He saw it as a healthy thing that she trusted him with her dog, then felt there was enough of a relationship between them to allow the guard to leave.

"What happened?" he asked as soon as the door closed. "How do you come to be here at the police station tonight?"

Camille shook her head. She didn't want to tell him. "They do that to people sometimes. Tonight it was my turn."

"Did something happen to make it your turn?"

"I don't know."

"Why don't you tell me about what you've been doing the last few days."

"What about them?"

"Oh, like how you spent your time the last few days before you came here to the police station. What's your routine? What are your days like?"

Camille thought for a long time. Then she said: "I'm decorating the house. That takes a lot of time."

"Is that the house where you live?"

"Yes." Camille looked down at Puppy. Puppy was lying limp in her lap. Camille stroked her.

"Who lives there with you?" he asked.

"Puppy."

"Anyone else?"

"Bouck does."

"Tell me about Bouck."

Camille shook her head. "He told me not to."

"Bouck told you not to talk about him?"

She was silent.

"Is Bouck the reason you're at the police station tonight?"

"No, Bouck hates the police. He says the police don't protect anybody. We have to protect ourselves."

"Does Bouck protect you?"

"Oh, yes. We have locks on all the doors and Bouck won't let me go out unless I'm feeling just right. And he tells me how I have to be careful on the street."

"The city's a pretty dangerous place," Jason agreed. "Have you ever been attacked or followed?"

Camille looked at him shrewdly. "No," she said flatly. "Have you?"

He made a tiny noncommittal motion with his head and went on. "Do you ever feel people on the street are dangerous?"

Again the shrewd look. "Anybody can be a mugger." Camille played with her hair. "You never know."

True enough. The woman wasn't stupid.

"What about salespeople in the grocery store or restaurants? Do you ever think they mean you ill, like they're out to get you?"

Camille laughed. "That's crazy. Do you think I'm crazy?"

She seemed lucid, didn't appear to be delusional. He went on without answering. "Sometimes people can hear voices when no one else is around."

"That's crazy, too."

Jason smiled. She was shrewd, didn't want to appear crazy. "Tell me about the last few days," he repeated. His stomach growled. Very discreetly he glanced at his watch. Ten hours had passed since he'd had something to eat. He remembered that April had promised him food. He wondered if she was out getting it for him.

# 57

The door from the kitchen to the hall was open. April saw a big man crowd Lieutenant Braun, trying to push him out. The man's cheeks were red and blotchy, his eyes wide with shock and fury. He was thick around the middle and had the threatening gestures and loud, hectoring voice of a bully.

"Who the fuck are you?" he demanded, looking like someone who would have no trouble punching a cop.

"Lieutenant Braun, Homicide, NYPD." Braun held out his badge.

Bouck didn't look at it. "Get out of here."

April glanced down at the bundle of Maggie Wheeler's clothes on the top basement step, her heart racing. The man was probably their killer. And he was up on something, really high. She'd seen guys like him so high, they didn't feel pain, couldn't be stopped by half a dozen officers with stun guns, or even a .38 slug. She was scared.

"Just calm down," Braun said. "We have a warrant to take a look around."

The guy had no intention of calming down. "Oh, yeah, what for?" he demanded belligerently.

"A woman in the shop across the street was murdered. We're investigating the case."

"Are you nuts? What does that have to do with me?"

"Like I said, we're investigating the case."

"Oh, no, you're not. Not in here." Bouck spun around. "Who the fuck is this?"

"Sergeant Roberts," Roberts's voice replied.

Now two detectives were in the hall. There were five in the house. Where were the others? Adrenaline pumped through April without showing her the job to prepare for. She needed to tell Braun and Roberts what she'd found, to warn them, but they were jammed into the narrow space of the hallway. She didn't want to provoke an incident. Where was Mike?

"You can't just bust into innocent people's houses in the middle of the fucking night. Are you nuts?" Bouck screamed at them.

"Unh-unh," Braun said conversationally. "We have reason to believe someone from this house may be involved in two homicides."

"You got to be crazy. No way," Bouck said furiously. Then as if surprised by the thought, "Who? Jamal?" That stopped him. For a few seconds, while he thought it over, he had nothing to say. Then he got his voice back. "No way."

He looked from one cop to the other. "Where's Camille?"

Braun didn't say where the woman was. His voice got cold and his confidence came back. "You want to see Camille?"

"Yeah."

"Fine. Then do what we tell you to do. Got it?"

Wrong thing to say. Bouck stuck out his arm and tried to push past Braun. "I want to see her now. Get out of my way."

"Hey, watch that." Braun stood his ground.

"I want to see Camille."

"Fine. Come with us to the precinct. You can see her there."

"You took that sick woman out of my house?" Bouck's voice rose to a shriek.

The three of them were in a tight space, two without much patience and the third walking off the deep end. April's thoughts whirled. She didn't know what to do. She didn't know Braun and Roberts, didn't have the language developed with them to say the man they were so busy provoking was probably their perp. Ducci had suggested the killer might be a cross dresser or a transvestite. Bouck was clearly the one in charge here, kept his girlfriend in a restraint in the maid's room. Maybe he was the shopper, wore the clothes on the racks upstairs. Maybe he signed Camille's name in The Last Mango's guest book.

April didn't have many options. She didn't see how she could warn them without making matters worse. If she just came out of the kitchen with the bundle, Bouck might freak.

Calamita, the detective who had been searching the living room, made the choice for her. He pushed into the hallway.

"Shit, what's that?" Bouck spun around and hit the banister.

"We have a few more officers here," Braun said. "So don't get excited."

"Jesus Christ. Gimme that!" Bouck screamed.

"What is it, Calamita?"

April stepped forward to see it. It was then she saw Mike at the top of the stairs. *No, stay where you are.* Now there was a fourth. Four against one, and the guy was going to resist anyway. Suddenly April realized that the bulk at Bouck's waist was not all fat. He had a pistol tucked into the waistband of his jeans. Shit.

Bouck grabbed for the open box in Calamita's hands. Inside was a 9mm Colt All-American. Fifteen-round magazine and 3³/₄ barrel brushing kit. One automatic, two barrels.

"Stand back," Braun told him.

"What is that? Where'd you get that?" Bouck's rage escalated.

"It was behind a false back in an old desk, sir," Calamita replied.

"Would everybody stand back, please." Braun's voice was tight. "Put your hands out," he said to Bouck. "I want to see your hands in front of you."

Bouck ignored him. "You brought that in here. You brought it in," he screamed. "I never saw it before. I don't even know what it is." He reached for it.

Calamita moved back.

The top stair creaked. Bouck turned his head and saw Sanchez. "Whaa—"

Instantly April was out the kitchen door, gesturing to Mike and Lieutenant Braun that Bouck had a gun.

"This is a frame," Bouck screamed at the sight of two more detectives. "You're going to be history. You took a sick woman out of here. You're threatening me—I'm not going anywhere. I didn't do anything."

"Give me your gun." Lieutenant Braun's voice was soft now. "We don't want anybody to get hurt."

Bouck froze.

April let her breath out.

"Come on, let's let the boys finish up in here."

"Unh-unh. You can't do this."

"Come on. Give me the gun. Don't you want to see your girlfriend?"

"Yeah, I do. Why don't you go outside and wait for me? I'll come out on my own." Bouck's voice turned cunning.

Braun shook his head. "It's not happening that way. You give me the gun and we all go out together."

Bouck tried something else. "What, are you nuts? I don't have a gun." He reached his hand across his body.

Roberts moved forward to grab him. Everybody changed position, moving in, moving back. Bouck's pistol was out. Someone shouted. Roberts lunged at it.

Two shots exploded in the small space. Bouck crumpled, shot in the back. Braun sagged against the banister, screaming that he'd taken a hit. Blood poured out on the floor from a neat hole in his right shoe. Braun slid to the floor. More people began crowding in.

"What happened?" Penelope Dunham, the assistant D.A., running late, plunged through the front door with the two cops who'd let Bouck in without stopping him. She skidded in a puddle of blood on the floor. "Dear God . . ."

For an instant Mike and April stared at each other. Then Braun pointed at them, told them to stop gaping and get the hell out of there.

# 58

"It sounds like you're under a lot of stress right now," Jason said. His notepad rested on his knee below the level of the tabletop. He made a quick note.

Camille lowered her head and nodded. "I'm worried," she said softly.

"Sometimes when people get tense and nervous, their ears play tricks on them. They hear things when no one's there."

Camille nodded again.

"Have you ever heard people telling you things when no one's there?"

"No."

"What are you worried about?"

Camille glanced down at where she'd bitten her arm. She was silent for a long time.

"I'm worried about Bouck," she said at last. "I'm worried about my relationship with my sister." She looked up at Jason. "I'm worried about my future."

"You sound blue." There was nothing quite like stating the obvious. It usually worked.

Camille's eyes filled with tears. She shook her head fiercely. "I'm not supposed to say."

"Sometimes when people get depressed and worried they feel they don't want to go on living. Have you ever felt like this?"

"Yes." Camille mouthed the word.

"When?"

She shrugged.

"Within the last forty-eight hours?"

"No."

"Have you ever felt life was not worth living?"

She bristled. "I already told you that."

"You said yes. Did you ever try to end your life?"

"I'm not supposed to say."

"Who told you that?"

She shrugged again.

Uh-huh. "You mean you did try to end it?"

"Nooooo, I mean I never went all the way." She brushed her red hair away from her face, looked defiant. "I could do it. If I tried, I could do it."

"So you went part of the way? What does that mean?"

Camille kissed the dog. "I have my baby to live for."

"Yes." Jason looked at the bloody marks on her arm. "But you can hurt yourself. You bit your arm."

"I got nervous. I was upset. I don't know why I did that. I feel better now. I don't think I'll do it again."

"What else do you do to hurt yourself, Camille?"

She glanced at the pocket where Jason's key chain with the knife on it was. "I cut myself. I burned myself." She chewed on her lips. "I break things."

"What about Bouck?"

"What about him?"

"Have you ever hurt Bouck? Or your sister? Have you ever hurt Milicia?"

She looked shocked. "No. How could I?"

"Anybody else?"

"What?"

"Have you ever hurt anybody else?"

She shrank back from the table. "You're just asking me that because I'm in the police station. You think I'm crazy."

Jason didn't say anything.

She gnawed on her lip.

"Have you hurt anybody else?"

"No. Only myself," Camille said firmly.

Okay. "You said you were worried about your relationship with your sister. You want to tell me about that?"

Camille shuddered. "My sister is making me sick."

"How is she doing that?"

"Ever heard of voodoo?" she whispered.

"Your sister is making you sick with voodoo?"

"Yes, you got it." She nodded vigorously.

"How does she do that?"

"It happened a long time ago, and she won't stop. That's why Bouck has four locks."

"What happened a long time ago?"

"I can't say."

Okay. "Is your sister doing anything to you now?"

Camille nodded fiercely, her face brittle with pain.

"What?"

Suddenly her eyes squeezed shut. With her wild mane of reddish hair, the trancelike expression, and the loose gauzy clothes, Camille looked like a parody of a fortune-teller struggling for an omen. "I'm not sure. It's hazy. I can't see."

Jason changed the subject. "Why don't you tell me about the last few days before you came here. What were those days like?"

Camille opened her eyes. "You want to know what I do?" She looked around wildly, as if for something to say.

"Yes. What time do you wake up in the morning? What do you do? Things like that." Jason sat back in his chair.

Camille took some time to answer. The dog pawed her hand for attention. It gave her something to focus on. She smiled.

"I have to get up early because Puppy likes to get up early."

Then her face clouded over.

"You take Puppy out for walks?" Jason asked.

"Sometimes," she said vaguely.

"Then what?"

"I read the paper. If the stock market's up, I go shopping."

So Camille read the paper and went shopping. He asked about the newspaper first. "What's your favorite section?"

"I like the stock market. But I read the whole thing. Then I put the paper on the floor for Puppy."

"What was the Dow today?" Jason asked. He didn't know what it was himself, but he'd look it up later to see if she was right.

"Thirty-five twenty-five," she replied without hesitation.

"Is that up or down from yesterday?"

She shook her head, looking at him shrewdly again. "You're trying to trip me up." Her shrill laugh was startling. "But you can't trip me up."

"Oh, why not?"

"Because I know the trick." Camille clapped her hands triumphantly.

"What's the trick?" Jason was careful not to frown. He was puzzled.

"You asked me what the market did yesterday."

He nodded. So?

Camille laughed. "Yesterday was Labor Day. The market was closed."

"Oh, yeah. It was." Jason smiled. One of his supervisors used to say, "Never underestimate the mentally ill. Just because they're sick doesn't mean they're stupid."

So, she wasn't hallucinatory, knew what day it was, followed the stock market. Might be slightly delusional. Focus drifted in and out. She thought her sister was hurting her with voodoo that started a long time ago. What kind of voodoo? Jason checked his watch. It was nearly midnight.

# 59

April Woo looked through the glass viewing panel and mouthed "Come out."

Leisurely, Jason got up, stretched, said something to Camille April couldn't hear, then moved to the door. April opened it.

He gave her a piercing look. "What's going on?"

April didn't answer. She was deeply aware of the brown stains on her shirt and the blood spatters from the gunshot wounds of Lieutenant Braun and Bouck on her shoes and trousers. There had been quite a bit of blood on the floor. She'd waded through it. There was a lot of other trace evidence all over her, too. From the upstairs, from the basement. Crime Scene would have a hell of a time putting together the last few hours of her day. Just a routine day that started with a dead girl on one side of Second Avenue, then segued right into a shootout among five officers and a suspect on the other side of Second Avenue.

Upstairs they were saying the bureau got their perp within twenty-four hours. Great work. They were heroes. There were only a few crucial things wrong with that though. They got him in the wrong twenty-four-hour period. After he killed Maggie Wheeler, they'd been looking for someone who knew her, not a stranger. So he had time to kill again. They'd been meticulously working the wrong angle. April felt kind of queasy. A lot queasy, in fact. Like everything about this case from beginning to end was all messed up.

Once in a while in social situations she'd indulge and have a beer. She hadn't had one since Sunday, when she ate part of a lunch with Dr. Dong, but now she felt as if she'd been drinking steadily ever since the case began just over a week ago. She was tired, thick-headed, and a little nauseated.

And now Jason Frank's eyes were boring into her, increasing her uneasiness. This was a guy who didn't just look at people. He looked into them. She'd seen this before in him. His gaze made her wonder if he could tell what she was thinking. It used to throw her off balance until she got to know him. Then she decided he was all right, couldn't read her mind after all.

"What's going on?" he asked again.

"End of shift is all." She answered his question evenly, but her face was stiff with strain.

Mike was in Sergeant Joyce's office, on the phone with the Captain. For some reason, the people downtown didn't think it was as great work as Captain Higgins did. They weren't happy. They were talking about an internal investigation of the shooting. That made Captain Higgins nervous. He knew his people could be made to take the fall somehow just because they were on the scene and it would look better. Wouldn't look better for the Two-O though.

"Thank God, we're clean" had been April's first words when they got in their car to return to the precinct.

She said things like that because thinking the American thing was a reflex action with her. At the same time as she thanked the generic American God that actually had no meaning to her, she had another thought. She worried about which of the many Chinese gods that Sai Woo claimed were hovering around in the air all the time, waiting to decide which moments to make danger and which to protect from danger, was appropriate to thank on an occasion like this.

"Not so fast," Mike replied. "They'll check our guns to make sure we're clean, and then what they find will show maybe we're not so clean after all." He rolled his window down.

"Better pray they find you clean," he added.

April was driving. She had the keys, and it was her turn. She saw Mike's hand drift up to the knot on his tie and knew he was reaching for the cross around his neck. She could tell he believed in God, and might even be praying to Him right now. She found that kind of puzzling, because it was clear when people believed that kind of stuff, they got in a lot of trouble.

She couldn't get over the fact that Mike's wife hung on to him for years, even though she didn't want him anymore. That wasn't like the Chinese. But the Chinese were different in lots of ways. Each had his own name, different from anyone else's. The Spanish all had generic names, like the generic God they worshiped. The men were all José or Alfonso, Jesus or Juan. The women were Maria or Maria Rosario or Maria Elena, or Maria Magdalena. It got confusing sometimes. All the women in Sanchez's life seemed to be just plain Maria. His mother, sister, cousins, the Maria who didn't want him.

The thought of Mike's Maria who didn't want him sliced through April's stomach like a knife through a bitter melon. She felt the mix: the bitterness of the melon and the sharpness of the knife. She didn't understand her feelings about Mike. Everybody else she thought about with her head. She felt Mike with her body. That was *boo hao.* No good at all.

She thought about her reaction when she realized Bouck had a weapon. She had broken into a cold sweat, her first thought of Mike, up on the stairs, unprepared and in the middle of everything.

After the shots were fired, she had wanted to rush into the melee and make sure he was okay. That was not good. A cop couldn't think with the heart, or any other part of the body. A cop could think only with his head. Anything else was dangerous.

And the way she reacted to Mike was all physical. Sometimes when she was close to him she got a sharp pain in the stomach. And it wasn't because she missed lunch. Sometimes it was a piercing pain behind the eyes. Other times, sweat. It occurred to her maybe Skinny Dragon Mother was right and some Chinese god had gotten to America after all, had personally homed in on her, and was making mischief.

One day in the car Mike told April his mother Maria wrote a letter every day to his dead father up in heaven to keep him informed of what was going on with his family down on earth.

April didn't have to ask how much postage it was to heaven. Postage to heaven was free, but apparently getting there wasn't always so easy. An unhappy wife stayed married because she was afraid a divorced woman wouldn't get in. April felt bad that she had known Mike for a year and it took Ducci to find that out.

Skinny Dragon Mother would say April wasn't much of a detective. And it was true she didn't know what to make of Spanish women. One writing letters to her husband in heaven because she didn't want to keep him waiting for the news. One thinking she could get there on a technicality, pretending she hadn't violated her sacred vows by leaving her husband. What kind of God would put up with tricks like that?

In trouble, though, Mike's hand moved up to his neck, where the small gold cross hung on a chain. She had seen it once after they had a scuffle with two thirteen-year-olds who'd robbed a corner store, shot the owner in the chest, and then led them on a chase down a crowded play street, through an open fire hydrant. By the time they and three uniforms stopped the kids, the gun was long gone, people were shrieking on the street, and everyone was soaked. Mike had shoved his wet tie in a pocket and opened his collar.

It was then that April saw for the first time a small portion of dark and hairy, barbarian chest and the cross. She had thought it must be easier with only one God to worry about, because she didn't want to think about the hair on Mike's chest and how sexy she thought it was.

The whole thing had made her sweat—the cross, the chest. The chase, the stinging cold water from the fire hydrant.

Jason didn't buy shift change as the cause of her tension. "Where've you been?"

April turned to take him upstairs to the squad room. "Out in the field," she said vaguely.

"Something must have happened. You don't look so, ah, great."

"Yeah, I'll tell you about it. How are you doing with Camille?"

"Oh, I'm about finished for now. I've sent the officer back in with her while we talk."

Jason followed her upstairs to the squad room. He'd been there before.

It was after midnight. No one was around. April glanced at Sergeant Joyce's closed door. She wondered if Mike was still in there with her, giving his statement. If that was the case, hers would be next.

She sat down at her desk, trying not to think about it. She had been working six different cases when the Maggie Wheeler thing came up. All of them had been put aside. They were sitting there on her desk, the folders untouched in a week. Everybody cared about his own case and wanted it dealt with right away. Quite a few message slips had accumulated. The pile looked a little messy, as though someone had gone through it.

April took a sidelong glance at it. The name on the top pink slip jumped up and startled her. George Dong had called at nine o'clock. Hastily, she shoved the slips under a folder.

Jason lowered himself into the visitor's chair beside her desk, grimacing as if everything hurt. "I'm really hungry, and I'm really tired, and there's blood on your shirt. What happened?"

"It's mole," she replied quickly, closing her jacket around the stains. She couldn't decide what to tell him, so she hedged. "You want food first or the story first?"

Jason smiled bleakly. "Why don't you tell me the story while we're waiting for the food?"

# 60

"We got a warrant to go over the house where Camille lives," April began. "Her boyfriend came back before we were finished. There was a confrontation. He shot a lieutenant from Homicide, and a detective shot him."

"What?" Jason's California tan turned a little green. "You mean the boyfriend, Bouck, had a gun? He shot a cop?"

April nodded. "And a cop shot him. In the back."

"Jesus, is he alive?"

"He was alive half an hour ago. He's probably in surgery by now." She checked her watch. It was really late.

Camille's friend got shot. Jason looked stunned.

"In the back?" he said faintly, not understanding how that might have happened.

"Yeah, well, the Lieutenant was in front of him and the Sergeant was behind him. When the Sergeant saw him going for his gun, he fired to protect his boss."

Jason thought about that for a moment. "A real gun?"

"You mean Bouck's? Oh, yes, it was very real. We found three guns, none registered."

The sandwich came. Jason unwrapped the paper plate, then stopped and regarded it doubtfully, like suddenly he didn't feel so hungry anymore.

"Go ahead." April nodded at the food. A huge pile of crispy french fries took up more than half the plate, so the huge triple-layer turkey club on white toast hung over the side. "That should keep you for a while."

"Yeah," Jason agreed. "Thanks."

She watched, amazed, while he added five packets of Sweet'n Low

269

and a full cup of milk to the half cup of coffee he had ordered in a large cup. Interesting ritual. She wondered what Freud would think of it.

"Want some?" he offered.

April shook her head even though the french fries looked pretty good. "No thanks. I'm on duty."

"You can't eat when you're on duty?" Jason took a bite of the sandwich.

That was her attempt at a joke. She shook her head again. The plate had a lot of food on it. It would take a while before he could talk. She looked away, letting her thoughts wander around in the fog of this case.

In the office were Mike and Sergeant Joyce, either talking to each other, or Captain Higgins, or somebody who outranked Higgins. In the hospital were Braun and Bouck. April's thoughts drifted to Albert Block, their first suspect. It occurred to her that Block was a B word, too. Block, Bouck, Braun. All B words. What did that have to do with it? Nothing. She told herself to get focused.

She pulled out her pad and made some notes. Check handwriting in guest book. Bouck's. Camille's. They could get handwriting samples out of the house. April had taken the hairbrush from the room. They could match the hair from the hairbrush with the hair on Maggie's dress. It might not be Camille's hair in the hairbrush, but might be Camille's hair on the dress. Maybe both Bouck and Camille wore the clothes at different times.

Jason finished the french fries, pushed the plate away, and picked up the coffee. "Thanks for the food," he said again, and seemed to make a decision about something.

"I want to review the whole case with you, and I want to talk to Camille again. But not now. I think for now I should give you my reading of Camille and wrap it up for the night."

April frowned. She was the detective. He was the consultant. He wasn't supposed to tell her how to manage the case. She told herself to lighten up. "So what's your reading?"

"At this point I can't give you a complete diagnosis, but I can tell you what she isn't."

"Fine."

"She isn't delusional. That means she doesn't hear voices. She's not hallucinatory. She doesn't see things that aren't there, at least not at the moment. She's not psychotic. She can tell the difference between what's real and what isn't. She's not paranoid and not violent."

April frowned. What was he talking about? The woman tried to eat her arm.

Jason smiled. "I know. You're thinking if they act crazy, they probably are. Camille is certainly very troubled, very frightened. But except for the rages she directs at herself, she's a gentle, nurturing person. She could not hurt anybody else. I don't think she could kill a spider."

Judging from the state of the kitchen, she couldn't wash a dish either. April thought of the straitjacket.

"The clothes of the first murder victim were found in the basement of the house where Camille lived," April told him.

Jason shook his head. "Poor woman."

April nodded. "It was a—pretty unhealthy scene. The place is a mess. Her room was upstairs. Looks like he kept her in a restraint at least part of the time. We found a lot of sedatives, sleeping pills, that kind of thing, in his medicine cabinet." She shuddered and fell silent.

"Look, she doesn't need to be hospitalized at this time, either voluntarily or involuntarily," Jason said.

"We can't hold her here," April protested.

"I know that, but she does need supervision. She's used to having someone care for her. Unimaginable as it may seem, she was attached to Bouck, and freedom from him will be threatening, certainly more than she can handle. Better call her sister."

April nodded. Yeah, the sister could take her off their hands. She looked at her watch. Twelve-forty-five. "Thanks," she told Jason. "I owe you one."

"Sure, sure."

She collected the garbage and threw it in the overflowing wastebasket by her desk, then walked downstairs with him. "I really appreciate this," she said again at the door. The season had changed. The humidity had lifted, and there was a definite bite in the air.

Jason yawned and nodded absently. "Keep in touch. We have to follow up on this one."

"Yeah." Two of the guy's victims were dead. But the one he kept in a straitjacket was still alive. Eventually, if Bouck lived, he'd be tried and Camille might have to testify against him. It would be somebody's uphill battle to prepare Camille for that. But not hers, thank God.

271

April took a final breath of fresh air, then climbed the stairs to the squad room. She dialed the sister's number. She should come for Camille. But there was no answer, and not even a machine to take a message.

The door to Sergeant Joyce's office was still closed. It made her mad not to know what was going on. Finally she muttered "To hell with it," went over, and knocked.

# 61

It was well after one o'clock by the time April pulled her car into an empty spot in front of the Woo house. The light by the front door was still on, and April could tell from the glow spilling out from the kitchen into the downstairs hallway that her mother was still up. She groaned.

She had left the house before ten that morning, was bone tired, and due back in the precinct in less than seven hours. That left no time for study, and hardly any for sleep. At this point it was the sleep April worried about. She had been back and forth across town a half dozen times that day, and had to cross again to get to the Queensboro Bridge. At this hour the traffic wasn't so bad, but all the way to Queens she worried about Chinese torture. The worst torture was to have to eat, and be deprived of sleep.

One thing April liked about her job was the perpetual growling hunger she acquired in the long hours when there was too much to do and no time to eat. As a child she had never been allowed to grow hungry, but always fed before the need came. To Sai Woo this was the sign of a good mother. By feeding April she could change the long history of hunger and famine in China, and ensure for April a good future, full of plenty. April was sure plenty on her plate at all hours of the day or night was her torture for being her mother's only child. Only child had to have special care for good luck.

Chinese didn't wear crosses or medals of tortured saints on chains around their necks. Good luck, not heaven, was the great Chinese pie in the sky, the thing most prayed for and revered. Good ruck, rots of money, rong rife. Those were the symbols most often stamped in gold.

Gold symbols made April think of Mike, or maybe it was the other way around. She wondered if the great generic God that monitored the North American continent might be punishing Maria for leaving him, and not letting him go. That was sure thing bad luck for everybody. No way to put a good face on it.

On the other hand, sometimes you couldn't tell good luck was coming even when it was right in front of your face. Like the breaking of this case. Woman comes in with a story her sister might have killed somebody, doesn't say how she knows. Police check the story out, and before the A.D.A. even has time to get there, before there is any exchange of information at all, two people get shot.

Then, when it turns out the sister Camille was a virtual prisoner of the boyfriend, the sister Milicia can't be found to come and take her away. So now they had an officer guarding the boyfriend in the hospital, and an officer in the house making sure the wacko made it through the night. And still no word from the sister who started the ball rolling.

Well, good luck and answers to all questions were like shadows in the mist. You had to know how to interpret them, and when to follow them into the murk. April turned off her headlights and sat in the dark for a moment. What she remembered most about the Sherlock Holmes story she read a long time ago was the part about the London fog so dense, policemen could lose their way following a suspect around the block. At NYPD she learned fast that almost every case presented such a fog.

In her early training the question was once put to her: "What do you do, Officer, when you get called to a scene where there's a body splattered on the sidewalk and you don't know the first thing about it?"

The correct answer was: "You look up, sir."

A lot of people would give different answers, but that was the right one. First things first. Use your head, see if you can determine where the body came from.

April sat there, trying to sift through all the thoughts whirling around in her head. What was she so apprehensive about? Her Sergeant's test in two days? The command from the Captain to get together with the A.D.A. and wrap up the boutique case in the morning?

Higgins actually suggested they go to the hospital and wait there till the suspect regained consciousness, then arrest him for the murder of Maggie Wheeler before he fell asleep again. Then they could relax and put the Rachel Stark case together.

Damn. The shadow of Skinny Dragon Mother crossed to the window, cracked it open.

"What you doing out there?" Sai Woo threw her best English out into the night, so the neighbors, if they were up to hear her, wouldn't think she was an immigrant.

Often when April was on the four-to-midnight shift, her mother waited for her to get home, then invited her into the kitchen to feed her and hear about her day. That's why April was sitting in the car. Hoping to avoid it.

"Just getting my stuff."

"Come in, come in. I have good dumprings. Your favorite kind. Been waiting all night."

"Okay, I'm coming, Ma."

"Not come soon enough. Best kind. Clab, flesh pea."

That was just great. April grabbed her two bags and got out of the car. Her father was top cook in an Upper East Side restaurant. He must have brought the crab and ginger delicacy to bribe *boo hao* daughter to sit in kitchen, middle of the night, discuss cases with Skinny Dragon Mother, who didn't have anything else to think about but making her daughter as miserable as possible.

Sai Woo's greatest amusement was to steal many precious hours from her daughter and use them to scold her for choosing a hard life when, if April only smiled a little, she could marry and have a soft one. In this way she passed the time happily by making her daughter's hard life a whole lot harder. April trudged up the short cement walk to the house.

Magically the window closed and the front door opened. Sai examined her daughter critically, noticed right away that April was wearing her locker outfit. "Change crows," she said, wrinkling her nose.

"Yes." April turned away, didn't want to discuss it.

" 'Nother dead body?"

"Yes."

"Bad?"

"Yes."

"Very bad. Can smell from here. The one on TV? I watch, didn't see you." Sai Woo led the way back through the living room to the kitchen. "Why you never on TV?"

"Ma, I'm very tired. I've got to go to bed."

"You got to eat first."

"It's late, don't go to the trouble."

"No trouber."

"I can't eat now, really."

"Got to."

April suddenly got a look at her mother in the light. Sai Woo was all dressed up, wearing her good gray silk dress, stockings, and shoes. Her face was carefully made up. April regarded her suspiciously.

"What's going on?"

There was a sly smile on Skinny Dragon Mother's face that April didn't like.

"I'm cerebrating."

All alone at one o'clock in the morning? Sure. "What are you celebrating?" April asked.

The smile got wider. Ha. Got her. "Your good ruck," Sai said triumphantly.

April stared at her mother. What good luck? Everything in her life was a mess. "What good luck, Ma? Did I win the lottery?"

Sai got tired of being looked at and shoved April along the rest of the way to the kitchen. "Sit down. Eat clab dumprings. Don't mess up."

April shook her head. "I don't know about any good luck. I don't want crab dumplings. I had a hard day. I want to go to bed."

"Eat clab. Clab good luck."

April shook her head again. She could stop a two-hundred-and-fifty-pound drug-crazed thug with a razor knife and a gun no trouble. But couldn't get away from her mother when she wanted to talk.

"All right, give me a hint. What's the good luck?"

Sai nodded her head approvingly. "My friend say vely good ruck. He don't rike nobody, rike you."

Oh. If her mother got all dressed up for that, she was going to have a long wait for the wedding. April sat down at the table meekly. She'd bet a thousand dollars that even though Dr. George Dong was willing to ask her out again, maybe even take her to a nice place this time, it was very unlikely to work out the way her mother hoped. She decided she'd better have a dumpling, make her mother happy while she could.

# 62

One after another the antique clocks around the apartment chimed the half hour. On the tenth dong another sound joined in to pierce the silence. It was a ringing deep inside the head, like the echo of a bad hangover. Jason rolled over and groaned.

Nine more clocks finished their roll call, but the ringing persisted. Shit. He opened his eyes. The vertical blinds were open enough for him to see that outside, the sky was just beginning to lighten with the dawn. Emma's alarm clock with the Day-Glo face showed that it was six thirty-two. That made it three thirty-two in California, too early to be a wake-up call from Emma. The loud, unruly sound was the bell of his oldest telephone, the kind that most people had replaced a long time ago with the kind of phone that burbled like a mourning dove. Jason didn't want to answer it. It was a half hour too early to get his brain in gear, and there wasn't a soul in the world other than Emma he wanted to talk to.

Shit. He reached for the phone. "Hello."

"Happy birthday. What is it—thirty-nine or forty?"

Jason groaned again. It was his birthday. "Same as you, Charles."

"What's the matter? Did I wake you up?" There was an edge to Charles's voice.

Jason sat up, rubbing his eyes. "No, I've been up celebrating for hours."

"Good, I wouldn't want to wake you up. Did you get my message?"

"No, I got in so late last night I didn't pick up the messages." He paused. "You didn't call at six-thirty to say happy birthday. What's going on?"

"Maybe you should tell me. Actually, I'm surprised you didn't call me in on this before." The edge sharpened.

Oh, it was about Milicia. Jason waited for Charles to explode. He did.

"I don't get it, Jason. Milicia is a friend of ours, a colleague. You met her in our home. The least you could do is keep me informed of a situation like this." Charles's voice was tight with anger.

"She came to me professionally, Charles. You know I couldn't talk to you about that."

"Milicia called me last night. She was so upset by the way you've handled things, she spent half the night with us." He fell silent, then added, "Brenda told her she could stay over, but Milicia said she couldn't."

A heavy accusation hung in the air. Jason didn't respond.

"Jason, is this true? Are you responsible for having Milicia's sister arrested for murder?"

"No, she has not been arrested. But she is a very sick woman. And she was brought in for questioning. I was at the police station for hours last night. They wanted a preliminary evaluation of her and didn't want to send her to Bellevue."

"I'm just astounded by all this. Milicia is devastated. She's afraid her sister will go to prison. She blames you for dragging the police into it."

"Charles, Milicia came to me because she was fearful that Camille was dangerous. Since then two young women have died. Milicia told me she believed Camille was responsible for their murders. What was I supposed to do? I had no choice. Absolutely no choice. Milicia had to go to the police with the information she had. Look, do you have a half hour sometime today? I'll fill you in."

"Jesus, Jason, I can't believe you didn't call me. Shit. What is this— Wednesday? I have a cancellation at one forty-five. We could talk then."

"Fine. I'll meet you halfway. How's Madison and Seventy-ninth?"

"That's more than halfway for you, thanks. Ah, Jason, where is she now?"

"Camille? She's at her home. Oh, and Charles—the suspect is her boyfriend. He had a gun, and apparently there was some kind of shootout." The words sounded strange in Jason's mouth. He didn't know the kind of people who were in shootouts.

"God! Was anybody hurt?" Charles sounded shocked.

"Yes, the suspect and a policeman, as I understand it. I don't know the nature of their injuries, but Camille has lost her caregiver. She's going to need a lot of supervision."

"Should she be hospitalized?"

"We'll talk about it later." Emma's alarm clock started ringing. "I've got to get going."

Jason hung up and stretched. He didn't like the way the bed looked, only a small slice of it mussed, and the rest still made up, the pillows untouched. Twice a week Marta, the cleaning lady he'd had for a dozen years, made the bed for him. The rest of the time he messed it up and left it that way. He kicked the bedcovers off his naked body and pushed them around with his feet. The sun was now pushing in through the blinds, clearly revealing a thick layer of dust on the slats. His body looked slack and soft to him. He was damp with sweat, and his bladder was full. He got up to urinate for the first time in his fortieth year.

# 63

It was supposed to be better at night. It was always better at night. Depression moved in on Camille in the mornings, rumbling into the city by the bridges and tunnels in a caravan of eighteen-wheelers that pitted and dented the streets so badly, no one was safe negotiating the potholes.

Starting at four or five on bad days, she could feel it coming. She could see in inches, how the blackness of night began to break up into little pieces. And like the night fading away, she disintegrated, too, as unrecognizable bits of herself plunged into the Bermuda Triangle of another dawning day.

Camille was constantly, perpetually afraid. The knot in her stomach pushed up from below, crushing her chest and heart. It was painful to breathe. An animal stuck in her throat, chewed away at her from the inside. Sometimes she saw it as a tapeworm, thick and gray, sometimes as a cloud of poison gas. Today when she shut her eyes, she saw a formless thing, all mouth, eating her heart out. There was nothing in her, no human organs, nothing. Her body was an empty package with a bomb inside. She could hear it ticking away.

Bouck was in the hospital. The doctor told her that, but she didn't cry. The policewoman at the police station said she couldn't locate Milicia to take care of her, and they couldn't keep her there, so they had to let her come home. Still she didn't cry. She was numb.

The doctor said he would talk to her again so they could figure out what happened.

"When?" she wanted to know.

"Sometime tomorrow," he told her.

No, she meant, "What happened when? What happened now or what happened a long time ago?"

He didn't say.

280

Camille and Puppy came home in a police car. Her heart pounded all the way. A policewoman, big as a house, guarded her in the back seat, then let her out. She opened the doors of Bouck's building with Camille's key, then walked behind Camille and Puppy up the stairs.

The pounding in her chest intensified when she saw blood all over the hall floor. There was blood on the walls, too, and sticky tape marking off the places where no one was supposed to go. No one had cleaned the blood up. It left a sick smell in the moldy place.

The bomb inside Camille exploded. She tripped and pitched forward. The policewoman behind her reached out to stop her from crumpling on the floor.

At her touch, Camille started shrieking.

She grabbed the banister, smearing the blood, a shrill sound of pure terror pulsing from her throat. "Don't touch me. Don't touch me."

The wall of blue recoiled. "Honey, I'm not going to hurt you—"

Not a second later the other one lunged through the door. "What's going on?"

It was the one who drove the car, a man. He looked nervous.

Camille screamed, a cop on either side of her. "No, no!"

The power that kept her safe was gone. Bouck wasn't there to protect her. "Get away from me!" she cried.

Her heart started pounding again. There was blood on her hands. "Where's Bouck?" she whimpered.

She didn't know what happened to Bouck. Puppy yelped, trying to jump out of her arms. The wall of blue moved closer.

Camille froze. Bouck must have killed a policeman with one of his guns and left all that blood behind. Or a policeman had killed him. She stared, bug-eyed, at the two cops.

For a moment no one moved. Then the woman said, "It's okay, honey. No one will touch you." She cocked her head at the cop by the door and moved away from Camille to show they wouldn't touch her. Then she looked around the warehouse of the second floor in amazement, but didn't get any closer to Camille, or say anything about the place.

Camille was too upset to tell her they were redecorating.

It took a long time before she could ask what happened.

The policewoman said she didn't know. Camille didn't believe her, didn't know what to do. She wouldn't go upstairs to the room where she slept, wouldn't stay on the second floor with all the blood. Finally she went to Bouck's room, to sit in the bergère she had chosen for him, the new one that he liked.

The policewoman sat by the door in a hard wooden chair she had brought from downstairs, and watched Camille all night. Her eyes didn't droop. Camille could feel them, wide open, gaping at her. All night she could hear another bomb inside her ticking away.

It was bad, very bad, by morning when the telephone rang. Camille listened to it for a while, not wanting to pick up. By the tenth ring she knew she had to pick up. It might be Bouck calling from the hospital. She reached for the receiver.

Milicia's voice came out of it like a snake out of a charmer's basket. "Bouck, what's happened to Camille?" Her voice was harsh and wild. "I'm so worried about her."

Camille didn't say anything.

"Talk to me. I know you're there."

Still Camille didn't say anything.

"You son of a bitch. You're responsible for this. If Camille is sent to prison, I don't know what I'll do. Poor Camille, you did this to her." Milicia was sobbing.

Milicia was crying for her. Camille didn't want Milicia to cry.

"Bouck, just tell me where she is. I want to see her." Milicia's voice was pitiful.

"I'm here," Camille said in her little-girl voice.

"What?" The crying stopped abruptly.

"I'm right here," Camille said.

"I thought—I came by, looking for you last night. There were police all over the place. They said you weren't there."

"Well, now I'm here," Camille said, watching the big policewoman by the door.

"Didn't they arrest you?"

"I didn't shoot. I think Bouck did."

"What? Are you crazy? They were hung, not shot. Don't play dumb. You know they were hung." Milicia sounded annoyed.

"They were shot, Milicia. There's blood all over the place."

Milicia thought about that for a second.

"Camille, let me talk to Bouck," she said finally.

"He's in the hospital." Camille started to cry.

"Which one?"

"They didn't tell me."

"Shit, are you alone there?"

"No. They're watching me." Puppy stirred at her feet, stretched, then squatted on the rug.

"Who's watching you?" Milicia demanded.

"Police," Camille whispered.

"Look, I'll be right over."

Camille shook her head. No, Milicia, don't come over. Don't. But Milicia had hung up. She was already gone. The policewoman started talking into the radio she carried on her belt. Camille couldn't hear what she said. She glanced at the puddle Puppy had left on the floor, then picked Puppy up and hugged her.

# 64

"Okay, what do we have here?"

The A.D.A. surveyed the room full of people, half of them with containers of coffee as well as their notebooks in front of them. They were all talking at once.

"Come on, let's see if we have a case here." Penelope Dunham was a no-nonsense kind of woman somewhere in her middle forties who looked as if she ate only on rare occasions, saving up her appetite the rest of the time for her opponents in court. Tall and excruciatingly thin, she had a sharp nose with half glasses perched on the bridge, short curly brown hair, intense brown eyes, and a perpetual furrow between strong, untweezed eyebrows. She wore a gray suit with a pearl-gray blouse buttoned all the way up to the neck, low-heeled gray pumps, no jewelry or makeup. Two heavy black bags sat at her feet.

"For those of you who don't know me, I'm Penny Dunham, the assistant district attorney on this case. Before we're through, you're going to know me better than you want to." After having been up half the night and giving herself no cosmetic help, she looked every minute of her age.

She finished shuffling her papers and turned her unflinching gaze on Sergeant Joyce. Joyce had had even less sleep and the additional job of getting two unwilling kids off to their second day of school. Still, she'd taken the time to put some rouge on her cheeks in approximately the right places, some lipstick on her mouth, and the drops she used in her eyes "to take the red out."

April had seen her struggling to pull herself together only moments before. April's own eyes, hidden in their Mongolian folds, looked as fresh and bright as always. She was lucky that way, and knew if she could keep enough fat on her body, and not wither away like her mother, she'd age better than anybody. Joyce, Woo, and Dunham were the only women in the room.

Penelope nodded at Ducci, who had made his second rare emergence from the police labs, and Dr. Baruch from the M.E.'s office. Penelope, with her Daughter of the American Revolution background, was an anomaly in a D.A.'s office, where most of the prosecutors were on their way somewhere else, were ethnically diverse with distinct New York neighborhood accents and a wide range of coloring.

April had never worked with her before, but Mike called her "lock-'em-up Penny" because he once heard her dismiss the testimony of a hostile witness by demanding, "Don't you think our police officers have better things to do than go around arresting innocent people?"

It was nine o'clock in the morning, the earliest they could get together. Dunham had requested that the detectives on the case go downtown to the D.A.'s office because it would be easier on her team—her second in the case, Mario Santorelli, and her investigator from the D.A.'s office, retired Lieutenant Bill Scott of NYPD, now just Bill Scott. Because of the delicacy of the situation and the number of people involved, however, it hadn't turned out that way.

Sergeant Roberts was off the case, being investigated himself for having shot the suspect. Bouck had taken a .38 slug in his right lung, which had made such a mess, he only just survived the surgery. He was as yet unable to speak, and his condition was listed as guarded. Lieutenant Braun was in the hospital, on a different floor, not feeling too good with a couple of mashed bones in his right foot.

But still there were a lot of people. In addition to the three from the D.A.'s office, there were six people from the Two-O, Ducci, and Dr. Baruch. There weren't enough chairs. Sanchez and two other detectives leaned against the wall.

Ducci scowled as if already he wasn't happy with the way things were going. "I got the stuff from the Stark case only yesterday. Haven't *touched* the bag of clothes from the suspect's house. Haven't got anything else from the house," he grumbled. He didn't mind people telling him what to look for, but hated being told what he had. He already told them he wasn't finished.

"—yesterday evening. What do you think I am, a magician?" Baruch's words rose to the surface, then he looked around and was silent.

"Supposed to be. Want to share the autopsy report with us or keep us in suspense?" Scott threw his two cents in.

"What do you want—the whole thing, or just the pertinent parts?" Baruch opened the report.

"What do you think?"

"Fine, the pertinent parts. Rachel Stark died by strangulation, same as Wheeler. Can't tell you the exact time. Sometime Saturday night, probably. Interesting thing. Recently she'd had surgery, had only one kidney. Had some pretty bad keloid scarring around her—"

"Anything else relevant to the case?" Penny interrupted. "We have a lot to go through."

"Bruises around the neck and shoulders. Makeup on her face like the other case"—he looked up—"traces, I mean. Three deep scratches on the right arm. Some dirt under her fingernails, nothing else. Looks like she was overpowered and died without too much of a struggle. Just like the Wheeler case."

"What about the blood on the floor?"

"She had her period. Must have bled right through her Tampax just prior to, or at the time of her death."

Ducci coughed. "What about the pattern marks on her right ankle?"

Baruch nodded and passed around some photos of Rachel Stark, naked on the autopsy table. Two blowups showed a small black curve with four tiny black dots on one side of it. "Looks like a bite mark. I've called a dentist to take a look."

Penelope studied one of the photos, then tossed it to her assistant, frowning. "What kind?"

"What bites on the ankle?" Ducci said sarcastically.

"What? Rats, mice? What?" Santorelli stared glumly at the picture. Little animals gnawed holes. None of the detectives said anything.

"Woof woof. Here comes the mailman." Ducci rolled his eyes.

"Oh, God, the dog." Penny slapped her forehead and looked around for Mike, who had been the one to brief her for the warrant the night before. The dog hairs had been part of the case. Dog hairs in the first victim's nose.

"You still got the dog, Mike?"

"The dog is not in custody at the moment," Mike said, glancing at

April, who got very busy making a note. She had acquired hair samples from the puppy, but had let Camille take the dog home with her.

"Better get that animal in here before it disappears," Penny said sharply.

"It isn't going to disappear." April spoke for the first time, though she wasn't as confident as she sounded. Pretty stupid to send the dog home with the suspect's girlfriend.

"What makes you so sure?"

"It helps with its owner's sanity."

"It could still disappear if somebody finds out it's material evidence in a homicide."

True. Camille's loyalty was more likely to be with Bouck than her dog. "I'll take care of it."

Penelope switched her attention to the first homicide. All they had were a few fibers, a few hairs, a signature in a store guest book, and the victim's clothes found in the basement of the suspect's house.

"Let me get this straight," she said finally. "You want to arrest this man Bouck?"

Mike looked at April and didn't say anything. Sergeant Joyce said, "Yes."

"But you don't have a case." Penelope took her glasses off and rubbed her nose.

"He had several unregistered guns. He shot a police officer." Joyce made this declaration with as little conviction as it deserved.

"He could have shot ten police officers, Sergeant, but that doesn't help with these two homicides. Unless you can come up with his prints, his hair and fiber—*something* to put him on the scene—the evidence you have here points to the woman."

April cleared her throat. "The psychiatrist doesn't think the woman could have done it."

Penelope looked up sharply. "What psychiatrist?"

"Ah, we were having some difficulty questioning the suspect." April paused. "Her behavior was erratic. She was out of control, self-destructive, incoherent. She didn't seem to know about the murders and had no idea why she was here. I called in a psychiatrist we've worked with before."

"Who's that?" Penny raised her pencil to write it down.

"Dr. Jason Frank."

Penny frowned. "He's not one of ours. I don't know the name."

"We've worked with him before," Sergeant Joyce said. "We know the name."

"Okay, we'll let that go for the moment. What was Frank's diagnosis?"

"He said Camille was more likely to hurt herself than someone else," April replied. "He hasn't had time to make a full report yet." And it was her neck if he didn't. April let Camille go with the material evidence in her arms.

"Where is she now?"

"She's under surveillance at her house." April shivered. She hoped.

Penelope made a face.

"It was a pretty weird scene over there," Ducci broke in. "We see it as the boyfriend dressed up in the woman's clothes. That explains the large sizes he put on the dead women. Maybe stuff he woulda liked for himself, you know?"

"And he carried the woman's dog?" Penny said sarcastically.

"So it would appear," Ducci said.

Penny shook her head. "What about a wig, shoes, underwear, Sergeant? You find all that?"

Mike spoke up. "We found an arsenal, a straitjacket. He kept that woman locked in the attic. His medicine cabinet was full of pills—uppers, downers, you name it. No wig. No women's shoes that would fit him."

"Then we don't have anything," Penny said.

"He shot a cop," Santorelli threw in. "We have that."

"Maybe he thought he was protecting his girlfriend. Took the fall for her."

Penelope shook her head. "We can't nail him for this without some evidence. Find out if he liked to dress up in women's clothes, if the neighbors ever saw him carrying the dog around. See if you can come up with a motive. Check the signature in the guest book. A red wig would help. And a confession. That's about it for now." She stretched and collected her papers. "And don't rule out the woman."

April glanced down at her own notes. Maybe she wasn't so triple stupid as her mother said. The night before she had written down the same questions. Except the one about not ruling out the woman.

# 65

"What are you doing here? I thought you were finished with me." Albert Block stood at his front door. He had a mug of coffee in his left hand.

"I was in the neighborhood," April said. "I thought I'd drop by to say hello."

"I don't think I believe that." Block was dressed in another plaid shirt and string tie, jeans, and his lizard cowboy boots. His face was bloodless, as if he'd been deprived of oxygen for the last day or so. He looked nervous and scared, and sorry he'd pushed the buzzer downstairs to let her in.

April glanced around the living room. It looked as if he had decorated it very recently from Ikea. The black-and-white area rug on the floor was so new, a piece of its price tag was still wired to the end. The white nubbly sofa against one wall had a white pillow at each arm and a squat blond wood coffee table in front of it. On the coffee table were two twisted candlesticks with unused candles in them, and a brass pot filled with what looked like a sheaf of wheat. A matching blond wood table with two chairs floated in the middle of the floor by the closed folding doors of the tiny kitchen. There was not much in the way of clutter. Everything was very clean, neat. April wondered if Maggie Wheeler had ever been entertained there. She guessed not.

Block followed her eyes. "You've already searched the place. What do you want?"

"I just wanted to talk to you. Do you mind?"

He shrugged. "Yeah, sort of." But he closed the door behind her anyway.

"Why's that?"

He shrugged again, put his mug down on the single mat that indicated his place at the table. The mat was some kind of black woven plastic. There was nothing else on it.

"I don't have anything else to tell you." He said this like a man who'd been thinking things over and decided for sure he didn't want to be a murderer after all.

"I think you do."

He shook his head. "I saw the papers."

April looked around again. She didn't see any newspapers. "So?"

"So, I know, uh—there's been another one. I didn't have anything to do with it. I didn't know her. Nothing." He waved his hand at the sofa. "You want to sit down?"

"Sure." But she didn't want to sit on his sofa. She pulled out the closest chair at the dining room table and retrieved her notebook from her bag, checked her watch. She had only a few minutes for this. She wrote the day and date, the location and Block's name.

"I'm not here about the other one. I'm here about Maggie," she said.

He played with the empty cup. He didn't want to talk about Maggie anymore.

"You and Maggie were friends, right?"

"I already told you that," he muttered. "I didn't kill her."

"No, I never thought you did."

"How did you know?" He seemed as surprised now as he had been before when they let him go.

"You're too short. The bruises on Maggie's body indicate her killer was a taller person." April played with her pencil, giving him a moment to calm down.

"You can tell that?"

"Yes."

"So what do you want from me?"

She cocked her head to one side, like an inquisitive bird. "You don't look like a happy man, Mr. Block."

"I told you. Maggie was my friend. I liked her."

"You told me you were in the store, and you saw her."

"Maybe I was—kind of imagining things."

"You *imagined* some parts of the scene pretty well. So we believe that you were there."

"She was already dead," he said quickly.

"How do you know?"

"She was hanging there. Her eyes were open. Her face was all . . ." Sweat broke out on his forehead. His fingers trembled as he reached up to wipe it off.

"Albert, do you know that doctors can do amazing things these days? Revive people who've drowned, transplant hearts. There was a mother who saved her kid. He'd been struck by a van and hadn't been breathing for six minutes. She administered CPR while a police officer drove them to the hospital. Only a few blocks away from here. Remember that?"

Albert Block looked doubtful. "She looked dead to me."

"Have you ever seen a dead person before?"

"No. But she was *hanging* there." His eyelid twitched, and he made a face to get control of it.

"Didn't it occur to you to try to help her?"

"You're not supposed to touch—you know—" Block looked away.

"She was your friend."

"I didn't think there was anything I could do!" he cried.

"There was a phone right there. You could have called nine one one. Why didn't you?"

He looked defeated. "I don't know. I keep asking myself that."

"Mr. Block, you left your friend hanging for three days without calling the police."

"I know. It was stupid."

"It was more than stupid. What kind of friend is that?"

Block hung his head. "I said it was stupid. What do you want from me?"

"For Maggie's sake, I want you to tell me the truth. How did you get into the store?"

"I had her keys. I took them off the counter when I asked her to have lunch with me and she said no. I fixed it so she couldn't go out for lunch without me."

"So you used the keys you'd stolen to get back in." April made a note.

"I rang first, but she didn't answer. So I used the keys."

"Where are the keys now?" They had searched his apartment and hadn't found any keys.

"I threw them away."

He threw them away. "Okay, let's go back to before you went to the store. What were you doing before that?"

"I told you—I was hanging around in the bookstore."

"The Endicott."

"There isn't another."

April nodded. "Were you looking at books, or were you looking out the window, watching for Maggie?"

"Both. I told you that, too."

"I know." But things were different now. "So you could see who was coming and going from the store."

Block shrugged. "Maybe."

"So who did you see?"

Block shook his head. "I didn't see anybody."

April found that she was holding her breath. "Nobody?"

"I wasn't watching every second."

"So what were you waiting for? How did you know Maggie was still there?"

"She always left at exactly seven o'clock. She was afraid of the old lady. She wouldn't dare close up before then. I got there about six forty-five." He was perspiring heavily.

April could smell his fear. "And?" She had stood by the window of the Endicott Bookstore and knew exactly what he could see from there. The man at the register knew Block and confirmed that he had been there that evening. She didn't let her breath out.

"And I hung around. I spend a lot of time there."

"You were in love with Maggie. Did you know she had a boyfriend and that she was pregnant? Were you standing there in the bookstore watching for her boyfriend?"

Block angrily shook the pain out of his eyes. "He was one of those hypocritical *Christians*." He spat the word. "He didn't want to use anything, and then when she got pregnant, he didn't want her to have an abortion. She was just so upset—" He crumpled. His tears splashed on the tabletop.

April went on quietly. "When you went into the storeroom, did you think he had done it?"

"No, I thought she did," Block sobbed.

"She? You mean the woman who was in there with her?"

"No, after she left . . ."

April let her breath out. There it was. "What she, Mr. Block?"

"*Maggie!* I thought Maggie did it because of him."

What? He confessed to murdering her when he thought she was a suicide? That didn't make sense. *Don't try to work it out,* April warned herself. *Just let it pass.* She went on.

"You saw somebody go in The Last Mango and then come out. Who did you see?"

"I don't know. Some woman."

"Come on, Albert. What did she look like?"

"I don't know. She was wearing a long skirt. She had red hair. Lots of red hair. That's all I remember." He shook his head. His nose was running.

"Mr. Block, do you know what a transvestite is?"

"It wasn't a man," he said sharply. "I'd know if it were a man."

"Sometimes they can be very convincing," April murmured.

"It wasn't a *man.*"

"How do you *know,* Albert?"

"She was wearing flats."

April waited. Now she was the one sweating. So, the woman was wearing flats. So what?

Block looked at her. "Men dressed up as women always wear high heels. It's part of the thing. The falsies, the lipstick, the wig, the tight short skirt, *and the high heels.*" He said it triumphantly. "This woman was wearing a long loose skirt, a loose top, and flat shoes. It was a woman."

"Did it ever occur to you the woman you saw leaving the shop murdered Maggie?"

"No. It didn't."

"Why not?"

"I don't know. It just—didn't."

Okay. "Would you recognize this woman if you saw her again?"

He shrugged. "I don't know. She was wearing a hat with a floppy brim. I didn't really see her face."

Oh, now she was wearing a hat, great.

"Then how did you know she had all that red hair?"

"I don't know. I guess I saw it."

"Well, would you recognize the hat? The shirt, the shoes, the blouse?"

293

Block shrugged again. He was a big shrugger. "I don't know. Maybe."

April looked at her watch. Twenty-five minutes had passed. Time to go. Had he clarified anything? Maybe he had. She told Albert Block she'd be back.

# 66

Milicia got out of the taxi a few yards north of Bouck's building. Nothing could calm her down and cool the rage she felt. Not the hours of talking to Charles and Brenda, not the Valium Charles had given her. Not the sleepless hours she spent tossing around on her bed. What if going to the police had not been the right thing to do? They never would have found Camille, never would have put together what happened. And even now they were all mixed up. First they took Camille away, and now they brought her back. What was going on?

The police car parked in front of Bouck's door puzzled Milicia. She didn't like the police. She felt a sharp pain in her mind's eye from the bad memories of police cars. They were on reels that played over and over. The worst ones showed the policemen making her father stagger along the yellow line on the side of the road all those times he had trouble driving at night.

"Let's go for an ice cream cone, girls," he used to say. Then, as soon as they were in the car, he suddenly remembered he had to meet somebody in a bar. He always said he'd be gone for just a minute. The girls were not allowed to leave the car. When he came out two, three hours later, he was always mad. He'd forgotten they were there.

Milicia approached the building cautiously, remembering everything, as if it were yesterday—she and Camille huddling under the old gray beach blanket that, year after year, no one ever took out of the car. The things they said—the whispering, wheedling, and whining. Crayon drawings all over the window. Cigarettes and matches in the glove compartment. Smoking. She wouldn't ever forget the burn marks on the car seat, on Camille's arm. Nobody ever figured out what the wounds were, even after they got infected and Camille had to go to the doctor.

Oh, yes. She remembered the police stopping them on the road. "You're going to kill yourself one of these nights, Mr. Stanton."

The bastard couldn't even stand up. That was the reason he never locked the front door. Once he passed out before he got it open. She and Camille found him sleeping on the lawn the next morning when they left for school. And there was the time a policeman brought them home in the middle of the night, and then had to take them away again. He rang the doorbell over and over, but their mother was lying asleep in the living room, her makeup messed all over her face, with a puddle of vomit beside her. They saw her through the picture window. Then they were taken away to spend the night in a shelter.

It took a long time for the policeman's predictions to be fulfilled. She and Camille were all grown-up. Daddy had to take Mother with him in the brand-new Mercedes the night of his crash. A few years earlier it could have been them. Milicia shuddered. And if Camille hadn't run away from her to Bouck, none of this would be happening now. Camille just wouldn't grow up. She was still a little girl dressing up in fancy clothes, doing destructive things. Only now they were worse things than drawing on car windows and mutilating herself.

Milicia could see that the front windows of the police car were open. Inside, a uniformed cop was eating a danish. For a few seconds she had the wild hope that maybe he had just stopped there outside Bouck's building to eat. But even as she thought it, she knew it wasn't true. If Bouck was really in the hospital, the policeman must be there to keep Camille from getting away.

Her mind raced. Her body vibrated with tension and fury. What happened in there? Did Camille find one of Bouck's guns, shoot him, and tell the police he'd done it himself? Milicia didn't know how she was going to manage this cleaning job. She was supposed to be at her office, supposed to be living a life. Instead, she was a wreck. Her face was bruised and puffy. She was having an anxiety attack. No, she was like an overheated car trying to dig its way out of a muddy bog. Every part of her was racing, and she wasn't getting anywhere.

She moved toward the entrance of Bouck's building without turning her head to acknowledge the strips of crime-scene tapes still stuck to the tree and the doorframe of European Imports across the street. She didn't look that way, but she knew from the night before that the store was still sealed up.

Last night, after she left the police station, she had walked around the West Side for hours, all the way down Columbus Avenue and back, debating what to do. She considered running away. She didn't want to think about the police going to Camille's house and ringing the bell a hundred times, trying to get in. She knew Camille would be in some upstairs room, cringing at the sound of the buzzer. And the puppy would jump around, yelping. She hated Camille more than anything in the world. And somehow she found herself walking there, back to Second Avenue, hoping to be in time to watch them take her sister away.

And then when she got there, it was too late. No one would tell her anything except that neither Bouck nor Camille was inside. Her head hurt worse. A huge generator was heating things up inside so her blood boiled, and she could hardly breathe. Milicia stood on the corner across the street for a long time, watching the police bring things out of the house in paper bags. Finally, she turned to the phone, called Charles and Brenda.


She reviewed all this in her mind as she tried to put her anxiety in another place. Her sister was a maniac who could kill salesgirls and get away with it. She had no choice but to walk up to the door of the house and deal with the situation.

Before she could insert her key in the lock, however, the policeman was out of the car, telling her it was a crime scene and she couldn't go inside.

# 67

April left Block's apartment and stopped at a pay phone on the street to try Milicia Honiger-Stanton's number again. At least the woman had gone home at some point. Her answering machine was back on. The voice on the machine told April this call was important to Milicia: "Please leave the day, date, time, and purpose of your call, and I will get back to you as soon as possible."

It did not sound promising, but she left a message anyway.

The woman who answered the phone at Milicia's office told April Ms. Honiger-Stanton wasn't coming in. She had called in sick that morning. April figured Milicia was home and just not picking up. Her apartment was not far away. April decided it was worth going over there to find out.

The building was right near John Jay College, behind Lincoln Center. It was big and plush, with marble floors and carpeted hallways. The surly-looking man behind the desk said Miss Stanton wasn't there. The name on his uniform was Harold.

"Do you know when she went out?"

"Are you a friend?"

April flashed her shield.

Harold examined it skeptically.

"Cop?"

"That's what it says." April smiled. "So, about what time did she leave?"

"Uh, she walked the dog at about eight o'clock. Then maybe half an hour later she went out."

"She has a dog?" April started to sweat again.

"Yeah, cute little thing. Poodle, I think it is. What's this all about? She not picking up its poop, or something?"

"Yeah, something like that." April paused for a new thought. "Does she ever wear big loose blouses, long skirts, and big floppy hats?"

"Nah, not her. She's got it, she flaunts it. Never seen her in pants neither."

"Thanks." April turned to go.

"You wanna leave a message?"

"No, I'll come back later." She looked at her watch and wondered if Mike was back from his hospital visit.

# 68

April had one of the older cars. It needed to go in for repairs. She could feel a vibration in the drive shaft. She tried not to think about that as she raced up Tenth, then cut over to Amsterdam.

"Sergeant Joyce's not at her desk right now," Gina had told her when she had stopped to call in.

"What about Sanchez?"

"He came in a few minutes ago, but he's not here right now. You want to leave a message?"

"Yeah, tell them to keep the Honiger-Stanton sisters separated until we've had a chance to question them. It's very important, Gina. I'm on Sixty-third Street. I'll be back as soon as I can."

Then, at a red light on Seventy-ninth Street, she considered turning left to Riverside Drive and stopping by Jason's building. That would be her third tangent of the morning. She was supposed to be getting the damn dog. But everything had gotten more complicated. She needed Jason to come and question Camille right away.

The light changed; April wavered. The problem with Jason was she couldn't just go over there and knock on his door. He wasn't the kind of doctor who'd drop everything and let her in. She'd have to leave a message on his machine and wait for him to call her back. She stepped on the gas, wishing she had a phone in the car, turned right on Eighty-second Street, and started looking for a place to park. Finally, she left the car double-parked in front of the precinct, the third in a line of three.

Upstairs, it was quiet in the squad room. Half the squad was working the case, canvassing the neighborhood with photos of Bouck and Camille, asking questions, looking for witnesses who saw either one of them on the Saturday night Maggie Wheeler was strangled.

They were deep into the second week of the case and already way backed up on their other cases. People called in, left messages, got mad. There were about a dozen messages on April's desk, in addition to the ones she hadn't been able to return the day before. The stack of pink slips next to the files of unresolved cases she hadn't had time to work on was the kind of thing that gave her a headache. She hadn't been able to study for her exam either.

Her whole body pulsed with anxiety. Even though she'd told the assistant D.A. she'd bring Camille and the dog back in, she'd put them on hold on the off chance Albert Block could identify the killer.

She didn't want to mess up on this one. She'd checked in with the surveillance team at Bouck's building three times to make sure Camille and the dog had stayed put and were all right. And still she worried. Penelope Dunham hadn't seen Camille. She didn't know how hard it would be to make a case against her. Right now they didn't have enough physical evidence to make a case stick against anybody.

Gina pointed in the direction of Sergeant Joyce's office.

"They're in there."

"Thanks." April smelled pizza or something coming from the locker room. She realized that even after a large meal of crab and ginger dumplings late last night to celebrate the continued interest of George Dong, she was hungry. She had to go to the bathroom, too, wanted to splash water on her face and calm down. She didn't have time to think about romance or anything else. She put her physical needs out of her mind as she headed toward Sergeant Joyce's office.

The door was closed, but from the other side she could hear an angry voice. "I want to see my sister. You can't stop me. This isn't some Latin-American dictatorship. You can't keep people under house arrest here. . . ."

April knocked on the door.

"Yeah, come in." Sergeant Joyce's voice.

April pushed the door open. Joyce nodded at her. Her face was a model of reason and grace under fire. Sanchez was in his usual place, leaning against the back wall. He smiled.

Milicia Honiger-Stanton sat in one of the visitor's chairs. She was wearing a severe gray suit, not unlike the A.D.A.'s but with a much shorter skirt. Her pose revealed the considerable length of her legs and most of her thighs. She didn't seem to be aware of her thighs at the moment though. Her face was redder than her hair, and her tirade continued on uninterrupted as the door opened.

"It's my sister, and I demand to know what's going on."

Sergeant Joyce raised her eyebrow at April. April cocked her head at the hall.

"Excuse us for a moment." Joyce crooked her finger at Sanchez, and the two of them followed April into the locker room. No one was in there, but a pizza box sat on the table. April touched it. It was still warm.

"So?" Joyce demanded.

"I went to see Albert Block. He says he was waiting for Maggie in the bookstore, watching from the window."

"No shit." Mike's nostrils twitched at the enticing smell of pizza.

"Albert says he saw a woman come out of The Last Mango. He waited for Maggie to close up and come out—or for her boyfriend to show up. He knew about the boyfriend. When she didn't come out, he went in looking for her."

"Huh? How'd he get in?"

"He'd taken the key from the counter earlier in the day."

Joyce sniffed at the pizza box, scowled, and turned her back on it. "He used the key, and he went in, and he found Maggie dead, is that it?"

"That's what he said."

"He saw the murderer, and he didn't call us?" Mike was incredulous.

April shook her head. "He saw a woman come out. He didn't think homicide. He thought Maggie committed suicide."

Sergeant Joyce's face also wrinkled with puzzlement. "He thought she'd committed suicide, then confessed to killing her?"

"I know he doesn't make a lot of sense," April muttered. "But I think he's telling the truth about this."

"How does he know it was a woman?"

"She was wearing flats."

Sergeant Joyce thought it over.

"Uh-huh," she said finally.

"He says transvestites always wear heels."

"Uh-huh. Sure, I knew that. Whose damn pizza is this?" Sergeant Joyce finally acknowledged the pizza.

Mike shrugged.

"Don't look at me," April said. "I don't have time to eat."

Like a light bulb, Joyce switched off the pizza again. "Okay, so where are we?"

"Block remembers the red hair and a long skirt," April said.

"What about the dog?"

"He didn't say anything about the dog."

"Can he identify her?"

"Maybe."

"Our forensic dentist took a look at Rachel Stark's ankle. He says it looks like an animal bite to him. He wants to make a mold of the dog's teeth to see if there's a match."

Sergeant Joyce shook her head. "Do you have the dog?"

"No. Something else came up. The Honiger-Stanton sister you've got in your office also has a poodle. I went by her building. She wasn't there, but I talked to the doorman."

"She wasn't there because she went over to see her sister," Mike threw in.

"So it appears," April said, still upset because she hadn't taken the time to get Camille's dog on the way over.

"But they wouldn't let her in. So she came over here."

Aspirante charged into the locker room. "You didn't touch my pizza, did you?"

"Yeah, we got hungry. We ate it," Mike said.

"Shit, you didn't!" Aspirante punched a locker. It made a nice metallic bang.

"It didn't have your name on it," Mike said, deadpan.

"It was *mine*." Aspirante pushed by him and opened the box. Three congealing slices with pepperoni and mushrooms were neatly arranged in the middle.

Aspirante turned away from Sergeant Joyce and mouthed the words "fuck you" at Sanchez.

Mike nodded.

"Cut the shit," Joyce said sharply. "We just left a suspect in the office."

Where the case file was. Very smart.

They trooped to the office. By the time they got there, they had a plan.

303

April turned to Mike before they went in. "How's Braun?"

Mike shook his head. "He'll probably limp for life—and get a citation. He said he missed you, wanted to know why you weren't there at the hospital, paying your respects."

"Nice. What did you tell him?"

"I said you were busy, but you were planning to come by first minute you got."

"Oh, wonderful. I'll remember that."

Sergeant Joyce opened the door quickly. Milicia sat there with her legs crossed the other way, drumming her fingers on the arm of the chair, trying to look as if she hadn't made a move since they left. The Maggie Wheeler file was where Sergeant Joyce had put it, under a stack of color-coded forms with her empty coffee cup that said LIFE IS A BEACH on top.

"Would you like a cup of coffee, Miss Stanton?" Sergeant Joyce sat down at her desk.

"I want to see my sister. I'm extremely worried about her."

"I understand, but we need your help first. Can you tell us a little about your dogs?"

Milicia stared. "What?"

"Your dogs. You and your sister have little poodles. We're going to need to know all about those dogs."

A muscle jumped in Milicia's cheek. She didn't speak for a long time. It didn't take a genius to see she wasn't prepared for any dog questions.

April glanced at Mike. His mustache twitched with the ghost of a smile. The ghost struck her in the heart. She left the room to make a call.

# 69

Max was having his first session since he got back from his vacation in Paris.

*"Bonjour,"* he said with a long face as he walked in the door. "It's shit to be back."

"Thanks very much, and the same to you," Jason replied.

Although Jason was several years older than Max, they had attended the same medical school and shared some of the same professors. Max was a surgeon who had been referred to Jason about five years ago when he plunged into a deep depression after losing a patient during a complicated breast reconstruction. His treatment with Jason had gone well. They'd terminated three years later.

The reason for his return to therapy, Max reported, was that his second wife, Lydia, wanted to get a divorce and take their three-year-old daughter, the only child he had, to another state to live. Max was bitter and didn't understand what was wrong with Lydia.

Since their last meeting, Max's hair had turned white. He'd gained about forty pounds, and was grossly overweight now. His face was round and full and looked like a bowl of vanilla pudding. Jason had been shocked. And that wasn't the only change. When Jason knew him he was married to a lovely woman called Alison who had worked in a bank to support him through his many years of training. The last Jason heard, Max was doing well, and Alison was quitting work so they could have a family.

Instead, he divorced Alison to marry the secretary he was sharing with his two partners in the practice. Now he was furious with Lydia for leaving him. And for insisting he purchase a big house for her in Virginia.

"So what went wrong?" Jason asked after he had heard the whole story.

All right, Max admitted, so he was fucking his surgical nurse. What was the big deal? Why did Lydia have to make this whole big *thing* about it? Why couldn't she just move into a modest apartment nearby where he could see his daughter every day? Why did she have to be a bitch about everything? Why couldn't she shut her mouth and just be nice? That had been the crux of his complaint for the past several months. He had to get to his complaint. He never started with it. And it would be a very long time before he could get past his complaints to the issue of his behavior.

True to form, Max lay down on the couch and started describing in minute detail the surgical procedure he had performed earlier that morning. Then he talked about Paris. Pamela, the surgical nurse, got some kind of bug and threw up the whole time. Max had found it all pretty disgusting.

Jason stifled a yawn. It was his birthday, and he wasn't feeling sympathetic. He looked at the clock on his desk and wondered when Emma would call. As he was wondering, the phone rang.

"I have to take this," Jason said. "I'm screening my calls this morning." He picked up before the second ring.

"Hi, it's April. Is this a good time?"

Jason glanced at Max's highly polished loafers at the foot of his analyst's couch. One was crossed over the other. The one on top jiggled impatiently. "I have a minute."

"We have a problem. Our only witness thinks the murderer was a woman. Is there any way you could come over and question Camille again?"

Jason's adrenaline kicked in. He didn't have time to be so deeply involved in this. He was supposed to meet Charles in two hours, and he had another patient before that. He looked at the clock again. Max's foot continued to jiggle. "It's not convenient," he murmured.

He didn't leave his office unless it was a medical emergency, a question of life or death. That was his rule. He never broke it.

"Murder isn't convenient for anybody. Look, I wouldn't ask if it weren't urgent."

"I know." Jason hesitated. He owed her. He'd probably be paying for the rest of his life.

"Please, just this once," April pressed.

It wasn't exactly a question of life, but he figured it was a question of death. "Okay, all right, I'll do it. But if you want me in on this, you'll have to fill me in on everything you have. I can't work in the dark."

"Fine."

They set the time for a meeting in forty minutes and hung up.

"What was that all about?" Max demanded.

"You know I can't tell you that," Jason replied mildly. "You were telling me about Pamela."

Max shook his head. "What do these women want?" he said bitterly. "Whatever you do for them, it's just never enough."

Jason watched the bobbing loafer express Max's frustration. It would take a long time to get anywhere with him. Max had some difficulty with his conscience. He seemed to have no shame. None at all.

An hour later, armed with his notes from the previous night, Jason sat facing Sergeant Sanchez and April Woo in the downstairs questioning room he was getting to know all too well. The tape recorder was on the table.

Even though the wired windows to the outside were open, it was hot in the green room with the cracked plaster ceiling and the dirty linoleum floor. They had gone over the thick Maggie Wheeler file with the autopsy report and dozens of transcribed detective interviews and reports, and the thinner Rachel Stark file. So far that contained only the autopsy and crime-scene reports. Splayed across the table were the crime-scene and autopsy photos of both victims.

On Jason's side of the table a full cup of cold coffee and the five empty Sweet'n Low packets he'd used in it were all that separated him from the macabre pictures of the dead girls. He couldn't drink the coffee and kept stirring it with a plastic stick, as if somehow he could mix it enough to get it right.

Until last spring, when Emma was kidnapped and April Woo was the detective on the case, he had known next to nothing about the world of police and perpetrators. He read and wrote scholarly texts about the kinds of pathology that incapacitated people, not made them killers. He didn't like sadistic films; he never read crime fiction. Now he was at the precinct again, this time studying photographs of what looked like two ritual killings the police wanted him to explain. Once again he felt out of his element.

During his career he had hospitalized and cared for very sick people. He had seen many kinds of tragedy. But dealing with many troubled people over the years, Jason had never felt personally touched by evil. Now he knew firsthand what it was like to have the most sadistic kind of madness directed right at someone he loved. He touched his hand to his forehead, as if to blot out the images in the photographs.

Sometimes the mysterious connectedness of disparate events overwhelmed him. Until last spring, the last thing he thought he'd ever do was to work with the police on a homicide case. Yet he had discovered over and over in his life that it was not possible to walk away from extraordinary events unchanged. Everything that happened opened a new door, a path to another dimension. He was not surprised that this kind of horror had found its way back to his door again, and unknowingly he had let it in.

"How is Camille's boyfriend doing?" Jason asked.

"He's in intensive care," Sanchez answered. "It doesn't look like he'll be able to contribute much for a long time."

"And you think a dog was at the murder scene?"

"We have evidence a dog was there," April answered.

"Can you determine which dog it was by the hair sample you have?"

Sanchez shook his head. "No, but teeth are like fingerprints. No two sets are the same, even in animals. If the bite mark on Rachel Stark's ankle matches the teeth of one of the dogs, we'll have something."

"But you don't have both dogs yet."

"No. We have Camille's. She'll have to give us permission to make a mold of the dog's teeth."

Jason kept shaking his head. He wasn't sure of the ethics of this situation. Milicia was his patient. When he called Charles to put off their meeting, Charles indicated to him Milicia felt betrayed and would not speak to Jason again under any circumstances.

At the moment she was upstairs, refusing to say anything and demanding to see a lawyer. Camille and her dog had been brought in and were waiting in another room to see him.

Without thinking, Jason swallowed some of the cold, oversweetened coffee, trying to digest the situation. They had found the possessions of one of the murdered girls in Bouck's basement. They had to establish whether or not Bouck ever dressed in Camille's clothes, whether he took the dog out on his own. If he had any other hiding places, like for shoes and maybe a red wig. They needed to know if anybody else, like Milicia, had a key to Bouck's building. They needed samples of Milicia's and Camille's handwriting to test against the guest book. They were looking for a blouse missing from The Last Mango.

The police needed Camille to answer all these questions for them, and they weren't able to get anywhere with her asking her themselves. Great. Was he violating a patient's confidentiality by interviewing her sister about the sister's possible involvement in a couple of homicides? He looked at the crime-scene photos again, one by one. Again he thought it was a fine line, but he wouldn't be crossing it.

He swallowed down the rest of the coffee. It was almost all milk and hardly tasted of coffee at all. Somehow being there he felt he was in the middle of a war. It occurred to him that it was always like this in a police station. A state of emergency every day. He pushed the pictures away.

April saw that he was finished, collected the pictures, and all the material.

"How do you think she'd respond to a video camera?" she asked.

"I think it would be a terrible distraction. Do you really need it?" Jason was alarmed by the prospect of himself with a murder suspect on tape. "Isn't the recorder enough?"

"She may not be competent to give her permission anyway," Mike pointed out.

"Fine, we'll go with the recorder. Are you ready?"

Jason tossed the coffee cup in the wastebasket. He noted that the basket had been emptied since the night before. Yes, he guessed he was ready.

amille let the woman blue wall pet Puppy's head on her second trip to the police station. The policewoman sat in the back seat with her. The other officer drove the car.

"That's a cute dog," the policewoman said.

It was okay to pet, but Camille wouldn't let her take the dog in her arms. Just because she hadn't let Milicia in the building didn't mean she was all right. Camille was sure she was going to jail. She shivered uncontrollably. A vibration deep inside of her wouldn't let up. *It was coming true, just like Milicia said.*

Whenever Bouck wrapped her up tight, buckled the straps so she couldn't move, and put her in the room upstairs that was hers, he told her this would be her future if she didn't have him to protect her. He told her that where she'd go, other people would own her body. They could touch her all the time, any way they wanted. And she wouldn't be able to stop them.

Without Bouck to protect her, Camille was afraid even to breathe. Every time she inhaled, it felt like a gasp. Don't let it happen again.

*"What's this, Milicia?" Camille was wearing their mother's long black velvet dress with the lace top. It had a funny smell—sour vomit, sweet perfume, powder. The dress was so long, it trailed on the floor. Milicia said she looked stupid. The lipstick on Camille's face was all crooked. She couldn't seem to get it right. Then she saw the Tampax on the dressing table and picked it up.*

*Milicia laughed. "It's for the bleeding, stupid. Don't you know anything?"*

*Camille examined it, feeling the thin paper over hard cardboard tube. "What do you do with it?"*

*"Pull up that stupid dress and I'll show you."*

*"But I don't have any blood."*
*"You will."*


The blood on the floor in Bouck's hall was a different color in the morning light. It had dried and didn't smear anymore when Camille touched it.
That morning after the police sent Milicia away, Camille squatted on the
floor for a long time, tracing the dark spatters on the stairway and the
wall. Bouck didn't call. The vibration in her body made her sure he was
dead, and she was starting to spin out of control.

He told her, "Guns are great." Sometimes he held one of them between his legs while he watched her put on her clothes. *Girl Dressing
While Artist Watches.* Just like a Renoir. He told her how to do it, sat in
his chair with a gun on his lap, watching. Sometimes he groaned and
made other noises, then said she was the one out of control. *Made her take
a pill, wrapped her up, and buckled her into herself so the furies were
contained.* Then he went out late at night, heavily armed with his guns,
looking for a fight.

Camille could see a fight on the floor in the hallway. She could tell
Bouck hadn't won. He told her bullets came in light loads and heavy
loads. Sometimes he took them out of their boxes to show her. Different
kinds of bullets made different kinds of holes in the human body. Sometimes he let her hold one of the guns, but never when it had bullets in it.
He was afraid she might shoot.

Guns weren't so great. She touched the dried blood on the floor
again, trying to connect it with Bouck. She couldn't do it. The blood was
like rust. It wasn't alive anymore.


The blue wall in the front seat talked to the blue wall sitting beside her
and Puppy in the back seat. Then the one in the front talked on the radio
like a taxi driver.

More storm clouds gathered in Camille's head. She didn't listen to
what they were saying.


In the police station, a different blue wall told her she could sit down at
the table.

"Do you want a cup of coffee, or tea, or something?"

Camille darted a quick look at her. She could see precinct cancer microbes crawling up and down the woman's face. Big ones. She turned away, covering Puppy's muzzle with the edge of her blouse, then pulled her hair over her face to hide from the enemy. *Don't let it happen.*

The door opened. Camille didn't move.

"Good morning."

Camille didn't move. That was the first lie. It wasn't a good morning.

"How are you doing this morning?" She heard the scrape of a chair. "I'm Dr. Frank. We talked last night. Do you remember?"

*Don't let it happen.* Camille pressed her lips together so no words could get out.

"How's Puppy this morning?"

Camille parted the curtain of her hair and peeked out. Dr. Frank was playing with the buttons of the recorder on the table. "No," she said sharply.

He looked up. "It's just a tape recorder. It won't hurt you."

"No," she said. "No is no."

"It's just so we can remember what we talked about."

"I am accused of a crime," Camille said, the shrewdness returning to her face. "You didn't read me my rights."

"I'm not a policeman," the doctor said gently. "I'm not accusing you of anything. I'm here to help find out what the truth is."

"No one can know the truth. It's too late." She pushed her hair back and studied his face. "Did you know you have a mole on your face, right in the middle of your eyelid? A big black one. You can get cancer from that."

The doctor touched his face. "Can you see it?" he asked.

"No. But I know it's there."

"Well, thank you for warning me. Now, can you tell me your name and where you live?"

"I'm not stupid. I did that yesterday."

"I know you're not stupid. If you don't want to say your name, why don't you write it down for me and then sign it?" He drew a three-by-five file card out of his pocket and slid it across the table. Then he found a pen in another pocket, put it down on the table.

Camille picked it up. It was a nice pen, brown and black. She took the top off and tested it on the paper. Black ink, medium point. She wrote her name and address, then added her phone number. Her handwriting was big and loopy. When she was finished, she began to decorate the edges of the card with vines and flowers. She signed it and handed it back.

"You can keep it," she told him.

"Thank you." He sat back in his chair. He had a black and white notebook. It sat on his knee. He put the card in the notebook.

"Do you know where we are?" he asked after a minute.

"The police station."

"Do you know why we're here?"

Camille petted Puppy very gently. She didn't answer for a long time. Her breathing hurt. She mustn't breathe in. "Somebody got killed," she said finally.

"Two people."

Camille chewed on her lips.

"The police have some ideas about who could have done it."

"Me?" Camille said in a tiny voice.

The doctor looked right at her. He didn't try to hide his face. "Several people could have done it. They don't want to get the wrong person. They want to know which person really did it."

"I don't know." Camille covered her face with her hair again. "I don't want to get precinct cancer," she added.

"I don't either," the doctor said. "So let's get going."

Camille tried to inhale. Her breath made a funny noise. She didn't want to think about this, had spent her whole life not telling. Didn't want to tell now. "What do you want to know?"

"Camille, does anybody ever take Puppy out for walks?"

She laughed suddenly, feeling a lot better. "Like who?"

"Oh, anybody. How about Bouck? Does he?"

Camille laughed some more, pushing her hair back a little so she could look down at Puppy. Puppy was asleep. "No. He says she's a faggot dog."

"What does that mean?"

"A dog for a fag. He won't be seen with her."

"Bouck doesn't like fags?"

"No."

"Camille, does anybody ever wear your clothes?"

She started nibbling her lips again. "Like who?"

"Like anybody. You have a lot of clothes. Are they all yours, or does somebody else wear them sometimes?"

She turned toward the door, her body twitching. There was a mirror on one side of the room. She didn't want to see herself. The window in the door was wired so it wouldn't break. Her body vibrated dangerously. She wanted to break the window and get out.

"Is that a yes?"

"Sometimes I've thought somebody did . . ." She didn't finish.

"Who wears your clothes?"

"I think they disappear sometimes." She hesitated. "But I'm confused—I don't always know."

"Is it Bouck who wears your clothes?"

Camille stroked Puppy faster, holding her tight. "Can't you see he's too big? He wouldn't fit into them."

"Have you ever seen him try on anything of yours?"

"No."

"Okay." The doctor looked down at his notebook. "I want to get back to what you were saying yesterday about your sister. You said your sister's dog and your dog were alike, just like you and your sister were alike."

"Two peas in a pod," Camille murmured.

"You're like two peas in a pod?"

Camille nodded. "Same hair, same eyes. Same curls. Same everything. People get us confused."

"Do you really look that much alike?" he said doubtfully, as if he knew they didn't.

"We used to, before—you know—puberty." She closed her eyes against the long dress and the Tampax. *It's for the blood. Don't tell or I'll wring your chicken neck.*

"In what way did people confuse you, Camille? Did you have the same personality, act the same?"

Camille shook her head, sucking her lips into her mouth, making herself toothless. In her lap, Puppy woke up. "I can't explain," she murmured.

"Were you together all the time? Were you good friends?"

"We had the same birthday," she said quickly, pulling a safer thought from the air.

"You were both born on the same day?" he asked.

Camille laughed at his look of surprise. "No, but we only had one birthday anyway. It was easier that way. One cake, the same party dress. The same present."

"Hmmm. How did that work out?"

"I thought it was twice as good. I had company to share the celebration." Camille squeezed her face into a frown. She could feel her heart beating too fast for itself. She shook her head and her hair stung her eyes and skin as it whipped across her face. Milicia broke her own present. Then she took Camille's, and said Camille broke them both.

Puppy stood on her lap and pawed at her swinging hair, wanting to play. Camille ignored her.

"She called me the she-devil for taking her birthday and her birthday present. I got punished," she said softly.

"How did that make you feel?"

"Every time something happened, I got punished. I had to get used to it."

"Did you get punished often?"

"I had to get used to it, or go straight to hell." *Take a hint.* Camille cocked her head. She decided to study the cracks in the plaster on the wall. "We looked alike. We dressed alike. People thought it was me stealing things. Hurting the dolls. Teasing the ugly girls and getting into fights at school. The mothers used to call home and complain."

"But it wasn't you."

*Take a hint.*

"No." Camille studied the cracks. One of them looked like the California earthquake. The big one, coming up any day now that would drown the whole state. "I wanted to be kind like Doctor Dolittle and talk to the animals."

"When there were these incidents, didn't your mother ever ask for your side of the story?"

"She was deaf and blind," Camille said flatly.

"Really? She couldn't hear or see?"

"She said I took her best pearls, the ones Daddy bought her from Japan, and drank her vodka. She—hit me. Once she bit my cheek . . ." Camille's voice trailed off.

"Did you ever tell anyone what was going on?"

"No." Whom could she tell? And now she was in a police station. She could get stuck here; she could catch the cancer.

"Camille, do you know you're in trouble?"

Camille looked at the doctor. She tried to look into him, but couldn't see anything in there. He could be filled with ants and worms, for all she knew. She didn't want to think about it. But he was forcing her. The dead girls, Bouck's blood on the floor. Everything was making her remember.

"Yes," she said. Bouck was dead, and she knew she was in trouble.

The doctor's face changed. "I'm going to borrow Puppy for a few minutes," he told her. "She needs to go out. We'll bring her right back, I promise." He stood and reached for the dog. Camille was too upset to protest.

# 71

"This better be good."

On her second visit to the precinct in one day, Assistant District Attorney Penelope Dunham looked less fresh and more than a little irritated. She took a seat beside Mike and dragged her glasses out of her purse. When she got them on, she nodded at April and Sergeant Joyce.

"You wanted to see your prime suspect," Joyce said. "Well, here she is. Camille Honiger-Stanton. That's Jason Frank with her. You know who he is?"

"Yes, the shrink from the Chapman case. I had some research done on him."

Penelope peered through the one-way glass at the scene in the questioning room. Jason Frank was an attractive man in a well-tailored gray suit, white shirt, navy tie with tiny white dots on it. Everything about the psychiatrist was conservative—his short brown hair, white shirt, clean-shaven face. He didn't look as if he'd been out much that summer. There was hardly any color in his face.

He sat at the table, writing occasionally in the notebook on his lap. His body was relaxed and his features did not register the bizarre behavior of the redheaded woman sitting across from him. At the moment she was making mewing noises; her hands picked at the air. Her left shoulder jerked up, up, up, three times before the right shoulder took over. Her huge mane of red hair was like a hay field, in and out of which her face bobbed and ducked. Across her lap lay a very small orange-colored poodle, its little butt in the air and its muzzle dangling toward the floor. In contrast to the movements of its owner, it was motionless.

"Is that alive?"

At the question, the dog's head flopped over. It looked drugged. On the floor a small plastic box thumped with the movement above.

317

Penelope pointed at it. "What's that?"

"A leash," Sergeant Joyce said sarcastically.

April glanced at Mike. He winked.

"It's like a reel. The dog has freedom to run around, but you can press a button and stop it from going any farther," he offered.

Penelope Dunham squinted at the leash intently. "Is that the murder weapon?"

Sergeant Joyce glared at her detectives. Neither said anything.

Jason Frank finished writing and looked up. He spoke in a precise, neutral voice. "Camille, do you have any idea why you're in so much trouble?"

After a moment the mewing stopped, and the woman parted her curtain of hair. Her hands clutched the poodle. "People . . . think I did a bad thing."

"What kind of bad thing?"

"They think I did a murder."

"Did you do a murder?"

She shook her hair back in front of her face. "No."

"Are you sure?"

"Yes."

"What about when you get really upset and have one of your fits? Do you hurt other people?"

"Only myself."

"Why do you hurt yourself?"

Camille looked straight into the mirror on her side of the wall, through which the people in the viewing room could see her, but she couldn't see them. She seemed to study herself for quite a while. "I'm bad," she said at last.

"Camille, do any associations come to your mind about what's happening now with these crimes?"

"Like what?"

"I don't know what. You have to tell me."

"Like when I was a kid," she said hesitantly.

He nodded.

"When people thought I did things and punished me and it was really Milicia?"

"Yes. Why didn't you tell anybody, Camille?"

Suddenly Camille's body became very still. "I thought . . . if she wanted me to be punished that much, she must have a good reason."

In the viewing room, Penny Dunham leaned forward.

"What was the reason?" Jason asked Camille.

Camille twisted a clump of hair around her fist. It was all tangled, looked like it hadn't been combed in some time.

"Do you know the reason?"

Camille pulled a clump of hair out by way of an answer.

"Don't do that," Jason said sharply, then more gently, "You pulled your hair out. Is there something you're worried about telling me?"

She looked at the clump of hair for a moment, then dropped it. It drifted to the floor. "Yes . . ."

"Something about Milicia?"

"Yes."

"Did you do whatever Milicia told you to?"

"Yes."

"You were accused of bad things and you took any punishment without telling the truth?"

Very small voice. "Yes."

"Can you tell me the secret?"

Camille's body became absolutely still. Her eyes filled with tears. "No."

Jason was silent for some time. "I need to know the secret, Camille. Two young woman are dead."

"I couldn't kill anybody!" she cried. The puppy in her lap stirred.

"Maybe someone wants to make it seem like you did. Why would someone want to do that? Does it have something to do with the secret between you and Milicia?"

"I don't know! I can't tell you what I don't know!"

"The victims were small women, almost like little girls. They were strangled, hung from chandeliers, dressed in party dresses way too big for them with makeup on their faces. What story does that tell, Camille?"

Camille let out a long, shuddering scream. "It's me. She made me dress up like a woman and gave me lessons to show me what it's like. Health lessons." The words came out an anguished wail. "With a Coke bottle and a hairbrush and—"

Camille put her head down on the table and sobbed. Her puppy didn't try to get away.

Ten minutes later, when it was clear Camille wouldn't be saying anything
else for a long time, Penny Dunham blinked a few times and got up from
her chair.

"Nice family," she remarked sourly. "You said the other sister is here.
Where?"

"She's up in the squad room." Sergeant Joyce's forehead was dotted
with perspiration. "Every time you think you've seen it all . . ."

Officer Paleo stood at the door to the questioning room. For a moment the A.D.A. made no move to open it. She seemed to be gathering
her thoughts. Then she asked Sergeant Joyce, "What's her story?"

"Her story is she went to the shrink to get help for her sister. On the
basis of what she told him, the shrink convinced her to turn her sister in
to the police. And now the police are questioning *her*. She thinks it
outrageous. She's demanding a lawyer."

"Did she call a lawyer?"

"No. Do you want to see her?"

"Not at this time." Penelope took off her glasses.

"Well, what do you make of it?" April asked.

"What do you think I'd make of it? You *still* don't have either the
witnesses or the physical evidence to make a case here."

She rubbed the bridge of her nose where her glasses pinched. "Even
if this wacko here is telling the truth and her sister dressed her up,
sexually abused her, repeatedly set her up to take the fall for antisocial
acts . . . Even if all that happened, there's no way to prove it or link it to
these murders." She put the glasses back on.

"More important, everything that happened in the past is inadmissi-
ble anyway. It has no bearing on the case. Right now what we'd have to
prove in court is that Milicia Honiger-Stanton, an attractive, successful
architect, murdered two young women so she could lay the blame on her
mentally ill sister. Why?"

No one answered.

"In addition, you'll have to show she had access to her sister's house,
took her dog, wore her clothes, and brought back souvenirs of the first
homicide to hide in her sister's basement—give me a break, officers."

"She has her own dog," Mike broke in.

"What?"

"I went by her building after our meeting this morning. The doorman told me she has a similar dog," April explained.

"Maybe it's the same dog. Maybe she walks her sister's dog sometimes." Penelope rubbed the bridge of her nose again.

April shook her head. "Then it would have to be a pretty magical dog. The doorman says it's up there now."

"What's your recommendation?" Sergeant Joyce asked.

The A.D.A. looked impatient. "Get more."

"So what do you want me to do with the suspects in the meantime?"

"Question them as long as you want. If you don't get a confession, let them go."

"Let them go?" Sergeant Joyce glowered.

"On what grounds can you keep them?" Penelope glowered back.

Nice to have someone helpful on their side. Sergeant Joyce turned to Mike and April. What was she going to tell the Captain? He wanted the thing tied up today.

"Why don't you let them go and see what they do," Penelope suggested. She lifted her arm and consulted the large black Swatch on her wrist. "I'm due in court in twenty minutes."

"One of them killed two people," Joyce pointed out.

"So don't leave them alone."

She strode off toward the lobby without another word. Officer Paleo, who was guarding the questioning room, turned away, pretending to be deaf and dumb. Jason Frank came out of the room and announced he was finished for the moment. The calm demeanor that had been so impressive a few minutes before was gone. Now he looked like he'd been torn apart by harpies.

## 72

ilicia was drenched in sweat. She could feel it all over her skin under her clothes. Her rage was so intense, she had to concentrate hard on keeping her body absolutely still, rigid, to stay in control of herself. She knew she must stay in control to survive. The smell of her sweat disgusted her.

Her mind jumped. She thought of Camille and the filthy lies that came out of her mouth, covering everything with bottom mud like a river that overflowed its banks in every storm. Camille lied to anyone who would listen. Bouck was in the hospital. He had to be crazy, crazier than Camille.

And the cops didn't have a clue what was going on. Milicia's foot tapped the floor. She could feel her hands clenching, too. Like claws. She told herself to be Buddhist about this. Let the universe flow over you until you're above it. It was just like long ago in the other police station. They'd keep her there because they didn't know what else to do.

They would keep asking her questions about the dogs, about Bouck, changing direction every few minutes to see if they could trip her up. But she knew better than to talk.

"I don't know. I don't know," she told them, keeping her green eyes wide with perplexity and pain. "I don't know what you want. I don't know what you mean." Sometimes she asked to see her sister. Sometimes she insisted on seeing her lawyer. Then they'd go away for a while.

Charles and Brenda told her to cooperate and tell the truth, but they didn't know about Camille. They didn't know how slippery Camille was, how her madness went in and out of the clouds whenever it suited her.

Milicia burned in her stomach and shivered on her skin. It was clear the police were deliberately keeping her and Camille apart. But she knew it could be dangerous to speculate why. It might not be for the reason she thought. With Camille, you couldn't ever be sure of anything. It could be this was all too much for her. Maybe she had retreated into one of her states when you could stick pins into her or light her on fire, and she wouldn't react at all. Maybe the police were just trying to figure out what to do with her. Milicia got the feeling they suspected Bouck of the murders. But why did they think he did it? How could he have done it?

She had been in this place for hours, first in the Sergeant's office, then on the bench. People were coming in and out all the time, standing around in clumps talking, before going out again. They didn't want her knowing what was going on, so they moved her to an empty room with a mirror in it. She knew they were spying on her. She didn't allow herself any movement except the tapping of her feet and the raising of her arm to check her watch every two minutes.

The Chinese woman came in around one-thirty. "You can go now," she said.

Milicia stood, trying to control her face. "If you keep your face serene in all circumstances, you won't get wrinkles" was what her mother used to say. Milicia could hear Mother's voice telling her that now. Okay, she knew how to keep her face serene. "I can go?" she said, her voice calm and low.

"Yes. Just write your name and address on this card and sign it for me, and we're all done for the moment." The Chinese woman held out a form.

Milicia was suspicious. "After you've kept me here all these hours?"

"Yes." She handed Milicia the form.

Milicia took it, wondering if it would be better to make a scene or go along with it and just get out of there. She examined the form, waffling over her options. Maybe it would be better to be indignant at the way she'd been treated. She glanced at the card. It seemed innocent enough. Name, address, phone, work and home, social security number. Signature line. She panicked when she saw the blank places for a picture and fingerprints.

"I thought you said I could go."

"Yes, you're free to go."

"What's this for?"

"Don't worry about that part," the woman said, and handed her a pen.

Milicia took a deep breath, trying to calm down. It seemed okay, but she had a feeling none of this was okay at all. This was going to hell. She wanted to change her clothes. She could smell her own fear.

"What about my sister?"

"She'll be able to leave soon, too." The Chinese woman now opened the door all the way, showing Milicia that she was free to exit.

"Really, she can go, too?" Milicia hesitated over the card. Maybe it was a trap.

"Yes, we'll be taking her home soon."

"I want my sister. Why can't I take her with me now?"

"I really don't have the information on that. I'm just reporting on what I know."

"I'm not a suspect?"

"Not at this time."

"Then why do I have to fill this in? You already have this information."

"It's just routine. There's a lot of paperwork. We keep information in lots of different places. Just complicates things, that's all. You want to go, you sign the piece of paper. That's the way it is." She shrugged.

Milicia was still suspicious. "What about my sister? Is she a suspect?"

"Not as far as I know."

Milicia snuffled through her nose. That was as far as she would go to express her disgust and disapproval at the whole stupid system. They didn't know what they were doing. She filled in the form quickly, signed it, and pushed past the Chinese woman on her way out. Half of her day was gone, and she wasn't sure what she should do next.

It was nearly two when she stepped out of the police station into the sun. It beat down hard, baking the city rot into the streets. Under her gray suit jacket, Milicia's sweat-soaked silk blouse felt cold and reeked of emotion. Milicia knew the odor, strong as horse sweat, would never come out no matter how many times the blouse was cleaned. She headed home to throw it out.

# 73

Jason and Charles lived and worked in the same latitude on opposite sides of Manhattan. Charles's office was on Seventy-ninth Street near the East River. Drawing a straight line across the island, Jason's was on the corner of Riverside Drive, facing the Hudson River. Charles had a view of the sunrise and Jason had a view of the sunset, but there were differences between them much deeper than who could watch the day begin and who could watch it end. Charles knew whenever he had the slightest feeling of unhappiness and promptly dealt with its source. He was unable to tolerate a moment's annoyance more than was absolutely necessary.

Jason often suffered vague uneasiness—even intense malaise—for weeks without acknowledging anything was wrong. He wanted everything to be all right with him so he could be strong for his patients and resisted giving his feelings of discomfort a name.

Since yesterday he had something new to be uneasy about. On the way across town in the taxi he kept worrying about the ethics of his situation. What was his responsibility in a case like this? This issue had come up with him before, once in a child abuse case and once with the unethical behavior of a colleague in treatment with him. Questions of patient confidentiality, a potential victim's right to be protected, and a moral responsibility to uphold the laws of the land were exceedingly tricky to balance. The bottom line, he knew, was that there was no elegant equation for the proper management of these issues. To satisfy one moral imperative, it was sometimes necessary to disregard another.

As Jason evaluated the things Camille had told him, he could see a clear picture of the escalation of her illness over the years, especially the years after puberty when the sexual abuse continued until Milicia left for college.

Sibling rivalry was an old, old story. The lethal greed and self-interest of the daughters of King Lear, and the bastard sons Edmund and Don John, were only a few of Shakespeare's dangerous, warring children. The

Bible had many more. In fact, aside from temptation and lust, sibling rivalry was the Bible's most-told cautionary tale. No invading enemy army could be as vicious, as insidious, or as dangerous as the voracious, grasping child desperate to be first and foremost in his parents' hearts.

In dysfunctional families like the one in which Camille and Milicia Honiger-Stanton had grown up, with a great deal of illness, little love, and no one watching, a brutal and sadistic war could rage on undetected for years. In this case it was continuing still, even after the death of both parents. Jason felt as if he had been caught in the path of a tornado with no place to hide from the howling wind and flying objects. It was not lost on him that the second victim, Rachel Stark, had died during a gale.

Unrestrained by conscience, human emotions could be as wild and destructive as nature run amok in fire and storm. Jason heard the venting of savage and vengeful feelings in his office daily. He was accustomed to patients' self-involvement so extreme, nothing else but their fury and desire for revenge mattered to them. Still, he did not find it easy to accept the possibility that someone he was treating could be close enough to that murderous edge to cross it without his awareness.

"You're not God, Jason," his first wife liked to scream at him. "Why can't you accept the fact that even though you went to medical school, you're not a king, you're not a god. You're just a man, and not a very good one." His first wife had been surprised and embittered when their marriage ended. She had no idea how she sounded, never heard a word she said.

About five minutes early, Jason stood on Madison Avenue praying for his nausea and dizziness to recede. As he waited, horns erupted at a sudden gridlock in the intersection. The Seventy-ninth crosstown was closed. It had been closed for over two years now, but a clot of traffic still got stuck several times an hour because drivers used to crossing there refused to adjust to the change.

He caught sight of Charles down the block, hurrying toward him. Charles had his complaining face on; his handsome features were furrowed with offense. If Jason hadn't felt so shaky, the sight would have made him smile.

"Where do you want to go?" Charles demanded without preliminaries when he reached him.

"How are you, pal?" Jason tried not to feel hurt that his old friend didn't offer his hand.

"How do you think I am? I feel like shit. I can't believe you kept me in the dark about all this. Brenda and I have been working with Milicia for a year. She designed our house. It isn't even finished. . . ." His voice trailed off.

"I know." Jason touched his friend's arm. "Let's sit down somewhere and have a cup of coffee, huh?"

Reluctantly, Charles nodded. "Fine." His lips were pursed at the thought of his big, unfinished house, and the outrage of his best friend involving his architect in a murder case.

They headed uptown toward a coffee shop on Madison, each deep in his own thoughts.

"It's hot," Jason offered as they trudged unhappily along.

"Yeah." Charles loosened his tie.

That was as far as they could get until they were sitting in the air-conditioned booth stirring Sweet'n Lows into frothy cappuccini. The tiny place was still crowded with an eclectic lunch crowd. They took a table in the window. A heavily made up old lady with a Walkman stuck in her ear sat at the next booth.

"I just can't believe you did this without talking to me, Jason," Charles said peevishly.

"Why don't we just review the situation?" Jason suggested. He tore open two more Sweet'n Lows.

"I trusted you," Charles muttered.

"I don't think it's me you're upset about."

"Oh, yeah? You took a step involving a colleague and friend of mine that will affect her for the rest of her life. You didn't inform me before you did it, and didn't inform me after it was done. How do you think I feel?"

"I think you're upset that you missed it." Jason took a swig of his steaming coffee. It burned like a son of a bitch. He felt like spewing it out in a great spray and splattering it against his old friend's hundred-and-seventy-dollar Turnbull and Asser shirt, custom-made blue banker's suit, and hundred-dollar Gucci tie. Charles was being such an asshole. But instead, he swallowed the mouthful, scalding his palate, tongue, and throat. Shit.

He thought of a case in Boston, or maybe it was Atlanta. A psychiatrist with a patient who committed a number of murders over several years while he was in therapy to ease his tension headaches. The patient fit the profile of a psychopath. He was a charming and persuasive personality with a high level of social perceptiveness who just had to break every rule he encountered. He hurt everyone around him, committing one destructive act after another and describing some of them with undisguised relish. But the psychiatrist who was treating him never associated him with the other more vicious crimes that were well-publicized in the area.

How did he miss it? The question was raised during a seminar on the antisocial personality at a conference Jason attended. His colleague's answer to the question was a shrug. "He lied to me," he said. End of story.

Hey, but the patient lied all the time. All patients lied. Everybody knew that. A good doctor was supposed to get beneath the lies. *Milicia sexually abused her sister for many years. She destroyed Camille totally. And Milicia never would have told him. Would he have figured it out eventually?*

"Okay, what's really going on here?" Charles demanded.

"Remember that day I came to Southampton?" Jason started slowly.

"Of course I remember it," Charles said irritably. His eyes drifted over to the dessert cabinet, where a lavish display of cakes and pies beckoned. "They'd just finished putting the kitchen cabinets in."

"I got there on Sunday. When did Milicia get there?"

"Oh, about ten-thirty, eleven on Saturday night. Something like that."

"Did she say why she got out there so late?"

Charles shrugged. "Something about having to work late. Why?"

"On Saturday night?"

"Why?"

"The first girl was murdered that Saturday night. The police think she died around seven in the evening, just after the boutique closed."

"So, what are you telling me?" Charles glanced at the desserts again. He was a hedonist, never able to let an appetite go unsatisfied for long.

"I'm telling you that Sunday night Milicia drove me home. We talked. I had the feeling she might be interested in a relationship, but I—didn't pick up on it. After I got out of the car, she said she wanted to see me professionally. I was surprised. I thought if she needed professional advice, it would be more natural for her to go to you."

Charles focused on that. "Hmmm," he said.

"I thought maybe you were hitting on her—"

"Jesus, our *architect*? What do you think I am?" Charles exclaimed.

Jason chose not to respond to that. "I thought she must need somebody neutral, so I agreed to see her. Charles, the whole thing was odd. She was seductive, clearly trying to manipulate me for some purpose that was unclear to me. I tried to get her to tell me what the crisis was. What event had occurred to cause her to seek help at this particular moment. She felt a great urgency, but refused to say why."

"So?"

"So, we met a number of times and she kept hinting things about her sister. But she gave me no real indicators that would call for any kind of intervention. She became frustrated and hostile. She was very angry at me for being unable to see her every day last week, but I was in Baltimore on Thursday. Friday I went out to L.A. for the weekend."

"You went to see Emma. How did that go?"

Charles changed the subject suddenly, throwing Jason off balance.

"Well. It went well," Jason murmured. But his visit with Emma seemed like a long time ago now.

"That's good. I like Emma."

Jason didn't say anything. He more than liked Emma. He loved her.

"Yeah, I know." Reading his thoughts, Charles looked sad for a moment. "Want some cheesecake?"

Jason shook his head. He felt old, was thirty-nine today and already he felt he'd crossed the line to forty.

"Then what?"

"Milicia called me several times while I was away, again about the sister. Again, nothing specific. We connected on Tuesday. Yesterday. It was then that she told me about the second murder. She said she'd heard about it on the news. You know how unnerving she is. You were the one who told me there was something about her—"

Charles nodded.

"Well, what?" Jason demanded.

"Little things." Charles gave up the fight. He raised his hand for the waiter.

The waiter had a huge handlebar mustache that did not come out quite far enough to conceal an ugly black mole on his cheek. The mole reminded Jason of Camille.

"I'll have a cheesecake and another cappuccino," Charles said. "Are you sure you won't?" he asked Jason.

"Nothing for me."

"Milicia was so upset last night, really wired. She felt she'd come to you in all innocence and you let her down in the end, sent her into the lion's den alone. And you were over there interviewing her sister the whole time. Unbelievable."

Jason took a deep breath and let it out. And Charles believed Milicia. That's how good she was.

The cheesecake came. Charles shoved a bite into his mouth. Jason waited until he'd swallowed.

"Milicia sexually abused her sister for years."

Charles dropped the fork.

"Are you sure?"

"All the indicators are there. Camille's illness, her dissociation. Self-mutilation beginning in adolescence . . . She's very sick, but she's not a killer."

"Do you think Milicia . . . ?" Charles couldn't bring himself to frame the question. He shoved his dessert to one side.

"The police are pretty sure the killer is one of the three of them. It could be the boyfriend dressed up to look like Camille. It appears Camille was set up."

Jason picked up his fork and reached across the table to Charles's plate, tasted the abandoned cheesecake. Then he told Charles about his sessions with Camille and the police, and filled him in on everything he knew about the case, including the ritualistic aspects of the crime scenes and how the careful design of the murders related to the ritualized abuse of years ago.

Cloudy with doubt for a long time, Charles's eyes slowly cleared to a hard intensity. From time to time as Jason spoke, Charles stopped him with a question, then nodded at the answer. Finally Jason finished.

Charles tapped his coffee spoon against the table, shaking his head at the cracked Formica tabletop. For a moment the two friends sat in silence as Charles searched for a response to a situation that was incomprehensible to him. The people Charles knew and treated suffered from a different kind of illness. They didn't do things like this.

"I can't believe it," he murmured, finally raising his head to look Jason in the eye. But even as Charles spoke in denial, Jason could see that all their years of training, and their long and close relationship, weighed more heavily than any doubts he could have. Charles did believe it.

Jason reached out to pat his friend's arm, then raised his hand for the check.

annabelle started barking the second Milicia opened the door. She was pretty good about staying in the cage and not making too much noise when Milicia was out, but the minute Milicia returned, the dog went wild, barking and scratching at the wire sides to get out. Milicia always let her out right away because she couldn't stand the racket.

She couldn't stand it now. "Shut up," she said sharply.

Suddenly Hannabelle was a liability. Milicia didn't know why the police were so interested in the dog. What did they know anyway? Even if they thought one of the dogs had something to do with it, how could they tell which one? Keep calm, she told herself. There was no way to tell which one. It was all a bluff.

But even so, the sight of Hannabelle made her sick. She couldn't remember now why the animal was there in her life. She didn't even like dogs.

"Ar, ar, ar." Hannabelle sobbed like a baby, deep inside her throat. *"Shut up!"*

Milicia stood in the doorway, studying the living room to see if anything had been moved. The doorman had told her a Chinese cop had been to the building looking for her, but had not asked to go inside the apartment. Milicia didn't trust the doorman. Maybe he had let the cop in and that's how the police knew about Hannabelle.

*Damn fucking dog.* "Shut up," she screamed at it.

Hannabelle barked louder, combining grating yelps with her intolerable whine for maximum effect. She wanted love, had to pee. Why couldn't she get out?

Milicia squinted through the slanting afternoon sunlight to see if the thin layer of dust on the antique tables had been disturbed. It didn't look like it. Then she crossed to the window, impatiently pulling off the jacket and blouse that smelled so offensive to her in the police station. She didn't see anything unusual on the street.

Her apartment was on the twenty-second floor. It was decorated with as many of her parents' antiques from the house in Old Greenwich as would fit in the two-bedroom rental. Milicia was very proud of it. Everything was dark wood, Queen Anne, with graceful curves and carved ball feet. She'd had everything carefully repaired after her parents' death. The nicks and marks and stains from all those years of abuse were gone now. The settee and wing chairs had new upholstery and no longer sagged in the arms and seats.

Now it was obvious what kind of people she had come from. This was how it had all looked in her grandfather's day, when the Stanton family was everything it should be. After her parents' death, the IRS made her pay tens of thousands of dollars just to keep the pitiful furniture she had planned to throw away. She hadn't known how valuable it all was until the lawyers showed her the tax bills the estate would have to pay to own it.

The Sotheby people said the highly polished silver tea service on the Queen Anne sideboard in the dining area was genuine George III, worth a fortune. By the time Milicia was an adolescent, it had long since been stuffed in the back of a closet, black with tarnish.

"Ar, ar, ar."

"Shut the fuck up, you little bitch." Milicia's face stiffened with rage as she looked through the kitchen door.

Hannabelle was standing on her hind legs with her muzzle poked through the wires. Her eyes were bright, black, puzzled. She pawed at the cage door, showing that she wanted to get out. When her mistress didn't respond, she cocked her head and raised the pitch of her wail. She weighed only three pounds, but she made a lot of noise.

Milicia threw her clothes on the floor, didn't care if anyone saw her in her bra through the window.

"Bitch." She stepped into the kitchen and opened the cage.

In a second Hannabelle had charged out and was circling Milicia's feet, barking happily, jumping up, her tongue out, lapping furiously at whatever she could reach. Milicia watched her for a second with utter disgust. Then, as Hannabelle pawed at Milicia's ankles, one of her razor-like baby claws snagged Milicia's panty hose. An ugly run snaked up her leg.

"Shit—" Milicia reached down for the little dog, scooped her up with one hand, and held her out at arm's length, scolding her furiously. The dog's woolly body was still, her legs hung down, her eyes were bright with despair and puzzlement.

"Bad dog!" Milicia screamed. "Very bad dog!" She brought Hannabelle to her chest, squeezing her hard so she didn't have to look at her. The dog was trouble. She didn't know what to do with her.

She wanted to get rid of her, but it would be suspicious if Hannabelle suddenly disappeared. The puppy clung to her, making pitiful mewing noises like a baby. Milicia smacked it hard, overwhelmed with the impulse to wring its neck. She thought about killing it for a long time, trying to decide if she should do it, while the puppy cried.

# 75

It was mid-afternoon, just before three o'clock. From inside 1055 Second Avenue came the sounds of running water and a dog barking. Downstairs, the chandelier shop was closed. Its heavy gate was locked with a massive padlock.

Two people had tried to enter 1055 in the last hour. A tall, bulky woman, well dressed in a designer suit, had walked back and forth in front of the building for nearly fifteen minutes, looking up for signs of life. She tried the bell a number of times, stepped back on the sidewalk, and looked up at the windows again. Her pale hair had recently been molded into a complicated style of swoops and swirls that didn't move when she did. Finally she took a key out of her bag and tried it on the inside door. A second later she was back out on the sidewalk, hailing a taxi.

The other person who came to the door of the brownstone was a black man with dreadlocks. He too rang the bell and tried to get into the building with a key that didn't fit. He too went away after a few minutes.

It was hot in the van. From time to time the whine of the dog came piercingly out of the amplifier.

Mike clapped his hands over his ears. "Ow, can't you fix that, man?"

Ben, the sound expert, adjusted a knob. "That better?"

The barking stopped abruptly. Now they couldn't hear anything.

"Uh-oh. Can you get it back?"

"I don't know. I'm not getting anything. Maybe she took the collar off." Ben played with the knobs.

"Shit."

"She didn't take it off," April said after a minute. "She just picked up the dog. It stops crying when she picks it up."

334

Discouraged, Mike sighed and stretched. "I knew this wouldn't work."

"We didn't have a lot of options," April murmured. They couldn't exactly put a wire on Camille without her knowing it. They couldn't bug the whole house. And they couldn't just let her go back in there alone while they sat outside without any clue what was happening inside.

For a few minutes, nothing emerged from the speakers. Then a kind of humming started—one long, disconnected note, another one higher in the scale. A third one, lower down.

"What's that?"

"Sounds like she's singing."

"Poor woman," April murmured. "She shouldn't be in there by herself." April was usually too busy to think much about what happened to people after their cases were closed. She was supposed to retain the relevant parts for her experience file, the fund of knowledge that made her a better cop with each case, and then let the personal part go. But she had a feeling this crazy lady was going to stay with her for a long time.

"I wonder what she's doing in there," Mike muttered.

Now some scratching as well as a humming sound came out of the machine.

"She's scrubbing something with a brush," Ben said. A small, wiry man with a shaved head, he was wearing shorts and a Grateful Dead T-shirt, Nike Airs with no socks.

The whole van smelled of his feet.

April shrugged. Camille didn't wash the dishes or anything else, but maybe this was a special occasion. Maybe she wanted to clean up the place for her lover's return.

When she left the precinct, Camille had wanted to get Bouck's sister to go with her to visit him in the hospital. She didn't seem to know where the sister lived though, and so far there was no lead on any sister. They had located an elderly father in Florida with Alzheimer's who no longer knew his own name, much less those of his relatives. He wasn't going to visit anybody. They had also located an older brother in California. When the brother in California was informed Bouck was in critical condition in the hospital with a gunshot wound, he demanded: "What the hell do you expect me to do about it?"

Maybe Camille meant her own sister would go with her. April stuck her nose out the cracked window on the street side to get some fresh air. A few hours earlier in the precinct Milicia had seemed so eager to be with her sister. They knew she'd show up.

But she was certainly taking her time getting there.

# 76

Milicia was wearing sunglasses, had pinned her hair into a tight bun and put a silk scarf on her head, tied around the back like Audrey Hepburn and Jackie Kennedy used to do. People turned to look at her. She knew she looked good. She was carrying her leather carryall and the Channel Thirteen bag with Hannabelle inside. She strode along Fifty-seventh Street, moving confidently now. The two Klonopin she took after her shower must have worked.

Usually, she didn't like taking pills of any kind. But Charles had told her that in really stressful situations, it was okay to get a little help to calm down. He told her the experience she was having now with Camille and the police ranked very high on the stress scale. She should have gone to Charles in the first place. This mess wouldn't have happened if she had gone to Charles instead of Jason Frank.

She glanced around casually. She wasn't stupid. She knew someone had to be following her. But who was it? She stopped in front of a restaurant with bottles of Chianti and piles of fresh uncooked spaghetti in the window and carefully studied the street reflected behind her. No one seemed to be watching her. But how was she supposed to know? It didn't have to be someone in uniform. It could be anybody. The person or persons following her could be Chinese or Hispanic, or black. The cop who had come to her apartment was Chinese, her doorman said. In the station house a lot of the police didn't look like police.

A feeling of unease drifted over Milicia as she thought of all those people looking like Haitian taxi drivers, and Indians on messenger bikes, who might really be cops.

She went into the restaurant. She took a table where she could watch the street from the window and ordered some spaghetti with tomato sauce and a glass of red wine. When the spaghetti came, she ate it slowly, thinking things over, sipping the wine and ignoring the unhappy dog scratching at the canvas bag by her feet.

After her meal she felt better. She paid her bill and headed east toward Second Avenue. Things looked normal around her. But still she had an uneasy feeling that anyone and everyone could be a spy.

On Second Avenue, unlike the night before, there were no police cars on the street. She did not know how this could be. They had sent a sick woman home by herself, a woman who was not safe without supervision. How could they do that? Weren't they responsible if they took her home in a police car, left her there, and something happened to her? She felt a surge of anger at the thought of something happening to Camille.

She scanned the street, looking for someone who appeared to be hanging around. She saw several dozen parked cars and vans: all were empty. None of the passersby paid any attention to her. As she approached the door of the building, it suddenly occurred to her that maybe Camille wasn't alone. Maybe they had sent a social worker or a cop with her, maybe she was somehow being supervised. Maybe she was under house arrest.

She glanced around one more time, saw nothing to arouse her suspicions, then opened the outside door. Inside, she had no problem using her key. Bouck was in the hospital. She knew that part wasn't a trick. She had called to make sure. He was in intensive care, couldn't even speak, the nurse had told her. His guns had been confiscated. She could go into Bouck's house anytime she wanted: She had no more reason to be afraid.

Milicia climbed to the second floor and opened the door at the top of the stairs. Inside, she stopped short. Camille was on her hands and knees in the middle of a lake of soap and water, scrubbing the floor, singing a tuneless little song.

At the sight of her sister, Camille stopped singing.

"Hi, baby," Milicia said, setting the canvas bag down. "I brought you a present."

## 77

"How did you get in here?" Camille was so startled to see Milicia come through Bouck's apartment door, she dropped the brush with a clatter.

"Baby, I can get in anywhere, you know that. I'm an architect. I know how everything works." Milicia made a face at the puddles of soapy water. "What do you think you're doing?"

Milicia's Channel Thirteen bag tilted and fell over. The dog inside tumbled out and shook herself. Puppy, who hadn't been acting right since the police station, suddenly regained her energy. She leapt out of Camille's lap, charged through a puddle, and hurled herself at her tiny twin.

"Puppy," Camille cried sharply. "Come back here!"

Puppy ignored the command.

"Puppy, it's your mother calling!"

"No." Milicia laughed. "It's her sister calling."

Milicia planted herself on the third stair. She took her scarf and sunglasses off, then peered through the banister bars at Camille, as if one of them were in a cage.

"Sisters are more important than mothers." She pointed at the dogs. "Look at them."

The two apricot fluff balls had launched into a frenzy of leaping and jumping and kissing and rolling all over each other with sharp yips of delight.

Camille was confused. Puppy had seemed so sick with precinct cancer, and now she seemed all right. "Oh, no." Camille smacked her cheek in horror. "Oh no, oh no." She'd taken Puppy's collar off when she started splashing water everywhere. The collar had been expensive, and she hadn't wanted to get it wet. Now Puppy was without her identification. Puppy wasn't listening to her, and Milicia's dog wasn't wearing a collar. What if Puppy forgot who she was?

"What's her name?" Camille cried frantically. "Call her, call her back—"

"Doesn't have a name. Look how happy they are to see each other." Milicia clapped her hands. "Isn't it cute. That's how sisters should be."

"Puppy's been sick," Camille said angrily. "I don't want her upset, you'll have to go. I'm too busy. I can't have you here." She picked up the brush to show how busy she was, spraying soap across the wet floor. "Take your dog and go away."

"Oh, don't be so mean, Camille. You're always so mean."

"I'm not the one who's mean." Milicia's sneaking in on her made Camille's head start to pound.

She kept her eyes on the dogs, now chasing each other up and down the hall, sliding in the soapy water and falling on each other. Puppy was staggering around a little, but seemed determined to play. *Go away, Milicia,* she thought but could not say.

Then, as Camille studied them, she could see they weren't the same at all, just like she and Milicia were not the same. The other dog had a tooth sticking out of its lower jaw that distorted its face just enough to make it look like it was always smiling. Puppy didn't have that tooth at all. She'd lost the baby canine on that side, and the new one hadn't sprouted yet. Camille knew this because one day a tooth fell out in her hand.

Camille reminded herself of the tooth so she wouldn't think about Milicia being nice to her. All those massages, when she rubbed little Cammy's tummy, moving her hand lower and lower, fingers wiggling between Cammy's thighs. *Like that, Cammy? Isn't it great?* Fingers slippery with Vaseline from the medicine cabinet. Back and forth, round and round with the soft, oily fingers until little Cammy was all throbbing and breathless and hot. *Yes, you like it. Yes, I'll do it again. Whenever you want.*

Yes, yes, comparing the two poodles point by point, Camille noticed Milicia's was darker around the head and ears, and Puppy's legs were longer. Puppy was taller. Her head still hurt, but she felt better when she knew which was hers.

"You're mean to me," Milicia said in a pouty voice. "I try to take care of you and love you, and whatever I do you hate me. Why do you hate me so much?"

That tone of voice made Camille's stomach queasy. Milicia's voice was like a pretty pond with a mud-sucking bottom. All sweet and sad, with an ugly, dangerous edge. *What did she want?*

"You better go. Bouck's coming back in a little while. He won't like finding you here." Camille pushed away the sick feeling in her stomach that kept warning her Milicia was there to be her boss again. Carefully, she scrubbed a spot on the wall she'd missed. "Can't you see I'm cleaning for him?"

"Bouck's not coming back." Milicia spoke gently. "He's dead. I'm the one who takes care of you now."

"No, stupid." Camille's eyes twitched. She was furious. "You can't trick me. He's not dead. He's coming back. I'm going to the hospital to pick him up in a few minutes."

"That's a lie. You don't even know which hospital. And you couldn't find it if you did. *You're* the stupid one."

Camille squeezed her eyes shut. Her head hurt. "Go away."

Milicia sat on the stairs like a queen and poked at her through the banister bars with her finger. "Unh-unh. You're stupid, and you're crazy, too. All your life you caused trouble. And now this. Look at this place. You can't keep house. You can't even find food. You're still little Cammy."

Camille trembled all over but didn't say anything. Milicia could do that to her, stop her from talking, stop her from breathing, anytime she wanted. The bad feeling in her stomach wouldn't go away. Milicia was here to do something to her. *What?*

Milicia's voice turned warm again. "You used to love me. Why do you hate me now?"

Camille shook her head. Her arms twitched.

*Give me a lesson, Milicia. I promise I'll be good.*

## 78

"What's going on?"

It seemed to get hotter in the van with every second. April was soaked with perspiration, her hair so wet it stuck to her scalp.

She glanced over at Sanchez, hunkered down on his heels like a cowboy or a Chinese peasant. He looked cool in spite of the temperature, smiled, and raised a shoulder at her. No answer.

April studied him suspiciously. Mike had talked with the Captain before they left the precinct. He might not know what was happening in the apartment, but he knew what was going on at the precinct. In fact, she was beginning to think that all these meetings with Sergeant Joyce and the Captain were getting to him. Sergeant Sanchez had been pretty laid back only a few weeks before. Now April could see that he was walking with a firmer step, his eyes set on the future.

She wiped the sweat from her forehead with a tissue, considering the situation. She knew these high-profile cases could change things. Lots of people in the department got assigned to one job and stayed in it for twenty years. But other people moved around, did different things. Got ahead. Now she saw how it happened. They called in somebody ahead of you, and that person messed up. You got to move up to their place. Just the way she and Sanchez were sitting in this van instead of Lieutenant Braun and Sergeant Roberts.

She knew what Mike was thinking, because people who worked together had a whole language worked out. Everything meant something. If they were questioning a suspect on the street and Mike said, "I'm hungry. Let's go for a pizza," it meant, "Cuff the suspect now."

Braun and Roberts had messed up and now April and Mike were in the van.

Mike smiled at her. "A peso for your thoughts."

April shook her head. "A whole lot of things. Taking the exam. Passing it and moving out of the Two-O. Failing it . . ." and staying in the squad. *His wife Maria dying in Mexico. His being free and finding another woman to love.* There were a whole lot of things to think about.

Mike's mustache twitched. He knew what they were and passed them right back, knocking her flat with the challenge to do what she wanted, say what she felt, be herself, and not some wet rag from a movie he'd seen.

"What is it with you Oriental women?" he had once demanded, swiveling around in his chair in the squad room one day when they were alone for a few minutes. "Don't you ever want to break out? Go crazy with love? Be wild, smash a wall? Tell your mother off? Get yourself off the hook?" He just had to let her know he'd gone to the damn movie.

"I'm out. What you see is all there is," April had replied mildly. She never told him she'd seen that cooking movie about Mexicans who went up in smoke when they fell in love. Or that she had thought it was dumb because nobody was *that* hot.

"Washrags," he had muttered. "I really wanted to slap them all."

"You want to slap me? Go ahead, try it. See how much of a washrag I am." She drew herself up and glared at him. "Go ahead. See how close you get."

"Damn you! You know what I'm talking about. You can tear apart a class-A felon with your bare hands. You just won't . . . I don't know . . . grab what you want, go for it." His hand slapped his desk the way he said he wanted to slap the women in *The Joy Luck Club.*

But he only shot her a piercing look. "When are you going to go for it, *querida*? You got to go for it yourself. It won't just come to you."

She shivered, not knowing what to say. "I'll go for it when I find it," she told him finally. "It's just old Chinese wisdom to look very close at the quality of everything before you decide what to take. You Latins just jump at anything that strikes your eye. You don't even know if it's first quality. Later, when you get what you think you want, half the time you're sorry."

That shut him up for a while. But now she could see the question coming back at her in the overheated sound van. She detoured around it. "There's nothing coming in here. Some great idea, bugging the dog."

Ben played with the knobs a few more minutes. "I think she took the collar off. I don't hear nothing. No breathing, no crying. Nothing. Did you tell her to leave the collar on?"

"She's supposed to keep the dog and the collar with her," Sanchez said.

"Maybe she disobeyed you." Ben sounded sarcastic. "Maybe the dog is no longer with us in this world."

"She wouldn't kill the dog," April said quickly.

"Maybe the other one would." He tried something different with the buttons. Nothing.

"Doesn't matter. They already took a mold of the dog's jaw. The dentist said it was an easy one. Sometimes they have to destroy the animal to get it."

"Nice."

April glanced at Mike. "One of those women is a killer. I don't want to sit here waiting to see which one walks out alive."

"Detective, are you saying in your considered judgment, the time has come to go for it?" Mike asked.

April wrinkled her nose at the smell of Ben's feet and nodded gravely. "Yes, Sergeant, I am."

"Okay." In one smooth motion, Mike stood, then slid the door open. "Let's go."

# 79

Milicia's voice was soft again, pleading. "You won't let me near you. You won't let me love you." She talked through the wooden bars, her voice trembling with emotion. "Why?"

Camille pressed her hands over her ears. The pounding in her head felt like Niagara Falls. She was rigid all over. Her body told her why.

"Why are you doing this to me?" Milicia asked sadly.

"Don't talk to me," Camille cried. "Don't—"

"Well, I have to, stupid. It's all your fault."

"No!" Camille pushed the old voices away, the old feelings: first so exciting. So much fun. What a secret!

*Let's make a tent with the sheets and hide. Come on, Cammy. Don't you want to be healthy and feel good? Yes, it does make you feel good. Only big people do this. Only smart people . . . Mommy doesn't like you. She wants you little and stupid. It's good too, isn't it? Means I love you.*

Camille inched backward until her spine touched the wall. Her hands brushed at the skirt covering her stomach, trying to wipe away the memory of Milicia's hair hanging over her bare belly so many times, tickling her until she squealed with helpless laughter. For a while so safe and exciting. Milicia being so nice when she wasn't mean.

Then not so nice when she thought of more things that gave Cammy a strange, unsettled feeling. Scary feeling. And more scary as Milicia took her secret place from her little by little, turning it into a torture chamber. It was Milicia who created a panic button right in the center of Camille's body, trying different things on it until Camille's secret place was Milicia's to invade any way she wanted. Cammy couldn't make it different.

*Milicia, it's your turn for a health lesson.*

*Nobody gives me health lessons. I'm already healthy. You're the one*

345

*who needs it. If you didn't need it, you wouldn't ask me, would you? Beg me, Cammy. Beg me now.*

Camille's head pounded. She tried to stop the voices in the tent, on the bathroom floor. In the back of the car under the blanket. But they rushed back at her. All of them crowding together in Bouck's hallway, where the frothing soapy water was now tinged pink with his blood.

"My head hurts," Camille whimpered.

"I can make it stop hurting," Milicia whispered through the bars. "You want to go upstairs. I know something new."

*If you don't stop bugging me, Cammy, you'll never feel good again. Is that what you want?*

"No."

*You can't have it this way forever. This is the baby way. You won't be a woman until you do it the woman way.*

"Oh, come on. What are you afraid of?"

"I can't be touched."

"That's silly. I'll hug you and make you feel better."

Camille struggled with the words. "The police know, Milicia."

Milicia looked surprised. A flicker of hope penetrated the cavern of Camille's terror.

"They know you killed those girls. . . ."

"You're crazy. How could I do that?"

"You know how to squeeze." With enormous effort Camille shaped the words. "Remember?"

"Did you tell the police stories?" Milicia was angry again. Her face through the bars of the stairway was fierce and very cold.

Camille covered her eyes with her hair so she wouldn't have to see it. "About what?" she whispered through her hair. "About the scarf game or the plastic-bag game?"

"I don't know what you're talking about," Milicia said, suddenly aloof and uncaring. "Come on. Let's go upstairs and have a rest. You'll feel better after a nap. I promise I won't touch you."

"What about the dog-leash game?" From behind the hair. "Those girls were killed with the dog leash, weren't they? That would be right."

"Shut up, Cammy, you're annoying me. You know I couldn't hurt anybody."

"You hurt *me*," Camille said in a baby voice.

"All right, I'm sorry. Is that what you want?" Milicia held out her hands in a gesture of contrition. "I didn't know I hurt you."

*Stop that complaining. If I said I won't hurt you, I won't hurt you. So take off your underpants, Cammy. Don't argue, or I'll never make you feel good again. Stop that. You can't get away. I have to do this for your health.*

Camille closed her eyes behind her hair. Milicia's hairbrush came from England. It had a handle curved to fit the hand. Narrow then wide then narrow. It was the first thing Milicia thought of to try. *No more Mr. Nice Guy. I don't care if you don't want to anymore. It's a medical problem. I have to fix it.* Camille had screamed and screamed, but the bathroom door was locked, no one was home, no one cared. Milicia had squeezed her neck to shut her up. *I'm the boss of you. I do what I want. Stop that stupid screaming, or next time I'll make it worse.*

"*You're* the one who killed those poor girls, Camille. Are you still that mad at me?"

The throbbing intensified. "My head hurts," Camille whispered.

"I can make it stop hurting."

"No . . ."

"Look, I said I'm sorry. Forgive me. I gave you a puppy, didn't I? Look at the puppies. Look at them, Cammy."

Camille hid behind her hair. Puppy had run away from her. She wouldn't look at Puppy anymore.

"Go on. Look at them. They're so sweet."

Camille turned her head toward the joyful yaps but would not part her hair to take a look.

"Do you want me to take them away? You don't have to have them if they bother you, Cammy. I'll take them away. I'll do whatever I can to help you. You don't want to go to prison, do you? We have to make sure that doesn't happen."

Camille made a slight move. Her hair swung from one side to the other. Didn't want to go to prison.

"Look at that," Milicia commanded. "See that. Perfectly natural."

Camille moved out of her hiding place to see what was going on. She parted her hair with one finger and glanced in the direction of the dogs. Just for a second. It was very quiet. Milicia's dog, very intent and busy, was nudging around Puppy's stomach. Obligingly, Puppy lifted her leg and stood still while her sister began sniffing and licking at her bottom.

"Time to go upstairs, Camille."

# 80

April and Mike stood crowded together at the top of the narrow stairs. She was so close to Mike she could see the hairs his razor had missed that morning and feel his heart racing about as fast as hers. They'd left the outside door open a little to let the evening breeze drift up the stairs. April's sweat chilled on her skin. The last time she and Mike had been in a position behind a door like this they'd almost gotten their heads blown off.

*Yip, yip, yip.* Dogs. Sounded like more than one.

She glanced at Mike. She could see that under his jacket the front of his shirt was damp.

He frowned. "Did you see another dog come in?"

"No. Milicia was carrying a bag. Maybe it was in the bag."

"Does it sound like two dogs to you?"

April pressed her ear to the door. There was a whole sound van downstairs on the street, and still she was listening at a door. What technique. "Yes, it does sound like two dogs . . . but I don't hear anything else."

*Yip, yip, yip.* The barking grew louder.

Mike came closer, put his hand high up on the door, and leaned into April, breathing on her neck. Damn him. She shivered and retreated, shaking him off, trying to concentrate. What were the dogs barking about? What was going on in there?

"What? Do I have bad breath or something?" Mike popped a Tic Tac in his mouth and offered April one.

She shook her head. "Get serious. We're on a job."

"I'm dead serious." He smiled. "I don't get more serious."

"Fine, then let's go in."

The barking grew frenzied. Mike leaned back against the wall, scratching his chin. "Are you sure that's the right thing to do, Detective? We don't exactly have a warrant."

"It's too quiet in there. Open the door."

"Unh-unh. What if nothing's happening?"

"Come on, Mike. The dogs are going crazy."

"Oh, what do you think is going on?"

"I have no idea. But there's an old Chinese proverb—"

Mike rolled his eyes. "Yeah, what is it?"

"He who ignores barking dogs misses boat."

"Sure." He punched her in the arm. She punched him back harder. Inside, something had definitely unhinged the dogs. They were screaming like abandoned babies. Maybe one of the women was torturing the dogs. To April that constituted a call for help.

"Let's go. If I'm wrong, you can say I needed to use the bathroom."

"Wonderful." Mike tried the door. The main lock offered no resistance to his key. None of the three additional locks were set. He clearly wasn't happy with B & E because of a barking dog. "Do you really need the bathroom?"

She shrugged. "Another old Chinese proverb say: Never miss an opportunity to pee."

Inside, one of the little dogs was running up and down the stairs in a barking frenzy. The other was not in sight. From somewhere above came the grunting and thrashing of several bodies in a savage, wordless brawl.

Mike took the stairs three at a time and got there first. But April was not too late to see Camille, with her big skirt and tangled mass of red hair billowing around her, sitting astride Milicia on the bed, grunting "Uh, Uh, Uh."

Bouck's beautiful room was in chaos. His elaborately fringed pillows were scattered all over the floor. The elegant silk brocade bedspread had been yanked off the bed. It was twisted around one of Milicia's legs, binding it like a bandage. She was on her back, bucking and kicking her one free leg as Camille tried to strangle the life out of her. The other tiny poodle stood on its hind feet, scrabbling madly at the side of the high bed, trying to jump up, failing, and howling its frustration.

"Stop! Police!" Mike shouted just before he plowed through the pillows to separate the two battling women.

The small pillows flew up in the air when he dove on the bed. A white lace heart sailed across the room, landing with a soft thump on the other side. At his touch, Camille's body went rigid. Falling abruptly silent, she released Milicia's neck. She looked stunned as he dragged her to her feet and quickly cuffed her hands behind her back.

Milicia sat up sputtering and gasping, her hands on her throat. "Oh, God—she's crazy. She—she just grabbed me. Just like that. We were—talking. She took me by surprise. She would have killed me." She untangled her leg from the bedcover and pulled her skirt down. Inched over to the side of the bed, away from her sister. April crossed to help her.

"It's okay. Stay where you are. I'll call an ambulance."

"No, no. I'm all right." Milicia rubbed the angry red blotches on her neck, looking over at Camille with total surprise and horror. "Did you see that? She was going to kill me. . . . Just like the others." She stroked her throat with both hands. "Something must have triggered it. I don't know what . . . I can't believe it. My own sister . . . I'm lucky to be alive. . . ."

Dazed and wobbly, Milicia pulled herself together and stood up. She took only a tiny second from her recovery to kick the whimpering dog out of her way. The dog yelped. Unsettled by the unexpected cruelty, April reached to scoop the puppy up in her arms. Instantly, it dropped its head to her shoulder and sighed. April was shocked by this sign of tenderness from an animal.

She turned to Sanchez. "Mike, you all set there?"

"Yeah. Call for an ambulance." He was ashen under his Mexican tan. He had Camille by the elbow, but it wasn't easy holding on to her. The woman's body and face had become a mass of tics and jerks that were beyond her control. Her torso trembled; her mouth was slack. So their killer was the psycho sister, after all. It was the kind of thing cops pray for: They'd caught her in the act.

Still holding the puppy, April glanced down at her watch. It would be a long night before they got it wrapped up.

# 81

"You aww light? No rook so good."

Sai Woo held the door open for April and swiftly bundled her inside. As soon as the door was shut and locked and chained—as soon as the outside light was turned off—she began scolding in Chinese. "You have big test tomollow. Why home so late? You clazy? How pass test with no sreep?"

Skinny Dragon Mother was wearing black silk pants and a bright red shirt, had been waiting up for her husband and daughter as usual. Tonight wasn't so late though. Only twelve-thirty. April knew her father wouldn't be home for another hour. There was deep red lipstick on Sai's thin lips, and her eyes were as shrewd as a Chinese gambler's. She studied her wilted daughter.

"Hi, Ma." April gave her a weak smile. "What's up?"

Sai did a little two-step, heading toward the kitchen. "Maybe no pass test. Maybe get malleed instead."

Maybe no pass test. No get married either.

"Uh-huh." Whatever you say.

"How's case?"

April frowned. "Case closed. Ma?"

"Yeah, who did it?" Sai realized April was still standing by the front door, eager to go back outside and up the stairs to her second floor apartment. Spiteful daughter was not respectfully following Wise and Helpful Mother into the kitchen. "Where you going?"

"I have a test tomorrow. I'm going to bed. . . . Ma, I have a question for you."

"Whuh?" If possible, Sai's eyes sharpened to an even greater degree of acuity.

"You remember how I always wanted a dog when I was little?"

351

Sai screwed her features into an angry scowl. "No rememba."

April tried again. "Remember you had a dog?"

"Long ago, in China. Come, have lice. We talk."

"The dog disappeared, and you thought the neighbors ate it." April leaned against the door. She was bone tired, as tired and discouraged as she'd ever been. She had just witnessed one sister's attempt to kill another. And even after seeing that—then going through all the paperwork, and the trip to Bellevue because the suspect appeared to be having a psychotic breakdown—she still couldn't get over the little poodle's curly head resting on her shoulder, the two poodles nestled together on the front seat of the squad car while a uniform sat with the assault victim in the back. At the moment the dogs were in cages in custody. Soon one might be without a home.

Sai nodded, the long-ago fury at her beloved pet's terrible end burning in her eyes. "So?"

"We're not in China anymore. No one will steal a dog and eat it here."

"So?" Sai didn't get it. What did that have to do with big test and getting married? Nothing.

"So I know a dog that maybe needs a good home. A very cute dog. A baby. You have a backyard already fenced in. Wouldn't even have to walk it. No work. Just open the door." April shrugged.

"You clazy?" Sai's voice sank to an anxious whisper.

"Maybe."

"Why want dog? Dogs nothing but troubber."

"No one would eat it here, Mom. It's a nice one, expensive. This kind of dog costs five, maybe six hundred dollars."

"Huh." Sai's penciled eyebrows jumped up. Money always got her. Then the slyness returned. "You still getting married?" she demanded in Chinese.

"We have to go out again first," April pointed out. "See if we like each other."

Sai thought about that, then conceded the point. "Who did it?" she asked at last, switching back to English.

April frowned. She didn't like this case. "A very sick woman." Didn't like it at all.

"You got a probrem?"

"More than one."

"You rant tell me? Mebbe herrp." Sai moved a few feet and sat stiffly on the modern sofa—very hard, no soft cushions to sink into—in the tiny front living room, then patted the place beside her.

April sighed and checked her watch. Five minutes, no more. She might be able to squeeze another hour of studying into this ruined night. She sat next to her mother. "Okay, it's like this: A crazy sister kills two young women who work in stores—"

"How?"

"Strangles them. Then sane sister comes in and reports her problem sister to the police. We investigate. Pretty quickly, we begin to think the crazy sister is too crazy to kill anybody. Then we find one murder victim's clothes in the crazy sister's house. We investigate more. We get the sisters in for handwriting samples. We test the bite marks of the crazy sister's dog. We come up with nothing on the crazy sister. Now we're wondering if maybe she's been set up, so we follow both of them to see what they do. Few hours later we catch the crazy sister trying to strangle the sane one. Got it?"

Sai shook her head. "I don't berieve."

"What don't you believe, Ma?"

"Tly not same as succeed. . . ."

"So, what do you think happened?"

"How I know? You detective . . . I just mother. Hey, *Ni*? You know stoly of ten thousand soldjuhs?" It seemed like a question, but it wasn't a question.

"No, Mom. What's the story?"

Sai settled back on the hard sofa to tell it. "Hundred, hundred years, peasants work rand. All lound rand good. One piece rand nothing can do. Clops no glow. No leason. All same rand. Peasants beg gods for leason, make many offerings. Give rand water, night soir. Nothing can do. Then mebbe hundred hundred years dig up bad rand to make city. Then find out what's what." Sai slapped April's arm. "Ten thousand cray soldiers buried on horses. That's what."

Yeah. April nodded politely. So what did that have to do with the Honiger-Stanton sisters and the two dead salesgirls?

"You take Sergeant test tomorrow?"

Again April nodded. *So?*

"Bad spilits. Now sreep—hey *Ni,* you rant dog?"

"Yeah, Ma. If I can get it."

Skinny Dragon Mother shook her head as if the spiteful daughter she had futilely named Happy Thinking so long ago had finally lost her mind.

April got up slowly. A lot of times her mother made her feel as if she were still three years old. Really small and not very smart. In fact, quite, quite stupid. She knew Skinny Dragon Mother had some important lesson in mind for her, but as usual she didn't know what it was. Once again she headed upstairs.

"See what I mean?" Sai said to her back.

"Yeah, Ma. Look for the ghosts making mischief."

*"Hnngh."* Right through the nose was the triumphant sound that followed April up the stairs.

# 82

It was almost midnight. In the dark, Jason sat in his favorite armchair, listening to the nine carefully restored antique clocks prominently displayed on bookcases and tables around his living room. The clocks all ticked in a slightly different rhythm. No matter how many times he adjusted them, he could not get them to keep exactly the same time. It took a full ten minutes of bongs and dongs in nine different tones before they all got through striking the hour. He had no idea which one, if any, had the correct time. If he wanted the correct time, he had to consult his quartz watch.

At this moment, some five, ten, fifteen minutes before midnight, he didn't give a damn about the correct time. He was waiting for the 108 strikes that would proclaim the end of his thirty-ninth birthday. He felt very alone.

One of the occupational hazards of being a psychiatrist was that very few of the people in his life, even those he'd seen regularly for many years, knew anything about him. Today not one of his patients had any idea it was his birthday. The day had passed with no office party, no congratulations, only a few cards, no cake. He did get a call from his parents bemoaning the fact that he had produced no children and never came to visit. It didn't occur to them to ask him, or take him, to dinner. They sat on extension phones in different rooms of their Bronx apartment where they had lived for forty-three years, talking at the same time. They promised to send Jason a birthday card as soon as they found one they both liked.

But all of that he'd sorted out long ago. What really bothered him was that even though he had spoken to her twice that day, he desperately missed Emma. And his best friend Charles was furious at him. Further, he seemed to have misread the Honiger-Stanton case right from the beginning and all the way through. That was puzzling. He didn't often get things wrong. He and April Woo had arranged to have dinner together the next night to talk the case over. He was looking forward to it.

Outside, it began to rain. Lightning snaked across the sky above the Hudson River, illuminating the New Jersey horizon for an instant. Thunder reverberated. Jason brooded about the case, about Camille under observation at Bellevue. Something worried him about the story April told him when she called from the hospital two hours earlier. He didn't see how the young woman he had diagnosed as gentle and nurturing just that morning—the woman who had told him she wanted to be like Doctor Dolittle—had made a very serious attempt at strangling her sister at five-thirty in the afternoon.

Camille had appeared frightened, vulnerable, fragile. How did he miss her rage? She must have lied. Well, all patients lied. Everybody he knew lied. Still, getting beyond the lies to the truth was his job.

Jason sat there in the dark, trying to work it out. Camille said she always did whatever Milicia told her to. Jason believed that was true. What if Milicia knew the police were outside and deliberately provoked Camille to violence? What if Milicia had threatened or attacked her in some way and Camille acted to protect herself? The thunder rumbled closer. Rain pelted down, drenching the city for the second time in a week. It was the storm season. Jason had the urge to call Emma, to thank her again for her gift. Find out how she was. Hear her voice again, no matter how much it hurt. The phone rang before he had a chance to decide if that was a good idea. He reached to answer it.

"Did I wake you?" Charles demanded.

"No." Jason was disappointed. He'd been thinking about Emma, more than half hoped it was her.

"Are you alone?"

"Yeah, I'm alone. What's up, Charles?"

There was a lengthy silence. "Look, I'm sorry I ripped into you today." Charles sounded sorry.

"That's okay. I'd probably have felt the same."

"We've been friends for a long time."

"Yes, we have. Thanks for calling."

"That's not the only reason I called."

"Oh, what's up?"

There was a short pause, then Charles spoke. His voice had a catch in it. "The shirt came back from the laundry."

"The shirt? What shirt?" Jason searched his memory for a shirt.

"Milicia gave a shirt to Brenda in Southampton. The Saturday night before you got there. The night the first woman was murdered. It was a weekend gift, a big white shirt. I have it in my hand."

"Was that the shirt Brenda was wearing the day I came?"

"Yes. Brenda must have worn it to appear appropriately grateful. It was way too big for her."

Jason remembered. "Yes."

"Look, I don't know if it's the one the police were looking for. It doesn't have a store label in it. But I wanted you to know. And Jason— happy birthday."

Jason closed his eyes. "Thanks, I appreciate it. I'll call the detective on the case and let her know."

The first clock began to strike the hour. Then the second. Suddenly the room went into its bonging frenzy. Jason took the portable phone with him and shut the connecting doors. Now he couldn't see the lightning, or the river, the trees on Riverside Drive shuddering in the wind, or the crooked horizon of New Jersey. He went into the kitchen and turned on the light. It was midnight, but Jason dialed April's work number anyway. The polite voice that answered said Detective Woo was not there, was off tomorrow. He had no idea what her home number was.

# 83

April swallowed down some hot lemon water from the mug that said GOOD LUCK, LONG LIFE in gold Chinese characters on the side. The mug was a thank-you gift from the sister of a man who'd been kidnapped upon arrival at Kennedy Airport by the people who arranged for his immigration. The kidnappers demanded an additional thirty thousand dollars for his life. April had located the man in an abandoned warehouse in Newark. In addition to the mug, she was given a bag of oranges and a live eel.

This important and symbolic morning she sat at her tiny kitchen table in her underwear, drinking from her lucky mug, trying to calm down and stop sweating so she could put her clothes on. It was just before eight. Her exam began at ten.

After two weeks of working what she now called the sisters case, it was over. It didn't matter if Camille Honiger-Stanton struck her as a victim, not a killer. This wasn't the first time she was unsatisfied with the resolution of a case. Probably wouldn't be the last. Anyway, the ghosts under the ground would surface sooner or later. There was still the evidence, the handwriting samples to match with the boutique guest book in the Maggie Wheeler homicide, the dog's teeth marks to match the bite on Rachel Stark. And who knew, maybe Albert Block could give them a positive ID on the woman he saw leaving The Last Mango before he discovered Maggie's body.

April couldn't calm down. How could she be afraid of answering a few questions? What was the big deal here? She'd taken and passed a lot of exams in her life. She'd testified in court. She'd inspected putrifying corpses, tussled with muggers twice her size. She'd been shot at and burned. She had a father who was an expert at the silent treatment and a mother who demanded answers to more questions, of greater depth and complexity, than any prosecuting attorney she ever encountered. How could a mere written exam, followed by an oral one in front of no matter how stony-faced a board of examiners, be any worse than a thousand things she'd already experienced? And yet she had to admit she was scared to death. Didn't want to fail and lose face in the squad. Didn't want to endure the contempt of her mother, let down Sergeant Joyce.

She'd hardly closed her eyes all night. She felt slightly nauseated and hung over, so tense that she almost fell off her chair when the phone rang. She was certain it was her mother.

*"Wei?"*

"April, it's Mike."

"Calling to wish me good luck?"

"Good luck, *querida.*" He didn't remind April that if she made Sergeant, she'd lose her job as a detective. She'd have to go back into uniform, would have to leave the Two-O, become a supervisor in some other precinct, maybe even go back to the street. He didn't say it, but April thought she could hear some conflict about that in his voice.

"Thank you. I'll call you later—"

"One other thing," Mike interrupted. "The forensic dentist just called. Seems like this guy's a morning person. He's already made a mold of the teeth of Milicia's dog and had it bite a few things, including some stuff they use that acts like human tissue."

April let her breath out. "And?"

"He says we got a match with the bite mark on Rachel Stark's ankle."

April was silent as her excitement mounted. She'd been right. It wasn't over.

"You with me?"

"Yeah. I'm coming in. I'll see you in twenty minutes."

"What about the exam?"

"I'll make it."

April hung up and hurried into the bathroom, adrenaline pumping in with every heartbeat. She prepared for battle, smeared on more deodorant, dusted her armpits with powder. She threw on the good-luck outfit she'd laid out the night before, then slipped out of her house without encountering a parent.

After last night's heavy rain it was a glorious day, finally crisp and cooling into autumn. The leaves on the trees outside the house were brown around the edges. Some were already on the ground. The rest of the leaves would fall early. April breathed in the fragrance of grass and damp earth. The season was changing. Her heart lifted as she moved toward her car. Suddenly it all seemed easy. All one had to do was dig a little deeper, like her mother said, and whole armies of ghosts would rise up from the earth to tell their stories. April wondered if maybe she were turning out to be an optimist after all.

The first thing she saw when she entered Sergeant Joyce's office at eight-twenty was the spatter of ugly rust-colored stains on her blouse. Exactly at the third button, between the Sergeant's generous breasts, the spray of dried coffee indicated a day of chaos had already begun. The second thing April saw was the dog kennel on the floor. It was a pale putty one, for a small dog, the kind people used for traveling. The apricot poodle inside was weeping like a baby, the heart-rending sounds pleading for release.

Surprised, Sergeant Joyce glanced up and scowled. "You're not here today. Aren't you supposed to be—?"

April swallowed. "Yeah, taking the exam. I have a few minutes. I thought I'd check in."

Sergeant Joyce frowned some more. "What the hell for?"

"I heard we got a bite-mark match in the Stark case with Milicia's dog." April's confidence still soared. She still felt good. They were going to nail the right person after all.

"So?" The dog's whine went up an octave. Sergeant Joyce's attention was diverted. "Shut up," she told the dog fiercely. The poodle didn't seem impressed. It didn't stop crying.

"So, we got the link. We got the evidence. It was Milicia," April said over the noise.

The dog's whine grew louder.

"*Shut up!*" Sergeant Joyce turned back to April, furious. "Can you tell *which* dog *that* is?" she demanded.

April shifted from one foot to the other, suddenly a little uneasy. "Well, no, not from here. Which one is it?"

"What's the matter with you? How the hell are you ever going to make Sergeant? What are you doing here? What are you *thinking*? Get out of here and take your test."

"But it was Milicia's dog that bit the victim." April felt her own irritation rising.

"Use your head. Let it go, Woo."

"But if it was Milicia's dog, it changes the case," April persisted.

"How the fuck do we know that? There are *two* damn dogs. They could have been switched at any time."

"But—"

"What are you—stupid?" Joyce's voice was a snarl.

April could almost see the sounds traveling into the squad room. The supervisor of the squad was calling her stupid. She flushed all over, hot with shame. Perspiration ran down her sides. The dog was crying. Her head was bursting. She had to get out of there. "I thought it would make a difference—"

"Well, it doesn't make a difference. It doesn't mean squat. There's no way to prove who carried that dog into the boutique. Try that in court, and you'd get chopped to pieces. Stupid," she said again.

April's jaw set. She moved a step closer to Joyce's desk. If she made Sergeant, she'd be out of here. If she failed, it wouldn't matter anyway. Her voice did not falter as, very deliberately and clearly, she said, "Don't ever talk to me like that again."

"What?" Sergeant Joyce looked surprised.

"I'm one of the best detectives you have. Don't ever call me stupid again."

*Awwwwwooooooo.* The dog wailed.

Sergeant Joyce pursed her lips as if preparing for another abusive outburst. Then, suddenly, her forehead smoothed out, and she turned her attention to the little dog in the cage. "Yeah, you're right. Why don't you get that animal out of here."

April picked up the kennel and muttered a few soothing words into it. The ear-shattering noise ceased. "What do you want me to do with it?" she asked.

Sergeant Joyce waved her hand toward the door. "Take it back. The tooth man is finished with it. Some idiot brought it here and left it before I got in. When I find out who, I'll cut his balls off."

April's head pounded. One confrontation a decade was enough. She didn't have time for another. Her exam was in an hour and twelve minutes. "Take it back where?"

"Take it back where it came from. This is the NYPD, not the ASPCA. It's not evidence. We can't keep it here."

"Where's the other one?" April said faintly, afraid suddenly it wasn't anywhere anymore.

"The other one is evidence. It's still being held." Sergeant Joyce waved her away.

"Oh." Still April hesitated. If this was Camille's dog, she couldn't take it back. Camille was in Bellevue. Bouck was in intensive care in the hospital. There was no one to take care of it.

"It's been released, April," Joyce said impatiently. "Guy called Jamal phoned for it. He's the employee. Take the dog over. Is that asking too much?"

Under the circumstances it was, but April didn't want to push her supervisor any further. She headed for the door with the dog kennel in her hand. As she closed the door behind her, she thought that she heard Sergeant Joyce mutter, "Good luck."

# 84

In the car, however, April had a change of heart. Should she have left the damn dog behind, just dumped it somewhere else in the precinct? She felt like an idiot with the bulky kennel on the front seat of her car. The puppy was quiet, but April was really rushed and anxious now. She had less than an hour to get to her exam. She muttered to herself all the way across and downtown.

"Calm down, calm down. We'll make it."

She drove more aggressively than usual, weaving in and out between double-parked cars and vans, speeding up in momentary gaps in the dense traffic. She did not look at the clock on the dashboard, didn't want to know.

When she got down to Fifty-fifth and Second, the iron grille was still in place across the front of Bouck's shop. In spite of all the antiperspirant she had used that morning, she broke into another sweat at the sight of it. What if no one was there to take the dog? How could she walk into her exam with it? She didn't think she had a choice here. The thing wasn't exactly NYPD property. The examiners would think she was nuts. She had to get rid of it.

April could feel her good-luck shirt sticking to her back as she pulled the car into an empty spot in front of a hydrant and looked up at the windows in Bouck's living quarters. The light was on in the living room. She could even see the crystals in the huge center chandelier sparkling faintly. The guy Jamal must be in the house.

April got out of the car, slipped her purse over her shoulder, then went around to the passenger side for the kennel. She figured she still had about forty minutes. It was almost a straight line downtown to One Police Plaza. She could take the FDR Drive and make it in thirty.

Puppy poked her muzzle out of the wire mesh and tried to lick April's hand as she reached inside the car for the kennel. April stroked her wet nose. "Hi, sweetheart. Someone wants you. Guess you'll never be mine." She hurried across the sidewalk to the door of the building and pressed the buzzer. "Didn't really want a dog anyway," she muttered.

The downstairs door clicked open instantly. Carrying the kennel in front of her, April climbed the stairs. At the top, she rang the doorbell. A few seconds later the door swung open. A smiling face greeted her.

"Oh, it's you."

April's jaw dropped. In the doorway, dressed in a lavender silk camisole and a long, loose purple skirt, Milicia Honiger-Stanton grinned at her.

"How nice of you to bring my baby back. Hi, baby." Milicia reached for the kennel and took it inside the apartment, where she crouched down to open the wire door and release the excited puppy.

April followed her in. "That's your sister's dog. A man called Jamal telephoned for it."

"No way, hon. This one's mine. Hi, Hannabelle." Milicia picked up the ball of fur and hugged it to her chest, laughing. "You think I don't know my own puppy?"

April frowned. "What are you doing here?"

"Oh, I came for Camille's things." Milicia cuddled the puppy. "I had to check up on everything, you know. I'm responsible. Will you look at this place?" Still holding the puppy, she led the way down the hall to the living room. "All this stuff. It's Camille's. She bought it all. A compulsive shopper. Camille has money hidden everywhere. It used to drive me crazy. I can't just leave everything here like this. Who knows what will happen to it? I'm so glad you brought my dog. I was so worried about her."

"Where's Jamal?"

"I have no idea. I've never heard of such a person."

Milicia stopped in the middle of the jumble of furniture. Here a space had been made for a huge mirror. It sat propped up on the top of green-leather-covered rolling library stairs two steps high. The mirror was almost seven feet tall.

"Get a load of this, will you." Milicia twirled in front of the big mirror with the dog in her arms. Her purple skirt swung out in an arc. The mirror reflected pinpoints of light from the sparkling chandelier above. Milicia smiled at the lovely vision of herself. "It just came the other day.

Isn't it gorgeous? Camille told me it's the best pier mirror she'd ever seen. Dates back to 1703."

April frowned, worried about the predicament Sergeant Joyce had put her in with Jamal and the puppy. Joyce had told her to return the dog to Jamal. And April was also intrigued by the change in Milicia. Yesterday the woman had been hostile, insecure, frightened of the police. Now she had invited the detective on the case into a house whose owner was in critical condition, was openly revealing her plan to remove what she wanted from the house, and chatting happily about the sister who had only the day before tried to strangle her.

"It's a real horror, isn't it?" Milicia preened in front of the mirror, at home in the cluttered room, much too comfortable with the situation. "Just the kind of thing Camille liked." She laughed softly.

April's scalp tingled. She shivered, uneasy about a lot of things. One was the way Milicia was now gripping the little dog. It clearly wasn't her dog. The puppy struggled in her arms, trying to get down. And time was passing. She was going to be late for her exam. April had no more than thirty seconds. She told herself to get Milicia to sign a release for the dog and get out of there.

Instead, she said, "You don't seem very upset about your sister."

Surprised, Milicia swung away from the mirror to look at her. "Oh, honey, I've been upset for twenty years. Do you have any idea what it's like to grow up with a wacko sibling? Believe me, I cried a lot. But I'm not crying anymore." She shook her head. "I'm sorry she's going to prison, but she hurt me. She hurt other people. She can't get away with it. That's what our laws are for." Her voice was suddenly harsh.

In Milicia's arms, the dog whined deep in its throat. Milicia glared at it, then abruptly put it down. Free, the tiny animal raced out of the room. April could hear it charging up the uncarpeted stairs. Probably going to the third floor, searching for its mistress.

"What happened yesterday? What made Camille turn on you?"

"I told them at the station. She was upset by all their questioning. She had a headache. I suggested she lie down and get some rest." Milicia's eyes glittered. "I helped her upstairs and turned down the bed. She didn't want to lie down there."

"Why?" April asked. "Why didn't she want to lie down?"

Milicia shrugged, raising her shoulders twice for emphasis. "How do I know what sets her off? The woman's crazy. Anybody can see that." She narrowed her eyes at April, frowning a little, her mood changing. "She's crazy. Crazy and violent. What more do you need to know?"

Now April shrugged. "Was she afraid of lying down?"

"What are you saying? What are you getting at?"

"I'm just wondering. Your sister just seems more like a victim than a murderer to me." April said it mildly, but she knew she was pushing it. Instantly, Milicia flared up.

"Are you accusing me of something?" She took a step toward April, suddenly revealing a powerful undercurrent of rage.

For the first time, April realized what a big woman she was. The skimpy camisole revealed how wide her shoulders were, how deep her rib cage, well fleshed, with round pendulous breasts. Her bare arms had the definition of someone who worked out with weights. The full skirt of crinkled purple silk, billowing out from her waist, only expanded her impressive bulk.

"Why the questions?" Milicia demanded. "What are you getting at? Don't you believe me?"

"Any problem with my asking?" April asked calmly. Still, she eased away from her, toward the door. She felt threatened by the woman, increasingly uneasy about being alone with her in the empty house. April was supposed to be somewhere else; she could almost hear the seconds ticking by as she lingered. Why didn't she just go? She glanced toward the door, willing herself to leave.

"I answered all your questions. I told you what happened. I told you *everything.*"

April edged another step toward the door. Time was passing. She must go.

"Don't back away from me," Milicia cried. "Why are you backing away from me? Why do you all do that?" A muscle in her cheek twitched.

*Why do you all do that?* Who was Milicia talking about? Who else had backed away from her? April felt the weight of her off-duty handgun. The gun was in her purse. Her purse hung by a strap on her shoulder, touching her hip. There was no unobtrusive way to get her hand into it. She was alone, off-duty, on her way to her Sergeant's test, couldn't get to her gun without alerting Milicia, couldn't seem to get out of the house.

Milicia towered over her. "Don't back away from me," she said hoarsely.

April stopped. "I'm not backing away from you. I have to go, that's all. You want to sign a release for the dog?" As if to get the release, she reached for her bag.

Now April could hear the dog pattering down the stairs. It hadn't found its mistress, was coming back.

"I didn't touch her. She backed away from me for no reason. *No reason*," Milicia said fiercely.

"Backed away? How did Camille back away?" April asked.

"Attack. I said *attack*. Can't you *hear*?" Milicia took a step closer to April.

Now she was near enough for April to feel her heat and smell the deep heavy perfume she wore. Milicia reeked of hot musk and fury. As April recoiled from the smell, her foot caught on the ornately carved ball foot of a table and she almost lost her balance.

"Hey, watch that," April said sharply. "Don't touch me, I'm a police officer."

Milicia made a sound like a branch snapping. Her long arm snaked out and grabbed April before she could maneuver around the cumbersome table.

"Let go!" April tried to recover her balance. "I don't want to hurt you. I said *let go*."

Milicia's grip was unexpectedly painful. April's breath caught in her throat. She could feel her terror mounting. Milicia had begun to shake her, like a dog with a sock. Her sharp fingernails bit into April's shoulders, right through her jacket. Her head snapped back as Milicia picked her up easily, and her feet left the ground. In the huge mirror April could see herself suspended, like a little Chinese doll.

The grotesque mirrored image of herself struggling in Milicia's powerful arms brought the last moments of the two dead girls into hideous focus. Also the ancient memory of an academy instructor, six feet four and built like a linebacker, holding her off the ground with one hand, laughing his head off at the sight of her helpless, flailing arms.

*You want to be a cop, little girl? Then don't struggle. Use your pussy little brain and kick the shit out of me.*

*I said,* KICK ME, *Officer.*

Yessir, whatever you say, sir. As she had done more than once in her life, April relaxed into a dead weight, then slammed her knee into the softest place of an opponent's body. In Milicia's case it was the stomach.

The vicious blow caught Milicia by surprise. She doubled over, gasping for air. Released, April stumbled backward, hitting her head against the crown of a column with a marble bust on it. Still propelled backward, she hit the hard brass corner of the bulky table with the ball feet. The table prevented her from crashing to the floor. She held onto it, fumbling in her purse for her gun.

"You're crazy. You kicked me," Milicia screamed as soon as she could find her voice. She hugged her stomach. *"You hurt me."* Her face was contorted with surprise and rage.

"You can't *hurt* me." Milicia started toward April as the tiny dog charged into the room. Finally free after twenty-four hours in the small kennel, perplexed by her missing mistress, and excited by the angry voices, the puppy started dashing around and around Milicia in a dizzying circle, barking wildly.

"Stop that," Milicia screamed.

The puppy continued to bark shrilly. Her sharp baby nails pawed frantically at Milicia's calf, giving April precious seconds to recover her balance and reach for her gun.

The dog wouldn't stop. It scratched at Milicia's panty hose, at the hem of her skirt until the panty hose ripped and the puppy caught a nail in the tear.

"Shit!"

Milicia jerked away, back toward the center of the room, where she stood reflected in the mirror under the enormous crystal chandelier, lashing out savagely at the dog attached to her leg by a thread. The dog finally tumbled away, but Milicia went after it. The second time her kick missed the yipping ball of fur, her foot slammed into the library stairs that supported the antique mirror.

"Noooo—" In the middle of a long piercing scream, Milicia could see the little dog turn and leap into the Chinese policewoman's arms. She could see that the policewoman had a gun pointed at her. She saw the huge mirror jolt, then teeter. The horror on the policewoman's face.

The mirror pitched forward, setting the sparkling crystals on the chandelier above it into a gentle swaying dance. And in the last shimmering, light-filled split-second before the full weight of five hundred pounds of wood and glass came crashing down on her, crushing her skull, Milicia understood it wasn't the policewoman who ended her life. It was the dog.

# EPILOGUE

April walked slowly out of the precinct, sucking in the crisp fall air with the relief of someone who'd been in prison for a long time and hadn't thought she'd ever be released. She looked up. The sky was a brilliant afternoon blue, scattered with the thinnest patches of pure white. She knew each kind of cloud cover had its own name, but until the names applied to some case she was working, she'd probably never learn what they were. Free. She was finally free to leave. Sanchez was somewhere behind her. She stopped on the sidewalk to wait for him.

At three-thirty in the afternoon the entire block of Eighty-second Street from Columbus to Amsterdam was double-parked with police vehicles, marked and unmarked. Many, many years ago the police union had bargained for the right of officers to drive their cars from wherever they lived and park them around the precincts where they worked, instead of having to travel on public transportation. From time to time, the lack of police on the subways and buses during rush hours and the glut of illegal parking around precincts engendered a swell of bad feeling, followed by some token action. None was in force today.

In addition to the solid line of double-parked cars, uniforms swarmed all over the sidewalk. Several nodded to April and called out to her. News traveled fast. She'd upset a prominent case that had been cleared only the day before. *"Police Detective Involved in Death of Former Suspect"* wouldn't look good in the headlines or on the evening news. The department had to get the story straight.

Since the ambulance doors had closed on the body of Milicia Honiger-Stanton, April had been questioned for many hours—despite a pounding headache and severe bruises—about the events that had occurred in the building on Second Avenue. For over two hours she had been isolated from Mike and Sergeant Joyce while each was questioned separately.

A mean-eyed Lieutenant she'd never seen before had a long list of doubts about her story. He kept asking why she had returned to the building today. His repetition of the question implied disbelief that she was following orders to take the dog there. How could that be the case? It was a day she wasn't even on duty. She had been scheduled to take her Sergeant's exam. What about that?

"I missed it, sir," April told him.

The Lieutenant continued to scowl at her. Not for the first time she had been uncomfortably aware of how the stale air always hung heavy in questioning rooms. Sometimes innocent people panicked in the closed spaces, looking guilty under the pressure of having to tell the truth, the whole truth, and nothing but the truth. Over and over until they got it right. She was also reminded how hungry-making this kind of stress could be. Sometimes the questioners fed people to encourage disclosure. Sometimes they did not. They had not fed her.

"We know you missed the test, Detective."

"I was working off the chart, but I *was* on police business. Will I have another chance to take the exam?"

He laughed sourly. "Maybe in five years— if you're telling the truth."

April flushed. Five years might be the next time the test would be offered. That would be too late. By then, she'd already have lieutenant's pay, and it would be a demotion no one in their right mind would dream of taking. What a system. You could be *promoted* to detective, but had to pass a test to be a sergeant or lieutenant. Once you became a captain, you could be promoted to any rank above. But with each promotion came a reassignment. For her it would mean she could no longer be a detective. She'd be reassigned to some other department. She might get to be a sergeant in the detective bureau sometime in the future, but then again she might not.

A lot of people in her position would not risk taking the test. She had the pay and the job. Getting the rank meant they could put her in uniform and send her out to supervise foot patrol officers in the Bronx. They could stick her with a desk job anywhere at all.

Maybe it was a power thing. Maybe it was a gender thing. Maybe it was an ethnic thing. All she was absolutely sure of was she wanted respect. She wanted the rank. She waited for the color to fade from her cheeks.

"I am telling the truth, and I'd like an opportunity to reschedule the exam now, sir."

The Lieutenant's fingers did a little dance on his knee as he thought it over. He personally might have nothing to do with it, but he scared her all the same because you never knew who had the juice to do what.

"We'll see what can be arranged," he said finally.

That's what made her think she'd be out of there by dinner time. It occurred to her then that the only way to make it in this world was not by being honey for the bees, as her mother advised, but by fighting for her rights every step of the way.

Mike came up behind her, took her arm as if he had ownership, and steered her out of the crowd. "You did good work, *querida*. You're a first-rate detective."

April forgot about the uniforms watching them from all sides. She squeezed his arm against her side. "Thanks for standing up for me in there."

Sanchez grinned. "What's a rabbi for?"

Oh, so now he was a rabbi again. "I don't know what a rabbi's good for. I've never been to church." April laughed. "How about food? Are you good for food? That son of a bitch gave me a little water but not a thing to eat. Must have thought I deliberately set out this morning to murder a woman twice my size."

"Fine. I'm good for food." They strolled to Columbus and stopped on the corner. "What do you feel like eating?"

It was a loaded question. April hesitated. In five hours she would be meeting with Jason Frank to have dinner and start working on the procedure to get Camille out of Bellevue, as well as appointing a guardian to see that she got the treatment she needed. April had promised Jason Chinese and was determined to pay for it.

The light turned green, turned red, turned green again while she thought about it. Finally she realized that what she wanted was to sit down with Mike and have a long, long talk about a whole lot of things: his dying wife, Maria, and his mother in the Bronx, what his hopes for the future were, and why he hadn't taken the Lieutenant's test a few months ago when Sergeant Joyce did. She wanted to breathe in his powerful spicy aftershave and . . . eat a burrito.

She glanced at him, a tiny smile teasing the corners of her rosebud mouth. Without a word, he nodded and steered her left for Mexican.